NO·AR MVFOL

THE SHARK CURTAIN

A NOVEL BY CHRIS SCOFIELD

BLACK SHEEP

This is a work of fiction. All names, characters, places, and incidents are the product of the author's imagination. Any resemblance to real events or persons, living or dead, is entirely coincidental.

Published by Akashic Books
©2015 Chris Scofield

ISBN: 978-1-61775-313-8
Library of Congress Control Number: 2014955097

Black Sheep/Akashic Books
Twitter: @AkashicBooks
Facebook: AkashicBooks
E-mail: info@akashicbooks.com
Website: www.akashicbooks.com

More books for young readers from Black Sheep:

Pills and Starships
by Lydia Millet

Changers Book One: Drew
by T Cooper & Allison Glock-Cooper

Changers Book Two: Oryon
by T Cooper & Allison Glock-Cooper

Game World
by C.J. Farley

What Is Punk?
by Eric Morse
(forthcoming)

To Ray,
first, last, and always

CHAPTER 1

PABLO, WHEN THEY'RE KISSY

Lauren laughs and points at me. "Lily's got fleas!"

I'm thirteen and I don't have fleas but I *have* been scratching and my fingers freeze like dinosaur talons over my arm. When I hold them up and make a face like a hungry T-Rex, my younger sister says I'm "weird," but she doesn't know a T-Rex from a T-Bird, or that all birds are dinosaurs, or that Mom's new car is a 1960 fire engine–red Thunderbird. The Thunderbird is a Mexican bird that went extinct before the dodo did.

"Dodo did." That's funny.

"Mom, Lily called me a dodo."

Our beautiful mother rolls her eyes. She stands at the breadboard making banana-and–peanut butter sandwiches for tonight's star party. "All right, Lima Bean. Thanks for the APB." APB stands for *All Points Bulletin*. Mom smiles at me and asks, "Itchy?"

Yes.

No.

I shake my head and stick my hands in my pockets one, two, three times. I consider the word "itch." It's *onomatopoeic*, which means the word sounds like what it means. I love words: big, small, musical.

Mom says I'm the smartest teenager she's ever met.

She wraps the last sandwich in wax paper and sticks it in the fridge. Second shelf, left side, piled one on top of the other, folded side down. I open the fridge and double-check that they didn't shift when she closed the door. I open the fridge and triple-check.

"You find something to wear yet, Lily?" Mom's distracting me on purpose. "Lauren?"

"Jeez, I can dress *myself!*" Lauren says as she paws through sweatshirts and cardigans, Gramma Frieda's ugly crocheted afghans, flashlight batteries, and rolls of star charts on the cluttered kitchen table. "Gross," she says, pushing aside an ashtray of lipstick-stained cigarette butts.

Mom says artists are messy: "It's as obvious as that." Her work shirt hangs on the back of her easel, on the floor a paint-splattered wood drawer holds tubes of paints and dirty rags. She rinses out the big thermos and sets it in the drainer; we're taking hot chocolate too.

There are three wineglasses in the sink (four yesterday, three the day before), all Mom's. She cleans them and puts them away. They were a wedding gift from Frieda (Dad's mom), imported from Portugal, the colors of stained glass. Mom ignores me when I rearrange them so red stands between the green and blue.

We had a late lunch and are saving our appetites until our midnight picnic under the stars. It's August and meteor season.

Dad walks in with a sack of powdered doughnuts. The "star party" was his idea.

"How much longer?" Lauren whines.

"You tell me." Dad points at the wall clock, then kisses Mom's neck, but she swats him away.

No one asks me, though I look at my watch and answer anyway. "Three hours, two minutes, and forty seconds." I like to be specific. I like the way some numbers are multiples of each other, and others reach into infinity.

The clock over the fireplace chimes. The antique dealer said it was from Eastern Europe, most likely Polish or Czech. Mom's people are Eastern European. Mom and her sister Jamie were Romanian Jews once, but now they're nothing. They were sent away, orphaned by the war; they even left their accents behind. The clock makes a deep distant sound like it's chiming on a mantel far away then bounces off a star in the middle of the ocean before finding our house in Portland, Oregon. The ocean is like the sky, only upside down, and meteors and comets are speedboats flying across it.

It's time for *Sea Hunt!* Repeats of course, but who cares? Time will crawl unless we keep busy. I dash to the family room and plop down in front of the TV.

Soon the whole family joins me.

Stupid ads drone on and on. When Edie Adams slinks across the set in a long tight dress, singing about cigars, Dad peeks over his *Sports Illustrated* and whistles.

"She's married to Ernie Kovacs," Mom says, sitting on the arm of his chair. "Bet they'd be fun at a cocktail party, don't you think, Paul?"

Dad shrugs.

Mom loves cocktail parties. Mom loves cocktails.

Finally the TV screen fills with a watery scene and a voice introduces *Sea Hunt*'s star Lloyd Bridges as ex–Navy frogman Mike Nelson.

Mom whistles this time.

It's a stormy day and Mike's out on his boat with two clients. One, a young guy with Poindexter glasses who doesn't know how to scuba dive, but his busty girlfriend does. She's a student of Mike's and today is graduation, but he suggests she wait a day or two before the final dive. He warns that the water is unusually choppy and muddied, but the girl starts college on Monday. "It's now or never," she insists.

Mike frowns. "Stay close," he says before slipping overboard.

Dad tsks. "Anyone else smell trouble?"

Mom and Lauren raise their hands.

Everything's fine until they can't see through the boggy blur of water. Mike spins around cautiously then gestures for her to stay close. A sudden movement behind him catches the girl's eye . . . and just the smooth gray cheek of a shark is visible before it disappears into the soupy water. Her eyes swell to saucers, and, unable to remember the hand signal for trouble, she points over Mike's shoulder, then toward the surface. When Mike looks again, he sees nothing. He shakes his head and gives her a thumbs-up.

"That's right, ignore her. Typical man," Mom mutters. "Haven't we seen this one before? Aren't they all reruns these days?"

"Turn around! Turn around!" I yell.

While the girl finally breaks for the surface, the sleek, gray, pin-eyed animal picks up speed, aiming itself at Mike like a torpedo, its giant jagged mouth ripping a hole through the blurry curtain of water between them.

I throw my hand over my mouth.

On the surface, Poindexter pulls his girlfriend aboard just in time to see the shark's fin skim by.

Underwater, Mike raises his spear gun and fires into the shark's mighty mouth. The animal jerks away, and quickly swims off, a trail of blood scenting the water around him.

"Whew," Mom says in an exaggerated voice, "that was close."

"It's all over now," Dad responds. "He's history once his friends get a snootful of blood. Right, Lily?"

Mom reaches for the *TV Guide*. "Another happy ending. What else is on?"

"Lily?" Dad repeats, but I'm still underwater, my air hose torn. Bubbles fill our family room.

Lauren throws a pillow at me and, startled, I yelp. "Dummy," she says.

"That's enough," Dad snaps.

Lauren's not supposed to make fun of me. It's a family rule.

I watch each TV show to the end of the credits, and when *Sea Hunt* is over, Dad calls us to the kitchen. "Okay, troops," he says, "meet here at twenty-three hundred, sharp. Take a nap if you need to, but be dressed for the big night."

Mom pours herself a glass of wine. "That's eleven p.m., girls. You've got . . ."

Lauren tears outside with her jump rope. It's summer and still light.

"She's like a grasshopper," Dad says. "Do you think it's healthy for her to jump so much?"

"It makes her happy," Mom says. "That's good enough for me."

There's a "shark curtain" in my bedroom closet. Every time I pull the string to the bulb overhead, I see only white and I have to wait for my eyes to refocus to see more. Bad things can happen while you wait. Until Mike Nelson finally saw the shark curtain, he didn't know he was in trouble.

Each room, as I head down the hall to mine, draws me in. I try not to look. Doors open, lights off, curtains closed to keep out the summer heat, darkness fills each room to brimming. Beyond it are more shark curtains, more blurry darkness.

At the threshold to my room, Mrs. Wiggins, our St. Bernard, lies on her left side snoring. "*Sea Hunt*," I explain as I bend down to pet her. Her tumor is hot under my hand and the old dog tenses before she relaxes and wags her tail. Maybe the cancer isn't as bad as Mom thinks it is.

Maybe Mrs. Wiggins just doesn't like to be touched sometimes. I don't.

When I flip on the overhead light, my fingers brush the framed picture of Jesus that Gramma Frieda gave me. His chest is open and His heart is wrapped in roses and thorns, but it doesn't bleed. He looks down at the art books Mom put on my bed: *Leonardo's Gifts* and *Pastoral Landscapes of the Romantic Age.*

Groovy. Mom never lets me look at her art books.

On the cover of *Pastoral Landscapes*, a golden sky turns black as it disappears into a blurry stand of trees, a place too thick and dark to make out what's happening inside it.

In the living room, Mom and Dad laugh and talk. My best friend Judy calls them Romeo and Juliet.

A rock hits my bedroom window screen. "Watch!" Lauren calls from the driveway. "Hot peppers, Lily! Watch!" I count thirty superfast twirls before she makes a mistake.

On the sidewalk behind her, Missy Crenshaw rides her new Schwinn bicycle, smiling and waving like a Rose Festival princess. It's a warm August night and still light at 9:17 p.m. Across the street, a phone rings and young, blond Mrs. Savage throws down her garden hose and steps inside. Somewhere a baby cries; a dog barks; a golden-oldie radio station plays "Mr. Sandman." Rusty and Sherman, each in coonskin caps, sit on the curb across the street, quietly loading their cap guns.

I watch Judy the longest. Slouched and sad, she sits in her front yard reading a magazine, but she never turns a page. "If things don't get better," she told me once, "I'm running away." So I watch her intently, looking for anything that would say she's finally ready to pack her bag and sneak off in the middle of the night. She's saved her allowance for six months, her babysitting money too.

Where would I go if *I* was running away?

Mom's books are big and heavy and full of beautiful glossy pictures.

In *Leonardo's Gifts*, I stare at Leonardo da Vinci's sculptures, focusing on their white empty eyes and marble sex organs; I always thought penises were bigger.

I trace one of Leonardo's flying machines, paste it into my scrapbook, and glue strips of Mom's "ratty old mink stole" to its wings. Then I turn to the centerfold of *The Last Supper* and trace that scene into my scrapbook too. I give the table a long tablecloth painted with stars and planets, and

11

fill the windows behind it with comets. I've seen the picture at Gramma Frieda's church and I know that Jesus's hand is raised (Dad says He's asking for the check), but when I look closer this time, I see powdered doughnuts on the table.

And powdered sugar on Jesus's face.

I slam the book shut and look at my watch.

Mom says I'm good at entertaining myself. She says my imagination is a work of art. *The Last Supper* is a work of art. Maybe my imagination is on the next page; I saw something like that on *The Twilight Zone* once.

When I dare to look at Jesus again, He raises an eyebrow and shrugs.

"Stop it!" I yell. Mrs. Wiggins moans and briefly raises her head.

On TV, people who hallucinate famous dead people (like Jesus) are taken to the hospital where they put jumper cables on their heads. They wear diapers and pajamas all day, and cry all night because they want to go home.

"Crawford Quarry is perfect viewing," Dad told us earlier. He knows all about the planets and stars, but he still calls Mom his "favorite heavenly body." He checked out books from the Multnomah County Library and drew star charts that we'll look at when we get to the pit. He bought us each a flashlight too.

Lauren and I've never been to Crawford Quarry, but when our parents told us about the huge pit where people dig rocks out of the ground with big Flintstone-style steam shovels, my little sister giggled. She loves *The Flintstones*.

At 23:00 (11:00 p.m. exactly), we meet in the kitchen. Lauren's been sleeping and she's hard to wake up, but I've been watching the clock—listening to the little ticks inside each tock and matching them to my heartbeats; visualizing every step between here and the entrance to Crawford Woods.

"Okay, kidlets," Dad says, pulling on his windbreaker, "it's time to go." Mrs. Wiggins looks up from the floor in the family room and wags her tail. "People are sleeping, but their windows will be open, so no talking. And Lily? Leave your watch at home."

"Why?"

"Because you look at it all the time, dummy," Lauren says.

"And none of that, girls, or we'll turn right around and come home. Got it?"

Lauren and I draw zippers across our mouths.

I grab Mrs. Wiggins's leash. "Not this time, honey," Dad says. The star charts crinkle when he pulls a rubber band over them. "Mrs. Wiggins is too sick to go with us. She can watch the house while we're gone."

"But what if we need her? Her breed is strong enough to pull people out of snowdrifts. Besides, she's used to babysitting us. She wants to go." Mrs. Wiggins wags her tail but doesn't lift her head.

"You're being selfish, Lily," Dad says. His words pierce my heart. "She's old and sick. You wouldn't want to be dragged around if you were her."

"I won't drag her around."

The cold water faucet whistles when Mom fills a glass for her evening "happy pill," and we all turn around to watch. Mom gets unhappy faster than Speedy Gonzales and the pill "gives her balance," Dad says. "We're lucky to live in a pharmaceutical age."

He puts his hands on his hips. "Okay, Asher family. Are we ready to roll?"

Mom smiles; Lauren claps.

"Home no later than three a.m.," he says. He also says something about the bogeyman and carriages turning into pumpkins too, but Lauren and Mom are already out the door.

I tuck my wristwatch in Mrs. Wiggins's bed, say a prayer, and draw a pie chart over her, blessing her the way a priest would. "I love you," I say in Pig Latin.

Dad puts his hand on my shoulder, but I shrug it off.

It's a twenty-minute walk from our home on Aiken Street, uphill past the fancy houses in Crawford Heights, to the entrance of Crawford Butte. As we pass the big houses, Mom points out her favorites. Against the dark blue sky, they look like outlines of giant ships. In daytime, they're all the same: big and white with used brick trim, bay windows, and fake columns, some in the Greek Ionic tradition, some in the Doric. Other columns look like Lincoln Logs or upside-down umbrella stands.

I'd like to build a table-sized Acropolis, paint scenes on the inside, then spin it like a zoetrope. Aunt Jamie said she'd help.

It's a beautiful night.

My family's quiet, though inside people's houses, dogs bark at us anyway. It's late but televisions light up most living rooms. Jack Paar was Mom's favorite late-night host but Johnny Carson's on now. Tonight's guests are Woody Allen and Ed Ames.

We finally arrive at the dark woodsy path leading to the quarry pit and Dad double-checks our flashlights. He checks that we're each still carrying a blanket too, and asks after the hot chocolate, tin cups, sandwiches, and powdered doughnuts in Mom's picnic basket. When he also asks if I zipped my windbreaker, I don't answer. I'll be fourteen in two months; I'm not a baby.

Trying to be funny, Dad runs his new binoculars up and down Mom's legs. "*Ooga, ooga,*" he jokes. Judy says he bought them with money he won at the horse track, but how does *she* know?

Dad walks ahead of us, kicking an empty can out of his way. It's motor oil, probably for the motorcycles that tear through Crawford Woods all hours of the day and night. There's an empty wine bottle in the bushes too, old yellowed newspaper, and dirty Dixie Cups.

"Litterbugs," Lauren says, leaning into me. Messes make her nervous.

Mom and Dad stop where the trees begin to darken and blur and I stop too. "Wait a minute," Dad says, turning around. He sniffs. "What's that?" It's his teasing voice. "Does anyone else smell it?"

Mom turns her flashlight beam on him. "Paul," she warns.

He sniffs again. "Is that . . . carrion?"

"What's carrion?" Laura asks.

"Come on, Paul. No ghost stories. You promised."

"All right, all right." He smiles, and taking Mom's hand finally leads the way into Crawford Woods. When they slip out of view, my sister and I hurry up behind them. Every five steps, I stop and listen.

"Mom?" Lauren calls out. "Lily's—"

"Use your flashlights if you need them," she interrupts.

The dirt trail is soft and dusty, and except for the picnic basket bumping against Mom's leg, Dad's crinkly star charts, and Lauren's heavy breathing (Mom says she needs her adenoids out), it's a quiet walk through Crawford Woods.

Up ahead is the basalt quarry, the bombed-out crater, the hole all the way to China. Up ahead is the giant mouth of the pit and the meteor-filled sky.

The path narrows and widens, narrows and widens, like the giant walk-through lung at the science museum. Where the trees disappear, the woods become a wall of black. I want to be brave like the Indians on TV, to ride into battle screaming my head off and eat the hearts of my enemies. I want to stop walking and look into the shadows where the shark curtain lives but I'm afraid. I'm afraid of places like the blurry landscapes in Mom's art book, where angry elves keep escaped circus bears as slaves, or gargoyles sit in the bushes watching me stumble by.

My fingers twitch as I "pretend type" a prayer on Frieda's typewriter. *God bless Aunt Jamie and Mrs. Wiggins and . . .*

The trail gets narrower, pressing against us. "How much longer?" I ask.

"Not long," Dad answers. He directs us to turn off our flashlights and "trust the stars, your eyes will adjust." For three or four minutes (it could be longer; I don't have my watch) Dad whistles the theme song to *The Andy Griffith Show.*

The woods smell like the sweet-and-sour soup they give you before the good stuff at Ming's Chinese Garden. "Smell the musk?" Mom asks. "It's nettles. Be careful, they'll sting."

I stop and sniff. The smell is strong and getting closer.

Nettles and soup, but more than that too. Something familiar that isn't the raccoon poop in Mom's flower bed; isn't Dad's wool army coat, dog chow, or the cold cement floor in the garage. Something else is in the air. A whole lot of something elses. I hurry a little and accidentally step on the heel of Lauren's shoes.

"Dummy," she mumbles.

Suddenly, a huge bird darts over our heads and Lauren gasps. "An owl!" Mom shouts and, pretending to be scared, hurries to Dad's side. I read that owls are warnings, sometimes of death, sometimes of danger.

The others walk on, but I stop, then take three short breaths and inhale deeply. Exhale. Repeat. Three short breaths (for the Father, the Son, and the Holy Ghost; for Mom, Dad, and Lauren) and inhale deeply. Exhale. Repeat.

The scent is some combination of familiar and unfamiliar, but sticky sweet and wet too. I open my arms like crucified Jesus, stretching my fingers and bugging my eyes, and make myself into a smell antenna.

The scent is coming toward us: the closer it gets, the more it fills my lungs ... The more it fills my lungs, the more the ground vibrates under my feet ... The more the ground vibrates under my feet the more the smell vines up my legs like a pea plant until the stink and sound and vibration slip through my ears and nostrils, filling me up, inflating me like a rubber balloon, or Jiffy Pop. Will I explode before it gets here?

"Mommmm!" Lauren flips on her flashlight and walks back to me. "Lily's being weird again."

Listen, can't you hear them ... ? Dozens of snapping sounds and growls, panting breaths, high-pitched barks, and finally the smell—I recognize it—the warm dusty smell of dry soft dirt, a cloud of it pushed ahead of their thrumming, drumming feet.

How close? I fall to my knees and press my ear to the ground.

"Lily! For God's sake, stand up." It's Mom. I see the toes of her dusty white deck shoes. They'll be washed and sitting in the morning sun by the time I get up tomorrow. "Lily!" I feel her warm worried hands on my shoulders. "Paul!" she calls.

"I'm okay," I say, or try to say. But dogs don't talk.

I smell their hot sour breath and wet fur as we race through Crawford Woods together, their thick muscular bodies brushing mine as we run side by side, feeling the tendons in my legs stretch and contract as I run—only I'm big and slow and sick and I fall behind the pack ... behind ... slowing ... slowing ...

Then find a burst of energy and rejoin them. My face is wet with the saliva that flies off the tips of their long speckled tongues. Their fur brushes my face, their musk fills my nose. When the hair on my arms stands up, they recognize me. I'm one of them. In a blur of dust and dirt, claws and fur, we nip at each other, yip, and bark.

"Lily!" It's Dad. "Can't we do one simple family thing together without you ..."

On my knees in the starlit woods I see what Mrs. Wiggins sees with her tired milky eyes; flying over stones and potholes, struggling to focus through the cloud of soft thundering dirt while dry prickly brush whips her face, she keeps going, putting on even more speed when she sees her family, us, up ahead on the trail.

The others will fly past us before she does, but somewhere up the trail the dogs will slow down. Then. Finally. Stop. They're only pets, after all, out-of-shape purebreds and mutts, not feral dogs, wolves, coyotes, or (their distant cousins) bears; no T-Rexes or Thunderbirds. Finally, they'll wander home (Mrs. Nelson is calling Offie right now), exhausted.

But proud they didn't forget: they were wild once.

They're nearing us! The heat of the pack, the yelping, the dust—

Suddenly Dad cries, "Off the path! Now!" And my family jumps, making startled complaining sounds when we land in the brush, seconds before the dusty snarling dogs race by.

I raise my head and watch Mrs. Wiggins lift off the ground. Floating above the others, she looks back at me with her milky eyes, and her warm cancerous breath heats my face.

"Thanks," she says in Pig Latin.

"Everybody okay?" Dad calls. His flashlight bleaches the trail. It finds Lauren. "Lima Bean?"

Lauren nods. She looks scared and confused. Her freckles spring on and off her face like Mexican jumping beans.

"Lily?"

The muscles in my legs relax as I pull sticks and vines out of my hair. The thick callous pads on my feet dissolve. I'm still panting from the run, and chilled by sweat I stand up in the bushes and press my hand to my burning chest.

"Okay?" he repeats.

Yes. No. "Okay," I say, clearing my throat.

"Kit?" Dad shines the light on Mom, curled around him. "There you are," he jokes, kissing the top of her curly auburn head. They found each other first; they always do.

Mom laughs too, then reaches for the picnic basket and says, "Whew! That was wild! Where'd they come from?"

I know. My eyes are good at night. I recognized some of them, dogs from the neighborhood: the German shepherd from Sherwood Court, two yellow labs, the old boxer, the chubby beagle, the short-legged Lassie.

At the entrance to the quarry, Dad unhooks the chain gate with the

No Trespassing sign and gestures us through. "Bet the dogs passed here hours ago," he laughs.

Mom smiles, but Lauren and I don't. We glance at each other. The dogs were cool but it's wrong to break the law like Dad is.

We follow our parents into the starlit open sky. The trees stand back from the big hole, silhouetted against the clear night sky like rows of spears. The heat of the day still clings to the barren ground. It's a weird place, like the surface of the moon in comic books. Lauren slips her hand in mine. She looks around for the Flintstones' steam shovels, but they're nowhere to be seen.

"Don't forget what I told you about . . ." Mom peers at the sky. "Look! There's one!" She points at the twinkling star mass. "How beautiful! There, did you see it? Stars, meteors, everywhere!"

Meteors fall around us without touching the ground; they hang in the trees and shine in Lauren's red hair.

When Mom calls the stars "kisses from angels," Dad grabs her and kisses her on the lips.

"Girls?" Mom starts again. "You remember what we discussed about the pit, right?"

Lauren puts her flashlight beam under her chin. "Do I look like a jack o' lantern, Mom?"

"I take that as a yes then?"

"Stay away from the pit," I answer for us both.

"Is that your jump rope?"

"It's my lucky charm," Lauren explains as we lay out our blankets. My sister doesn't go anywhere without her jump rope. Sometimes she loops it over her bicycle handles or wears it as a belt; tonight she carries it in her afghan.

Lauren jumps rope, chews gum, sucks her thumb, and throws up because of anxiety, bad ears, and motion sickness. When Mom told Dr. Goodnight that Lauren was a "nervous child, a perfect candidate for ulcers," he smiled and wrote Mom a prescription for more happy pills.

"A rabbit's foot would be smaller," Mom said to her.

I got in trouble for burning my rabbit's foot, even when I explained that it was the only way the foot and rabbit could be reunited. I read about it in *Aboriginal Tales*.

"Ladies!" Dad barks. "Can we please be quiet and watch the stars? Isn't that what we came for?"

That's not a real question; neither one of them are.

Lauren and I don't get close to the pit. Okay, maybe just a little. On top of Gramma Frieda's afghans we pretend to be astronauts; the starlit white rim of the pit is the outline of the moon. My blanket is a flying carpet, a floating island where I sit and walk my fingers across the sky, leaping over meteors.

Mrs. Wiggins loves the sky. When it's a full moon, I don't have to look outside, check the tide chart, or *The Old Farmer's Almanac*, because Mrs. Wiggins jumps on my bed and stares out the window, so I know it's full. Now that she's sick and old, she pees a little when she jumps, so Mom covers my bed with old towels.

I wish I could read Mrs. Wiggins's mind. I tried her on a *Ouija* board once—shoved it under her nose and waited for her to nudge a series of letters that would spell out something—but she didn't like it. She's private, like me. After school one day, I found its chewed-up pieces in her dog bed.

When we finish our picnic, Lauren and I lay back, counting meteors out loud and laughing. After a while, we hear our parents whisper and Lauren shines her flashlight on them.

"I knew four flashlights were too many," Dad says, turning his back to the beam. Mom lies beside him. He gives her a noisy kiss.

"Oh, Pablo," Mom giggles. She calls him Pablo when they're kissy.

"*Oh, Pablo*," Lauren mimics, making loud smoochie sounds on her arm.

"Girls!" Dad snaps.

With my index finger I connect a series of stationary stars, and draw Mrs. Wiggins's outline in the twinkling sky. A new constellation: Canis Wiggins.

"Lily, do the dogs run through the woods every night?"

I shrug but Lauren isn't looking. I guess she asks me questions I can't answer because I'm older than she is. Plus, our parents are making out, so she can't ask them either.

"*Mommy and Dad-dy, sitting in a tree,*" she sings as she jumps rope. I smell the dust kicked up with every twirl. The ground thumps when her feet land together. "*K-I-S-S* . . ."

In the dark, on another flying blanket far away, Mom giggles.

"*First comes love, then comes marriage,*" Lauren continues.

Mrs. Wiggins's water dish is in the stars too. And a cartoon bubble over her big square head that reads, *STAY AWAY FROM THE—*

Suddenly there's a skid, and the rope stops turning. A thump. A moan.

Lauren! I jump to my feet.

"Lily?" she whispers.

"Lauren?" I whisper back.

"Girls?"

"Mrs. Asher, please!" Dad is being silly. "Your lips, the stars. Your lips, the stars."

"For God's sake, Paul, let go!" Mom flips on the flashlight and hurries toward us. I'm blinded by the glare. She quickly puts it down, and turning the beam away illuminates the gray scraped wall on the opposite side of the quarry.

"What's going . . . Where's . . . Lily, what are you doing?"

On my stomach.

Hanging my head and arms over the lip of the big black hole.

Reaching for my little sister.

My body flexes and stretches, the muscles lengthen, tighten, and grow strong; I smell the dogs' musk, and feel their deep excited growls in my throat. Somehow I have one end of her jump rope. When I tug at it, Lauren looks up. She's easy to see under a sky of bright stars that light her pink barrettes and the shiny tip of her sun-blistered nose. She stands on a tiny shelf, just out of arm's reach, and clutching her end of the jump rope leans against the quarry wall, breathing heavily.

"Lauren!" Mom gasps as she kneels beside me. "Oh, Jesus!"

Dad turns his flashlight beam on Lauren, who blinks and closes her eyes. "It's okay, Kit, we'll get her out. She's right here on a ledge, only a couple of feet away. She's fine." He clicks off the flashlight and hands it to Mom. "Daddy's here, Lima Bean. I gotcha."

He straddles me and wraps his hands around mine.

Doesn't he see me? I'm not invisible.

"Lily, let me do it. I'll pull her up."

Lauren's eyes shine with tears. "I'm scared," she says quietly.

"I know," I tell her. "When you feel me pull the rope, hold on real tight, okay?" Lauren doesn't answer. "Lean against the rock and I'll pull you up. If you feel another ledge, step up on it."

I can do this. *We* can do this. I feel Mrs. Wiggins crouch beside me; I smell her hot rank breath.

"Lily," Dad says sternly, "give me the rope. Let it go slowly."

I ignore him. "Lean against the rocky wall, Lauren," I say. "I'll pull you up."

"But it's dirty." Lauren hates being dirty.

"I know, but you can take a bath when we get home." Mrs. Wiggins's wet nose smudges my leg. Her toenails scratch the dirt. Somehow she's behind me, ready to pull with me. "Just hold on really, really tight."

"Lily," Mom says, "let Daddy do it. He's stronger than you."

"No."

"This is no time to be stubborn!"

"NO!"

"*Please*, Lily! Lauren's in danger!"

"I am?"

"Lily!" Dad barks.

"NO!" I yell at them both. "Go back to your stupid kissing!" I don't take my eyes off Lauren. "I won't let you fall," I tell her quietly. "Promise."

I scoot backward and pull on the jump rope. The dirt and gravel scratch my stomach and then I do it, we do it, somehow we pull her up—Mrs. Wiggins, and maybe Dad and Mom, but mostly me—and Lauren slides up over the edge, out of the pit, flat on her belly, dirty and scared and whimpering.

Mom hugs Lauren to her big soft boobs. "Are you all right?" she asks while looking her over with the flashlight. Finally she looks at me. "Why must you always challenge us, Lily? Why can't you do what we ask? The rope could have slipped from your hands, and then what? If your father hadn't been there to pull her up . . ." Mom starts crying all over again. When Dad pats her shoulder, she lets go of Lauren and grabs his hand. "Oh God, Paul."

Shouldn't my sister be more scared than Mom?

Lauren climbs out of her lap.

"If you won't listen to your father, Lily, then listen to me. We can't protect you if you don't do as we ask."

"But you were kissing," Lauren says. She twirls the jump rope, walking instead of jumping, stepping over it when it stops at her feet.

"Lauren! Put that damn thing down!" Mom says. "You're the older sister, Lily. How many times have I told you—"

"Yeah." When Mom yells at me, my voice gets small.

"*Yeah?* What the hell kind of answer is that?" Mom sniffs. "We're your parents. If you don't listen to us here, how can I trust you at Peace Lake?"

Peace Lake is our favorite family vacation spot. It's also where Aunt Jamie swims. And me. And sometimes the whole swim club, the one thing I do with kids my age besides go to school. I'm a good swimmer, one of the best on our team; there's a competition next month, but even if I win no one will care. No one talks to me at school or on the swim bus. Lauren says it's because I'm a "weirdo."

"Lily!"

"Okay."

Dad carries Lauren on his shoulders as we walk out of Crawford Woods. She's ten years old and "too big," but he does it anyway. She carries the unopened star charts and every once in a while looks back at me. The jump rope is draped over her shoulders. "Dummy," she says with a smile.

"Dummy," I smile back.

The night air is thick and stuffy. *Humid*, Mom calls it.

The woods are throwing us out. They've had enough, they want us to go. We embarrass them with our clumsy, weirdo, pill-popping, gambling stuff. When Dad says, "I'll bet each one of you a Hostess Cupcake it's after two a.m.," Mom throws a dirt clod at him. He pushes a button on his wristwatch and announces, "It's two thirty."

That's one hundred and fifty minutes past midnight.

Back home, drawers stick out and closet doors stand open.

We should hurry. *Things get out if you're not careful, things get in.*

What I wish had happened next:

"Let's all sleep in," Mom suggests. Then, "Waffles with whipped cream and strawberries at ten!"

Mom talks a lot when she's tired. Or scared. Or excited. She talks a lot on our way out of Crawford Woods that night. Mom talks about being nearly trampled by a pack of dogs. She calls me her "hero" for rescuing Lauren, and sings, "*Hi-Lili, Hi-Lo . . .*" I blush, but I like her singing. She talks about school starting in three weeks, and how Lauren and I need new coats.

"Let's go shopping tomorrow," she says.

"Yippee!" Lauren yells. She loves to shop.

I hate shopping, but maybe I'll go this time.

Minutes later, with Mom in the lead, we sing "Kumbaya" as loudly as we can. She balances the picnic basket on her head, like one of the African women in her paintings, while comets fly through the trees.

We talk about Maxwell Smart's old phone-in-the-shoe trick, and *The Man from U.N.C.L.E*, and Mom asks Dad to say something with a Russian gangster accent. "Oh, Pablo," she swoons, and everyone laughs.

What really happened:

After a while, Lauren yawns and leans against Dad, half asleep.

"The Perseids are beautiful," I say to no one in particular.

Mom's still mad. Dad whistles the first few bars of *The Andy Griffith Show* song, then stops.

I see something in the bushes and fall behind.

"Lily?" Mom calls over her shoulder.

"Got to pee. Just a minute."

"Good job, kiddo," says the voice in the dark. I can't see His face but I know it's Jesus; His voice is quiet and deep like in Bible movies, and stars light the shoulders of His robe.

I don't answer. Maybe if I ignore Him, He'll go away.

"Saving Lauren," Jesus repeats. "Good job."

If I talk to Him they'll put jumper cables on my head, stick me in pajamas and diapers, and I'll never go home. Never eat waffles again or get a new school coat.

"Lily?" Mom calls again.

"Coming!"

If Jesus were really here right now, I'd ask Him why He didn't help me save Lauren; the Bible is full of bigger miracles than that. I'd ask Him what's wrong with me; why even my skin feels weird these days. If Jesus were standing in front of me in the woods at three o'clock in the morning, congratulating me on saving my little sister, like He is, I'd ask Him why He's bugging me.

Does He want me to wear jumper cables?

Doesn't He love me like the Bible says?

"*Now*, young lady," Mom calls.

I turn and start up the path.

"Sure, go ahead," Jesus says behind me. "I'll catch up with you later. Say hello to Mrs. Wiggins for me." I hear a twig snap as He heads off into the brush. Why doesn't He fly? He walks on water, doesn't He?

I rush to Mom and fall in step behind her.

CHAPTER 2

THE SWIMMING RIBBON

Three things have happened since Jamie last came to Sunday dinner:
1. The pit.

2. I saw Jesus riding on the back of the garbage truck.

3. I lied about the swim contest at Peace Lake. No one knows I lied, and my lie didn't hurt anyone, but it still bugs me. I want to be a good person, and Aunt Jamie says, "Lies make your guts hurt."

My guts have been hurting for days.

"It's lush and lanky Lily Lou!" Jamie cries as I open the door. She likes words too. When she sees our old dog standing beside me, she kneels down to face her. "And the wonderful Wanda Wiggins," she says quietly. "Can't leave you out, can we, girl?" When Mrs. Wiggins whines and wags her tail, her hips tip to one side and she stumbles a little. "Poor thing."

"How do you know what her first name is?" Lauren asks.

"She told me." Jamie winks. "Nice pink umbrella. New?"

The umbrella over her head, Lauren twirls in place on her tiptoes, humming "Waltz of the Flowers." She wants to be a dancer. Or a dentist. Or a Southern belle; she's just seen *Gone with the Wind*.

"Why, yes it is," she says in her best Scarlett O'Hara. "Mother took me to the 99-cent store and said I could have anything I want. I just *love* the 99-cent store."

"Me too. Especially the bins of cheap imported toys."

When something bad happens, Mom goes shopping. She took Lauren the day after the pit.

"I heard about what happened at the quarry," Jamie says. "Everybody cool?"

In the kitchen Mom winds the oven clock, then takes down the Sunday china and stacks it on the counter.

"We're cool," Lauren smiles. "Hey, are you a beatnik, Aunt Jamie?"

"A beatnik?" Dad calls out. "Not our Jamie! Maybe a hippie—"

"More like a bohemian, I guess. A nonconformist." Jamie smiles at me. "How's my favorite mermaid?"

"Fine," I lie. My stomach is wringing out towels.

"The big family day at Peace Lake is tomorrow, right? It's smart of your family to go on a Monday; you'll probably have it all to yourselves. You can bring your pink umbrella, it'll keep you from burning," she says to my fair-skinned redheaded sister, "and you," she beams at me again, "can swim out as far as you want. Excited?"

"Yep," Lauren says. "Want to see me jump rope? I did thirty-six hot peppers without messing up."

"Thirty-seven," I correct her.

"Later, maybe," Jamie says to both of us. "Excited about school?"

"Yep."

Jamie sniffs the air. "Chicken and dumplings?"

"Yep."

"*Yep* is not a word, Lauren," Mom lectures from the kitchen. "Do I hear the voice of higher learning? Has my sister finally arrived?"

"Come in! Close the door." Dad's at the dining room table reading Dale Carnegie's *How to Win Friends and Influence People*. It's a loan from our neighbor Mr. Marks, Judy's stepdad.

"For God's sake, Paul," Jamie giggles, "ever heard of fresh air? It's seventy-three degrees out."

"Better be warmer tomorrow, if anyone's going swimming."

Lauren, Jamie, and I take our positions at the dining room table. My sister looks at the salad bowl and crinkles her nose.

"Come on, Kit, let's eat!" Dad bellows. "It's dangerous to keep a hungry man waiting."

Jamie shakes her head. "I thought my sister had you better trained. I swear, I'm never getting married."

"Unless, God forbid, you fall in love," Mom says, appearing in the doorway with a tureen of chicken and dumplings. Everyone applauds. It's my favorite giant soup bowl—its two long-eared white rabbits serve as the handles.

"Wait, wait, I almost forgot," Jamie says with excitement. Mrs. Wiggins slips under the table as Jamie dashes to the family room to dig through her satchel.

Mom sighs. "Can't it wait until—"

"Absolutely not! I thought it would be fun to talk about something different over dinner. Find out what the *girls'* opinions are for a change." Jamie is the grooviest aunt ever. When she sits down again, placing a thin black book next to Mom's fancy salad bowl, a curtain of long red hair falls forward, brushing her arm. Jamie is beautiful. Even Mom says so.

"A book?" Dad lifts an eyebrow. "Okay, James, talk. But if my dinner gets cold, we're eating at your house next time."

"Before we dig into another one of Kit's beautiful meals, I want to present Lily with this gorgeous homemade ribbon for taking first place in last week's Race to the Pilings!" Pressed in the book is a purple ribbon with my name in silver glitter. "Ta-da!"

My stomach does a backflip, nearly knocking me out of the chair.

Lauren reaches for the ribbon. "Can I have one too?"

"Only when you become a master swimmer like your sister, Lima Bean. Only when you brave the dark, cold, treacherous waters of Peace Lake," Jamie says dramatically, "to reach the half-submerged pilings of the ancient Floating Doughnut Shack."

"Ancient?" Dad says, pouring wine. "It only burned down ten years ago."

"We're talking halfway across the lake, Paul," Jamie says. "That's impressive at any age."

Mom's suspicious. "What have you two been up to?"

Jamie looks at me. "You didn't tell them?"

Mom doesn't like it when Coach Betty moves swim practice away from the YWCA. "The team went to Peace Lake," I say.

"Again? I don't remember being notified. What if—"

"No what-ifs. No big deal," Jamie says, helping herself to the Waldorf salad. "Other moms came along; there was plenty of supervision. I was up there already. It was a beautiful day—just a hint of fall in the air."

Mom looks confused. "Did you bring a slip home, Lily? Did I see it?"

I nod.

"Did I sign it?"

I nod again. It's true but my stomach hurts times pi. The only thing worse than lying is making Mom feel bad.

We take turns passing her our plates and watch quietly as she serves each one of us a dumpling that she smothers with chicken and gravy. She finally slips into her chair. "Huh," she says, surprised at herself.

Mom forgot to buy gas last week too, and a tow truck brought her home. Her car was full of groceries and when the truck guy helped bring them inside, Mom said he "made some crack about all the wine I bought. He thought we were having a party. It's none of his damn business what I buy."

Everyone eats until Jamie pats Mom's arm. "I forget things all the time," she says, finishing her second glass of wine. "It doesn't matter. The lake was great, Kit. The water was delicious and the girls are such strong swimmers. Of course, Lily took the cake."

Lauren perks up. "We're having cake?"

"You'd have been proud of her, Kit!"

Don't be proud of me. I didn't get to the pilings; I had to stop. My body weighed a ton, and I was out of breath. I dog-paddled in place until Theresa and Carol swam by, then joined them swimming back to shore. They reached the pilings but I didn't. On the beach, Jamie stood next to Coach, clapping her hands and whistling. Mom and Dad like it when I do something with "kids my age," but it only mattered that Jamie applauded. When she did, I forgot all about the pilings.

Kind of. If I had a time machine, I'd take back everything that happened that day.

"But Peace Lake is hell and gone," Mom says. "I should have remembered."

"It all worked out," Dad says. "No harm done. Lily's an ace swimmer, remember?"

"Don't patronize me, Paul. It's important that I remember."

"Ta-da!" I hold up the ribbon. This time it says, *Liar.*

Lauren loves round things. Eggs, baked onions, pancakes, Cheerios. She wolfed down her dumpling, made circles in her gravy, and pointed at Aunt Jamie's book. "Are we going to talk about your book?"

"Yes," Dad says. "What is it?"

"Only the most *amazing* thing with the most *amazing* pictures you'll ever see," Aunt Jamie announces. Her eyes twinkle.

"Have you considered a career on stage?" Dad asks.

Jamie pats the book like Reverend Mike does after he reads a Bible passage to the congregation. "It's called *A Child Is Born*."

My parents exchange looks. "That's really not appropriate for the dinner table," Mom says. She picks it up and puts it down again. "Were you actually going to explain all this to the girls? These are things we talk about as a family. You should have asked us first."

"It's about the miracle of life, not the act of procreation." Jamie takes a big gulp of wine.

"I know what it's about," Mom says.

Ever the copycat, Lauren says, "I don't want to look at the book."

"See?" Aunt Jamie shakes her head. "Ignorance is contagious."

Mom sighs. "More salad, girls?" Lauren and I both stare at her. We're kids; we don't eat rabbit food. "Garlic bread?" Mom unwraps the foil log. "Still plenty left."

We all reach for it.

"Do you know," Jamie says, tearing off tiny pieces she quickly stuffs in her mouth, "that we're all one sex until Mother Nature decides what she needs us for?"

When Jamie says *sex*, Lauren covers her ears.

"Chromosomes determine our gender, but before XY and XX play out, the fetus has everything it needs to be both sexes. The embryo is male *and* female. We even have tails like tadpoles do, for a while anyway. Far out, huh?"

Maybe I'm a boy *and* a girl. Maybe my tail is stuffed up inside me. "Yeah," I say. "Far out." I lean forward with excitement, resting my elbows on the table.

Mom points at my plate. She wants me to eat up but it feels wrong to eat chicken right now. We studied chicken embryos in class, even though the incubator was accidentally turned off one weekend and all the eggs died. Frieda said something was wrong with the baby chicks and God didn't want them to live. Mom said the custodian probably tripped over the plug.

"It's called . . ." Jamie looks at the ceiling. "Um . . ."

"I'll look it up," I offer. "Is it in the book?"

Mom holds her index finger to her lips to shush me. She's worried I might get "too excited." Maybe it's the boy chromosome in me that makes me do stupid stuff. Sherman and Rusty do stupid stuff all the time. "Have another glass of wine, sis. It'll come back to you."

"Go ahead, James," Daddy laughs, "enlighten our impatient little naturalist-in-training. Explain how the same sex glands and genitals develop in both sexes."

"*Dad-eee*," Lauren whines.

Two embryo-shaped dumplings do the backstroke in the cooling soup tureen.

Jamie slaps his arm. "It doesn't matter what it's called, Paul. It's just a word, but the idea, the scientific fact, is deep. That we create each other is amazing! Isn't it, girls?" She takes turns smiling at all of us.

"It's a miracle!" I cry, and accidentally kick poor Mrs. Wiggins under the dinner table. She moans; I must have hit her tumor.

Mom drops her fork. "Is the dog under the table, Lily? I said no, didn't I? Mrs. Wiggins is sick. She smells bad. You know better."

"That's a perfect example," Jamie says. "Science is bursting at the seams. In the future, Mrs. Wiggins could be cloned. We have the capacity to do so many incredible things! What if people had the option of being both sexes? Or neither sex? What would being human mean if we could reshuffle the chromosomes and be something completely different?"

Dad laughs. "You mean like a hermaphrodite?"

Mom throws her napkin at him.

This is the best, most grown-up conversation of my whole life.

"We could reinvent the world, create new foods that could save mankind! What if," Jamie says, turning to Lauren and me, "there were real mermaids and giants and DayGlo jungles? And lichen tasted like coconut, and we could take elephant rides on the moon?"

"Wow!" Lauren says.

Mom smiles. "*Wow* is the word, all right. You've been reading way too much science fiction, sis."

Jamie takes a big gulp of wine. "Okay, maybe I'm exaggerating a little, but if we have the science for it, why not the imagination? What are we afraid of? What's so special about all these overpriced toys, anyway?" She glances around the room, holding out her arms like the TV game-show model Carol Merrill. "When we could have a more meaningful and . . . *interesting* life. You're an artist, Kit. Don't you want that?"

Mom scowls at her. "They're not toys, Jamie. We work hard to have nice things. There's nothing wrong with nice things."

"I know, I know, it's just that . . . we have to change, Kit. It's almost too late already. We waste energy making things we don't need or even want once we get them home. We're destroying the planet."

"Let's not go into that over dinner. You're frightening the girls."

"No she's not!"

"Lily!"

"Why shouldn't the girls be part of the discussion? Their generation could save the world. They could save us from ourselves."

Mom gestures for our dirty dishes and we pass them, surprised when she starts scraping them right there at the table. She never does that. They make an angry sound.

"As fascinating as the book is," Jamie continues, "as amazing as the birth process is, our importance is overrated. We've messed things up. Mother Earth is polluted, and overpopulated. Her resources can't support—"

"Stop it!" Mom cries as she picks up the stack of plates and storms out of the room. "I've had enough Mother Earth for one night."

I slump in my chair. Sometimes I think Aunt Jamie is my real mom. Over her shoulder is the china cabinet where my swim-meet ribbons are kept, along with Lauren's first-through-fourth-grade attendance diplomas, and fragile little things no one's allowed to dust. Aunt Jamie's swimming trophies are in there too; Mom's keeping them for her until she moves out of "that damp little house on the old coast highway."

I braid the tablecloth fringe until Mom arrives with the dessert tray and coffee.

"Love your bread pudding and hard sauce," Dad says, wiggling his eyebrows. But when Lauren turns up her nose at it, Dad announces that it's eight thirty and sends her to bed. "Take the dog," he adds.

Mrs. Wiggins groans as she struggles to rise up then wobbles across the room. She'll feel better when we get to the lake tomorrow. Mrs. Wiggins loves Peace Lake.

"Thirty minutes, Lily," Dad reminds me. "Maybe you'd rather watch TV than listen to all this boring grown-up conversation."

"No thanks."

Mom pours coffee. "My God, that dog smells," she says. "You'd think she was still in the room."

"Shall we talk about eyebrow mites? Or bed bugs?" Aunt Jamie laughs, taking a sip of wine. "The way they live off us is so smart, so evolved—"

"You're talkative tonight." Dad gives her an impatient look. "Feeling the booze?"

Jamie glares at him. "You sound threatened, Paul. Does it hurt to stretch the old cerebral cortex, or are you just being sexist?"

I thought they liked each other.

"Okay you two," Mom says, clearing her throat. "I appreciate that we're taking a break from politics for a change, but can we talk about something that isn't creepy crawly for a while?"

Dad pushes his dessert aside. "Why stop now? We're just getting started." His eyes turn black and deep. "I know. Let's talk about Frog Boy."

"Let's not," Mom says.

"Frog Boy?" Jamie asks.

"I'm surprised you haven't . . . Oh, that's right, you read *The Socialist Worker* instead of the silly little magazines we do," Dad says.

"Paul!"

Jamie blushes.

"There were pictures of him in *Look*." All eyes are on Dad, who drains the last of his beer before saying, "Frog Boy isn't man or woman. Or a child. He's a freak. You can hold him in your hand. Is he happy? How the hell could he be happy? He's a mistake. He lives in the circus and people stare at him all day. I hope he doesn't have a brain. I hope he isn't aware of a damn thing."

Why is Dad being so mean?

"There are pictures of Frog Boy?" I ask. "Can I see them?"

Dad looks startled to hear my voice. "No," he answers quietly. "They'll give you nightmares." He clears his throat and smiles at Mom. "Great dinner, honey." He picks at the beer label. "We love you, James, but for a college graduate you're insufferably naive."

There's an uncomfortable silence before all three grown-ups laugh.

I don't understand. "Maybe Frog Boy likes living in the circus," I say.

All three grown-ups laugh again. Jamie pats her mouth, and smiles into her napkin. "It's the wine, Lily. Not you," she says, taking my hand.

Her fingers are cold. Maybe she's a lizard, with boy and girl chromosomes and a hidden tail, like me. Maybe like Frog Boy too. "Your folks are right. I'm a dreamer." She smiles at me. "You, however, are something special. You're an original, a one-of-a-kind without even trying. *And* a master swimmer to boot."

"No I'm not."

But Jamie doesn't hear me when she touches the pink quartz stone at the center of my crucifix. "Pretty," she says. "But why do people wear the symbol of Jesus's death around their neck? Why not His life?"

I've wondered too. Maybe I shouldn't wear it, maybe it makes Jesus sad, maybe it makes *everybody* sad.

"Blasphemy!" Mom laughs. "You're lucky Frieda isn't here."

Gramma Frieda gave me the necklace. I press it to my chest. "Dad says we make our own luck."

"Maybe," Aunt Jamie says, "but I believe that if there is a God, He doesn't know good fortune from bad, or Jane Russell from Frog Boy. We're all the same in His eyes, inside and out. All born of the same cosmic gasses, Einstein's star stuff," she points at the book, "slime, ether, clusters of cells." Jamie leans closer and breathes wine stink in my face; usually she smells like Doublemint gum. "Between you and me," she whispers loudly, "I think Mary and Joseph are crap. The Old Testament too. I'd rather be related to a flatworm."

"I thought we were," Dad says. "Unless you've given up evolution for something more romantic." He's in a good mood again.

The four of us sit quietly together for a while until Dad looks at his watch then leaves the table. A minute later he returns with Jamie's sweater and satchel.

"Subtle," she says, scooting her chair back. "Guess I've worn out my welcome, huh? Well, somebody had to corrupt the kids, so why not their favorite aunt?"

"Their *only* aunt," Dad says, holding out *A Child Is Born*. "I'm not throwing you out, James. You said you needed to leave before nine, remember? And you're still an hour from home."

"Yeah, I forgot. I was having such a good time."

"Don't leave your book behind."

"Keep it for a while. You know, in that fan of magazines on the coffee table: *Time, McCall's, Redbook,* explicit photographs of fetuses in utero, *Sports Illustrated.*"

"No thanks," Dad smiles.

I touch his arm. "Can't we borrow it?"

"It isn't really about *s-e-x*, Paul. It's about the wonder of life. All life."

"You don't have kids, James. Everything is about *s-e-x* when you have kids." He holds out her sweater while she threads her arms through its sleeves. "You okay to drive home?"

She hiccups. "I'm fine. I'm subbing for American Poetry first thing in the morning. Thank goodness it's community college *and* freshman level."

"Dad . . ."

He nearly throws the book at me. "All right already. I don't want to make it a bigger thing than it is." He rubs the back of his neck. "Sorry, kiddo, I'm tired."

Mom gives her sister a hug. When she says something in (what I think is) Romanian, they hug even harder. It's their secret language.

"Thanks for coming," Mom says in English.

"Thank *you*. Everything was yummy." When Mrs. Wiggins pushes in to sniff Jamie's pant leg, the old dog wobbles and nearly tips over again. "Poor Wanda Wiggins. I hope she's staying home tomorrow."

"Lily wants her to come," Mom says.

Jamie looks surprised.

"We'll see," says Dad.

I still hold the ribbon Jamie made me. She's smart but Mom's a better artist.

CHAPTER 3

PEACE LAKE

I leave the ribbon on the dining room table that night; Jamie made it for me so I can't throw it away. The glitter twinkles, the satin shines. The next morning, when Lauren asks if she can have it, I say yes, but Mom says absolutely not, and sticks it in the china cabinet.

We always stop at Elmer's Pancake House on the way to Peace Lake, and sit in a booth by the window to keep an eye on Mrs. Wiggins. This year she's too sick to climb in the front seat, or hang her head out the window, so I don't see her over Dad's shoulder when he raises his juice glass in a toast.

"To the master swimmer!" he announces, then winks at me. The people behind us look over their shoulders. I raise my glass too, only my arm's heavy, like it was at the lake the other day, and I put it down right away.

Mom looks at me. "You already full?" She's worried that Lauren and I won't eat enough of the chocolate chip pancakes, fresh bananas, three strips of bacon, and OJ we each ordered. I eat most of it but when I wrap my bacon in a paper napkin to give to Mrs. Wiggins, Mom says no. "It's too hard on her stomach, Lily."

Dad didn't want to bring her, but Lauren and I whined until he gave in. I whined more because Mrs. Wiggins is my best friend, even more than Judy. Dad loves the old dog too; he gave her to Mom on their first Christmas together. I felt terrible when he lifted her in the car this morning and she groaned with pain.

In fact, the longer I sit beside her in the back of the car, the guiltier I feel.

Dad looks at me in the rearview mirror and smiles. "Bet you can't wait to get your feet wet, huh?"

Yes. No. "How much longer?" I miss my watch.

"About forty minutes." He clears his throat. "How's the pooch back there?" Lying between Lauren and me, her giant head is in my lap; my legs are numb.

"Should we pull over so she can wet?" Mom doesn't like us to say "pee." She waves her cigarette around the car. It almost covers the bad smell coming from Mrs. Wiggins and her blanket which Mom washes every week, "in its own load."

"No, no, keep going!" Lauren answers.

Mrs. Wiggins doesn't want to smell bad. It embarrasses her. She turns a big brown bloodshot eye at me and moans.

"Did I ever tell you kids how your mother and I fell in love?"

"Yes," Lauren pretends to be disgusted, "one hundred billion times."

I start: "Mom was a bathing beauty ..."

Lauren loves this part. She tells everyone that our mother is the most beautiful mother in Portland, Oregon.

"That's right," Dad says. "At a photo shoot at Rooster Rock, modeling swimsuits for Jantzen swimwear. I hadn't seen her in years. Who would have guessed she didn't know how to swim? She was made to wear a Jantzen!"

Mom whacks him on the shoulder with a rolled-up magazine. "You're not exactly Johnny Weissmuller!" she laughs.

Johnny Weissmuller?

"You know, Tarzan? He won five gold medals, girls. Anyway," Mom explains, "it was the polio scare. Everyone thought that swimming in a lake, even in a pool, could make you sick. You know, Frieda was an excellent swimmer in her day too, and—"

"Mom tripped over you. Right?" Lauren is eager to get on with the story.

"Right, she didn't see me. She fell for me all right," Daddy says. "Flat on her face!"

Lauren laughs.

"Just call me Grace," Mom and I say simultaneously.

Mrs. Wiggins moans.

Lauren colors, while I listen to the usual joking our parents do on car trips: Mom teases how she should have married "that good-looking Barton boy," who became head of surgery at St. Francis Memorial Hospital, rather than a "skinny knucklehead." Dad teases how he never had a girlfriend until he met Mom, or "maybe one, but she was blond and went to Hollywood"; he's forgotten her name. "Marilyn-something, or something-Mansfield maybe," he wasn't sure. He had a French pen pal too, "one of the Bardots, I think," but they lost touch over the years.

Mom and Jamie rarely talk about growing up in Romania during the war, or what happened to their parents when the girls were sent to live at a Christian school in Bulgaria. Mom will sometimes discuss how Frieda's church brought them to Portland, and how she and Jamie lived with several families when they got here, even about how they took elocution lessons so "we could fit in," but usually she just says, "We were lucky," and changes the topic.

Mom tells one story from "the Old Country," though. It's my favorite too, about her dead cousin Albert and how something was wrong with his body, but he still got married, then his new wife ran away during their honeymoon, and he committed suicide. They found him dead in a bathtub.

"With all his clothes on too," Dad chimes in. "He didn't cut his wrists. He didn't drink himself to death. He *drowned* himself. How the hell do you drown yourself?" He shakes his head sadly. "Whatever drove him to it must have been a god-awful thing."

"I only met Albert once," Mom says. "Everyone said he was a funny duck." Mom called me a funny duck once. "He kept to himself a lot." Mom says I should make more friends. "Always so serious. Carrying the weight of the world on his back." Mom says I'm too serious.

"Poor Albert," she continues, looking in the visor mirror. Lauren turns a page in her coloring book. "I wonder what it was. Maybe," she winks at me, "maybe he had an extra toe so the army wouldn't take him. Or maybe . . . an arm growing out of his stomach!" She turns quickly in her seat. "Boo!"

Lauren's still coloring. Mrs. Wiggins woofs.

I stare. It's not funny.

"Lily . . ." Mom moans, "I'm teasing."

"Dummy," Lauren mumbles. "She's teeeez-ing."

I slug her arm, then turn my back to her and open Aunt Jamie's book and concentrate on seeing a human being in the lumps of blind dough and bug-eyed guppies in each picture. I smile at the pretty pregnant girl in the photographs and wonder if the fetus is healthy. Is it a boy or a girl or a hermaphrodite? Will it have Down syndrome like Aunt Cass? There's weird stuff in our family and Judy says weird stuff gets passed down. Maybe Cousin Albert had a tail.

When I turn to the eighth week, I gasp.

It's me, inside out: the single-celled-something-weird that becomes a mud frog, a newt in Mother's rock garden, a fish, a monkey, or Adam and Eve. At eight weeks and one inch, my heart has been beating for a month. Draped in an egg-white shower curtain, I'm a shrimp, a tiny hunchback with webbed fingers, plastic doll joints and black bullet eyes. My head is stitched together like a baseball. The picture is me on the inside: a fuzzy cashew floating in a starry galaxy.

What happens next month to Lily Elaine Asher of Portland, Oregon, West Coast, United States of America, Northern Hemisphere, Planet Earth, Milky Way Galaxy, in Forever and Ever, amen? Stay tuned, readers!

"Do fetuses have feelings?" I suddenly blurt out. "Do they know right from wrong? I mean, in a fetus kind of way?"

"Did you bring that damn book?" Mom asks impatiently. She lights another cigarette.

"I brought Jules Verne too."

Dad touches Mom's shoulder. "You're the best read kid I know, Lily Lou," he says. "No. Fetuses are too busy growing and changing to know right from wrong. Their brains are just developing."

The radio crackles. It's mostly fuzz except for some guy answering phone calls far away. "I'll be damned," Dad says, twisting the dials. "It's Joe Pine, all the way up here!"

All the way up here and out the car window, Lauren holds up her Brownie Starlight camera and takes blurry snapshots of tall dark trees pressing against each other, crowding out even Bambi. I get dizzy trying to hold my eyes in one place and focus, looking for a path through the dense undergrowth to a hideaway in the bushes.

And wait.

If no one sees me, and I wait as quietly as I can, for as long as I can, something will happen there. Something special. I know it.

Lauren's asleep with her hand on the camera when Dad drives around a slow-moving red jeep pulling a matching red rowboat. Jesus waves a bottle of Coke at me from the backseat. He smiles and picks up His tackle box, waving that at me too.

Jesus?

If He's "always on the job," like Gramma Frieda says, shouldn't He be feeding all those starving kids in China?

Okay, so He's taking the day off, going fishing. Big deal.

"Where's the funeral?" Dad laughs as he turns into the lane in front of them. Does he see them too?

Mr. and Mrs. Potato Head sit up front, their eyes (and upside-down noses) on the road. I haven't seen the Potato Heads for a while—Lauren lost most of their eyes, noses, and mouths last year, which is fine with Mom because real potatoes are messy and smell bad after two weeks in my closet. I was experimenting: If potatoes grow underground, they're used to the dark. How much would they grow in my dark closet? Is water more important or dirt? I was taking notes, even talking to Mr. Alsup (my science teacher) about it.

I keep an ant farm in my closet too. The ants climb to the top, where the clear plastic sky meets the green plastic frame, trying to get closer to God, so He can hear their prayers. Judy says that's why Asian people build temples high in the mountains. Judy's family has a miniature Japanese garden, so she knows stuff like that.

Where my bedroom wall meets the ceiling is where *my* prayers run, like ticker tape, like a locomotive, around and around my room, rattling and smoking, barely making the corners sometimes.

If I were Jesus, I wouldn't sit in the backseat of the Potato Heads' jeep. I'd drive instead, and fast. It's not like it would kill Him.

My parents don't mention the jeep's strange passengers. Mom flips down her visor, touches up her lipstick, and checks me out in the mirror. "Lily, are you still looking at Jamie's book?"

I want to answer, but at eight weeks, one inch, my brain is still developing and I don't know what to say.

"Peace Lake!" Daddy announces when his Pontiac rattles onto the gravel road that winds down to the lake basin. Mrs. Wiggins moans and squeezes her eyes shut. She opens them again when we pull in. There are only two cars in the parking lot.

"Great! Nobody's here," Dad says, as he unloads the trunk. He hands Lauren the beach towels. Mom tells me to leave my books in the car. Judy says *Twenty Thousand Leagues Under the Sea* is a boy's book, but I don't care. I wish I were Captain Nemo and had my own *Nautilus* to explore Peace Lake, and then I wouldn't have to swim.

"Let's draw, shall we?" Mom hands me her sketchpad and a pencil. "You can draw what you see here at the lake," she suggests. "Or dinosaurs! Aren't you studying dinosaurs in school? Just not imaginary scenes from the life of Jesus, okay?"

Gee, I only did that a couple, five or six, times. "Okay," I mumble, and tuck the pad under my arm. "Thanks."

While Mom unwraps the blankets swaddling her portable bar, Mrs. Wiggins walks past me to the beach, slower than usual. All of us watch her teeter and stumble through the rocks and driftwood before losing sight of her. We know she has finally reached the water when a flock of noisy ducks fly up and over our heads. A few minutes later she slowly brings me a stick.

Dad's right, we shouldn't have brought her.

"She got the stick. Maybe she isn't as sick as we thought," Mom says. She looks disappointed. Maybe she wants another pet. Chester, her favorite parakeet, used to sit on her easel while she painted; last year he sipped Mom's turpentine and died.

"She's slow," Dad says, "but she seems to be enjoying herself. She still loves being here." Lauren laughs when he grabs the kindling ax from the trunk of the car, takes a deep breath, and strikes a pose like Paul Bunyan. "Beware the sharks!" he warns before heading off to collect firewood. Dad always jokes about sharks, in Peace Lake—at the YWCA, even in Lauren's old wading pool and the bathtub at home; any place there's water.

"You girls know sharks don't live in fresh water, right?" Mom asks.

Sure, but I talked to Mrs. Wiggins about it anyway. About *Sea Hunt* and Crawford Woods and all the dark blurry places I've noticed since then, but she just opened an eye and closed it again, reminding me that she'll protect me and there's nothing to worry about.

My sister and I pull off our shoes and socks and race across the sharp gravel toward the beach. Lauren runs ahead of me, slowing only to toss back the long lacy vines of the weeping willow where our parents first kissed. They came here on their first "official" date.

Lauren and I fill our pockets with shiny rocks, and stand knee-high in the lake eating barbecue potato chips until Mom yells at us for ruining our appetites.

Minutes later, I sit on a rock with my feet in the water. Mrs. Wiggins lies in the cold sand nearby, panting hard, the stick beside her. "Please, Jesus," I whisper to my picture of the guy with a halo sitting on the back of a dinosaur, "watch over Mrs. Wiggins."

Creepy Frank Sinatra sings "Strangers in the Night" on the portable radio Mom placed on the tablecloth, and Dad scoops her up, dancing her to the water's edge. They walk up the beach hand-in-hand, while Lauren makes drippy sand towers for her sandcastle, and I draw.

Lauren and I eat lunch while they're gone. There's no time to waste when you have to wait thirty minutes before going in the water.

Not that I'm going in.

Not that I couldn't if I wanted to.

Some animals have super-duper hearing. So do I. I try to ignore my parents' conversation about me. I try to pretend I don't hear them say that I'll need "special help" in school if things don't change. I try not to listen when they say I should see a therapist.

"Stop talking!" I shout, but no one notices except Lauren who yells, "You'll get cramps!" when I stomp into the lake.

I don't need a therapist, or special help. All I need is to be left alone. In my own room.

The cold water startles me at first, but I swim out quickly then turn around to face the shore, kicking my feet to keep afloat. The sun is high and hot and dries my shoulders and face instantly. Mom and Dad are back; they sit with Mrs. Wiggins on the sand, looking toward me. Lauren dances with her new pink umbrella.

The water feels good.

I count fifty strokes, divide it by half, swim twenty-five more, cut that in half, and break off midstroke. I was the best at long division; good at making decimals out of remainders too, even if I was sent to the office twice in May for "an overactive imagination." The first time, I pretended everyone in my classroom was dead so I didn't have to talk to them. And once, after lunch, I spoke to Miss Pendergrass through a milk straw because it was hard to breathe when I was locked inside Houdini's steamer trunk. She gave me an F instead of an A on our last spelling test, when my answers were in fake hieroglyphics. I gave her a key to them, and I spelled each word correctly after class, but she still called Mom. When

Jamie saw all the watery squiggles and fish shapes I used, she called them "hydro-glyphics." *Hydro* means *water*, she told me. She also told me I was smart, probably even smarter than Miss Pendergrass.

I love to swim.

Maybe it doesn't matter if I lied to everyone.

When I pass Duck Island, the swampy nesting place Lauren and I looked at through the binoculars, I realize I'm farther out than I've ever been. Farther than the swim team, maybe more than halfway across the lake, and I'm tired. If Jamie were here she'd say it was okay that my body is heavy. *Just float on your back for a minute. Relax.* It wouldn't matter that my feet tingle like they're asleep, or that my arms are tingling too. The cold is in my ears and behind my eyes; it's giving me a headache.

Is the lake punishing me for lying about swimming? Maybe it wants to show me "who's boss," like Judy is always threatening to do.

Somewhere around here are the rotted half-submerged pilings of the Floating Doughnut Shack. I wish I were eight weeks and one inch so I could start over again. I wish I could turn back time like some adventurers do in Jules Verne books.

Suddenly I've forgotten how to swim.

I roll onto my back but I can't float forever.

On shore, Mrs. Wiggins paces back and forth in the shallow water. She wades out a little, looks toward me, comes back in, sits down, watches some more, then paces again.

Don't look, I tell myself, and glance away. I don't look at Mrs. Wiggins, or my family "rusticating" (Mom's word for "taking a break from the suburbs"), until Lauren suddenly yells, "Missssss-usssss Wiiiiigg-uunnnssss!"

I roll over and bob in the water. The sick old dog is headed my way, the stick in her mouth.

"No!" I yell. "Go back! No stick, no!" But she keeps coming. Behind her, on the beach, Mom, Dad, and Lauren wave their arms over their heads. I wave back, and Mom puts her hands on her hips.

She won't make it; I'm out too far.

I hold up my thumb and index finger; Mom's the size of a circus peanut. I roll on my back again, and kick my feet. At least I think I'm kicking; it's hard to tell when most of me is numb.

I wish I weren't a weirdo and a liar, and hadn't stomped out into the lake when my parents started talking about me. Peace Lake is big; no wonder it's where Aunt Jamie trains for the Olympic Trials. No wonder everyone clapped for the girls on my swim team. Dad says Jamie and I have the "swimming chops" in the family, but right now I don't have *any* chops, and when the sun slips behind a dark cloud, and the water becomes an even colder black soup, I'm more scared than I was when Lauren slipped into the quarry pit.

"Mrs. Wiggins?" I say out loud. When I speak the cold water spills in, filling my mouth, running down my throat, making the rest of me even colder. I try whistling but I can't. I look for Mrs. Wiggins's bobbing head in the dark water.

Maybe she went back.

Down in the meadow in a little bitty pool
Swam three little fishies and a mama fishie too . . .

Mom used to sing that song.

"Mom?" I call.

My teeth chatter. *Swim back!* I tell myself. *You can do it! Tell them you're a dummy and a liar and the lake wants you to apologize. Do it!*

Only I stay in place.

Bobbing in place. I'm not going anywhere.

Mrs. Wiggins? Where are you?

On shore Dad wades into the water, waving at me to come in. He points to the sky at the exact moment a bright light flashes. Lightning! Is it close? I listen for thunder, and count out loud like he taught me: "One, one thousand" for every quarter-mile away. "Two, one thousand. Three, one thousand."

Nothing.

"Stop!" said the mama fishie. "Or you'll get lost!"

"Lillleeeee!" Mom calls in a scared high-pitched voice. "Hold on! Daddy's coming!"

Dad runs to the pier where a rowboat is tied. I watch him jump in, pull the rope off the piling, and start rowing toward me. With one paddle.

He pauses to search the bottom of the boat for the other, then looks toward me again. One boat, one oar. It'll take awhile, but he's coming.

I slip under, but the cold startles me and I pop up again.

So the three little fishies went off on a spree
And they swam and they swam right out to the sea . . .

I'm tired and think of my room, rearrange the books beside my bed, pull out the scrapbooks from underneath, and begin going through each page.

Boop boop dit-tem dat-tem what-tem chu!
Kick kick kick. I'm kicking! I feel it!
Boop boop dit-tem dat-tem . . . kick kick . . .

When I get home I'm adopting one of those little African kids on late-night TV, the ones with flies in their eyes.

The sky tears open.

Brightly lit drops of rain pop and sizzle like the bacon on the grill at Elmer's this morning. I wish I were there right now, eating chocolate chip pancakes with Lauren. I wish I'd worn the new culottes Mom sewed for me too—bright, flowery ones that match hers and Lauren's. I wish Mike Nelson, from *Sea Hunt*, would swim by in his black rubber leotard and save me.

Boop boop, dit-tem dat-tem what-tem chu!

What color was the ribbon Jamie made me?

Purple. Purple?

Am I still kicking? I don't feel my legs anymore. They don't tingle, they don't anything. My arms are empty sleeves that lay limp on the surface of the lake.

I've.

Stopped.

Moving.

And they swam . . .
And they swam . . .

I slip under again. My heart is on a trampoline without a spotter.

Is this when you say the Lord's Prayer for real?

Our Father . . . I can hold my breath for a while, just not as long as Theresa and Carol.

My stomach fills with a thousand macramé knots as I slip underwater. Instantly, my lungs push against my chest. They want out, they want to swim up for air. Numbness is all I feel between the stormy surface and the sandy bottom of Peace Lake.

"Even strong swimmers can drown," Coach Betty told us.

Up ahead is the shark curtain.

"I'm going to die, aren't I?"

"Nah," Jesus says, looking up at me from a rusty barrel at the bottom of the lake. "Mrs. Wiggins is dying, not you." He looks at His bare wrist. It's half past a freckle. "She's almost here," He says, then dissolves like fish flakes in the goldfish bowl back home.

And suddenly, like the Chief Pontiac hood ornament on Dad's car (or stories of dolphins saving children in Aunt Jamie's favorite storybooks), Mrs. Wiggins dives for me and I'm face-to-face with her big wet head and bloodshot eyes.

Am I dreaming? Is this really happening?

"Grab my collar," she says, though it's hard to understand her with a stick in her mouth. So I do, and pressing myself against her we fly through the shark curtain, through bright stripes of stormy light and warm currents of water until we burst onto the surface of Peace Lake, spitting and coughing.

Once upon a time . . .

Mrs. Wiggins saved me. I slip my hand out of her collar and we bob on top of the water. Her head is bigger than mine, and with her mouth open, her abscessed gums and rotting teeth, her cancer smell is everywhere. She trembles with cold and pain because the stick is cutting into the corners of the black lips that outline her bloody grin. Three dark teeth stand on their heads, connected to her bottom jaw by a spit-glittered thread of skin. She can't chew anymore. She hasn't eaten kibble in a week.

"Give me the stick," I say, reaching for it.

The old dog pulls away. She's scared; I see it in her eyes.

"Drop the stick!" I scold, but she doesn't and starts paddling toward shore. "Wait!" I yell, and somehow muster the strength to lunge at her. She yelps and turns around, flailing at me with her paws, scratching my face and mouth. It's a blur of water and movement, her legs, my arms, sky, trees, Daddy's rowboat nearing us. She thinks I'm trying to hold her down, she thinks she's drowning.

Then it's over.

I'm breathing, the sun is warm on my face, and Dad is calling "Lil-EEEE!"

My body's awake. I feel everything, and wave at his boat. "I'm okay!" I shout.

It's over.

"Mrs. Wiggins?" My heart beats like crazy. The water is still. "Girl?" But she's quiet and her eyes are glazed. Her mouth stands open, the bloody stick wedged in its corners. Her breath smells like roses, and I remember reading that sainted people smell like roses when they die. A small pool of blood floats between us; in its center is one of her sick teeth.

"Take it," she says, though it's still hard to understand her with a stick in her mouth.

"Don't die," I sob. "I'm sorry."

"It's okay," she says. But it's not. Jesus said she was dying, but I killed Mrs. Wiggins. I demanded she come to Peace Lake; I swam out too far.

She bobs a little more, and then tips to one side; the water buoys her. "I'll take you back," she says.

"I'm sorry," I repeat, draping my arms over her. With my chin in her wet thick hair, I clutch her tooth and, looking straight ahead, paddle us toward shore. Panting and crying, we pass Dad who stands up in his rowboat, staring.

Mom and Lauren wait for us on the beach. I see them.

"We're going to make it!" I tell Mrs. Wiggins. "We're almost there!" Panting. Kicking. I'm alive. "Mom!" I call. Mrs. Wiggins saved me.

Down in the meadow in a little bitty pool
Swam three little fishies and a mama fishie too . . .

When I'm close enough to see Lauren point at us, I feel a whoosh of energy and know the dog's scared brave blood is in me now. It slipped into me through one of her cuts, like in werewolf movies, making one blood where there was two; one new person: inside and out.

Mrs. Wiggins and I chase each other around the house, both of us barking, until Mom says to stop. We run like football players, long watery strides, until we fall into the summer grass, exhausted and giggling, Mrs. Wiggins underneath me, chewing on me with her soft gentle mouth.

A final wave pushes us onto the sandy beach, and I throw myself off the old dog and smile up at Lauren and Mom. With the sun behind their heads, their faces are dark, their bodies outlines.

I lay there long enough to run around the house again.

Something's wrong. "Mom?" I finally ask. She doesn't move except to cover her mouth with her hand.

I hear a splash behind me. "Lily?" Dad tosses the oar on the sand, and stumbling, exhausted, wades toward Mom.

I see them now. All of them. The rowboat floats away.

Little waves slip under Mrs. Wiggins's body, rushing in and out of her ears, making her lips flutter like they do when she sticks her head out the car window. I clutch her tooth in my hand.

Lauren shakes. When she cries, "Dummy!" I get goose bumps.

I sit up, take the stick from Mrs. Wiggins's mouth, and throw it down the beach.

"You killed her!" Lauren cries. The sun lights her hair like a match.

I killed Mrs. Wiggins. I'm a liar and a killer.

When Mom picks up Lauren, she collapses and sobs so deeply Mom's whole body shakes. Daddy pats my sister's back, hands her his hanky, and says, "It's going to be all right. She was an old, sick dog. Everything's going to be all right."

Mom spins around. "All right? All right? Are you kidding me?" Her nose flares (like Ferdinand the Bull) when she turns toward me and says, "I guess I was right: we can't trust you."

I try to say something but I'm an eight-week-old fetus again.

"For Christ sake, Lily, you almost drowned out there."

What name does Jesus use when *He* swears?

Mom jiggles Lauren up and down like a baby. "If you'd come when we called—"

"But I was too far out."

"That's exactly the point . . . If you'd listened, Mrs. Wiggins wouldn't . . ." We all look at the dog covered in sand. Mom turns away first and sets Lauren down. "Why are you doing this to us?"

"What do you mean?"

"Easy, Kit," Daddy mumbles.

"I'm serious, Paul. I want to know." She glances at her portable bar. "The doctors don't know, her teachers don't know, maybe *she* knows. Do you know, Lily? What's wrong with you?"

"Kit!"

"Shut up, Paul."

My sister and I aren't allowed to say "shut up." Lauren sticks her thumb in her mouth; back home, sucking her thumb would cost her a quarter.

Jesus stands in the bushes. Except for the white robe and fishing hat with bright-colored doohickeys all over it, He's almost invisible in the brush and willows, like a puzzle in *Jack and Jill* magazine—"Find the Bunnies" in the March issue, "The Pilgrims' Hats" in November's.

If I'd died, Frieda would have said He had a plan for me.

"What happened out there?" Mom asks.

"I . . . don't . . . know," I say, keeping an eye on the bushes. Tears roll down my cheeks, fat hot salty tears that make me flinch when they race across my scratched face. I feel my tail trying to get out.

"That's not good enough, Lily." Mom glances at the bar again. "Don't you see what you're doing to this family?"

"That's enough, Kit."

I know what happened out there. I know Mrs. Wiggins saved me, not Jesus. Before Jesus evaporated like fish food, He stood up and turned away for a second. When He did I saw a Chatty Cathy pull-string peeking through the back of His robe and seams, where His plastic molds were fitted, running down the back of His arms and legs. When the water lifted His hair I saw what Mom calls root plugs, and a sliver of dark Holy Land skin peeking through the white at the back of His neck.

He's a doll.

He's a phony.

Mrs. Wiggins saved me. I close my eyes and press myself against her. "*Wiggins wiggins bo biggins,*" I cry into her wet coat.

For a minute I'm alone with her on the beach. We live here, just the two of us, and my family only visits when we send them smoke signals, which they can't read, so they never ever visit, which is fine with us, just fine.

"*Banana-fana fo figgins . . .*"

When I open my eyes again, Mom kneels beside me. "Oh God, Lily," she says, "I'm sorry . . . I was so scared. I didn't know if you were alive or dead, and then the way you . . . and the . . . dog . . . The whole thing is so awful. I shouldn't have talked to you like that, Lily. Thank God you're all right, thank God . . ." When Mom touches my shoulder, one of her tears falls on my arm.

In fairy tales, tears change everything.

Lauren stands behind her, her arms crossed on her freckled chest. Her face is red and swollen from crying.

A wave laps the back of my legs. It shifts Mrs. Wiggins a little, making my sister jump. I press a bare foot against the dog's thick wet body so it won't move. The cold water washes over my feet, squishing the gritty sand between my toes before it's sucked into the lake again.

"I hate you!" Lauren suddenly yells, and runs to the weeping willow where our parents first kissed.

Mom rocks me, whispering what sounds like a prayer in Romanian.

Dad sits beside us. After a minute he asks, "Would you like a drink, Kit?"

Mom nods.

I sneeze.

"Bless you," they both say.

Later, I sit between Mom's long tan legs, facing the lake. Her breasts cup the back of my head, and I feel her heart pounding while she combs my hair with her fingers, checking my scalp like she checked Lauren at Crawford Quarry, the way monkeys on TV nature shows check each other for fleas. "Trauma to the head" is Mom's biggest fear. "Something could be happening in there and we'd never know until it's too late."

Dad brings the first aid kit from the car and disinfects my scratches and cuts.

When Mom wraps the dry wool blanket around me even tighter, I realize that she's forgiven me for killing Mrs. Wiggins.

I can't forgive myself though. I've killed my best friend. I push the sharp end of her tooth into the center of my hand, but it resists going in.

"You okay?" Mom asks.

Yes. No. "Yes," I whisper.

If Mom and I sit like this until morning, never fall asleep and never move, we could turn back time. Mrs. Wiggins wouldn't have died, and then, even if nothing were ever right again, Mom would have loved me once, just once, as much as she loves Dad.

"Can you keep a secret, Lily Lou?" She breathes slowly and deeply to keep from crying. I nod and look over my shoulder. Her cheeks are shiny with tears; she's cried off all her eye makeup. "Sometimes I don't know what to do," she says quietly. "Sometimes things happen . . . and I don't know what to say, or how to fix them. There's no instruction book, you know. I blurt stuff out without thinking. I hurt your feelings. Or your father's. I'm not a nice person sometimes."

"Yes you are," I say quickly. It hurts to talk and I touch my lips. The salt on my fingers makes it worse.

Up the beach I hear the shovel digging in the sand. Dad and Lauren are burying Mrs. Wiggins.

When I open my eyes again, the lake is dark, and the sunset skips across the water. Dad has built a fire, and it pops and crackles, sending sweet-smelling sparks into the air. Mom calls them "fireflies." Her portable bar sits in the sand beside us; the fire highlights the vodka bottle and a half-full plastic cup.

"She was old, and sick," Mom says. How long have we been talking? The cold penetrates my clothes and wool blanket, and I press myself into her for warmth. "The water, the swimming . . . it was just too much for her." Mom sniffs. "I know you, and you'll think about it until you make yourself sick. Listen to me, Lily, okay?" I listen to the waves lap the beach. "It was an accident. Accidents happen, sometimes awful, unfair things happen. Terrible things. You're too young to take on the world's heart-breaks. Nobody's shoulders are that big."

Mrs. Wiggins?

My embryo tail swells and lengthens, pushing out of me, digging through my skin and clothes, planting me like Mom and Dad's kissing tree, deep into the beach at Peace Lake.

"Mrs. Wiggins saved me," I say. I clutch the dogtooth extra tight.

Mom sighs and kisses the top of my head. "I know," she says, then leans away, reaching for her purse. "Listen, now that you're awake, I'm going to stretch my legs." She digs out her cigarettes, stands up, and brushes off her pants.

I watch her walk to the water's edge and stand there. Even from the back, Mom is beautiful. Prettier than Aunt Jamie, prettier than anyone. "Mom?" I say quietly. I know she can't hear me.

Dad's long shadow, carrying the shovel, appears between us. "Doing better?" he asks me.

I want to tell him that lies hurt so much that sometimes you can't lift a juice glass or swim back to shore, but I don't, and he tells Lauren to sit with me while he smothers the fire and puts our things in the car.

She sticks out her tongue, begging me to slug her.

So I do.

It's dark when we leave Peace Lake. I'm thankful for the headlights that focus my attention on the long, slow drive out of the lake basin.

Dad swerves to miss a dead deer.

"We're not coming back," Mother announces. She lights a fresh Kent off the one she hasn't finished yet. Her hands are shaking.

"What . . . to the lake?" Dad asks.

"Of course to the lake. What else would I be talking about?"

"No, Mom, no," Lauren whines. "We love Peace Lake. It won't happen again."

"Damn right it won't," Mom mumbles.

I know I should say something, but I can't. I'm still in the lake, still staring at Mrs. Wiggins's milky eyes, still breathing her cancerous breath when she said to me, "You didn't do anything."

But I did.

Dad pats Mom's leg. When she looks at him, he smiles weakly. "I'm serious, Paul. I'm done with this place; it's dangerous. I should have listened to Jamie when she said the lake was haunted."

"Haunted? I thought you were the sensible sister."

"You remember the story about the Indian children drowning when their canoe capsized, don't you?"

"A cautionary tale, Kit. It's probably happened in every lake in America." Mom looks out the window. "No comment, kemo sabe?"

"Lily nearly died out there."

"Kit . . ."

"No, Paul. We're not coming back, and that's that."

"But Mom, we love the lake!" Lauren cries out. She scowls at me. "You ruin everything," she says, pinching me. Hard.

"Lauren . . ." Daddy warns. "Kit, listen. You know who should stop coming up here, don't you? Jamie. Driving four hours twice a week just to swim up here, alone. It's dangerous. And crazy. Think of the relationships her swimming has cost her. But Lily? Lily just bit off more than she could chew today, that's all." He catches my eye in the rearview mirror. "And Mrs. Wiggins did what came natural to her breed. She was a good dog." He pushes the button on his wristwatch; a small green light briefly colors his face. "It's been a long day but we'll be home by ten."

"Good!" Lauren says.

Jesus races by in the bright red jeep I saw earlier; a raccoon tail waves from the radio antenna. He's alone this time, and it's dark, but I know it's Him. "Woo-hoo!" He yells as He passes, then He really hits the gas.

What happened to the boat? Did He leave Mr. and Mrs. Potato Head tied to a tree and steal their car?

Why didn't he save Mrs. Wiggins?

Don't my prayers mean anything?

Mom throws her cigarette butt out the window, checks her lipstick, and snaps back the visor.

"Imagine what the kids will write when they get back to school next week," Dad chuckles. "'What I Did on Summer Vacation.' Let me see, Lauren fell into the quarry pit, Lily nearly drowned . . . and all that in a couple of weeks. Quite a summer."

Lauren's right.

I ruin everything.

Mrs. Wiggins is buried at Peace Lake but her heart, inside the tooth in my pocket, beats all the way home.

CHAPTER 4

LICKETY-SPLIT

Mom stops painting, rinses her brush, and dabs it on her shirt. She's barefoot and her nails are red as valentines. "We've talked about it before," she says. "They're growing pains, Lily."

Over her shoulder, Sherman presses his stupid ten-year-old mouth against the sliding glass door, inflating his cheeks and crossing his eyes, before running off. It leaves an impression that instantly evaporates.

"Lily, are you listening? You said your body hurts sometimes, right?"

I shrug.

"Of course it does," she says. "Mine did. You just turned fourteen. It's puberty. You're going to feel strange for a while, but you'll get used to it."

It isn't puberty, it's the tail. I felt it before Peace Lake, but since I killed Mrs. Wiggins, it wakes me up at night with bad dreams. Sometimes I feel it all day long.

"You're growing breasts, aren't you?"

Not that again.

"Yes, but—"

Frieda said I was born with a calcification at the end of my spine. She said the baby doctor shaved it down, or cut it out, or off, or whatever he did, lickety-split. In fact so lickety-split, I didn't even miss a nursing. "Maybe it's . . . growing back," I say, and swallow hard.

"There's nothing to grow back, sweetheart. Your grandmother is a wonderful woman—sometimes anyway—but she's a storyteller. You like telling stories too, don't you?" I do? "Remember when Frieda told you and Lauren that we'd found you under a cabbage leaf?"

That doesn't count. That's not the same thing at all.

Mom smiles and motions me to her stool. When she hugs me, her heavy, tanned boobs push into my stomach and leave indentations like I'm made of clay or wet papier-mâché. She smells of perfume and cigarettes, wine and turpentine. She's beautiful in her paint-speckled toreador pants and baggy work shirt. I want to look just like her when I grow up.

"I guess it's okay if it hurts," I say. Then, remembering my first day at Frieda's church, I add, "God doesn't give us anything we can't handle."

Mom stiffens. "Listen," she says, "if you really want me to, Lily, I'll take a look."

Yes. No. "Yes."

It's weird to feel something growing inside you; something that's attached but still wants to get out. What if it keeps growing? Caesar, the biggest German shepherd in a three-block radius, got Judy's poodle, Fifi, pregnant. Even though Judy is three years older than I am and says she doesn't believe in magic (or God), we've been burning candles, making up spells, and saying prayers in Pig Latin and Spanish (Judy's taking Spanish in school) so Fifi won't die giving birth to oversized puppies.

Good thing Lauren isn't around. She's a blabbermouth and would tell all her friends at school about my invisible tail.

I shake as I follow Mom to the bathroom.

What if she pulls down my pedal pushers and my tail plops out and she screams bloody murder until the neighbors call the police? They have to, don't they? Dad said you should never be afraid of calling the police. "That's what they're there for." Maybe it's even written on the side of their cop cars when they squeal into our driveway and wrap bright yellow police tape all over our house. *Danger. No Trespassing*, it reads. Our neighbors stand together in their front yards watching while Mom is led out of our house, crying and shaking, by a nice policewoman who looks like Ethel Mertz on the TV show *I Love Lucy*. I watch while the police put on gas masks and pull bats and shields from the back of their cars before entering the house where they look for me.

I'm a freak like Lawrence Talbot in the old werewolf movies, half-man, half–murderous dog.

A horse-drawn wagon appears in our driveway. An old gypsy woman slips a feedbag over the horse's nose and waves at me standing in my window.

I stop at the threshold to the bathroom. Inside, Mom sits on the edge of the tub, waiting. "If you don't want me to look, Lily, I've got other things to do." After I pull down my pants, she tenderly presses the skin around my tailbone. "Does that hurt?"

I grit my teeth. Yes, I'm growing a tail, why shouldn't it? "No," I say. "Is there anything back there?"

"Nothing, sweetheart. Still, I think I'll call the doctor."

No! Dr. Goodnight's a kid doctor and I'm not a kid anymore. He didn't believe me when I told him about the tail last time I was in, which I did when Mom was out of the room so I wouldn't embarrass her. My tail hides from Dr. Goodnight like it hides from everyone.

"That's okay," I call after Mom as she heads to the kitchen. "It feels better now."

I pull up my pants and touch each tile with the toe of my shoe. There are things to be counted all over the house: the Swiss Dot curtains over the utility sink, the straws of the garage broom, Gramma's collection of faceted cranberry glass.

Mom is talking on the kitchen phone. "Yes," I hear her say, "I'll hold." She opens the fridge, and sets something heavy on the counter. A wine bottle, I think.

Outside, the metal mailbox rattles when the postman sticks something inside it.

"Lily?" Mom calls. "Will you bring me the mail, please? I'm on the phone."

Mom loves mail. Today's mail consists of two bills, a *McCall's* magazine, a postcard from Aunt Jamie (she's visiting friends in Boston), and the new *TV Guide* with the cast of *I Dream of Jeannie* on the cover. Mom said there's a fight over Jeannie showing the jewel in her belly button. She says the TV censors are afraid of women's bodies.

"Here," I say, handing it over.

Thank you, she mouths, then holds her index finger to her lips. "Yes," she says into the receiver, "Wednesday afternoon would be fine." There's a folded piece of paper in front of her. She's not talking to Dr. Goodnight. It's a psychologist named Dr. Madsen, it says so right under the phone number and his photograph. He has a very long neck, spiky blond hair, and looks like a giraffe. I reach for the paper but Mom snatches it away, then thinks twice and blows me a kiss.

The crisscrossed paintbrushes in her curly auburn hair look like antennas in the TV show *My Favorite Martian*. Dad calls me his walking, talking *TV Guide*.

Mom refolds the note and sticks it in her pocket.

I've seen psychologists on TV. They ask stupid questions, cost a lot of money, and never smile. Seeing a psychologist means your head is screwed on wrong; it means I'm more than just a weirdo. Mom says "it's a good thing to be different," but I don't want to be different like that.

"I feel better," I say. "Really, Mom, you don't have to call anybody. I'm fine."

I grab her arm to get her attention. It's slick with mineral oil from tanning. Before cleaning her brushes she laid outside on the chaise longue. It's a warm day in late September, but in Portland, Oregon, that's no guarantee it won't rain. "You get the best tan between eleven in the morning and one p.m.," Mom says in the same voice she used to teach Lauren and me how to set the dinner table for guests: the short fork on the far left, the water glass to the right of the wineglass, linen napkins folded edge in.

"Mom! I'm fine."

"Please, Lily, I'm on hold again and . . . That's right, she just turned fourteen. No, she hasn't started her period yet. Yes, I know. Uh-huh. Perfectly healthy, except for . . . That's right, Lily Asher," Mom says patiently.

She hangs up the phone and takes a wineglass out of the cupboard.

Mom told me her family's last name once. It was long with lots of vowels, and when I finished writing it, she asked me to burn it. She said it was fitting that she'd married a man named Asher.

There are lots of secrets in my family.

Dad's real last name isn't Asher either. It's something "that was changed at the immigration office a long, long time ago," he said. Something Gramma Frieda swore she'd never tell anyone.

Rusty, Judy's little brother, says our real name is probably German for *smelly butt*. If Frieda doesn't want us to know it, it must be really bad. Like Hitler.

When I asked Mom about it, she smiled. "Someone's got to be Hitler, I guess. I wonder what happened to his family." She stared at a magazine ad for Hai Karate cologne and said, "I feel sorry for them." Mom's nice; she feels sorry for everyone. Dad says she needs to protect herself, but Mom says she just "feels a lot. My family were empathics."

Dad says he's a secular humanist "like Steve Allen."

I know who Steve Allen is but what's a secular humanist? "Do you think they had plastic surgery like in that Humphrey Bogart movie?" I ask her.

"Who?"

"Hitler's aunts and uncles and cousins."

"Maybe. Or moved to South America. At least changed their names."

"Do you think we could be related? I mean, if they changed their names and we don't know ours, maybe we're related. Maybe our families got married and had kids. Maybe the kids were retarded." My voice crawls into a box. "Or crippled, or something."

Judy says it's against the law for cousins to get married. It leads to idiocy or birth defects. Or Down syndrome like Aunt Cass.

"You think too much, Lily," Mom says. "You worry too much."

The boys at school call me "Asher to Asher," like the "ashes to ashes" they say at funerals on TV. Paul McCartney's girlfriend is Jane Asher. She has long red hair like Jamie and Lauren. Even though she's British, I wonder if Jane Asher's grandparents are German too. I'd rather be related to her than Hitler.

When Judy gave me a bunch of old teen magazines, I cut out all the pictures of Jane Asher, pasted them on my notebook, and told the kids at school that she was my aunt.

What's in a name, anyway?

I looked up *Adolf*. It means *noble* and *wolf*. Hitler could have been something else if he'd wanted, something grand.

I looked up *Jesus* too. *Jesus*, with a *J*, is short for *Yeshiva*, *Isaiah*, or *Joshua*, all meaning *salvation*. There's a Joshua on our school bus. He thinks it's funny to wipe snot on everybody.

I didn't need to look up *Lily*. *Lily* is for Easter flowers, for coffins, for the prayers of the living that their dead loved ones will rise again like Jesus did.

We read W.W. Jacobs's "The Monkey's Paw" in English class last week. In the story a woman, in mourning for her dead son, makes three wishes on a wizened (*shriveled with age*, Germanic origin, Oxford Dictionary) little monkey paw. Jesus might not think so, but maybe the dead are best left that way.

Once, when Lauren and I were little, Dad tried to scare us with a story about enlisting in the US Army and how, on induction day, an army doctor told every eager young recruit to strip naked and bend over. Dad didn't say what he was looking for, but the doctor quietly confirmed each man was healthy until he suddenly dropped his clipboard and cried out something about a tail.

Everyone looked of course, and the guy pulled up his pants but not before Dad, and some of the others, saw it. "Like a monkey's tail," Dad explained, "only shorter. And fleshier and not very hairy. Like a monkey's tail." I remember his repeating this because he wanted to scare us, but Lauren only ran outside to play and I smiled.

People were monkeys before they were human, so it made sense to me. The man's monkey tail was a mutation, an evolutionary throwback, maybe something in a time warp H.G. Wells, Ray Bradbury, or Rod Serling would have created.

I forgot about Dad's story until Mrs. Wiggins died. A tail started growing inside of me right away. *Things get out if you're not careful, things get in.* I feel it push against my spine. It wants out.

Sometimes I like the idea of having a tail. Using my school pictures, scraps from Mom's ragbag, and pages from *National Geographic* or *Arizona Highways,* I make pictures of myself hanging by my tail from the London Bridge, the Grand Canyon, or in kivas dug by Anasazi Indians.

I read that in some societies, being freaky or ugly or weird, even schizophrenic or retarded, made you special, and special made you important. In those societies growing a tail was no big deal.

But it wasn't that way for Mom's cousin Albert who drowned himself on his honeymoon.

It wasn't that way for Frog Boy.

Or the man at the induction center.

At a tea party in my closet, I shuffle their place cards (and corresponding nut cups) and put Frog Boy next to Jane Asher, a shy young art student named Adolf Hitler (who dies before he's twenty) next to drowned Cousin Albert, and Mrs. Wiggins next to John Merrick, the Elephant Man. And instead of prayers, Tarzan (Earl of Greystoke) instructs us in pounding our chests, and perfecting our yodels.

Spider monkeys and all fifteen varieties of howler monkeys join in, their tails wrapped around tree branches and each other.

In my room, tails and disfigurements don't matter.

Names don't matter either. They're just words, squiggles on a page.

In my bedroom, you can be what you want.

CHAPTER 5
THINGS I'VE KILLED

I keep Mrs. Wiggins's tooth in my bedroom dresser. It glows through my underwear when I open the drawer.

This morning its holy light pours down the dresser like lava and runs to my open closet where it puddles under the big plastic One Hour Martinizing bag. Inside it is the one-piece Big Bad Wolf Halloween costume (minus the mask) Mom told me to throw out two years ago.

Before Mrs. Wiggins died, I draped the costume over my shoulders and sat on the bed beside her, the two of us staring at the moon. She liked it a lot and, leaning against my long hairy arms, she smelled and licked the fake fur like it was a real wolf. Dogs are related to wolves, and wolves mate for life—I saw it on TV. It made her happy, so I didn't throw it out.

I wish I had though.

The bag shivers and shakes with anger. It knows I'm scared; it knows I don't want to have a tail. I quickly shut the closet, and push my desk and chair against it.

Things get out if you're not careful, things get in.

I know that a glowing dogtooth, an angry Halloween costume, and a dresser that spews lava sounds like fairy tales, but since Peace Lake, weird stuff happens every day.

When Dad's gone, Lauren, Mom, and I eat whatever we want for breakfast.

Mom makes herself a screwdriver, a cup of black coffee, and a stack of honey-drizzled Roman Meal toast she puts on a tray and sets next to her easel. She's working on a picture of a bookstall in Paris, she even put my name on one of the bindings. Mom's been smiling since she got up. When Dad's away on business, she covers the kitchen table with newspaper and tubes of paint and works all day. This morning she wears her hair in a scarf, powders her face, and dabs her cheeks and lips with bright red lipstick. "Like a geisha," she explains.

Lauren pouts until Mom makes her a geisha too.

While our mother paints, we eat cereal in front of the TV. I'm too old for Saturday-morning cartoons, but today is Halloween and Dad and I have a bet about the kids in the studio audience. I say there'll be more pirates than cowboys, but he disagrees. Dad and I make little bets all the time. I usually lose my allowance to him, but it's back on my desk next time I look.

Dad plays poker with "the guys from work" each Wednesday. There're dice with his pocket change on top of his dresser, and he always has a pack of fresh cards whenever my sister and I need them.

Lauren laughs when Huckleberry Hound tells Quick Draw McGraw he needs a girlfriend. Boys make her giggle.

Mom doesn't care what dishes we use as long as we clean up after ourselves. Lauren eats Trix with a wooden spoon out of a small saucepan; I eat Cocoa Krispies from the gravy boat.

I hear a howl from my bedroom closet, a long, lonely howl like in the werewolf movies.

Is it calling Mrs. Wiggins? Or me?

Dad says my imagination is a national treasure. Mom says, "People need all the quiet they can get after a traumatic experience." What happened at Peace Lake was a traumatic experience, she explained. She even gave me a Valium to sleep that night, but the pill got stuck in my throat so I taped it in my scrapbook instead. If it were smaller, like the dust mop–looking protozoa thing we learned about in science, maybe I could have swallowed it and then peed it out the way Frieda passes a kidney stone "every time I turn around."

The howl is for me. The old wolf costume is calling.

I try to ignore it but, when it howls for the third time, I can't.

I'm human, and it's fake fur and rubber, I remind myself as I hold the costume at arm's length and tiptoe down the hall past the bathroom toward the back porch and trash can.

Lauren's in the bathroom singing, "*We will fight our countries baa-A-tles, in the air, on land and sea . . .*" She loves the "Marines' Hymn" and marches in front of the mirror, saluting herself, as she sings. She stops when she hears the floor creak beneath me, and peeks through the crack in the door. I walk faster.

"Don't!" I try to warn her, but it's too late. When she opens the door and steps out, the costume digs its claws into me.

"You still have that old thing?" She just turned eleven, but Lauren sounds like Mom. "You were supposed to throw it away. It has bugs."

"It does not!" I say, but my words become a growl that rolls over my long black tongue, drenching my sharp yellow teeth in saliva, curling my lips like Elvis.

Usually Lauren's stronger than me, and when we pinch, scratch, and pull each other's hair, Mom tells us to "stop rough-housing," and that's it. This time is different though. This time the wolf skin crawls up my arm and when it wraps itself around me, I jump on Lauren, growling, barking, and snapping. When she tries to get away, I don't let her up.

"Stop it!" She kicks and slaps, while squirming underneath me. "Stop it! Lily!" She pulls at the fur but it's part of me now. "MoMMMM!"

Inside my Keds, thick hair sprouts on the tops of my feet, and pushes against the laces. The muscles in my arms and legs grow tight and strong. Two bloods pulse inside me now, one on top of the other. Dog blood. My blood.

"Get OFF me!"

She's scared and angry, but for the first time ever I don't care. I'm stronger than her and I like it.

"MmmOOMMM . . . MmmmOMMM!"

Suddenly, Mom stands over us, slapping at me with a bathroom towel. "Lily! Stop it! LILY!" And finally I do, freezing in place on all fours. Lauren crawls out from under me, crying and afraid. "For God's sake, Lily," Mom says breathlessly, "what's gotten into you?"

Lauren sits on the toilet lid and Mom looks her over. Thoroughly, too, like Lauren at the quarry and me at Peace Lake; like she'd forgotten something or left something behind.

"You okay?" she asks. There's lipstick on her teeth.

Lauren nods.

Sweaty and panting, with the hairy hide twisted around my neck and shoulders, I smell like Dad's BO after playing tennis. I must have bit my tongue; I taste blood.

"Stand up, Lily!" Mom barks, then reaches down and jerks the costume off me. "You told me you threw out this damn thing." She looks at her hand. "Dog hair. That sick old dog slept on it, it's filthy." She catches her reflection in the mirror and quickly looks away. "The garbage truck will be here in the morning."

I struggle to stand. "I'll put it out!"

"No you won't. I will." Mom starts rubbing her forehead. "You're not a little kid anymore, Lily. You could have really hurt Lauren." I reach out for the costume but she throws it on the bathroom floor behind her. "You will never bring another . . . animal costume into this house again, do you understand me?"

"It's not a costume," I tell her. "It's a werewolf." It's scary to say out loud, but she needs to know. "Information is power," I add. I heard that on TV.

"It isn't a werewolf," Lauren says, wiping away a tear. "It's a Big Bad Wolf costume."

"I threw away the stupid mask!" I scream. My eyes are on little bedsprings that pop in and out of their sockets.

Mom pauses then looks at me with concern. "Lily?"

"She thinks she's Mrs. Wiggins," ratfink Lauren says. "She told me! She said she's got Mrs. Wiggins's blood inside her! It's gross."

"Shut up! I did not!"

"You did too. Liar!"

I am a liar. I did tell Lauren about Mrs. Wiggins's blood.

I told Judy too, but when I swore her to secrecy, she laughed at me. "Who would I tell?" she asked. I immediately thought of her blabbermouth girlfriend Karla who definitely would tell, and then Mrs. Wiggins would have to be dug up and tested for rabies, "and probably have her head cut off," Judy said, and then I'd have to get really painful shots in my stomach that would hurt so much "you'd wish you were dead just like your dog."

I lied about swimming at Peace Lake.

I lied about Aunt Jamie's microscope too. I said I gave it back months ago, but I didn't. It's in my closet. Jamie doesn't mind. When she comes to Sunday dinners, she brings me dead bugs, pods, diseased leaves, and strange wet stuff in pill bottles to look at with the microscope after she's left. Things look different when you see them close up. Even black goop from Mom's eyelash curler has teeth. There are tiny worlds with big monsters everywhere.

I hear clip-clopping outside, and look down the hall toward my bedroom. I imagine the hairy face of the werewolf popping up at my window. Behind him, in the driveway, an old gypsy woman holds the reins to a horse-drawn wagon. "There really are werewolves, Mom. They live in dark foggy places you can't see from our house."

The costume lies in a tangle behind her. "Monster movies," she mumbles.

"Werewolves aren't monsters. They're normal people who—"

"I know what they are," Mom interrupts. "I grew up with that nonsense, and I will not have it in this house."

Lauren sniffs.

Outside, the gypsy's horse poops on Dad's new steam-cleaned driveway. The werewolf collapses in Mom's flower bed, crying in pain while his spine stretches and bows like the land bridge we learned about in school, connecting the old world to the ice age and back again. The werewolf is changing into a man named Lawrence Talbot.

I'm changing too.

"Go to your room, Lily," Mom says.

"It doesn't matter if you throw it away," I say quietly. "It's still mine."

"Your *room*, Lily."

Lauren sticks out her tongue at me.

I'm sorry I hurt my sister, but it doesn't matter how old or big I am—I can be a werewolf or the Big Bad Wolf or anything I want. It's a free country. I'll have to apologize and promise to do Lauren's chores for a week, but I don't care. Next time she goes outside to play, I'll pee in her closet.

That's what a wolf would do.

Mom runs a hot shower for me, and asks me to join her in the kitchen when I'm done.

I lean away from the sticky plastic shower curtain when I wash. Lauren comes in and lifts the lid to the toilet. "Hey finkhead," she says. After she pees she turns off the fan, says, "Watch out for sharks," and slams the door shut.

The bathroom is small and steams up immediately.

I can't see past the curtain . . . where laughing baby Lauren sits on the countertop while Mom changes her clothes. It's years ago and Lauren and I just took a bath together.

I'm still in the tub.

Winding myself tighter and tighter in the thick plastic folds of the large shower curtain, I make funny faces at her. She laughs and points her fat finger at me.

I.

Can't.

Breathe.

"Isn't she funny?" Mom teases, lifting Lauren into the air. She doesn't look at me. "Lily is . . . so . . . so . . . funny!"

Lauren laughs.

I sit Indian style in the cooling bathwater. The curtain sticks to my forehead, the end of my nose, and my shoulders, and presses my arms against me, holding me in place.

"*A taste of honey . . .*" Mom sings with the radio. "A taste, much sweeter than wine . . ." Her back is to me.

I twist. I splash. I kick the side of the tub, jingling the metal rings on the shower bar. Each exhale makes the curtain crackle then steam up, erasing my view of Mom and Lauren. When I hold my breath, a little window clears in front of me, and I see her legs and apron strings. Inhaling, I smell bubble bath and the Pine Sol–scrubbed shower curtain.

Mom?

She giggles, pretending to bite Lauren's stomach.

"*Marv Tonkin Ford's got the deal for you!*" the radio blares.

"*Shark shark bo-bark . . .*" Lauren sings as she opens the door again. She flips on the fan. "*Banana-fana fo fark . . .* Better hurry up!" she says, brushing her teeth. "Mom's making chili dogs for lunch."

"Lily!" Mom finally cries and, putting baby Lauren on the floor, quickly untangles me.

Dad takes care of Lauren that night, while Mom sits on the floor next to my bed, smoking cigarettes and rocking back and forth.

My arms stay stuck to my sides for hours.

Mom's on the phone.

"I told him to go. *For goodness sake, go to Chicago, Paul. It's the chance of a lifetime.*" She's talking to Mrs. Marks, Judy's mom. "Of course, I don't mind a few days to myself either." She laughs.

I'm painting eyes and cutting them out for my Halloween costume. Cat eyes, doll eyes, human eyes.

"Lauren's a princess this year. She's in the bathroom doing her makeup. Uh-huh . . . Lily? She's going as a potato. That's right, an Idaho spud. She's sitting at the kitchen table right now, making eyes for it. Then she'll staple them to some brown butcher paper, stuff it with newspaper, and climb in . . . I know, isn't she? . . . Uh-huh. Well, whatever else, we never doubted her creativity. What about your kids? . . . Well, of course she's too old. Judy's always been old for her age, hasn't she?"

Then it dawns on me: I don't want to be a potato. "I've changed my mind," I announce. "I'm going to be a gypsy."

"Just a minute, Connie," Mom says, covering the receiver. Her smile falls. "A gypsy? Your potato costume is clever. Be clever, Lily. Strut your stuff."

"But I don't want to be clever."

"Can we have this conversation when I'm off the phone?"

I start ripping up the eyes I've organized in piles according to size and type.

Mom sighs. "Let me call you back," she says.

"*First to fight for rights and free-EE-dom, and to keep our hon-OR clean,*" Lauren sings, marching into the kitchen. Mom and I stare at her. Her tiara with red and blue rhinestones is beautiful and I like all the plastic flowers in her hair, but Frankenstein's Bride must have done her makeup.

"I want to be the old gypsy woman in the werewolf movies," I say. Without thinking.

"No! Absolutely not. There's been enough wolf business around here." Mom wets the corner of a dishtowel and begins wiping Lauren's face.

"But Mom . . ."

"If you don't want to go as a potato, you can stay home. End of discussion."

"But . . ."

"The end."

* * *

Lauren goes out with Rusty and Sherman, while I stay home with Mom.

Three adults in costumes come to our door before dusk. The man in a suit and hat with face and hand bandages holds out a UNICEF box. "The Invisible Man," Mom smiles. "May I give an invisible donation then?" The quiet man shakes the tin box. Raggedy Ann and Andy stand behind him.

"Hi, Kit," Raggedy Andy says in an embarrassed voice. It's mean Mr. Marks, Judy's stepdad.

Mom laughs. "I see she talked you into it. Very cute, Connie." Raggedy Ann curtsies. It's Mom's phony voice. She doesn't mean it.

The Invisible Man walks off. Maybe it's the full moon. Dad said yesterday that Halloween on a full moon is a double whammy. "Chock-full o' nuts," he laughed.

After the Markses leave, Mom and I light the jack o' lanterns and sit together on the couch. "I bet the lake seems like a long time ago now, huh?" she says.

"Sort of."

"Almost four months. We've gotten used to life without Mrs. Wiggins, haven't we?" She lights a cigarette. "Life goes on."

"I'm sorry about hurting Lauren," I say.

"Of course you are. I know you, Lily. You're a good girl." She takes a puff. "Are you sleeping better? I mean, since the lake?"

I nod. I lie. I don't sleep much at all. My body feels different, even my feet wiggle like they're running down the street without me, and I itch everywhere.

Lauren bet Sherman and Rusty she could eat half her sack of candy before eight o'clock, and she won. She also barfed so much it made her cry.

Mom assigns me to the last trick-or-treaters, and when Dad calls at nine she's still in Lauren's room, so I pick up.

"You won," I tell him. "Two pirates. Three cowboys; triplets even!"

"What are the chances?" Dad laughs. "That's seventy-five cents, Diamond Lil."

I smile. He can't see me of course. "I got in trouble today."

"I know. Mom called earlier. Better now?"

They don't know what to do with me.

"Yeah."

Sometimes I like Dad better than Mom.

Dad didn't tell anyone about Peace Lake, but Mom did. She told her closest friends and Aunt Jamie, of course, but she even called old friends she doesn't usually talk to. Women she met in a writing class at Lewis & Clark before dropping out "because I have nothing to say," and the mah-jongg group she left because they were "a bunch of gossiping old hens."

After tearful pauses, Mom ended each call with, "It was awful. I can't talk about it anymore." After Dad yelled at her for buying a whole carton of cigarettes, she didn't talk to anyone on the phone for a week.

Sometimes I like Mom better.

At night, I hear her walk down the hall to the kitchen, take down a glass, and fill it with the last cubes from the ice bucket. The door of the liquor cabinet, over the refrigerator, doesn't like to open; it's stickier than the others, even after being cleaned. Daddy told me that once he put gum in the catch, a "gob stopper" he called it, to "tease Mommy," but she pulled the handle so hard it knocked her right off the stool.

She didn't fall last night. I heard her turn on the TV and sit on the couch. I imagined her lighting a cigarette and pulling her knees to her chest, to keep herself warm. I imagined tiny reflections of Johnny Carson on her freshly polished fingernails when she brought first the cigarette, then the wineglass, to her mouth.

Mom never watches more than fifteen minutes before going to bed. Sometimes, in the summer when she and Dad fight, she doesn't watch TV at all. I hear the sliding glass door open and the clatter of a metal lawn chair on the patio when she turns it to face either the moon, or the newlyweds' house. She calls it the newlyweds' house because they're always getting new furniture and cars, or taking trips to beautiful places. "Pretty girls get lots of nice things when they're young," she tells me.

After twenty minutes, I blow out the jack o' lanterns and lock the front door.

When I listen in at Lauren's door, everything is quiet; Mom must have fallen asleep too.

Back in the family room, it's my turn to curl up on the couch and watch TV.

"A wolf? A gypsy woman? A murder? What's going on here?" asks an old English guy with a mustache and pipe.

Poor Lawrence Talbot turns away, tears in his eyes, wringing his hands. Only a skinny flat-chested woman notices. She touches his shoulder and asks if he's all right.

I scoot closer to the TV. Will he tell her he's a werewolf this time? It's okay if he does. Everybody likes Lawrence Talbot; he's big and quiet and sweet, just like Hoss Cartwright. He doesn't want to hurt anyone.

I don't want to hurt anyone either. So I never tell Mom how, after the gypsy lady tracks the werewolf into the dark foggy woods and hides him in her buckboard, she drives the wagon right up to the movie camera and looks at me. Me. Lily Asher of Portland, Oregon.

Or how, after I go to bed, I pray that God won't change me into something everyone is scared of. Even though that would make it even-steven because I killed Mrs. Wiggins and fair's fair.

A few minutes later, Mom sits down next to me on the sofa. "Horror movies on Halloween, that makes sense. You tired yet?"

I shrug. "Do I have to turn it off?"

"Are you okay? You've had a long day."

"I'm okay."

Mom puts her head on my shoulder. "Why do things always happen when your father's out of town?"

"I don't know."

Even though Mom smells like the regular stuff—cigarettes, wine and that special shampoo Dad says is too expensive—she seems different. Her body is wider and heavier, her voice sad and tired. If Mom isn't herself, who is she?

Did Jesus kidnap the real Mom while I was in the lake? Is He buying her lobster dinners and new art supplies? Judy says a boy cat will eat his own kittens to make a girl cat come into heat again. Would Jesus eat Lauren and me?

What if He falls in love with her? "Everybody does," I've heard Dad say.

Suddenly Mom bursts into tears. "Your father and I thought if you girls learned how to swim, everything would be okay. But if it isn't one thing, it's another. You're struggling to . . . be yourself and . . . find your way, and then there's the lake and Mrs. Wiggins, and even these monster movies—they get under your skin, don't they? They get under *mine*." She reaches for my hand in the dark. "I'm so sorry, Lily."

Mom doesn't usually apologize. "You didn't do anything. Besides, I can still swim a little."

"You mean dog paddle. *Dog* paddle! Like the whole thing with Mrs. Wiggins was some kind of sick ironic joke," Mom sniffs. "If I talked less and listened more, if I kept an open mind . . . Jamie said I'm small-minded. I guess I am."

"No you're not."

"And today? With the Halloween costume? Sometimes I think I have no maternal instinct at all. Jesus." Mom glances toward the kitchen. The wine calls to her the way the costume called to me. "You and I are family but we aren't even on the same page, sometimes. How can that be? Maybe if I didn't . . . You're the most interesting person I know, Lily. I could learn from you."

Page? Interesting? Learn? "I'm not a book."

Mom sits up. Her body stiffens when she says, "Of course you're not."

The next night, Dad comes home from the airport in a taxi, with new roller skates for Lauren, origami papers for me, and a big bottle of perfume for Mom. He tells us over dinner that "the newlywed couple is selling their house. Did you notice? How much are they asking?" He suddenly stares at Mom. "Jesus, Kit, you look beat."

"Thanks," she says, pinching her cheeks for color. "I am. We've been busy." She tells him about our special lunch that afternoon. How she put out a lace tablecloth, and filled the brandy snifters with red Kool-Aid and frozen fruit. And made deviled ham sandwiches with the crusts cut off, and served us big slices of grasshopper pie with real Oreo cookie crust. "There's plenty of pie left in the fridge.

"Good." Dad smiles at Lauren and me. "Good. Sometimes I think our little house on Aiken Street is the only place in the world that makes sense. An oasis, an island. Asher Island."

"Like Gilligan's," Lauren smiles.

"I get to be Ginger!" Mom says. She's happy again. "What a figure!" Dad whistles.

I'll never get off Asher Island. Dr. Madsen, a.k.a. Dr. Giraffe, says to be patient—that I'll be winning swim competitions again in no time, but I know better.

I don't even miss it.

I wait until everyone falls asleep and enter my parents' room. I smell their fear when they realize something or someone dangerous is standing in the shadows.

Mom is naked and I see her big tanned boobs when she sits up.

Dad's brave, and when he jumps out of bed his protective blood makes a big whooshing sound, like the walk-in heart at the science museum.

He's scared but ready to defend Mom. I pounce on them both. Lauren's blood already smears my face; her body is in shreds in the hall. Her guts all over the fancy grass wallpaper and Mom's new shag carpeting.

I wake with a start. My room is dark and quiet.

Dad's home. Mom cut up my old Halloween costume and threw it in the trash. "There's nothing to be afraid of," she said.

I touch my crucifix and feel a small patch of dog fur growing underneath it. Jesus died for our sins. What did Mrs. Wiggins die for?

I pull out the scrapbook from under my bed and make a new list.

The Things I've Killed:
1. Lots of flies and mosquitoes.
2. Peace Lake.
3. Mrs. Wiggins.

CHAPTER 6

JESUS'S SECRETARY

The open window at the end of Judy's bed is covered with a rice-paper shade. It looks out on a small Oriental courtyard, with the miniature bridge we used to walk our Barbies across before they had a tea party under the bamboo.

We're both too old for dolls now, but I sometimes think about Barbie, *my* Barbie, who lives on a tropical island but drives her speedboat to the mainland where she plays piano in a jazz bar.

The magnolia tree in Judy's courtyard is in full bloom today and shades the front door. Her mom planted it for her the day she was born but Judy hates it. She hates her room too, with its mile of rosy wallpaper between her bed and the small churchy window near her ceiling. Judy hates lots of stuff these days.

I hear them yelling at each other as I stand outside their house. Judy's voice is loudest. I don't want to go in but I have to: Lauren's with Jamie, Dad's out of town, and Mom's taking a class at Portland State.

I knock quietly. When the yelling stops, I knock louder and Mrs. Marks finally opens the door.

"There you are," she smiles. "Come in," she says, while holding out a plate of homemade sugar cookies. The house smells warm and sweet, and even though she made cookies, her apron is spotless. My mom can't even walk through the kitchen without getting something on her. I step inside and take a cookie.

"Go ahead, sweetheart," Mrs. Marks nods to Judy's door down the hall. "She's waiting for you."

Every room in the Markses' house is modern, colorful, and neat. Especially Rusty's room, which is weird because in person Judy's brother is a real slob. He even buttons his shirts wrong. When I walk into Judy's room, she hands me a bottle of smelly fingernail polish and directs me to sit on the edge of her bed, take off my shoes and socks, and stick cotton balls between my toes. Her hair is in rollers but her bangs are trimmed, straight and shiny.

"I've never painted my toes," I say.

"It's easy. Just don't use much." Three toes later she asks, "Who do you think is the cutest: Adam, Little Joe, or Hoss?"

Judy always asks me that question. It's our way of saying hi. Sometimes when we're watching *Bonanza* the Cartwrights burst through the burning map of the Ponderosa Ranch, stop their horses right in front of us, and smile into the camera wondering the same thing.

"You always ask me that question. Cutest? Adam is, I guess."

"You guess?"

I look at her guiltily with the little pink brush poised over my big toe. "He's handsome," I say, "but he's a snob." Even though Judy thinks Adam is "moody and self-centered," she still likes him best. She likes *me* best when I agree with her, but sometimes I just can't. "I don't like Little Joe either. Dad says he's 'slick' like the guys who sell cars downtown."

"No he's not," Judy grumps. "If Adam died, I'd marry Little Joe."

Not me. I love Hoss. I want him to love me too. We'll build a little ranch in the middle of the pines, have a baby, and live happily ever after. Some Sundays we take the bouncy buckboard to the Ponderosa Ranch, and eat lunch in the kitchen with Hop Sing. Outside, after lunch, I rest my head on Hoss's chest, and he wraps his big arms around me and tells me my hair smells like warm biscuits with butter. Later, we sit in the living room with the stone fireplace. "There's my big boy," Grandpa Ben says when we pass him Hoss Junior. Adam stands off to the side, one foot on the hearth, thinking of something moody or self-centered to say.

Hail clicks and clatters against Judy's window. It never hails on the Ponderosa.

"Hoss," I smile. "Hoss is my favorite Cartwright."

Judy sighs. Then, with tears in her eyes, says, "I don't get you sometimes. Why do you always have to be different? Why can't you like what I like?"

She looks at me funny, and for a minute I think she's going to say something important, maybe even share a secret (like why she's so mean these days), but then her mom walks into the room. Mrs. Marks carries a basket of folded laundry and sets it on Judy's bed. On top of the clothes is a tray holding two small glasses of milk and more sugar cookies; underneath are neatly folded pedal pushers and a pink two-piece swimsuit.

"Your new *Seventeen* came today." Mrs. Marks smiles and tosses the magazine on Judy's bed, then holds out the tray.

"Thanks," I say, helping myself to the cookie plate. "You sure are a good cook."

"So is *your* mother, Lily."

"My mom is jealous of your mom," Judy says.

"Huh?" I stop biting a star shape in my cookie.

"My mom says your mom is beautiful and artistic . . . oh, and happily married."

Judy talks like her mom isn't standing right there, blushing.

I smile at Mrs. Marks, nervously. She's small and skinny with a pointed chin. Mom says she has an "interesting face" which means she'd like to paint her someday. Judy says her mother looks like the Wicked Witch of the West.

"No treat, Judy?" Mrs. Marks asks, still holding out the tray. "Have some milk."

"I'll take water, Connie." When did Judy start calling her mom by her first name?

"I like it better when you call me Mom."

"Okay, Connie, but no cookies for me. I don't want to gain weight before my trip to San Diego."

Mrs. Marks turns and walks out. When the dishes rattle on the tray, I realize she's shaking, a small nervous tremble like the vibrato Aunt Jamie showed me on her violin.

"Why are you acting so . . ." I start to say, then change my mind when she steps up on her bed, stretching on tiptoes to reach the high church window. Judy calls it "the jail window." Only her fingertips touch it but she keeps stretching.

"Milk and cookies are fattening, Lily. And water's important," Judy sniffs. Is she crying? "People are 85 percent water. The earth is 76 percent water." Judy's smart. She always gets As in science.

"If there's so much water inside us, why do people die of thirst?" I ask.

She ignores my question, plops down on her bed, and opens the latest issue of *Tiger Beat* to its centerfold of teen idol Bobby Sherman.

"Don't you think it's weird that we're full of water but we still need more?"

"Lots of stuff is weird," Judy says.

I know that. But, "Why aren't people born with enough water inside them?"

"How the hell would I know? You talk a lot, Lily."

"No I don't." I look at my toenails. "Just to you." I don't like the color. "What color is this, Pukey Pink?"

Judy sniffs. "Yeah, I puked in it. I put snot and scabs and pus in it too. And blood—that's where the color comes from. I thought you'd like it."

"I do. Thanks." Usually when we gross each other out it's funny, but we're not joking this time.

"You talk about God a lot too."

"No I don't."

"Yes you do. You believe in Him, right?"

"A little. Sometimes." God is okay, it's Jesus I have problems with. He's a selfish ratfink who doesn't save drowning dogs or children. I pull Judy's sewing basket into my lap and begin arranging and rearranging the threads, first by color and then alphabetically. Judy doesn't mind; she never uses them.

"Do you think if something was wrong," her voice is softer now, "you know, bad or evil or something, that Jesus would help me even if I don't believe in Him?"

"I guess. Maybe."

"Because I saw His shadow on my bedroom wall."

"Huh?"

"Jesus was outside my window last night."

My heart beats faster. "Maybe it was your stepdad," I say. Judy turns red. Did I say something wrong? "Or Rusty, or Sherman."

"No," Judy says impatiently. "It was Jesus. Alan saw him the other day too." Alan is Judy's boyfriend; they're going steady but he hasn't kissed her yet. Next weekend, after Judy gets back from San Diego, is their first official date; Alan's father is driving them. "Alan saw Him in Bible study, just for a second, standing at the blackboard."

There's an illustration of Jesus "standing at the blackboard" in the kitchen at Gramma Frieda's church too. I saw it when I helped cut pie one Sunday.

"Maybe it was a picture," I say.

"No, he swore it was true. Do you think, you know, that maybe Jesus came to my house because He wants to help me?" Judy asks. "You said He might help if things were bad."

"No I didn't. I don't know if He'd help you; I'm not Jesus's secretary." I can't concentrate on organizing the threads, so I put aside the sewing basket.

"But you go to church, Lily, and you wear a crucifix, and . . ."

Why was Jesus at Judy's house? *I'm* the one who almost drowned. *I'm* the one who killed my dog. *I'm* the one who saw Him in the woods, in the jeep, at the bottom of Peace Lake.

Judy crosses her arms on her chest. "Stop looking at me funny!"

"I'm not!"

"You are too. I'm not lying about seeing Him, you know."

Which means she probably is. "I know," I say. I flip through her new *Seventeen* pretending to be interested, then close it.

Jesus was looking for me, and got Judy's house by mistake. All the houses in our neighborhood look alike, it's easy to get confused. My hands are sweaty. "How'd you know it was Him if all you saw was His shadow?"

"You'd know it was Him if you saw Him," Judy answers, snapping her gum. "He wore one of those boy dresses like in the Bible, and He had a beard and long hair."

"How long?"

"Longer than Prince Valiant's." I smile despite myself. It's a secret that Judy and I both like Prince Valiant; everyone else thinks he looks like a girl, or one of those sissy Dutch guys on cigar boxes. "He didn't have a crown of thorns though."

Good, I hate that.

My sweaty fists stick to the glossy magazine cover. When I lift them off the paper they make little prints of baby feet, without toes, that quickly evaporate. "Were you scared?"

Judy shrugs, then burps long and loud from deep in her throat like boys do. I wish I could do that.

She's three years older than I am—old enough to take a week off from school and go to San Diego with her stepdad. Mr. Marks is the West Coast sales rep for Kenmore. Every time a new furniture or appliance store opens between Seattle and Los Angeles, they send him out. Judy and Mr. Marks leave tomorrow, before school starts, for the biggest appliance convention of the year. But Judy isn't excited about getting out of school for five days, or buying new clothes; she doesn't want to go to San Diego, or "anywhere else with my stupid stepfather." Judy told me she wished he'd never married her mom.

I don't like Mr. Marks ever since he asked me to check his heart with the stethoscope I got for Christmas, then stuck his tongue in my mouth. "I didn't know doctors tasted so good," he said. Gross. When I told Judy about it, she got mad at me as if *I'd* done something wrong.

Mom must like Mr. Marks though, because when Dad said she flirted with him at the New Year's Eve party, she turned red. "I know you didn't mean anything by it, but people gossip," he reminded her, "and his first marriage ended in a big ruckus. His own daughter—"

"You know how families are," Mom cut him off. "And Paul? It was my third martini. We were *all* pie-eyed, don't you remember?"

Mrs. Marks made Judy put her hair up so she'd "look nice at the convention's big dinner" tomorrow night. I stare at the four soup-can rollers down her part line, the four stiff brush rollers—two on either side—and the three neat rows of pin curls at the nape of her neck.

"You're staring at me again!" Judy says, pushing her white and pink rhinestone glasses up her nose. "I don't like people staring at me!"

"Okay, don't have a cow!" I pause. "Did His shadow have a halo?"

"No," Judy says. "Halos don't have shadows; they're invisible unless you look at a sainted person just right." Did Jesus wear a halo when I saw Him? I don't remember. Still, Judy reads a lot; she probably knows. She's taking two fat library books on her trip.

I hear the front door open and Mrs. Marks step outside. "Rusty!" she yells for Judy's little brother who's playing across the street. "Stop wrestling with that dog! Do you hear me? Rusty!"

He loves to play with Louis, the neighbor's black lab; they even sleep together when Rusty stays over, which he's doing again tonight because Mr. Marks's back is acting up. Judy's mom says Rusty is too loud and "active" to be inside when the weather's nice. He and Mr. Marks fight a lot so it's a good idea.

"Look what I did," Judy says, drumming *Tiger Beat* magazine with her pencil. "I filled out the contest form to win a 'Dream Date with Singer Teen Idol Bobby Sherman!' This and this are true," she adds, pointing at her neatly printed name and address, "but I fibbed about my age." She points at *18* on the *Your Age* line. "If you're eighteen you don't need your parents' permission." She hugs the magazine to her chest.

I wish it were Mrs. Wiggins sneaking around the neighborhood. The bump, where my tail grows, itches. I try to sound casual when I ask, "Half-person, half-dog. That's a werewolf, right?"

Judy runs her finger over glossy Bobby Sherman's glossy lips.

"A dog bite, or a scratch . . . If its blood got inside you—"

"You're talking about a werewolf, right? There's no such thing. You just got cut up when your dog drowned, and even if her blood got inside you, it still wouldn't make you a werewolf. God, Lily!"

"But I killed her!" Suddenly I can't breathe.

"Okay, you're a dog murderer! Does that make you feel better?"

I stare at Judy's starched white dust ruffle.

"Listen," she says, "you're not a werewolf. You're nothing, just a dumb girl like me." She throws her magazine on the floor. "I'll never win a dream date with Bobby Sherman." She sticks her fingertips under her glasses and presses her eyes. "I'm so stupid."

"No you're not. I'm not either."

"You are if you think you're a werewolf. Maybe you like Hoss so much because you're both stupid."

Mrs. Marks sticks her head in Judy's room and says, "Your father's home. Sloppy joes in half an hour." She doesn't look at either of us. After Judy's mom leaves, the room feels funny.

"I'm sorry, Lily," Judy says. She lies on her bed, holding her knees.

I wish Mom didn't send me over. I don't need anyone to watch me. Be nice, I tell myself. "I like sloppy joes," I say. Judy must have them all the time; she's glaring so hard at the closed door she could burn right through it like Superman. "I wonder if Jesus ever ate a sloppy joe. I bet Hop Sing could make them. He could probably make a Baked Alaska too. And one of those fancy chocolate cakes like I get at Rose's Delicatessen on my birthday. Does your dad like sloppy joes?"

Now I'm talking too much.

"He's not my dad," Judy mutters.

"I know." Judy's real father died in Korea.

"Hey, Judy," I say, arranging the magazines by date, "was there Baked Alaska before Alaska was a state?"

Judy turns red. "Shut *up!*"

My skin starts to itch. I scratch hard, making my hand into Mrs. Wiggins's claw.

"Stop scratching!" Judy shouts at me. "Jeez! Have you got fleas?"

Kind of. Only it's Mrs. Wiggins this time. "The dead want to be remembered," Frieda says when she explains why she talks to dead Grandpa.

"I can't help it," I explain.

Judy closes her eyes. "I'm too old to be your friend anymore. You're weird."

I wish I hadn't said I'd stay for dinner. "Stop being mean to me! I'm going home if you don't stop!"

"So go! I don't care. Go home to your beautiful family! I don't want to talk to you anymore! I don't want to talk to anyone!"

"I don't want to talk to you either!" I yell, as I lock myself in the bathroom across the hall.

I open the medicine cabinet, take out Judy's red toothbrush, and spit on it. The cabinet's shelves are neat and clean, no powder, toothpaste, or cough syrup rings. The Markses have lots of pill containers, some with *Judy* and *Rusty* right on the labels.

"Lily?" Mrs. Marks says, tapping gently at the door. "You okay?"

"Yes," I squeak.

"Dinner, girls," she announces. She presses herself against the bathroom door. "Lily, sweetie, why don't you give Judy a few minutes to think things over and join Mr. Marks and me in the family room? It's almost time for *Bonanza*. You'd like that, wouldn't you?"

I stand on the edge of the tub and stare longingly out the window up the knoll toward our house and Mom's new redwood fence.

Jesus is a jerk, Mrs. Wiggins is dead, Judy doesn't want to be my friend anymore, and I can't go home until after dinner. "Mrs. Marks?" I ask through the crack in the door. "Would you please tell Judy I'm sorry?"

"Ah, sweetie, don't worry. Judy's just, our family is kind of . . ." She walks away without finishing her sentence.

Judy joins us while the Ponderosa map is still burning. She kisses her stepdad, but ignores her mom before sitting down in front of her cold plate of sloppy joes.

Mr. Marks gives her a mean look. "For God's sake, Jude, do you have to wear those damn things to dinner?"

Judy touches her rollers nervously.

Mrs. Marks pours him another beer. "You want her to look nice for tomorrow night's big dinner, don't you?"

He smiles and turns to me. "Did Judy tell you that we're flying to San Diego in the morning?" He looks at her. "It's the annual convention. There will be salesmen from all over the country, old friends, new products. Should be lots of fun, huh, kiddo?"

Judy stares at the TV.

"Just the two of us. A special father-daughter time."

"*Step*father time," she corrects him.

Everyone eats quietly, watching TV.

I've seen this *Bonanza* episode before: A big strong guy standing at the bar is a famous boxer from Ireland. When Hoss and Little Joe, who are in town for supplies, wander into the saloon, the Irishman walks up to Hoss and tells him to "put up his dukes." Hoss tries to talk him out of it. He even offers to buy him a drink, but once the saloon is hooting and hollering and placing bets, Hoss takes off his hat and shirt and agrees to fight him. When there's a big saloon scene like that, I start looking for the tattletale who'll run out of the bar to tell the sheriff. Sometimes it's the town drunk. This time it's a little kid who sticks his head in the door when he hears the excitement.

Judy frowns at me before saying, "Lily likes Hoss Cartwright best."

"Me too," Mrs. Marks adds. "Such a sweet man."

Mr. Marks laughs. "The man is a pig! Look at him! What about Little Joe? Or Adam. All the girls think Adam is sexy, don't they, Jude?"

Judy looks down at her plate. "I guess so," she says. "Hoss is fat." Maybe Judy isn't a liar. Maybe she's a copycat like Lauren, like how she and her friend Karla wear the same outfits on the same day.

Suddenly there's a TV news bulletin about a civil rights demonstration in Memphis earlier in the day. Dr. King, a young Negro minister, locks arms with other Negroes and a few white people and walks right down the middle of the street, singing and chanting. When they approach a diner, the group is surrounded by police and everyone is arrested.

Mr. Marks pushes his dinner plate aside and lights a cigarette. He points it at the TV. "Can't they read the goddamn sign? It says, *No Niggers*, plain as day."

He said *nigger*. At school, kids get sent to the office for using that word.

Mr. Marks likes Cassius Clay, Jackie Robinson, and Nat King Cole; all the grown-ups in our neighborhood do. What's wrong with Reverend King?

"They knew what would happen when they walked in there, didn't they? I hate to see any man treated like a dog, but I don't feel sorry for them."

"It's been a hundred years," Mrs. Marks says. "Negroes have the right to more than just . . ."

Mr. Marks glares at her.

"I'm just saying—"

"Let's call a spade a spade, shall we?" He chuckles to himself. "Those brilliant men that signed the Constitution had slaves. I bet *they* called them niggers."

"Things are better these days, Mom," Judy says.

"I can't believe you two," Mrs. Marks says, choking back her words. "You're quite the team, aren't you. You two really are . . . you really are . . ."

"Change takes time, Connie. I'd like somebody to explain to me how giving uneducated, backward-thinking poor people the same rights as the rest of us is good for this country. Can you do that, Connie? Can you explain why them sign-toting niggers—excuse me all to hell—*Negroes* should . . ."

I'm shaking so hard I can't eat. Before I know what I'm doing, I stand up. I feel Mrs. Wiggins stand up beside me, looking at Mr. Marks too when I say, with a trembling voice, "*Nigger* is a bad word."

Mr. Marks puts down his cigarette and gives me a hard look. "A man's home is his castle. I'll say whatever I damn well please in my own house, young lady."

"You're being hateful and prejudiced and mean. On purpose." It feels good to say what's true. "I want to go home."

"White people still have rights in this country. Go home if you want to; I won't stop you." His eyes grow tiny and dark when he picks up his cigarette and takes a long slow drag on it. I've never talked to an adult like this before. My heart's beating so fast it fills my ears and I almost don't hear him when he says, "Maybe you're in need of a semantics lesson, Lily. Lesson one: there are polite words and coarse words, but they mean the same goddamn thing." He throws his head back, finishing his beer. "I've got a bad back, right? I could say it feels like . . . *shit*, and wonder why the *fuck* I got such a raw deal and still have to work my *balls* off." His words are slow and sharp like he wants to hurt me with them. "While some people carry a goddamn sign all day. Niggers or Coloreds or Negroes, same thing."

"*Nigger*'s just a word, Lily," Judy says.

"No it isn't!" I yell at her. "Liar!" I feel myself turn hot and red all over. "Liar!" I repeat. "You didn't see Jesus either, did you? You lied to me."

My friend blushes and looks away.

"You said you saw Jesus?" Mr. Marks laughs. "What's gotten into you, Judy?"

I glare at him. "She doesn't want to go with you on your stupid old trip, either."

Mr. Marks drops his smile. "What have you girls been talking about?" But before Judy can answer, her mom appears with another beer and a clean ashtray and says, "That's all right, dear, girls talk," and Mr. Marks changes his expression.

I pick up my plate and milk glass, but when I fold up my TV tray and place it in the stand next to the TV, I don't hurry to get out of his way. I want to block the TV. I want him to see me the way the Negro protestors want the angry white people to see them. I feel him frowning at me but I don't care. I'm going home.

Mrs. Marks walks me to the door, trying to convince me to stay for dessert and forget what was said. "It's the beer, Lily. And the pain pills for his back. Don't be too hard on him; he'll be a different man in the morning."

But in the morning Mr. Marks is going to California with Judy. They'll stay in a motel for five days, swim in the pool and the warm ocean, eat at restaurants, go to the zoo. Judy can wear a swimsuit under her clothes all day long if she wants to, and she's not even taking homework with her, just two fat books from the library.

Her mom gives me a hug; I feel dampness through her blue blouse. "I'm sorry, sweetheart. Tell your mother I'm sorry too, will you?"

"Don't be mad at me, Lily," Judy says, suddenly crying.

But I don't look at her when I slip on my jacket. "Thanks for dinner," I say over my shoulder. I feel strong, like Martin Luther King.

Walking home, I'm not as scared of the dark as I usually am.

I pretend I'm with the Negro marchers, arm-in-arm. We walk slowly, like they did on TV, down the sidewalk toward my house. I hear Mr. Marks's bad words rise up between our chanting and singing, but we keep walking anyway.

At home, we squeeze through the front door. "Lily?" Mom calls out. "You're home early. You want to watch *Bonanza* with us?"

"No thanks," I call, and squeeze down the hall with Reverend King and the others, walking past Lauren's bedroom with the matching pink-and-white–striped bedspread and curtains. When I whisper how her room is the cleanest room in the house, the marchers nod their heads in respect.

After Mom tucks me in that night, every shadow that races across my room makes me jump. Every sound gives me the willies.

Waiting for Jesus is scary. What does He want?

I lie in bed and listen for His footsteps in the flower bed outside my window. It's like waiting to get spanked: you don't know how bad it's going to be, you just want to get it over with.

Where is He? Jesus was once lost in the desert for forty days, so He must not have a good sense of direction. Maybe He needs glasses. I'll make Him a map.

I get up, sit at my desk, and reach for the *Bonanza* pencil cup I got at Carson City two years ago. Dad didn't want to leave the casino so we were too late for tickets to tour the Ponderosa that day. "Next time," Mom promised. She's already looking at brochures, calling up motels, and talking about how Bobby Darin and Bob Newhart are performing in nearby Lake Tahoe this summer. Sammy Davis Jr. sold out the first week.

Lauren loves Sammy Davis Jr.

Come on, Jesus, where are you?

I run my finger around the cold tin lip of the cup with its picture of pine trees and horses, and Ben, Adam, Hoss, and Little Joe. When I trace Hoss's ten-gallon hat, he smiles at me.

Most nights, at 11:55, if Jesus were to look through our living room window, He'd catch me racing through the house in my underwear, checking all the closets and cabinets—opening drawers and closing them again.

Someone has to check. *Things get out*—I imagine telling Jesus when He cups His hands around His eyes for a better look—*things get in.*

Most nights, when I'm done, I dash down the dark hallway past my sleeping parents' room, past my sister's with the hissing humidifier, and into the bathroom where I push the pee out as fast as I can (even if I don't have to go). Standing at the threshold to my bedroom again, I make my arms into bony wings for a broad jump and leap from the hall rug across the watery carpet, to the rag rug island in front of my bed, to the sanctuary of my blankets, before the twelve deep tones of the living room clock are finished.

Things happen if you don't pray right too—if you forget the order or lose your place during the who-to-thanks and what-fors. I press my palms together until they forget which one is right and which is left, and I start my eyes high on a corner of the bedroom wall and pray. My fingertips jump with the words, pretending they remember what I practiced on Gramma Frieda's typewriter. My prayers are long and wrap themselves around the room, over and over, like ticker tape. I apologize for being selfish. I apologize for worrying and embarrassing my parents. I apologize for hurting my sister and Judy. I apologize for being a weirdo and having a big imagination. And then I add out loud, "Please, God, don't let the bomb drop on our house."

I'm scared of the bomb most of all. Before I killed Mrs. Wiggins, the bomb prayer was the biggest. It wrapped itself around the room dozens of times and I had to bite my arm to stop it from swallowing everything up.

Tonight, though, I'm too scared to run around the house. Waiting for Jesus, I'm too scared to get up and check on things, too scared to leave my bedroom in case He's sitting at my desk or hiding in my closet when I come back. Maybe He's a "practical joker" like Mom says Dad is. Maybe Jesus is sad inside, like Judy. After hearing prayers for a thousand years, He probably is.

Either way, I'm mad at Him for two major reasons:

1. He took away Mrs. Wiggins and made me a murderer. Gramma embroidered a bunch of pillows with the Ten Commandments and gave five to Lauren and five to me for Christmas last year. *Thou shalt not kill* keeps falling off my bed.

2. My body's changing. I don't like it, but there's nothing I can do about it.

That's big stuff for any kid. Even a teenager.

So tonight, when I kneel beside the bed with my mouth in the covers so no one else can hear me, I talk to God instead—not Jesus—because I heard you go straight to the top when you need extra help. I need a big prayer because big stuff keeps happening.

With every word the prayer train picks up speed, zooming around my bedroom like a toy racecar, knocking smaller prayers into the bushes. Until there's a tap at my window and I jump with surprise.

But not really.

So Jesus found me, so what? Still, I bet He doesn't go around scaring Reverend Martin Luther King, Jr.

I take a deep breath and, thinking of the Negro marchers, decide to ignore the tapping. I can be brave too, so I push my knees into the floor extra hard, and press my hands together till they hurt. Until finally, I peek between my praying fingers and watch as Jesus, inside my room now, throws shadow puppets on the wall over my bed. The more I look at Him, the more I feel my brain turned upside down, erasing everything on top like an Etch A Sketch.

"Hi," I say, trying to sound casual. "Jesus?"

"Well, I'm not Bobby Sherman," He laughs.

My heart's beating so hard I barely notice the long hair and halo Judy mentioned. And He doesn't look like Prince Valiant at all. He's smaller than I remembered from Crawford Butte or Peace Lake, and skinnier. Maybe His body is changing too.

"What do you think?" Jesus asks, nodding to the shadows. Even though He's showing off and I don't like show-offs, I'm impressed. All I can make is a rabbit, but Jesus makes Ben, Adam, Hoss, and Little Joe bursting through the burning map of the Ponderosa with His hands. "You like Hoss best, right?"

"Yeah," I answer quietly. "But I like Martin Luther King better."

Jesus instantly walks the Negro marchers down my bedroom wall. Dogs lunge at them from the crowd, and white people spit and turn fire hoses on them. "Why don't you help them?" I ask. "Why don't you help the Negroes?"

Jesus puts down His hands. "Martin's doing fine without me," He says. "Besides, who said I wasn't helping?"

"Lily?" Mom knocks on my door. "I see your light's still on. Judy's mother called. I'm sorry you didn't have a good time, sweetheart. Listen, I made some Jell-O. How about a midnight snack?"

I look at my clock-radio. "But it's only 10:15. I mean 10:16."

Lauren opens her door and sings, "*Jell-O Jell-O bo bell-o, ba-nana-fana . . .*" She's a perfectionist and worried about her homework. She can't sleep either.

Everybody's up. We're having Jell-O at 10:18 and thirty-five seconds. I bet they're not doing that at Judy's house.

"Go," Jesus says, making painful faces as He backs through an insect-sized rip in my window screen. "It's Jell-O. Wish we'd had Jell-O when I was a kid."

I want to feel sorry for Him, but after Mrs. Wiggins I just can't.

CHAPTER 7

STEALING MOMMIES

We follow Dad as he gets up from the breakfast table and, singing, *"All day, all night, Marianne,"* shuffles calypso-style down the hall toward the bathroom where Mom puts on her makeup.

"Hon-ey," she giggles when he grabs her by the waist and plants a noisy smack-kiss on her long tan neck.

"These are your beauty secrets?" he teases. "Lip liner? Green eye shadow?" He sticks them in his pocket and dances back to the kitchen. "Watch out, Kit," he calls back, "you'll be the most beautiful woman at the Rose Festival Parade. Then what?"

Lauren and I look at each other with concern.

"Keep an eye on her, girls," he says, as we slide behind our cereal bowls again. "She's a wild one."

We laugh.

Aren't our parents supposed to keep an eye on us?

"All day, all night, Marianne . . ."

Mom doesn't tell us we're picking up Aunt Cass.

When she takes the freeway exit to Good Shepherd Home, Lauren and I roll our eyes at each other.

Aunt Cass is family, even though she doesn't look anything like our parents or Frieda or Uncle Po. Cass is forty years old and has Down syndrome. She used to live with her brother Uncle Po (I don't know his real name), but she's been at Good Shepherd for years now. Other folks with Down syndrome live there too, and people who never get out of their wheelchairs, people who'll die much younger than Po who Dad calls "as old as the hills."

Good Shepherd Home is at the end of a long country road. Someone ran over a skunk, and Lauren plugs her nose.

It's only 7:20 a.m. The parade doesn't start until nine. Maybe Cass isn't up yet.

She's up.

"No bra," Mom moans as a "helper" walks Cass out to our car.

Her boobs are big and hang almost to her waist because she refuses to wear one of the bras Mom buys her at Fran's Foundations. She's short and chubby, and beige-pink like Bazooka bubble gum. Her cotton-candy hair is sticky with hair spray she doesn't need but uses anyway, "covering the bathroom mirror with most of it," Mom says. Cass still has her baby teeth, which are tiny and square like kernels of white corn, only when she smiles she keeps her lips as tight as a coin purse and never shows them.

She piles in the front seat next to Mom, which Lauren and I aren't allowed to do anymore after Mom got new seat belts, the first in the neighborhood, and had them installed in the backseat just for us.

Forty minutes later, when the four of us pull into the parking lot closest to the Rose Festival Parade route, Cass has fallen in love with Mom all over again. They hold hands as we cross the busy parking lot to the Midway, passing a line for the roller coaster, and signs advertising corn dogs, pie-eating contests, the dime toss, gypsy fortune tellers, and *Sno-Cones, 45 cents*. Mom ignores the carnies who wolf-whistle at her and shake huge teddy bears at the rest of us. Lauren pretends to ride a Lipizzaner stallion, weaving in and out, her head held high. Lauren saw them perform last week; now she wants to train horses.

Cass pushes me away when I get too close to Mom. "No, Lily, no," she says. Like I'm a dog or something.

We keep walking. Mom leads the way through the noisy crowd headed to the street with their lawn chairs, thermoses, and blankets. People look at her because she's beautiful, and Cass because she's strange. Mom says I'll "grow out" of being embarrassed about Cass. She also says that Cass is "old for Down," which means she should have died by now, I guess.

As we near Burnside, Lauren and I run ahead, claiming the curb for the best possible spots, standing or sitting. We position ourselves on either side of Mom like kid models in a Butterick pattern book, only we're really her guards. Dad asked us to keep an eye on Mom, who lights a cigarette and says, "Beautiful day, isn't it, girls?" Shading us with her flawless tan and sunglasses, I almost forget Aunt Cass is standing behind her.

A minute later, Mom moves her in front. She rests her hands on Cass's shoulders and points out clowns on tiny motorcycles and kids and dogs. Mom's finger passes over another Down syndrome adult, across the street. He looks more like Quasimodo than Cass. He wears lederhosen and laughs like a donkey.

Does Cass notice him too?

On our side of the street, people fan themselves with parade programs and look up the road excitedly. Edges of metal folding chairs glint in the sun. Babies cry. A big greasy guy pushes a grocery cart of balloons and stick toys. Little kids run into the street and point. "It's coming!" they cry, even when it's not.

Soon enough, kilted bagpipers strut by. Their music fills my chest with vibrating depth charges, like the recorded sounds on the battle submarine we toured at last year's Rose Festival. Marching girls my age, in short skirts and white-fringed wrist cuffs, throw twirling batons in the air at exactly the same time. After every float is another high school band in matching uniforms with shiny instruments.

In the Rose Festival Parade every float is made with flowers, even the one of Packy the Elephant. "Pink zinnias!" Mom exclaims, as the huge flowery elephant lifts his mechanical trunk and sprays the street with confetti.

Six bright red convertibles, each carrying a festival princess, are next. This year's queen is from Grant High School. Every year Mom cuts out the newspaper photo and biography of each high school princess, and bets Dad five dollars that she can guess who'll be chosen queen. She's only been wrong once.

My favorite thing each parade is the Alpenrose Dairy float with real goats, sheep, and rabbits. I cringe when Cass yells, "Goat!" and the woman standing next to us smiles and says, in an exaggerated voice, "That's right! Good for you!"

"Look!" Lauren yells at the blue-green float carrying a giant starfish with a bearded Neptune on one arm. Mermaids lie on raised steps at his feet. They wave, like slow windshield wipers, and Mom points at one with a sash across her chest. "She's runner-up to the Rose Festival Queen this year," Mom explains. "Melanie Collins—four-point student and citywide high school swim champ, Lily. Isn't that neat?"

I'd rather be a troglodyte and live in a cave. I think I'm getting too old for the parade. I'm definitely too old to hang out with Cass.

The old-time swimmers are next, tossing beach balls and pretending to swim as they walk along. When a woman in a little black dress stops to kiss a man in a striped one-piece swimsuit—showing off his hairy white legs and wiggling his black cardboard mustache—the Keystone Kops run in. Blowing their whistles and shaking their small black bats, they chase the swimmers through the street, but the crowd laughs hardest when the fire brigade arrives, pulling carts of wooden barrels behind them. One of the girl swimmers stops in front of us and plugs her nose. When she raises her fingers 1-2-3, and slips to the pavement, Cass says, "Uh-oh."

Suddenly the Wicked Witch from *The Wizard of Oz* is standing over her, cackling and calling, "My pretty!" Two boys behind us dash out and swat her butt, then run back into the crowd again.

While people across the street squeal when a "fireman" stops to spray them, I look for Quasimodo. "Watch out!" someone shouts behind me, and everyone pulls back. Mom, Lauren, and Cass jump away too, leaving nothing between me and the fake fireman who stands there.

Spraying me. With the hose. It's real water this time.

"Sorry, kid," he says before moving on.

I can't move. The water burns through me.

Mom smiles, then hugs me and lights a cigarette. "You're fine, Lily. Don't be a sourpuss. It's a hot day. Your clothes will dry in no time." She waves at a friend across the street. The man standing next to her thinks it's for him and waves back.

"Sourpuss," Cass echoes, and I pinch her. Hard. "Owww," she says, looking at me with surprise.

Cass has Down syndrome; I shouldn't have done that. She rubs her pinched arm and smiles at me anyway. Cass is okay. In some ways we're even alike: our insides don't go with our outsides.

"They're here!" Mom suddenly cries.

It's the Grants Pass Cavemen.

I step back in horror.

The Grants Pass Cavemen are ugly and frightening. They scratch themselves like monkeys at the zoo, then stumble around like drunk cartoon fleas. They wear scary wigs, bedroom slippers, and *Flintstones* clothes.

One caveman waves a club at a cowering cavewoman with long blond hair and she runs away, screaming. Barney and Fred would never do that.

The cavemen throw candy and a piece lands at my feet, but I leave it there.

Their jail arrives, on wheels, pulled by two prisoner cavemen, each dragging a chain and bowling ball around his ankle. Inside the jail are people, real people, women with their fingers wrapped around the bars. A woman standing beside us touches Mom's shoulder. "You're pretty," she smiles. "I bet they take you."

Lauren slips her hand into Mom's. "Don't go," she pleads. But Mom doesn't hear her. She would have gone with them last year if Lauren hadn't screamed and the caveman said something about "controlling your kid" which made Mom mad. She will go with them this year; she has to. "You'll be the most beautiful woman at the parade," Dad said at breakfast. "Then what?"

When the cavemen disappear down the street, their jail remains. But they're sneaky; a few wandered into the crowd: they're around here someplace. Except for the man pushing the popcorn wagon, and some guy who looks like Jesus walking down the middle of the road wearing a sandwich sign that reads, *Repent! The End Is Near!,* people are quiet.

Two hairy guys pop up in front of us and Lauren and I scream, but Mom laughs. When they pull on her wrists to join them in the street, she's still laughing. She wants to go, and we know we should let her, but we can't. We hold tight to her waist and legs and yell, "Stop it!" at the kidnappers, while people around us laugh.

It's not funny. I know they're not real cavemen, but the more Mom slips from our grasp, the more frightened I am. "Leave her alone!" I cry, gripping her with one hand while hitting the cavemen as hard as I can. "Don't let go!" I yell at Lauren.

"Jesus, kid," one of them says to me. He covers his head. "It's a joke. We're not going to hurt her."

"Everybody, please!" Mom cries. "Stop pulling on me!" Lauren lets go but I don't. "It's all right," Mom says, blushing and happy. "It's just for fun, Lily. I'll be right back." She clears her throat. "Now, let go."

"Let go," Cass repeats in her dead dull voice.

Mom blushes. "Hold onto this for me, will you?" She hands me her favorite straw purse.

I don't want it. Mom never goes anywhere without a purse.

"You have your wristwatch, right? I'll be back in fifteen minutes—okay, boys?"

The cavemen grunt and flex.

Mom wants to go. She wants to leave us. Maybe she doesn't want to come back. Trini Lopez sings, "*If you wanna be happy for the rest of your life, don't make a pretty woman your wife.*" Dad calls it his theme song.

When I finally drop Mom's hand, one of the cavemen picks her up and throws her over his shoulder. She laughs while they rush her away and people around us applaud and whistle.

"Hold it, Frank," the guy calls out, gesturing toward Mom. "We've got another one." When they finally set her down, Mom walks, of her own free will, up the wooden plank of the jailhouse.

I feel Lauren and Cass standing beside me, quiet and still.

The cavemen are stealing mommies. One of them, pretending to be gallant, removes his hat and wig when he opens the jail door and Mom walks in, smiling. She blows us a kiss through the bars. The cavemen lurch and scratch and grunt like monkeys when they walk farther down the block where fainter cries explode from other unsuspecting kids and moms.

Mom said she'd be back. She said not to worry, that it's just for fun. She said fifteen minutes, but I know better. I won't even look at my watch.

Everyone wants Mom: Lauren, me, Dad, the cavemen.

Maybe some nice lady will take Cass home and I won't have to say anything when she looks at me with her skinny Martian eyes and says something I can't understand because she has Down syndrome and mumbles half the time.

There's a hole in the parade. I look down the street. "Hurry up," I whisper. The faster the parade passes, the sooner Mom will be back. I hug her bright straw purse to my chest. She got it in Mexico on her last wedding anniversary; Frieda took care of us while they were gone.

"Lily?" Lauren says.

"It's okay," I tell her. "I've got her purse. She'll be back."

"She'll be back," Cass repeats.

"I want to hold it," Lauren says.

"Mom told me to hold it for her."

"I don't care. You're not my boss." She snatches it away.

It's getting hotter. Lauren burns easily. Maybe there's lotion in Mom's purse.

"You're not my boss," Cass repeats.

"Shut up!" I shout at her.

I pinched Cass and now I've yelled at her. I am not a nice person.

No, I tell myself when I look at her. We're not alike. We're not alike at all.

Thirty-five minutes later Mom returns, laughing and red-faced, three balloons in her hand. When she asks if I want one, I pretend like I don't hear her.

When we climb in the car after the parade, and Mom announces that all of us are going to Oscar's for lunch, I can't believe it. Oscar's Oyster House is my special birthday place. Just Mom and me.

"Oscar's! Oscar's!" Lauren chants. Dummy. She's never even been there before.

Okay, I'll go, but I won't have fun, no matter what. I'll punish Mom for sharing the place, for ruining its specialness. I just hope Oscar's doesn't have the usual Shirley Temple paper dolls that come with the Shirley Temple drinks she'll probably order for Cass and Lauren. Lauren will want to come here on *her* birthday too.

Outside Oscar's is a newspaper box. *Negro Boycott Meets with Violence*, reads the front-page headline.

"*A . . . B . . . C . . .*" Cass says slowly.

"No, Cass," Lauren interrupts. "*N . . . E . . . G . . . R . . .*" She wants to be a teacher.

And a stewardess

And a horse trainer.

For the last three years, on my birthday at Oscar's, a tall man in a long white apron leads Mom and me to our table in the corner. He removes the *Reserved* card, smiles, and takes Mom's order for a dry vodka martini with a twist. We eat steak and onion rings and salad with Thousand Island dressing, and talk about Dad and Lauren and books and our favorite TV shows. But this isn't my birthday, and I don't recognize the maître d' who leads Mom, Cass, and Lauren to our table. I put my head down and follow them slowly, like people do at funerals.

When Cass spills her water, I excuse myself to go to the bathroom.

"Here," Mom says, reaching across the table with a fifty-cent piece. "Give it to the nice Negro lady in the powder room." I like Bill Cosby on *I Spy* and Reverend Martin Luther King, but I've never really spoken to a Negro before.

The women's restroom is across the bar at the end of the hall. I walk through slowly, passing two quiet men on stools. The bar smells like cigarettes and air freshener. Behind a saloon door, dishes clatter, pots bang, a mixer whirs; cooks and waitresses yell at each other over the sounds, and the kitchen smells are meaty and sweet.

In an animated sign for Dad's favorite beer, a small humming motor makes a fishing boat rock gently on bright blue waves. Sitting in the boat are the Hamm's Bear and Jesus, both of them in silly hats and vests, holding fishing poles and smiling. A half-submerged string of fish hangs off the side of the boat, a case of Hamm's bobs along next to it. Jesus throws out His line.

Up ahead are the *Buoys* and *Gulls* restrooms, separated by a cigarette machine.

Then I see the picture. Over the cigarette machine.

A dark smudgy hill of water faces a dog that's only visible from its shoulders up. I stand on tiptoe to read the nameplate under it. "*Drowing Dog. Francisco de Goya,*" I say out loud. Has it always been hanging there? My pulse fills my ears. I smell the cold lake water, Mrs. Wiggins's cancerous mouth and wet fur. I'm in the lake with her again. Drowning. Scared. The shark curtain an arm's length away.

A man leans over my shoulder. "Woof!" he laughs, ducking into the Buoys' room.

"Woof!" I repeat, just like Cass would do. Startled, I rush into the Gulls' restroom.

The dimness is nice at first; I can't see anything, and it can't see me.

Slowly my eyes adjust, and when they do, everything is different.

I like the blue glass floats in fishnets suspended from the ceiling and how, when I stand in front of the mirror, I suddenly hear seagulls flying overhead. When I turn on the faucet to wash my hands, I hear crashing waves. I remember the wall-embedded sensors at the science museum and run from sink to sink triggering the wave sounds. Watching myself in the mirror, I back away until the seagulls stop, then, standing on the lip of the sensor, I rock back and forth on my heels, starting and stopping the bird sounds again. The tiny spotlight over all three sinks stays lit.

My brain watches my body run to one sink then another, opening the tap, starting both the gull and wave sounds, in various combinations. Music! Maybe I'll be a composer someday! I don't stop until, kneeling on the counter, I touch the starfish painted on the mirror and say, "*Drowning Dog.* Goya."

In the brief silence after my words, I hear someone clear her throat behind me, and I freeze in place.

"Excuse me, miss," a woman's voice says from the dimly lit room. "You might break the thing, doing it like that."

I jump off the counter, shaking. "Sorry."

"The machine," she says. "The sensor." I see her now. The "nice Negro lady" sits in a chair in the corner of the powder room, smoking a cigarette. When she crosses her legs, she reminds me of Mom.

"Were you . . . watching me?" My heart's in my throat.

"Yes ma'am. Me and Jesus sitting right here, taking a break. Being entertained by you, we surely is."

Jesus? He follows me everywhere.

The woman wears a crucifix too and touches it with her long black fingers. "You got a lot of energy, young lady. You know that? Your mind working all the time, I bet. I see you, I do. You're a smart one."

Most grown-ups tell me I'm pretty or confused, but not smart.

I feel the half dollar in my sweaty hand. It's a long slow walk to the woman in the chair.

"It's okay," she says, seeing me coming. Her voice is gentle. "I won't bite."

"I know," I mumble. I feel myself blush and hope she can't see it. I hold out the coin. One hand on the cigarette, the other on the arm of the chair, she looks like a queen when she leans forward to peer at the fifty-cent piece.

"That's all right, miss. You keep it yourself," she says. "I didn't earn it; I been sitting right here doing nothing." When she takes a puff, the burning ash highlights her starched white collar.

Lauren suddenly opens the door to the Gulls' room. She stares at me and says, "Mom said you better have fallen in, or else she's coming to get you."

"Okay, okay, I'm coming."

Lauren spots the woman. "Hello," she smiles. "My name's Lauren."

"How do you do, Lauren? I'm Mrs. Evans."

"Are you a Negro, Mrs. Evans?" Lauren asks.

I blush.

"I surely am," she says.

"Sammy Davis Jr. is a Negro too. He's my favorite entertainer."

"You have good taste, Miss Lauren. He's my favorite entertainer also." Mrs. Evans laughs as Lauren runs out again.

"I guess I better go."

"Your mother's waiting."

"May I ask you something first?"

"You may." She lights a fresh cigarette.

I pause before asking, "Do you like cavemen?"

"Cavemen? Like *The Flintstones*?"

"Yeah. But not funny cavemen." I straighten my shoulders. "What if your mother was kidnapped by them and she was gone for a while—not for a long time, but kind of long."

Mrs. Evans leans forward and clears her throat. "You okay, miss?" Her voice is serious. "Something happen? You in trouble?"

"No, it's just that . . . we were alone for a little while. And something *could* have happened."

"Something could *always* happen, miss. Sometimes it does. That's life. But your mama came back for you, didn't she? Isn't she waiting for you right now?"

"Yes."

"Well, then you just thank the Lord for sending her home, no matter what she's been up to."

I smile. "Here," I say, holding out the coin again. "My mom wants you to have it."

"All right then, if your mother said so. I can surely use it." I give her the money but keep standing there. "There something else you want to say?"

"I'm . . . sorry," I say quietly.

"For what? What have you got to be sorry for?"

"For the hoses. And the dogs. And the mean white people. I saw the demonstrations on TV."

Mrs. Evans disappears into the shadows again, and for a few seconds I don't see or hear her at all. Then I hear her sniff. The chair squeaks when she stands up. She's older than I thought, and bent over a little bit, nothing like Mom at all.

"Don't you apologize, young lady," Mrs. Evans says. There are tears in her eyes. "You nothing like those bad people. Standing right here, I feel God's love inside you. You feel it too, don't you?"

"Yes," I say, surprising myself. God's love, and Mrs. Wiggins.

Mrs. Evans smiles. She takes a rag out of her apron pocket and walks slowly to the sink where she begins to wipe my fingerprints off the mirror. "Go on back to your table, miss. And thank your mother for me."

"Okay."

"You keep that good heart, now."

Should I tell her that I don't have a good heart? That I drowned my dog, called Jesus bad names, and pinched Aunt Cass really hard?

When I open the restroom door she says, "I seen you working those sensors, young lady. You do something with the way you see things, all right. It's unique, I swear."

I hear Aunt Cass scraping her salad dish before I even get back to the table. She never has to be told to eat her greens; she eats everything. Dad said she'd "eat the paint off the dishes."

"That's enough," Mom says, grabbing Cass's fork, then frowns at me when I sit down. "Why were you gone so long?"

"You were gone too," I reply. "At the parade." She throws back the last of her martini and doesn't answer. "Sorry, I was talking to—"

"She was talking to Mrs. Evans," Lauren says. "Mrs. Evans is a Negro."

A Negro waitress stands beside us with our lunch. Mom blushes. When the woman hands out the plates, Lauren cries, "Goody! Fish and chips!"

"Goody!" Cass mimics. Cass acts like a kid only she doesn't know it, and I don't know I'm acting like a kid until I see her do it.

When Mom reaches for her bucket of steamed clams, I realize she's ordered me a whole fish. It stares at me with a boiled eye, its mouth midword. "Lily," she says, "you said you wanted fresh fish, right? And iced tea?"

Yes. No. Yes.

The pee-colored glass of tea is sweaty. The fish is trying to tell me something. I watch and wait. Maybe it'll say something in Aramaic or Latin and I can look it up at the library.

"No lunch, no dessert," Mom reminds me.

"Everything all right then, ma'am?" the waitress asks. Mom nods, and the platter holding the fish stays where the woman places it.

Untouched, until time to go.

Cass sits between Lauren and me on the drive back to Good Shepherd Home. There's an invisible line in the backseat that separates the two sides of the car (Lauren's and mine), and we watch as Cass's big soft body tips back and forth across it.

At Good Shepherd, Cass's roommate walks out to Mom's car.

It's weird but kind of neat how they look alike. It reminds me of the girls uniforms at St. Rita's, and how Mom says, "When students look the same on the outside, they're better students on the inside." Cass's friend hugs her and the two of them hold hands when they walk back inside together.

The backseat is extra-big without Cass. Lauren and I are quiet and hug our corners while we head home.

Mom clears her throat and asks, "Did you give the nice Negro lady her tip?"

I nod.

Eight, scratch that, nine minutes later, Mom looks for our eyes in the rearview mirror and asks, "You were okay, girls . . . weren't you? I mean, after the cavemen took me away?"

Lauren looks out the car window.

I'm the older sister so I say, "Sure," for both of us.

Mom's forehead wrinkles. "Good," she responds. At the next stoplight she freshens her lipstick.

At home, Mom browns the marinated pot roast in the frypan, then sticks it in the oven at 325 degrees. She peels potatoes and plops them in a pan of ice water in the kitchen sink. "What do you think, girls?" she smiles, looking out the kitchen window. "Can I squeeze another hour out of the sun?"

She doesn't expect an answer as she dashes to the bathroom, scurries into her two-piece swimsuit, and rifles through the drawers for her small blue eye-cups, hair net, and bottle of mineral oil.

Soon, Mom stands beside me watching the sky, a towel draped over her arm. She hesitates for a moment and rubs a bare foot up and down her long shiny leg. Mom loves to sunbathe. She positions the chaise longue like a sundial, prepared to chase the sun around the deck. She lies down, drops the bathing suit straps off her shoulders, and fifteen minutes later, when the portable oven timer goes off, she turns over. I imagine her big boobs breaking through the green plastic ribbing, and nursing dogs on her, like the puppies across the street, or Romulus and Remus who we learned about in school.

Lauren and I clean the bathroom and vacuum, then sit in the family room watching Mom tan herself. Soon Dad slams the car door shut, singing as he opens the door, home again: "*All day, all night, Marianne . . .*"

"Fix yourself a drink, honey," Mom yells, raising her head off the chaise longue, "I'll be right there!"

"How was the parade?" Dad asks.

"We had quite a day!" Mom giggles. They talk about Dad's work, and the parade and the cavemen and Oscar's, while Mom bastes the roast, mashes the potatoes, cuts wedges of iceberg lettuce and tomatoes, and tucks the red linen napkins through the napkin rings.

When she places the silverware in the middle of the table, Lauren separates the little fork, big fork, knife, and spoon, and sets them out. I fill the water glasses and light the candles, making fingertip cups with the warm wax. After Lauren leaves the room, I crawl under the table. I like sitting under there, though when I hear Dad talk impatiently to Mom, I wish I were back in the Gulls' room with Mrs. Evans instead.

"It's not just leaving Lauren there," Dad says. "It's not just Cass, either." He crosses the room, and back again. "It's Lily. We don't know what to expect from her anymore, do we? Do we, Kit?"

There's a pause before the freezer door opens, ice tumbles into a glass, and Mom says, "All right, dear, you made your point. Now . . . would you like a drink or not?"

Under the table, on the bottom of Peace Lake, I hold my breath longer than any other teenager in history, then swim to the surface and back to shore again all by myself. I'm an excellent swimmer so my parents don't worry.

Our family eats s'mores around an open fire, and Lauren listens really hard when I explain where the word *s'more* comes from. How Hershey is a town in Pennsylvania and Pennsylvania was named for William Penn, an early settler.

We look at pictures of fetuses and discuss how America was a fetus once too, just ideas and laws and witches and preachers who ignored the Indians who already lived here. We discuss how every pilgrim and explorer, every settler and slave owner and cowboy and gold rush guy, should have turned around and gone home.

Who would we be if we never left Europe? If there was never a Portland or Peace Lake, a Hoss Cartwright or an appliance convention?

I talk and they listen.

There is no drowning or sandy burial, and Lauren holds my hand all the way home.

"Dinner! Ten minutes!" Mom calls.

When she looks away, I crawl out from under the table and walk-swim into the family room where Lauren's watching Mr. Moon on TV. Mr. Moon hosts the local TV cartoon show.

I blush when I hear his voice.

Last night I dreamed Mom won a "Dream Date with Mr. Moon." For their date, he flew over the telephone lines and raised Mom's bedroom window. "*Come fly with me, let's fly, let's fly away,*" he sang like Frank Sinatra, cool, snapping his long white fingers. His big head was so bright it lit up the side of our house. While Dad slept, Mom took Mr. Moon's hand and the two of them flew out of the yard into the night sky. The next month they were *Tiger Beat*'s "hot couple." They shared the cover; only his full-moon, deep-crater face hid most of the graphics. Mom looked good; she looked like Jean Shrimpton, the model.

When Mr. Moon goes to commercial, I turn the station.

"Turn it back!" Lauren yells.

"He's ugly," I say.

"No he's not."

"Yes he is."

"Hey!" Dad walks into the room, scowling at both of us, then looks at the television. "Good," he says, falling into his favorite chair. "The news."

The Rose Festival Parade is on.

A policeman rides horseback behind a group of kids on unicycles and stilts. People applaud the Rose Festival Queen who waves like the Queen of England.

When a Grants Pass Cavemen sticks his face in the camera, Dad turns the station.

CHAPTER 8

PISSING IN THREE ACTS

Act I

Heather, Artis, and Lorraine are the toughest girls in ninth grade. It's strange to be standing with them, behind the cafeteria after school, while they smoke and talk. When I step out and look past the office, parking lot, and ball field, I can just make out the road.

If Mom drove by, demanding I come home immediately, I wouldn't mind. The girls make me nervous. They say I'm "weird but cool," and make me promise not to tell anybody about their cigarettes.

They just want my Beatles cards. I have ten on me; only three more at home. Collecting cards is kinda square but they'll sell them at the flea market and make money for grass. Marijuana, I mean.

"You don't have cards worth shit," Heather says with disgust. "Who wants Ringo, anyway?" When she blows smoky Os, she throws back her ironed-straight black hair. Her ears are pierced.

The others look up from their go-go boots discussion. Artis snatches Heather's cigarette and takes a deep puff.

All three girls check out my twin Ringos, untouched George Harrisons, and dog-eared Johns and Pauls. "How come you taped plastic wrap around George?" Heather asks, wrinkling her nose like she smells something bad.

I shrug.

"Shit," she giggles like she just made up the word. Made it up then pissed on it like one of Aunt Jamie's lost dogs.

Jamie calls it pissing and explains that dogs do it "to mark their territory."

"All animals do," she explains, as I help her put out salt licks for the deer that will wander through her dying apple trees at dusk. "Sometimes even females."

Jamie loves animals and sometimes rescues dogs that have been hurt or dumped off on the old coast highway where she lives alone in a little yellow house with red shutters. She built the kennel and the dog yard fence all by herself. She teaches English and poetry at the community college, writes songs, and swims, of course. Aunt Jamie does lots of stuff. Dad says she'll never settle down.

We listen to Peter, Paul and Mary on the stereo while we sit on denim-covered cushions in her bay window, eating banana bread and sipping peppermint tea. She puts a sugared lemon slice in my cup. Outside, two of Jamie's dogs, the ones she calls the "Heinz 57s," push around a small three-legged terrier named Percival.

"Poor thing," I say.

"They're not bad dogs, Lily. They're just showing him who's boss. They're saying, *You're a cripple and a stranger. We were here first. This is our property and this is how it's going to be.*"

Frieda said God made animals simple and accepting to give us an example to live by. "But they're being mean," I remind Jamie.

"If we went out there and stopped them, they'd just figure out a way to beat up Percy when we weren't looking. It's nature, Lily." Jamie smiles. "But there are things we *can* do something about. Bigger things, important things." She blows a little wave across the surface of her tea. "The war in Vietnam is wrong. Poverty and prejudice are wrong. It's time to stick our hands in the dirt and pull out the rotting stuff."

Healthy green vines frame the inside of her bay window and turn their leaves to the light outside.

"I met this guy named Kevin. We're joining a few friends from Reed College and going downtown tomorrow. Goldwater is in town. He needs to know that not everyone in Portland is cool with his opposition to the Test Ban Treaty. You up for a little civil disobedience, Lily? I won't let anything happen to you."

"Tomorrow? You mean Monday?"

Mom would kill both of us. Still, I might go if it were just the two of us. No Kevin. No friends from Reed College. "No thanks," I say. "Maybe next time."

"I hope there isn't a next time," Jamie says, taking our dishes to the kitchen.

I love Aunt Jamie's house. While she cleans up, I explore her living room. A big poster of a stooped Indian on horseback, with the setting sun behind him, hangs over her lumpy green couch. Tie-dyed lace doilies sit on the arms of two overstuffed chairs; a paisley-printed cloth is pinned to the ceiling. On the coffee table is a pile of strange-looking newspapers called the *Berkeley Barb*, and a little incense pagoda with strawberry-smelling smoke coming out its windows. In an ashtray is a half-smoked hand-rolled cigarette; it smells funny. Is it pot?

"Ahhh-CHOO!"

"Gesundheit," Jamie calls from the kitchen. "Did you know that means *healthiness* in German?"

Yes.

The mantle above Aunt Jamie's fireplace is covered with framed photos: Jamie in cutoffs, holding a fishing pole; Jamie hugging a gargoyle on the roof of Notre Dame (with the Eiffel Tower in the background); Jamie with her arms around guys with long hair and mustaches; Jamie when she was a little girl, sitting on Santa's lap, sucking her hair like Lauren used to do when she was nervous. There's a picture of Lauren and me in the spinning teacups at Disneyland too, and one of Mom and Dad cutting their wedding cake. Even a framed photograph of a chimpanzee.

"It's a joke," Aunt Jamie explains, standing behind me. "We're all related to the monkey, aren't we?"

"What about Adam and Eve?" I ask.

"If you find me a picture of them, I'll put it on the mantle."

I point at a glossy magazine photograph of Joan Baez and Bob Dylan, people cheering in the background.

"They'll do," Jamie says.

The folk singers smile big, showing all their teeth and the whites of their eyes, and point their guitars at the camera like machine guns.

"Think they'll get married?" I ask.

"That's what the magazines say," Jamie laughs. "They won't get married if they're smart. If you're smart, you never get married. Men like to piss on women too, Lily. Don't forget."

Act II

I should be cleaning my room, but sitting in the kitchen, watching

Mom iron, is more fun. "So you never liked swimming?" I ask.

"I never learned how," Mom says, pressing the collar of a blouse. "It's a beautiful sport, don't get me wrong. It just scares me a little."

"But you could take lessons and—"

"Nope. Not. Interested."

I know I've asked too many questions when Mom's answers blink on and off like the little traffic lights at Bert's Bumper Cars. Mom doesn't like Shari Lewis and Lamb Chop either. "They give me the creeps," she said once. "A lamb chop is meat. Shari Lewis is talking to something she wants to eat. I know it's a kid's show but it's creepy."

Mom hangs up the blouse, runs her hands under cold tap water, and splashes her face. She's been cooking and ironing all morning; the kitchen is hot. Sweat drips off her chin as she fills the iron with water from the Pyrex measuring cup, then spreads out one of Dad's dress shirts on the ironing board. "I guess I'll have to clean up your room then, huh? I can't wait to get my hands on that closet."

"I'm going," I say, finally standing up. "Does Lamb Chop still give you the creeps?" I pretend I'm a puppet and stare at her without blinking my eyes.

Mom points the iron at me, and mists the air. Her cheeks shine. "It's going to get *really* creepy around here if you don't do your chores, Lily. Now."

The phone rings.

I call out, "Topo Gigio gives me the creeps," touch my doorknob at twelve, three, six, and nine, like a clock face, then turn the knob back and forth making clicking safecracker sounds.

"All right," Mom says into the receiver, "I'll look into it. I'll make sure she gets back to you. Sorry for the inconvenience . . . Yes, yes, of course. No problem. Thanks for your call."

Immediately, the phone rings again. "Uh-huh, yes," Mom sniffs. Her voice is worried. I stand up and listen. "Yes, we'll be there as soon as we can. Tell her we're coming. Please tell her," she says and hangs up.

Did Lauren do something?

"Mom?" I call out. She doesn't answer but I hear her take a wineglass out of the cupboard.

Click click click, three to the right. *Click click click click,* four to the left. I wiggle my bedroom doorknob. Did I forget the imaginary code?

I can't get in. I want in. Something's wrong. I need to get in.

Mom says hi to Dad's pretty new secretary on the phone, and asks to talk to "my husband." Mom always forgets her name (it's Toni).

"She went up there this morning," Mom tells Dad. "I don't know, Paul. I don't know. Just come home, okay?"

What's wrong? Where are they going?

"Lauren's outside playing. We're all going, of course. We'll be ready to leave when you get here. Hurry!"

When Mom's upset, she forgets things. While she steps outside to yell for my sister, I tiptoe into the kitchen, unplug the iron, and hurry back to my room.

Dad's home in twenty-three minutes.

"In the car, kiddo, and bring a warm jacket. We're going to the lake."

"Peace Lake? Can't I stay home? Mom said I have to clean my room."

He opens my door and scowls. "The car, Lily. ASAP."

"ASAP, SWAK, RSVP, PTA, STP, COD, UFO."

"Lily!"

His voice unsticks me. "But I won't leave the house, or answer the door. I promise."

"We're going. *All* of us. Lauren's already in the car."

"But Mom said we were never going back." I grip my book harder. I can't go. I haven't been to Peace Lake since Mrs. Wiggins died.

But there's no discussion. Dad's already in the hall closet, changing jackets. A minute later he's starting the car.

"Lily?" Mom calls from the bathroom. She's peeing with the door open; she never does that. "You heard your father. Please, sweetheart. Aunt Jamie needs us."

I love Jamie, but I'm scared. "Why do all of us have to—"

"Lily!"

Sometimes when Mom gets mad, I turn into a picture Lauren drew of me when she was little. My eyes are big and far apart like a fish's, and my face is smeared with streaks because she erased my nose and mouth a lot, and her hands were sweaty. My arms and legs are ten-foot stilts and I stand on the very bottom of the page, surrounded by razor-sharp blades of grass and lollipop-shaped trees with beach ball–sized fruit. Overhead is a cloudless sky with a bull's-eye sun, and a flying mustache Lauren explained was a bird.

Mom stands in my doorway. "Windbreaker, Lily, and a sweater." She takes a deep breath. "You remember the old man who rents the boats at Peace Lake, don't you?"

I nod.

"Well, Jamie asked him to call us. She wants us to come get her." Mom smiles weakly. "We all love her, but *you* have a special relationship with her, Lily. You want to help her, don't you?"

"Yes," I whisper, so quietly Mom doesn't hear the word that plops, then sinks, to the bottom of Peace Lake.

"He said he rowed out to Jamie's boat but she wouldn't come in and she wouldn't take a blanket. She was talking in a different language, but she asked for me, for us. I know you're scared, but I want you to come with us, Lily." There are tears in Mom's eyes. "Now," she says firmly.

She says something else about killing two birds with one stone, then hurries to the kitchen where she quickly gulps down her wine.

On the way upriver, I learn that the first phone call was from a reporter for the *Oregonian* who was writing an article on Aunt Jamie as a "role model for young women athletes." Jamie was one of the first female swimmers in Oregon to ever earn an athletic scholarship to college. After that, she swam on various city teams, and this year competed freelance to win a spot in the Northwest Regional Finals. Only Jamie didn't show up for the reporter's interview, she wasn't at the pool for preliminaries, and she didn't call to cancel either date. Not showing up means she forfeits her spot in the finals.

I look out the car window for Jesus and Mr. and Mrs. Potato Head, but it's the regular stuff this time: the forest, the cars, and the painted white line that separates them.

Mom smokes cigarette after cigarette. "You're going to make yourself sick, Kit," Dad says.

"He had our number already. We're listed as her emergency contact. He should have called us earlier."

"Relax, sweetheart. Everything's going to be fine."

"You and your *fines*," she mumbles.

My parents are nervous. They don't even turn on the radio. They talk about weird stuff, like the Savage Boy who delivers our morning newspaper. Sometimes you hear him in the street past midnight, even on school nights. He drives the neighbors crazy when he leans against their mail-boxes or combs his hair in the side mirrors of their cars. Mike Savage is the youngest of three brothers and too young to smoke but he does it anyway. When Mrs. Sheehan left her purse in the front seat overnight, he helped himself to her wallet. At least that's what everyone said. Dad says Mr. Savage works three jobs, and with a new baby, his wife has "enough on her hands" so he doesn't blame them for raising "savage Savages."

While Lauren holds her transistor radio to her ear, I practice my times tables over and over, reciting every third equation in Pig Latin. Mom turns around, pressing her finger to her lips. "Everything's going to be fine, Lily. We'll pick up Jamie and drive straight home, okay?"

"Nine times fifteen is one hundred and thirty-five," I answer.

Finally we turn off the road and drive down to the boat basin. I'm the first one to spot Jamie's car next to the café where they rent the rowboats. We rent boat number 12 and five life preservers, then row toward the middle of the lake.

The breeze blows shivering whitecaps against our boat. Mom and Dad take turns with the oars, look straight ahead, and don't talk. Lauren twists the handles of her lucky jump rope. I hold tight to Mrs. Wiggins's tooth, and snuggle into the bright orange collar of my life preserver.

I'm safe on top of the water with my family, and lean into the rhythm of their rowing the way Jamie taught me to ride uphill on a horse.

A sudden flap of wings overhead makes everyone jump. Ahead of us, a duck runs along the lake's surface. Lauren points, then quickly puts down her hand.

"It's okay, Lauren." Mom tries to smile. "You're right. No matter what, Peace Lake is still a beautiful place."

A heron fishes in a nearby marsh. A man and a woman sitting on a sun-lit boulder wave at us, but they might as well be on TV; none of us waves back.

Then something scratches the hull of the boat, under my tennis shoes, right below me, and my heart jumps in my throat.

They're snags, I tell myself, fossilized trees holding onto the bottom of the lake, a water forest whose tops scrape the surface. I look at Mom and Dad, their eyes locked on the distant boat with a tiny unmoving figure inside. They don't hear the scratching scraping sounds that slowly spell out *L-I-L-Y*, the sounds, the letters, I feel through my whole body the way I used to feel Judy spell out *S-E-X* or *H-E-L-P* on my back when I slept over.

I press the pointed end of the dogtooth into my hand, not stopping until it hurts. Is that you, Mrs. Wiggins? Did you float out of your sandy grave? Are you caught in duckweed, or tied to a tree in the underwater forest?

I-A-M-S-O-R-R-Y, I write back with the toe of my sneaker.

"Weirdo," Lauren whispers.

The late-afternoon sun highlights clouds of tiny insects around us. The bugs are dinner for the swallows that fly in and out of the swarms, and for the fish I hear splash but never see jump. The oars gently slice the water and the boat pushes a glistening V in front of us.

The old man told Mom that Jamie has been here since nine a.m. She rented the boat and rowed out, but didn't go swimming and didn't come back in. What has she been doing?

"Jamie!" Mom cries out.

Alone and hunched up, my aunt looks up.

Dad finally rows us alongside number 8, and holds the boats together while Mom steadies Jamie so she can board. A dry white bath towel slips off Jamie's shoulders when Mom helps her step into our gently rocking boat, and I notice how thin Jamie is in her black one-piece swimsuit, her skin as white as Mr. Moon's. Her long red hair is braided, her muscular legs are covered with goose pimples, and her teeth chatter.

I've never heard teeth actually chatter before, so I listen closely to what they're saying. It might be a code.

Mom drapes a wool blanket from the car around Jamie, slips a life preserver over her head, and pats the seat next to her. Lauren and I squeeze together, forcing me closer to the edge of the boat and the water.

Jamie looks at us self-consciously while Dad ties her rowboat to ours. "It's the whole fam-damily," she says and smiles, though her eyes are strange. She's changed. Dad takes up the oars again.

"Ah, James," Mom coos, cupping and rubbing her sister's hands.

"I don't know what's wrong with me. I've been trying to get into the water all afternoon. I'm sorry, Kit."

"Don't worry about that. I'm always good for a little TLC, aren't I?" *TLC, ASAP, SWAK.* "Everything's going to be fine." *Fine fine bo-vine. Moo.*

"No. It's not," I blurt out. A bomb could fall on us at any minute, Mrs. Wiggins is dead, Jesus is a jerk, and now Jamie's afraid of the water.

"Lily," Dad says, shaking his head slowly.

"You didn't go swimming at all?" I ask. Why did I have to come back to Peace Lake? Until today, we were never ever coming back. "What about the regionals? And the newspaper interview?"

Lauren pokes me with an elbow.

Dad scowls, then looks at his watch. "Listen, the boathouse is closing, and we've got fifteen minutes to get in before they charge us for another day."

Jamie doesn't look at me when she answers, "The regionals . . . Lily . . . I don't think . . . I'm probably not . . ."

"Sshh," Mom says, hugging her closer. "Never mind that now."

It's slower crossing the lake without Mom's help and Dad rows hard, grunting and huffing as we glide through the water towing Jamie's boat. No one talks again until Jamie says, "The water, Kit. It isn't in me anymore."

The waves stop licking the boat; the lake holds its breath.

It isn't in me anymore, either.

I shouldn't have been mean to Jamie; I push the sharp end of the tooth into my hand until it hurts.

Dad clears his throat. "Got your keys, Jamie? Why don't you ride with Kit and Lily, and Lauren and I will drive your car to your house, okay? I'll meet you there."

Jamie takes a key out of her swimsuit bra and hands it to him.

Finally docked, Dad tethers the boats, grabs Lauren's hand, and dashes to the café. Mom heads to the car while I stare at the lake. The water's a mirror of the "abalone sky" overhead. That's what Mom calls the fading "blush of pink and robin's-egg blue" we sometimes see from our porch at dusk.

"Lily! Your jacket!" she calls, but when I grab it, Mrs. Wiggins's tooth falls into the bottom of the rowboat where it instantly shines like a polished agate. Does Mrs. Wiggins want it back? I look across the lake at the sandy bar where she's buried.

Should I throw it in the lake?

At the end of the pier, Jesus wrestles His tackle and ice chest out of the boat.

"Lil-EE!" Dad calls. "Stay with your mother!"

I wish people would stop yelling at me.

The *Closed* sign is hanging in the café window, but the jug-eared old man stands outside waiting for Dad, who hands him our life preservers and a bill from his wallet. Lauren sits on a rock nearby, listening to her transistor radio.

Jamie leans against her car while Mom threads Jamie's white goose-bumpy legs through a pair of long pants she brought from home.

We made it.

Jesus smiles and waves a long string of fish at me. Big deal. Everybody knows He's a fisherman.

I grab the dogtooth and run to the car.

On our way to Jamie's house, Jamie and I sit in the backseat, staring out the window. "I'm sorry you had to go to the lake, Lily," she says. "I know it was hard for you."

"She wanted to come," Mom answers. "Lily was worried about you. We all were."

I smile.

When Mom turns away to light a cigarette, Jamie leans toward me. Her usually bright face is drained of color, just outlined in black like an untouched drawing in a coloring book. "I used to be a mermaid," she whispers.

When she says it, I'm mad at Jesus all over again.

A minute later Jamie falls asleep and pees. Most of it soaks into the wool blanket Mom wrapped around her, but a warm trickle runs along the stitching. I scoot forward to get out of its way. She must have been holding it for a long time.

I put Mrs. Wiggins's tooth in Jamie's open hand, count to fifty backward, and snatch it back.

Dad takes us home while Mom stays with Jamie for a while. She gives her a hot shower, sticks her in clean pajamas, puts her to bed, and arranges for the neighbors to watch her animals. Jamie sleeps for three days. She never tells us what happened on the lake that day, or why, after watching her weight so closely, she left a half-eaten quart of chocolate ice cream melting in the foot well of her car—a white plastic spoon stuck in the middle of it.

At breakfast the next day, when Dad says his muscles are sore from rowing, Mom kisses his cheek and pours him another cup of coffee. When he complains how Aunt Jamie always needs extra attention, she bursts into tears.

After lunch, Mom and I sit in a sunny window and draw.

Even looking upside down at Mom's sketchpad, I recognize Peace Lake, the rowboat, and a dark figure in the water. "Why did you draw Jamie in the water? I thought she didn't—"

Mother abruptly stands up and stretches. She touches her toes and looks out the window at the picnic table where Jamie's wool blanket is drying in the sun. "She wanted to be in the water, Lily, so I put her in the water. You can make things up when you draw. Imagination is a wonderful thing, as long as you're the one in control."

"So Jamie's . . . not in control?"

Mom sits down to draw again. "Aunt Jamie is fragile sometimes. I don't know how to explain it; some things can't be explained." She wets her thumb and rubs it across the paper, smearing the dark waters of Peace Lake. "Romania has the Black Sea, of course, but we are from Sibiu. Jamie calls us landed mermaids." Mom smiles. "Maybe that is why we have the occasional . . . issue with water. It makes us—you and me and Jamie— different. Like someone in one of your books. Different isn't so bad, is it, Lily?"

All three of us are weirdos?

"Every family has problems," she says. "Judy's family, for example—" Mom suddenly stops talking. She draws a circle in the sky over Peace Lake. A sun, a moon, or a hole in the sky, I can't tell.

I don't want to be fragile. I don't want to have a problem with water or anything else. I draw a heron fishing in the reeds, or maybe it is in mud like the "special mud," the primordial ooze we all come from.

Aunt Jamie keeps a collection of fairy tales on her nightstand.

Once, when I stayed over, she read me several stories about mermaids. "When a mermaid grows up," Jamie explained, "she has to choose between the water and love. She can't have both. If she tries, she'll be unhappy the rest of her life. The world's full of women who used to be mermaids." She turned the old leather-bound book to the back. "I want to show you something."

When she unfolded the sheet of water-stained paper, sand spilled from it. It smelled of saltwater and tide pools, fish and wind and dead stuff on the beach. I took a deep breath.

"You smell it too?"

"Ocean?"

"Tears."

Act III

Aunt Jamie's in love with Kevin. They're getting married in October.

Mom says Kevin's always in a "big fat hurry." Too busy to help Jamie with her rescued animals, garden, or chores; too busy to read her poetry or spend more than a weekend at her house, or even come to our house when Dad builds us a kite or Mom makes lasagna. Kevin's too busy to do anything but fly Jamie to strange exotic places that she loves and never wants to come back from. Kevin has his own plane and promised to teach her how to fly it someday.

"Are you ever going to swim again?" I ask her.

"Why should I?" Jamie smiles. "Kit told me *you* stopped. It doesn't matter, I don't need it. Kevin makes me happy now." I smell patchouli when she hugs herself then twirls around like that scene in *The Sound of Music*. The long pink underwear and knee-high moccasins under her patchwork skirt remind me of the tiny pink hollyhock dolls she used to make for Lauren and me.

Jamie stops and weaves in place. She grabs the back of the chair for balance.

"Won't you miss it?" I ask.

"Swimming? What's to miss?"

When she smiles her cheeks stand up, making her teary eyes squint. *Chinese, Japanese, knobby knees, look at these.* I bet Kevin saw more than titties and that's why they're getting married.

"But you said if a woman was smart she never gets married."

"It's a woman's prerogative to change her mind, Lily." Jamie got after Mom for saying that once. She said there was no such thing as a woman's prerogative; that it was that "kind of talk that keeps women down."

"But what about the dogs?"

"Dog. There's only one left." Jamie looks toward the sliding glass door that empties onto the porch where she grows tomatoes, peppers, and herbs in whiskey barrel halves. "I'll miss all the animals, wild and tame," she says. "I miss them already."

Past the porch and down the hill, Percival, the abandoned three-legged terrier, stands at the gate, barking at the mail truck. Jamie said that Mitch the mailman never worried about leaving his truck and walking up the road until Percival tore his pant leg. He liked Jamie's animals, even the peacocks, but he was especially fond of Ray, Aunt Jamie's blind llama, who used to stand by the fence waiting for a head scratch. I only saw Ray once before a drunk hunter shot him dead, but I liked him too. Today, Mitch sticks the mail in the box and drives off.

"What about Percy?"

"I found him a home." I stare at my beautiful aunt. "What, don't believe me?"

Nope. She lied about never getting married, why wouldn't she lie about finding a home for Percival? No one wants an old three-legged dog anyway. She's probably taking him to the pound.

"I'm in love, Lily. I want a different life now." She cocks her head. "There's nothing wrong with that. You aren't mad at me, are you?"

"No," I lie.

Each Christmas Lauren and I get water stuff from Aunt Jamie: umbrellas, rain boots or brightly colored slickers, beach towels, flip-flops, snorkeling gear. She promised to buy us scuba-diving lessons when we were "old enough," so we can explore "the underwater ruins of Alexandria, the Turkish coast, and the Red Sea."

Now it'll never happen.

I look around Jamie's place. It's almost empty. No music playing, no incense burning. She stopped baking and gave away her sourdough starter. Her posters are rolled up; her books and records, pictures of friends, and tie-dyed doilies are packed in boxes.

"Cup of tea, Lily? I'm having one."

"Sure."

I wrote a story about Aunt Jamie. When Jamie walks away, I stick it in a book by Emily Dickinson. In my story . . .

Jamie has fish scales and wears leotards to hide them. Her toes are webbed, and a small gill grows under each arm and behind each ear.

When she's not writing poetry, Jamie sits in the bathtub for hours and never has to dry off; she doesn't even own a towel. In fact, except for the floor-to-ceiling bookshelves in every room, the bathtub is the biggest thing in the little yellow house with the red shutters off the old coast highway.

Her skin and hair twinkle with salt crystals. Empty glass salt-shakers are scattered everywhere. At night, Jamie's glittering skin lights her way to a cliff overlooking the ocean. As the wind blows her long red hair, ships looking for landfall mistake her for a twinkling constellation of stars and crash into the rocks.

She gets in trouble, and they put her in jail.

While she's locked up, Kevin falls in love with a waitress and leaves town. After Jamie gets out, she moves in with us, and everyone lives happily ever after.

Lauren wrote the last sentence when Jamie announced her engagement.

"You know, after we're settled," Jamie calls from the kitchen, "we'll come back to visit. If your parents say it's okay, you could join us on a trip sometime. Wouldn't Africa be great? Would you like to come to Africa with us?"

Of course.

Kevin's helping Jamie sell the house. "Don't know where we're going, but we're going," she told me. She was happy when she said it; maybe even twirling around on the inside like dumb old Julie Andrews in *The Sound of Music.*

"Mom says you don't have to sell your house," I remind her, while she shows me her ring. "You could rent it for a while, in case you want to come back."

"But I don't want to come back. To stay, I mean. I'm tired of being alone."

"But you're not alone," I say, wiping away a tear.

Jamie stands up and heads to the kitchen. "I'll miss you too," she calls back. She pops the lid off the imported cookie tin Kevin gave her and places two teacups on the empty counter.

"Did Kevin make you give up the animals and swimming and stuff?"

Jamie fills the kettle and sets it firmly on the burner. "No," she finally answers, standing in the doorway with her hands on her hips. "Why is everyone so damn suspicious?" She glances around the room. "Can we talk about something else? Please?"

I just chewed off my two longest fingernails. They're not as long as Judy's, but they were getting there. "Do you think there's a curse or something? You know, about our family and water, I mean?"

Jamie sighs. "Sure. Your mom and I joked about it for years."

Joked?

Jamie hands me a jar of sugared lemon slices. "I made them for you," she says, finally smiling again. "Want to know what I *really* think about the water curse, Lily?" I nod. "Water-schmahter."

Jamie is beautiful and groovy and smart.

"Hey, do you like the Beatles' song 'And I Love Her'?" She sways in place and sings, "*A love like ours . . . could never die . . . as long as I . . . have you near me . . .*" Jamie turns her head when three-legged Percival barks again.

"Do you know that *dog* spelled backward is *God*?" I ask her.

"I heard that somewhere, yeah." Over her shoulder, dead sunflowers tilt in the breeze. Jamie grows the tallest sunflowers I've ever seen. "Listen, Lily Lou, Percy will be fine, I promise. Dog-spelled-backward will take care of God-spelled-backward."

I saw a photograph of John Lennon holding a sunflower once. "I like George. Who's your favorite Beatle?" I ask.

"Kevin. Want my Beatles cards?"

CHAPTER 9
THE SAVAGE BOY

I'm just waking up when the mermaids, printed on my wallpaper, drag themselves onto the rocks of Copenhagen Harbor to sing.

Each mermaid has two voices and their songs sound like hunger growls, tinkling glass, and crying. Mermaid songs are easier to hear with your eyes closed. The brighter the sun, the harder I squeeze out the light. Without opening them, I know the wallpaper is littered with little numbered rowboats too. Aunt Jamie sits in each one, waiting to be rescued.

I keep a harmonica under my pillow and, taking it out, I match the mermaid songs by holding two notes as long as I can, hoping they reach Peace Lake, Copenhagen Harbor, and Jamie's empty house on the old coast highway.

"I *thought* I heard something," Mom says, standing in my doorway. "Breakfast."

Startled, the mermaids slip underwater.

Mom's hair is perfect. Lauren and I went to the salon with her after school yesterday and watched a chubby woman in a tight pink smock do Mom's hair and nails while talking about her oldest boy, a pimply faced high school junior who hasn't been to class on time "all year, swear on the Christ Child!" The woman looked at Lauren and me. "I keep a tire iron in the hall closet to pry him out of bed each morning!"

Lauren flipped through the glossy pages of *Today's Hair* but I listened intently.

"Just kidding, sweetheart," the hairdresser said. "You're Lily, aren't you?"

Down the hall, the kitchen radio advertises "unheard-of deals on new Mustangs." Mom opens Lauren's door next. "Up and at 'em," she says, then announces that even though it's Sunday, "No church. It's *your* day. Do what you want."

Mom's in a good mood. Yesterday was their sixteenth anniversary.

They had dinner at the London Grill and grabbed a brandy at The Benson on the way home. Dad gave Mom a dozen red roses and she gave him a bottle of fancy champagne she'd hidden in the laundry room for weeks. Lauren and I stayed home alone for the first time, and were asleep on the couch when they got in. I left a detailed list of everything we did on the kitchen table.

"Paul?" Mom calls. "Paper's here!"

It's only 8:22 a.m. but the *Oregonian* is late again this morning, even though Dad called the circulation desk last week to complain. That's when he found out we were the last house on the Savage Boy's route. Dad says he dropped out of school, and Mom calls him a "hood." He stole a strip of Christmas lights off our laurel edge last Christmas; Mom saw him. He's sixteen, has his driver's license, and looks like TV idol Tab Hunter if Tab didn't take a bath or wash his hair for, like, six months.

One time, when his parents weren't home, Judy and I climbed a tree overlooking the Savages' backyard and watched him and some of his friends jump off the roof onto a pile of mattresses, sleeping bags, and furniture cushions. He did backflips and cannonballs, which Judy says he probably learned from his father who is a high school gymnastics coach. I got shivers when he stood at the edge of his house; his bare toes curled over the eaves trough and, leaning out, he threw himself into the air.

There's a thump outside my window.

A dog barks.

A car door closes.

Maybe Rusty's volleyball finally fell off the roof.

Maybe it's Jesus; I wish He'd use the door like everyone else.

I look at the window from the corner of my eye. That's how you see fairies, but there's nothing there, no Jesus, no sprites or leprechauns.

Mom once said, "Fairies live in the woods and use flowers as umbrellas when it rains. They never grow old, and they're always in love." Someday I'll move to the country I see out of the corner of my eye, and fall in love with a boy who loves me the way that Dad loves her. We'll fly to Paris for dinner and sit at the top of the Eiffel Tower where there's nothing but stars until a giant balloon drifts by, showering us with Cracker Jack toys and yellow rose petals.

I make a pirate's spyglass with my fists and run the view over the room.

I spy . . . Mrs. Wiggins's tooth on the floor at the end of the bed where it fell from the pocket of my jeans.

I spy . . . Frieda's new picture of Jesus, His arms wide open to the plump happy children who gather at His feet.

I spy . . . the wallpaper. Quiet Copenhagen Harbor, and the bronze statue of the Little Mermaid with a fleet of colorful fishing boats docked behind her. A seagull flies overhead. The water is still, not a ripple anywhere. It's wallpaper, from floor to ceiling, and the scene is repeated sixteen times; four across, four down. Mom's painting over it tomorrow. "A nice pink," she says, "to match Lauren's room." Mom loves to decorate. "Now if your father would just replace the window screens."

I wish she wouldn't. I like my "busy wallpaper." I like old houses left to grow old, unpainted walls, empty rooms, crumbling chimneys. Jamie said there's life everywhere: under a rock, on a rusty bumper, in a bare corner.

Lauren explodes from her bedroom fully dressed, and flies into the bathroom. No one's seen her in underwear for years. Mom says she's shy about her body.

Two days ago, I sat beside Judy in her front yard.

"I'm bored," she said. Judy's bored a lot since she came back from the appliance convention. She doesn't want to talk about the trip, or the fight we had either.

Sherman rode up on his three-speed. He's twelve years old, like Lauren, but he enjoys hanging out with Judy and me because "older women are more sophisticated." Mom laughed when I told her.

"Sounds just like Jim," she said. Jim Newell is Sherman's "handsome new stepfather." He's also a pharmacist with his own business who made enough money last year to have a bomb shelter built in their backyard.

Dad said the Cold War is over and there's nothing to worry about, but how does *he* know?

Sherman likes to gross us out. The subject that day was dog penises. I put my fingers in my ears and sang, "*La la la,*" but Judy only laughed. "Dog penises are ugly," she said. "Boy penises are ugly too."

She's seen boy penises?

Sherman blushed and looked down at his new handlebar grips.

"What's wrong?" she said in a tired voice. There was a pimple on her chin. "Isn't *your* penis ugly, Sherman? Or is it too small to see with the naked eye?" Huh? "Lily, go get your microscope. Let's examine it." Why was she talking to us like that? "Boys always want girls to look at their penises, don't they?"

They do? Sherman and I stared at her.

Suddenly, the Savage Boy rode up on his new ten-speed. Standing up on the pedals he rode back and forth in the same concentrated space, making a deep muddy hole in Mr. Marks's thick, weedless grass.

"What are *you* doing here?" Judy asked. She sat up straight. "Heard the word *penis* and had to be part of the conversation?"

The Savage Boy leaned back on the narrow black bicycle seat that jutted between his legs, crossed his arms on his chest, and smiled. "Whose penis?" he asked. He smiled at me. "You look nice, Lily."

"Sherman's," Judy said. " We were discussing its size." She paused. "Is it bigger than a cat's?"

The Savage Boy laughed.

"Nothing to add, Lily? No additional mammals of comparable size or scientific classification?" Judy was sweaty and nervous; I could tell when her glasses (with the rhinestone frames) slid down her nose. She looked at Sherman and me. "You two are such weirdos," she said.

Where were all the moms? They're usually everywhere.

"Let's go, Lily," Sherman said, climbing on his bike. He didn't wait. Riding off he yelled, "You're a bitch, Judy Marks!"

His words gave me goose bumps and I stood up and stared at the top of her head. Does she know she has dandruff? I remembered the duet she taught me once, how impressed I was that she was older and smarter, and her freshly painted fingernails clicked the piano keys—they made their own music. Now Judy's angry all the time.

"Sherman's right," I said. "You have dandruff too."

"Who cares?" she said, storming off. A second later, her front door banged shut.

The Savage Boy looked around. "Where is everybody?"

"Lauren's home."

"Where's Rusty Nail?"

"Rusty and Mrs. Marks are . . ." I put my hands on my hips. "None of your beeswax." The Savage Boy's arms were tanned and strong. Even though it rains a lot in Portland, he's always outside, smoking cigarettes, popping wheelies on his bike, or working on his older brother's car. When he scooted his bike closer to me and leaned across the handlebars, he smiled like he did when he threw himself off the roof.

The Savage Boy is brave. Maybe people were wrong about him.

I was close enough to see that he had freckles like Opie on *The Andy Griffith Show*. I was still counting them when he asked, "How many penises have *you* seen, Lily? You're old enough. Pretty enough."

Huh?

"Want to see mine?"

"No thanks," I said, hurrying across Judy's yard toward home.

"*No thanks*," he laughed, mimicking me as he slow-pedaled along the sidewalk. I felt his eyes on me when I climbed the little rise to our house and slipped inside, hiding behind the living room drapes. I counted by twos to one hundred, before looking outside again and finding him gone.

Inside the TV was on, and Lauren sat in front of it, digging through her cigar box for the right crayon.

"Lily?" Mom called, and I followed her voice to the bathroom where she stood in front of the sink rinsing out nylons. I sat down on the edge of the tub and sighed.

"Everything okay?" she asked. "Things better between you and Judy?"

No. Yes. "No."

"Do you want to talk about it?"

"No."

So, Mom and I talked about how Sandra Dee should have married Troy Donahue instead of Bobby Darin because they'd have had beautiful blond babies, but then neither one of them was a natural blond so it didn't really count. Mom said Pamela Tiffin married James Darren but James married Miss Denmark 1958, and Pamela someone rich we'd never heard of.

I didn't correct Mom. I didn't care what we talked about that afternoon as long as it wasn't penises.

I stand in front of my mirror, making my mouth into a big O like the Coppertone girl in the billboard sign on the way to Rooster Rock.

Yes, I'm growing boobs. My nipples hurt even when I accidentally brush them. Mom says my period will be here any day. She bought me a bra and slip to celebrate and I model them in front of the closet mirror, holding them over my knee-length cotton nighty.

Across the street, someone opens his garage door. Someone else drags his trash can to the curb; he's early—pickup is Monday.

Down the hall the coffee pot perks, Mom opens the fridge, Dad pulls back the drapes. On the morning after their sixteenth anniversary, he whistles *All day, all night, Marianne,* over and over. A moment later I hear the squeak of his favorite kitchen chair and the newspaper's crisp pages when he gives it a snap open. "Good coffee," he says.

Mom turns up the radio. She loves Arthur Godfrey.

There's that sound again.

My room's on the sloped side of the house and sometimes phone wires, dead birds, tree branches, balls, and rackets get stuck in the shingles overhead. Usually a breeze will bring them down but this is different.

There's movement, a figure. Someone outside my window.

"Dad?"

"Lily." It's not Dad *or* Jesus. The window screen is old and dark. It needs replacing.

"Lily." It's a boy's voice, a man's. Quiet, secretive.

"Who is it?" I whisper when I kneel beside the window. I see no one until . . . the Savage Boy peeks around the corner of the window frame.

I cry out in surprise and fall back. "What are you—"

"Hi," he says quietly. "I'm sorry about the other day. I shouldn't have said what I said."

"That's okay." I pull my nightgown over my bare knees.

"You look nice this morning."

"Thanks." I guess he's being polite; I haven't gotten dressed yet.

"Nice day, huh? Hey, I saw your bra and slip. Did your mom get them for you?"

I don't answer.

"Would you model them for me?"

"No."

Why isn't he going? He already apologized. His arm is moving. He's holding something in front of his pants, something alive that's trying to get away. "*Hi-Lily . . .*" he quietly sings. "*Hi-Lily . . . Hi-Lo.* I bet you like that song, huh?"

"No." When I stand up, my heart's pounding so hard, I'm dizzy and grab my bed frame. "I'm not supposed to talk to you. Go away or I'll call my dad."

The boy's arm stops moving. "You talked to me the other day. Besides, your parents can't hear you, they're on the other side of the house. So's your sister. The radio's up, no one can hear us."

Maybe it was the Savage Boy who peeked in Judy's window, not Jesus.

Mom says there's a Peeping Tom in the neighborhood. I heard her laugh that it wouldn't be so bad. "Really," she said to her girlfriends over cocktails last week, "we'll never be so young and sexy again!" And all the moms giggled and clinked their martini glasses.

I don't want anybody peeking through my window. I head to the door.

"I won't hurt you," the Savage Boy says. "I said I'm sorry. I'll leave in a minute, I promise. I'm just lonely. Can't we be friends?"

"It's easy to be nice to nice people," Gramma Frieda told me. "We do God's work when we befriend the unfriendly." I stop and turn back. The Savage Boy must have stepped up on the faucet because he's taller now, and when he cups his hands around his face and presses himself even closer to the screen, I see his eyes, teeth, lips, and the front of his white T-shirt where a big white shark is pictured above the words, *Monterey Man-Eater, California.*

A curtain falls between me and the Savage Boy. I smell Mrs. Wiggins's cancerous breath.

"Like the shirt, huh? My old man finally took us someplace." He sticks a hand under the T-shirt to make the shark move. "Spooo-oky, huh? You like to be scared, Lily?"

"No," I say firmly.

"I'll give you my shirt if you come closer."

He's not going to leave. "Mom?" I say softly.

"She's making breakfast. Her sweater slipped off her shoulder so I saw her bra strap. Your mom's sexy." The Savage Boy's moving his arm again.

The lake's current pulls at my legs. I press my toes into its sandy bottom.

"Mom?" I say louder.

"Don't bug her. She's tired, remember? They were out late last night.

You and Lauren were alone in the house while they were gone." He was watching us? "Besides, like you said: you'll get in trouble for talking to me, and you don't want to get in trouble, do you?" His teeth shine through the watery curtain. "Come here," he whispers. "Pull up your nightgown."

"Lil-ee?" Dad calls from the kitchen. He turns down the radio to say, "Five minutes, or I'm dragging you out of there!" He turns it up again.

"Go away," I tell the Savage Boy.

"Sharks have perfect lives; they swim and eat all day. They're man-eaters. Or, in my case, a girl-eater." The Savage Boy leans his forehead against the screen, licks it, then begins to pant. Faster and faster, like his arm.

At the front of our house there's a knock at the door. "Get your paper this morning, Asher?" It's Mr. Marks. "The kid's bike is leaning against the telephone pole but he didn't . . ."

"They know you're here," I say quietly. "Go away."

"I will if you show me your panties. Do it, Lily. Come closer and show me your panties." His voice is deep and serious. "Do it, Lily," he repeats. He breathes even heavier now.

Is he sick? Does he have a disease?

"Please, please, Lily. No one will ever know you talked to me. They'll never know I saw your mom's tits."

"Shut up!" He saw Mom's boobs? "Leave her alone!" I say as I lift my nightgown and show him my underwear.

"Now pull them down with the other hand."

"No," I say, but I grab the waistband anyway.

"You're so pretty. Prettier than your mom. That's right, pull them down, Lily . . . A little more, that's it."

I drop my nightgown and glare at him.

His hands stop moving. "Do it or I'll tell everybody that you wanted to show me your pussy. Everyone will believe me too." His voice is calm and quiet, like Dr. Giraffe's when he's telling me something "important," something he wants me to remember.

My eyes fill with tears. "No they won't. They won't believe you."

"Yes they will. You're retarded. You killed your dog and you go to a shrink."

"No I'm not! *You're* the retard! *You're* the Savage Boy!"

"Lily?" Dad calls. He's standing at the end of the hall, waiting. "Two minutes and counting!"

Mom turns off the radio.

"Do it, Lily." The boy's voice is soft and sweet. "Do it for the Savage Boy."

But I don't, and when I don't he takes out a pocketknife and rips at the hole in the window screen, the hole Jesus climbs through when He visits.

"I'm coming in, Lily," the Savage Boy says. He digs at the screen with his knife then his mouth, widening the hole. Using them both, he pants and moans, ripping the metal mesh open, pulling up woven threads with his teeth, tearing aside great hunks of the screen. Stabbing at it with his bloodied fingernails and knuckles, he tears the shark curtain wider. Spit rolls down his chin.

I stare in disbelief, terrified and fascinated.

His eyes burn through the watery scrim, beady, black, and small, and he gurgles and pants as he chews it open, its sharp metal ends tearing his lips and gums. The metal makes angry stubborn sounds; tears and sweat streak his scratched face as he gnaws the screen like Mrs. Wiggins used to gnaw on bones. There's blood everywhere, but he doesn't stop.

What is he doing?

Why is he here?

I should have locked my window. *Things get out if you're not careful, things get in.* The house has fallen silent. Behind me, on the wallpaper, sixteen sharks pull sixteen Little Mermaids off sixteen rocks. Little air bubbles appear in the same place in each scene and pools of blood slosh against the fishing boats.

His heavy breath gurgles when he stops to stare at me.

The hole is bigger.

He's coming in.

He's *getting* in.

"Dad!" I finally yell.

Mrs. Wiggins's tooth appears in my hand. There's a hard thump when it hits the metal screen in front of me and tears at the Savage Boy's face. He falls back in pain. I'm quiet as I stab the screen again, harder and harder, until there's more than a scratchy sawing sound that I taste in my fillings, more than a rip. I taste *his* blood too; it mixes with mine and Mrs. Wiggins's. My hands are red with it.

"Paul!" I hear Mom cry out when Dad bursts in and rushes past me to the window.

"You son of a bitch!" he screams, running out again.

Outside, the Savage Boy struggles to stand up. I hear a zipper and Dad's cursing as he dashes around the house.

I've ruined his screen. I talked to the Savage Boy. I hold Mrs. Wiggins's tooth tight and, without asking, take three giant "Mother May I" steps backward.

There's a loud tumble in the front yard, curse words, and more panting. Dogs bark. A car horn honks. Doors open and close, and Mr. Marks yells, "You got him, Paul!"

"Lily?" Mom stands in the doorway.

I turn to face her. Slowly. I want to take it back. All of it. Everything that happened in my bedroom this morning . . . and you do that slowly, going backward, taking back time.

My feet are as heavy as the cement pier blocks under Gramma's porch. My hair is stuck to my face in sweaty strands. The palm of my hand is bleeding and I think of the stigmata. Why wasn't Jesus here?

Suddenly, Lauren races down the hall toward us. "Mom, Mom!" she shouts. "Dad's hurting the paper boy!"

"It's fine, sweetheart." Mom doesn't take her eyes off me.

"But Dad's on top of him and—"

"It's okay. Your father knows what he's doing."

"But he put the boy's arm behind his back, and they're shouting at each other, and Mr. Marks and Mr. Davis are—"

"Lauren!"

Mom takes baby steps toward me, then pulls me in, wrapping her arms around me, carefully, the way she handles her fancy art paper. I rest my head on her shoulder; I'm almost as tall as she is.

"I'm sorry," I whisper. "You're tired. You were out late last night."

Mom looks at me funny. "I'm fine," she says, crinkling her eyebrows. Her makeup is old; she isn't as pretty as the Savage Boy thinks.

Dad calls the police first, then Mr. and Mrs. Savage. Later he orders new locks and new screens for all the windows. After everybody "calms down," he goes to the office for a while. Mom says it helps him relax.

"I'm okay," I repeat even to Dr. Giraffe, who doesn't mind Mom calling him at home on a Sunday, but she gives me a Valium anyway, and treats my scratches and cuts.

"The pill will make you sleepy," she promises, then makes me a bed on the couch in front of the TV, brings me a big icy glass of 7-Up, and says, "Better get you a tetanus shot," before leaving the room.

A minute later Lauren runs in, drinks most of my soda pop, and sings, *"You're getting a tetanus shot, you're getting a tetanus shot."*

"Jerk," I mumble.

"Dummy," she says.

I dream I'm sitting on the Savage Boy's roof, howling at the full moon. Below me is an ocean of empty rowboats. Suddenly he's sitting beside me. He hands me a cigarette, even though I don't smoke.

It's not a scary dream but I wake up anyway. I can't get back to sleep, so I walk to the kitchen and look around.

On the counter by the phone is a scratch pad, and on it—in Dad's writing—the name *Mike Savage*, with *Mike* underlined.

Savage. Mike Savage. His name is Mike.

"Mike," I say to myself. "The Savage Boy. Mr. Mike Savage. Mrs. Mike Savage. Mrs. Lily Savage."

I feel strange inside.

Scared but excited.

In the center of the kitchen table is the empty champagne bottle with two red roses stuck in its throat.

On either side of the bottle are paper-doll cartoons, Mom's cartoons, of Dad and her. *Pablo*, it says on tiny Dad's tiny shirt. *Marianne*, it says across tiny Mom's. They face one another and each hold out a cardboard hand toward the giant bottle between them.

CHAPTER 10
IF IT WEREN'T FOR KEVIN

Aunt Jamie died in a plane crash in Kenya during a photo safari with Kevin.

In a description at the bottom of her death certificate, which the government sent to us by courier, Jamie was *located approximately twenty feet from the fuselage*, and *died on impact*, her body *crumpled*, though even in death, it was determined that *the victim was a young female Caucasian*. Mom cries like crazy when she reads it out loud. And rereads it, over and over, until Dad tells her to stop.

The form describes Kevin, at the crash scene, as *unconscious and pinned between the pilot's seat and the crushed console. Currently hospitalized at Kwame Tsongi Convalescent Clinic for a concussion, two broken legs, and one broken arm*, he *requests contact with his fiancée's family*.

"Fat chance," Mom mumbles.

I close my eyes and see Jamie's body facedown and splattered like a water balloon on the hot, dry African dirt. I rub suntan lotion on her shoulders and move her arms and legs, tracing and retracing a chalk outline around her like the murdered people on *Dragnet*.

The thirsty plants in the ground underneath her soak up her 86 percent water and start growing immediately, and when Mrs. Wiggins and Jamie's Heinz 57s drag her into the thorny African brush, seedlings pop up through the soil and wave at the sun.

Crunching, tearing, chewing noises come from behind the couch where I sit with Mom and Lauren who are hugging each other and crying. Mom soaks her shirtsleeve and two of Dad's neatly pressed hankies with her tears. Her eyes are swollen, her shiny cheeks streaked with black mascara. Lauren cries too, even harder when she looks at Mom.

I cried when I first heard the news. I try to cry more, but I can't. Losing Aunt Jamie is deeper than tears. I don't know what to do, so I just sit there.

Dad sits across from us. Every once in a while he sniffles and wipes away a tear, or says, "It's one of those freak things, Kit," or, "I'm sorry, sweetheart," or, "We're really going to miss her, aren't we, girls?" which means Lauren and me, of course, but we don't answer either, and while I sit there like a paper doll, Lauren hugs Mom even tighter.

Finally, he goes out for a bucket of fried chicken. "Gotta keep up our strength," he says.

An hour later he's back with the food, a pack of cigarettes, and a new bottle of vodka. He pours Mom a glass and sits down across from us again.

Later, when Lauren falls asleep on the sofa, he carries her to her room.

It must be around eleven thirty because Ed McMahon is introducing Johnny Carson on TV. I wait until Johnny swings his imaginary golf club before I glance at the clock again.

I've been quiet for two hours and seventeen minutes. No has told me to go to bed yet. I want to feel special about it, I want to think that Mom and Dad are letting me stay up with them because I'm older and I loved Jamie more than Lauren, but when I finally ask, "Should I go to bed?" no one answers and I realize I'm invisible.

They don't see Mrs. Wiggins either, but her slobbers are all over my hand.

My parents have forgotten I'm here.

The three of us stare at the TV until 11:54 when I walk into the kitchen and check the drawers, closets, and cupboards. Mom doesn't say anything, but when I start on the living room, Dad tells me to stop.

"Now you're opening them first?"

Sometimes I do.

Things get out if you're not careful, things get in.

"Closing them isn't enough?"

Is he mad at me? He doesn't sound mad.

"Not tonight," he says, as he walks me down the hall. "Not tonight, Lily Lou."

I only want to keep my family safe.

Aunt Jamie would understand. She loved dogs and smiled when they dragged her body into the dry thorny brush. Her long red mermaid hair threads its way through their guts.

The next time they bay at the moon, they'll remember her little yellow house with the red shutters, and how she boiled their dog bones with a tablespoon of brown sugar because she loved them so much.

I like to pretend Jamie didn't die.

She moved to England instead.

She swam there, across the Atlantic all by herself, breaking world records as she went. She was in movie newsreels and on TV, and after reading about it in the *London Times*, a rich handsome merman fell in love with her and they got married.

A merman. Not Kevin who became infected with giant African worms and died.

Jamie's alive, we just don't hear from her anymore because phones and mail are illegal in England. It's a silly law and something left over from the war that Jamie works to repeal in her free time (not that she has any).

When she does, she'll fly to another country and call us, but her life as mistress of a manor house (with tall stone turrets, hidden rooms, and walk-in fireplaces) in the quiet English countryside keeps her busy until then. So do the flowers, fruit trees, and berry plants people send her from all over the world. It takes time to trim the boxwood to look like elephants and chess pieces.

It takes time to feed the black swans, peacocks, and rabbits that wander over the big lawns, where Jamie and her husband put on fireworks shows for their new friends, and play croquet with pink mallets that look like real flamingos (but aren't).

When their friends stay overnight, the servants (who aren't Negro) bring feather mattresses outside so the guests can sleep under the stars— except for Jamie and her husband who sleep on big lily pads on a pond clogged with cattails and tiny yellow fish that shine in the moonlight. They have a movie theater and a bowling alley and a bomb shelter in the manor house too.

There are big dogs everywhere: Irish wolfhounds, greyhounds, and Great Danes with silly names like Sir Otis Fig and Lord and Lady Ticklebutt. And hanging in the entrance hall, between big oil portraits of people who once lived in the manor, is a portrait of Mrs. Wiggins, with real jewels sewn onto her painted collar.

There's no church, though. No crosses on the wall; no one's even heard of Jesus. And when someone dies, even one of the dogs, they hang black ribbons on the gate and drape all the mirrors and windows with black cloth. I like that. I read it somewhere.

If Jesus were really the Son of God, He wouldn't have let Jamie die on a photo safari in Africa.

That makes Him make-believe.

Just a story, like Jamie's.

"You okay, Lily?"

It's bedtime again and Mom's come to tuck me in. Since Jamie died three weeks ago, she checks on Lauren and me all the time.

"I'm fine," I smile, tucking my hands underneath me.

Mom doesn't smile back. "When Kevin got out of the hospital, he had her cremated," she says. "That's the way she wanted it, I guess. He said she didn't want to take up any space. Take up any space? She was here, wasn't she? Why *shouldn't* she take up space?" Mom's eyes fill with tears. "Jamie . . . signed something, he said."

"I know."

"He's going to send us some of her ashes."

I know that too. Mom is repeating herself.

I want to hug her, but fire engines wail, a dog barks, and my hands are turning into paws; if I touch her she'll see them. Instead I say, "When she gets here, where are you going to put her? The . . . ashes, I mean."

Mom stares at me and asks, "Don't you cry anymore, Lily?"

Down the hill, in town, noisy ambulances and police cars join the fire engines. One by one the neighborhood dogs start howling. It's a high-pitched sound that hurts my ears and tickles the back of my throat. My muscles tighten. Even the pulsing hardness at the end of my spine, where my tail grows—and doesn't grow, grows and doesn't grow—stops to listen.

I pretend to stretch, like I'm sleepy. Maybe Mom will take the hint and say goodnight. Maybe if I close my eyes, she'll be gone when I open them again. Only she isn't even looking at me. She's sad and staring at her hands, remembering her sister. She isn't moving, she isn't leaving my room.

I have to stretch, I have to move, I have to throw back my bedcovers and kneel on all fours.

I have to. And she isn't going to like it.

My eyes are glued to the window. I try to think of something else; I try not to listen to the noisy dogs outside. I try to sit down on the bed instead of kneeling, but my body doesn't listen. I feel myself blush when Mom looks at me. I hear her gasp, and feel her hands reach out for me, then hesitate and pull back.

She's scared.

I'm scared too. Something is inside me, something that wants to come out, like barfing or hiccuping, only bigger. Something that's going to come out, no matter what.

I'm sorry, Mom, but I have to howl.

I'm going to howl.

Any second now. I swallow to keep it in, but I can't.

And finally, finally, I tilt my head back and . . .

"Oooooowwwwww!"

It feels good; better than anything I've ever felt before.

Lauren pounds on the wall. I'm bugging her again.

When Mom jumps up and stares at me, I want to say, *I can't help it*, but dogs don't talk. Except for Mrs. Wiggins, of course.

Mom's face changes. "Lily," she says slowly, "sweetheart, I'm going to get your father. Okay? I'll be right back."

Alone in my room, I hear them talk through the walls. Dogs have good hearing. I'm exhausted, but I'm still on my knees when they come in. Dad closes the door, and stands next to my bed while Mom hugs herself.

What do they see when they look at me?

Am I half-animal, half-person like the Savage Boy?

Am I still Lily Elaine Asher of Portland, Oregon?

It's done. It's over.

"I'm sorry," I manage to say, and finally sit back on my heels.

But I'm lying. I'm not sorry. I'm tired, out of breath, and scared. I'm a scared, tired, out-of-breath liar.

"I must have been dreaming," I say. "I fell asleep and dreamed I was a dog."

"She wasn't asleep," Mom says. "She was wide awake, Paul."

Good. They recognize me. My words make sense. I'm still me, still Lily Asher, neighborhood weirdo.

"Do you think it's Tourette's? I've been reading about it, Paul. Maybe it's Tourette's."

Dad touches my shoulder. "It's okay, kiddo, we'll figure it out. We'll see Dr. Giraffe—I mean Dr. Madsen—in the morning, okay? Lily?"

"Okay."

Across the street, Mr. Davis opens his front door. Frosty, his late wife's miniature poodle, tears into the front yard barking. The neighborhood is still, the sirens long gone. Frosty is old, like sixteen or something. He's always the last dog in the neighborhood to do anything doggy. He's crippled and mostly deaf, but he must have heard me howl.

Mom says Frosty has been a lap dog so long, he's more human than anything else.

Dr. Madsen is tall and thin with a long neck, red spiky hair, and blotchy skin.

Like a giraffe, a talking, know-it-all giraffe.

I tell him everything: how I killed Mrs. Wiggins; how Aunt Jamie died; how I felt about stabbing the Savage Boy with the tooth, how I've felt about him since. How, despite what Frieda says and what Jesus promised, Jesus keeps turning His back on me. He even turned His back on the big apartment-house fire in town last night. A five-month-old baby and her teenage mother died.

"Did He punish her for having a baby out of wedlock?" I ask, but Dr. Giraffe only says, "What do you think?" So I decide yes. Yes, He did. And then I tell Dr. Giraffe how even my outsides and insides don't match anymore.

Mom calls it puberty—which the dictionary says has more to do with a chrysalis turning into a butterfly than having your period and bleeding all over your white pants. Judy says girls "should never wear white pants."

I'm growing a tail, I tell Dr. Giraffe. Sometimes, anyway. Mom doesn't believe me. "You still have ten fingers and toes," she says, "and that makes you human no matter how much you want to be Mrs. Wiggins." I don't *want* to be Mrs. Wiggins.

Finally, I tell my psychologist that howling was the "best thing I ever felt, ever."

Dr. Giraffe nods his head when I say it and makes lots of notes. I tell him that howling was okay with Aunt Jamie because she loved dogs. "They don't pretend," she told me. "They are what they are."

"If it weren't for Kevin," I say, "you could call her up right now and ask her yourself."

If it weren't for Kevin.

"I only howled once," I repeat.

Dr. Giraffe smiles. And makes another appointment.

CHAPTER 11
LEGLESS CUCKOOS

Since Jamie died, Mom's been weird. She calls Frieda every day and writes long letters she throws away. She sent a box of shiny yellow pears to a friend she hasn't seen since high school, and she's painting a picture of a big family dinner in our backyard. An imaginary picnic on an imaginary day. She put Jamie between Lauren and me, and adds strangers and people I've only seen in Dad's family albums. They don't look so old when they're laughing and reaching for a bowl of supersized strawberries.

When Dad said Mom was "rewriting history and someday people will think it really happened that way," she said, "It's art." When I ask about the old, sad-looking couple at the end of the table, she cries.

Dad says she's still mourning Jamie. He says to give it time.

Mom says "genes" are everything. "You are what you get from your family. When you don't know who you are, look around."

Now that Jamie's gone, the only family I see, besides Mom, Dad, and Lauren, is Frieda. And sometimes Aunt Cass. Rarely Uncle Po.

We're headed to Po's right now.

It will be the second time Lauren and I stayed over, and Mom said it'll be our last. "You girls are getting older and so is Po. Your visits exhaust him but he wanted to see you one last time."

Exhaust him? We've only been there once and we just sat around, reading and playing cards. One last time? "So he's dying?" I ask.

"He's old," she says. Then, "Aunt Cass will be there."

Lauren rolls her eyes.

Mom reminds me it's my turn to sleep with Cass. She reminds us of the phone in Po's kitchen and the emergency phone numbers in the kitchen and bathroom "in case you need help." Lauren leans forward, straining her seat belt; she wants to be a nurse. Or a private detective like TV's Honey West.

Does Cass know her brother is dying? Mom once said she's like a dog, kind and sweet though not very smart, but Jamie told me animals understand their world better than we understand ours.

The three of us listen to the car radio for the remaining 17.2 miles it takes to pull into Po's driveway.

"Don't worry," Mom says to the rearview mirror, "you'll have a good time."

When we let ourselves in, Po's asleep in his rocker in front of the big brown gas heater. The house is hot. Mom says old people's houses are always hot.

He looks more like King Tut than the handsome young man in the sepia portrait I've seen. Po used to be a farmer, but he never got married. He never cared that Cass had Down syndrome and can't read or write either, or that she scrapes her plate over and over until it hurts your ears, then burps so loudly it even embarrasses Mom.

Lauren looks around the living room and whispers to Mom, "Do we have to spend the night?"

Cass inches out of her bedroom, sees Mom, and smiles. There's a sweater over her arm. Behind Cass stands her tall brass bed, with the two wooden steps leading up to it.

"It'll be fun," Mom replies in an exaggerated voice. "Your father and I will be here first thing in the morning." They're driving to the beach overnight; Mom says they need a getaway. "You girls can play cards, and read all you want. Won't that be nice? Did you bring everything?"

"Yep," Lauren says, holding up her old Chatty Cathy pajama bag. Inside is her doll Irene. Lauren's too old for a baby doll, but Mom says it relaxes her. She brought other stuff too: *Black Beauty*, a small loom for weaving potholders, flip-flops, underwear, pedal pushers, pajamas, two sweaters (one red, one blue), and a tube of Bonne Bell lip gloss.

"Yep," I say, though my "everything" is way less stuff than Lauren's overstuffed bag.

Cass points at Po and knits her eyebrows saying, "Quiet," in her slow flat voice. My sister can say, "Yep," but I can't? Does Cass still remember me pinching her? She walks toward Mom who helps her with her sweater.

Mom kisses Po on the forehead and the two of them head out. "Going to grab some groceries, be right back," she says.

"Groceries," Cass echoes. As the door closes, the clock strikes twelve and Po wakes up.

"High noon," he announces, sitting tall. Then looks us over. "Kit's girls." Then he singles me out: "You look just like her."

"Who do I look like, Po?" Lauren asks.

He rubs his stubby chin. "Alice," he answers. Alice? Who's Alice? "If you need anything, shake me." He rocks three or four times, rubs his stockinged feet together, and closes his eyes again.

There are curtains on the closets but no doors on the cupboards. Not a picture on the wall or a book anywhere. Po's work clothes hang on nails in the kitchen near the rust-stained kitchen sink. On a shelf by the window (where an emergency number is posted) there's a row of pots with green seedlings just breaking through the dirt. In a basket are six rotten bananas. There's a mousetrap on the counter.

Lauren stands beside me and whispers, "I don't like it here," then heads to her book, passing Po and the ticking popping heater, the piano with its locked keyboard and piles of bundled magazines on the bench, into Cass's room.

Dad says Lauren's a nervous Nellie, but everything is different here, even Po's magazines.

Cass's room is sunny and clean, and tucked into the mirror over her chest of drawers are school pictures of Lauren and me, and an autographed color glossy of Rock Hudson.

Lauren squeals when I untie a magazine bundle and pass her a *Photoplay* with "The Rat Pack" on the cover. She flips through the pages until she finds a picture of Sammy Davis Jr. standing between Frank Sinatra and Dean Martin, the three of them laughing so hard Dean almost spills his drink. "Do you know Sammy has a glass eye?"

"Yeah."

"I think he's cute."

"I don't."

"I guess *this* is your boyfriend then," she says, pointing at a grainy black-and-white photo of a blond boy on the cover of *True*. Behind him is a giant swastika and the words, bold and red: *Discovered Photo Cache!* He wears a Nazi uniform and taller older boys in uniforms stand with him. All three are laughing. Before them is a pit of naked twisted bodies.

Lauren thumbs through *Photoplay*. She doesn't see the bodies. The naked bodies. Of dead people.

"Look, Lily!" Her hands are under her sweater, making gun-barrel nipples with her index fingers. In front of her is a color photograph of Diana Dors in a red two-piece swimsuit.

When the Nazis stand on their tiptoes to look across the bed at the movie star, Po's heater suddenly roars, and I jump.

"Nine times ten is ninety. Nine times eleven is ninety-nine. Nine times twelve is one hundred and eight." Nines are the best.

Lauren puts down her magazine. "You okay?" She sounds more and more like Mom.

I take *True* into the living room and plant myself beside Po's rocker, staring at the heater's window, wondering what old men dream of.

"Open the magazine and find out," says a tiny voice like Colonel Klink's on *Hogan's Heroes*. "What are you are afraid of?"

I'm not afraid. They're just pictures, like pictures in *Photoplay* or *Life* or *Look* or *TV Guide*. Scary pictures, ugly terrible pictures, but still just pictures.

The heater whooshes, and even though I whisper my nines again, forward *and* backward this time, the magazine falls open to the center, to the place I don't want to look, to the pictures I shouldn't see, and my sticky hands hold it there.

My heart races. I try closing my eyes but they spring open like cartoon window shades.

So I look. At the face of the same handsome blond Nazi from the cover: the Savage Boy, Tab Hunter, Troy Donahue, James Dean. He smokes his cigarette down to a stub and throws it in the pit of dead bodies; it lands in Diana Dors's platinum hair and sizzles.

Jesus died for our sins, so that everyone is forgiven, and Mom always says, "You can't judge a book by its cover," so I put the boy in a baseball outfit and set him at Mom's picnic table.

She sends Lauren and me to the house for iced tea with umbrellas.

The sun is high and hot. "Pleez pass duh strawberries," the boy says politely. His accent is thick, but his English is good. "Is der any cream?"

Women in high white collars and men in walrus mustaches drop their spoons and stare in surprise until the sad-looking man at the end of the table stands up. "What are *you* doing here?" he cries, pointing at the boy. "Get out! Get *out!*" and the boy, startled and blushing, stumbles to his feet, grabs his rifle, and—

Shoots.

Every.

One.

The picnic table becomes the pit, and my family—whoever they were, wherever they're from—instantly, quietly slump against each other. Their faces twist in pain and surprise like dead Jewish pickup sticks, all bony knees and cauliflower ears, bruises and baggy skin, twisted feet and pelvises like snow shovels. Skeleton faces with eyes so dark and deep they drill holes all the way to China. They fall and tumble, more naked than they've ever been, and I see their boobs and penises and hairy patches—private places they'd have covered up when they were alive.

I slam the magazine shut, and Po snorts himself awake.

"Lily?" he asks, scratching his whiskers. He knows my name.

My heart pounds like crazy. Should I talk to him? He's old, he knows stuff. Instead I answer, "Hi," and watch his eyelids grow heavy and close again.

Over Po's shoulder, sunshine pours through the café curtains, lighting the plastic tablecloth on the dining room table and a three-story card house.

Everything is winding down at Po's. Po, Cass, even time is dying. If the clock isn't wound each day it stops. Every hour, on the hour, a small wooden door flies opens and the cuckoo, glued to a tiny red perch, pops out, singing and trying to free himself. He worries he'll be stuck inside, forgotten, abandoned when Po dies, so he takes a big gulp of air and pulls up his legs, trying to break the grip before he's jerked back inside again. If he succeeds, he leaves his legs on the perch; if he succeeds, he flies but never lands because that would kill him too.

Po's cuckoo clock is from Germany but there are pits of fallen legless cuckoos all over the world, their bellies scraped bloody, their wings broken, their beaks frozen in counting.

It's hard to give up counting. I know.

There's a noise on the porch, conversation, someone wiping their shoes on the boot brush, and I jump up, stick the magazine under the sofa cushion, and rush behind Po's rocker, shaking his shoulders. "Po!"

He jerks awake as Mom walks in. Back with groceries and barbecue, she announces, "Ribs!"

I'm not hungry.

Cass likes to "cuddle," so when we go to bed I make myself small and lie on my side at the very edge. When she rolls over, a big soft boob rests on my arm and I wonder if it's freckled like her face and hands.

In the middle of the night Cass mumbles, "Water," and gets out of bed. I climb to the foot of it to watch her pad her way through the house. When she shuffles past Lauren, asleep on the couch, the flame in the window of the heater stripes her thick white ankles. As she passes the cuckoo clock, she bumps the corner of the dining room table, collapsing Po's card house; it falls on the damp plastic tablecloth he washed with a sour dishrag after dinner. Cass takes a card and holds it up to the moonlit window.

"Black," she says out loud. "Club." She counts one through six then says, "Seven." The seven of clubs.

I wander around the house at night too. I guess we *are* related.

Po's quiet house is lopsided; the floors are higher in the bedrooms, lower in the kitchen and back porch. Glasses clink as she takes one off a kitchen shelf and holds it under the faucet.

"Uh-oh," she says when the water splashes off a teacup, getting her nightgown wet.

Gulp mumble, gulp mumble, she drains the glass and sets it in the sink before walking back through the house like a circus bear. There must be a diagram in her head; Cass never turns on a light but she sees everything. From here to there, and back again, like an Arthur Murray dance chart: blue arrows and yellow feet that direct her to the kitchen, yellow arrows and blue feet that take her back to bed.

In the bathroom, the toilet seat squeaks when she sits down. When she's through, she washes her hands and walks to Po's room. I watch her when she stops and peers in. His room is small, only big enough for his white iron bed and the window behind it. The moon pours through the window tonight, falling like a spotlight on Cass. She doesn't move until Po turns over in his creaky bed, and then she says, "I love you," as clearly as I've heard her say anything. Ever.

A voice I've never heard.

I crawl back into bed.

Cass's thick, flat feet make a sticky sound when she walks in, and she grunts when she climbs up the steps to her princess bed and lies down again.

She reaches for the radio and turns on a golden oldies station: Perry Como is singing, "*Catch a falling star and put it in your pocket. Never let it fade away . . .*"

Jamie said history bounces off stars. On one star, a Tyrannosaurus rex runs through the Everglades, on another Jesus sits down to the Last Supper.

"We're all time travelers," she said. "That's what déjà vu is."

Mom said World War II feels like yesterday to her.

Before Jews became prisoners or skeletons, the world was a different place. Maybe on the closest star, like the one sitting next to the moon tonight, the Nazi boy was different too, and stood in his brother's doorway saying, "I love you," just like Cass.

CHAPTER 12

BARBIE ISLAND

The last time I was ever in Judy's room, there were stacks of *Brides* magazines next to her bed. On top of one stack was the extra-fat June wedding issue featuring miniskirted models in white silk coats, lacy hose, and big-bowed shoes. One model's platinum hair was braided with white rags while the other wore a wagon wheel–sized hat draped with a gauzy beekeeper's veil.

It was beautiful and, while Judy stood in her doorway waiting, I stared at the magazine cover for 2.5 minutes.

Judy doesn't read *Seventeen* or *Tiger Beat* anymore. She gave away every toy and old book, and hangs out with her girlfriend Karla now, introducing me to their other friends as "my next-door neighbor."

But most of the time, Judy ignores me.

I gave my Barbie to charity, but sometimes I think she's still here.

I hear her practicing her scales.

She lives by herself on an island with dogs and horses, and plays jazz piano in a bar on the mainland. Every night, no matter how late or dangerous the weather, she ferries herself home again. Sometimes Barbie brings Ken back with her and they drink wine and eat grapes while they sit on the miniature rattan lawn furniture and watch the blinking lights on the opposite shore. Then they kiss and Ken does a one-minute push-up on top of her, but they never have kids or get married. Barbie makes eggs Benedict for him in the morning, but mostly she forgets about him being there. While Ken reads the sports page, she rides her black stallion along the beach or drives her sports car really fast past coconut palms and banana trees, right up to the edge of a high, rugged cliff overlooking the ocean. Sometimes she takes off all her clothes and dives off it—like they do in Mexico. Then she goes to work again.

She likes work. She likes playing the piano.

Maybe Barbie will bring a different Ken home this weekend. There's a bunch of sunburned, blister-lipped Robinson Crusoe Kens who forage for nuts and berries on Barbie Island. Sometimes they steal ripening bananas off her porch or cooling jars of pineapple jam off her kitchen windowsill. At Christmas, Barbie makes them snickerdoodles and leaves them on a tree stump in the jungle, but they eat them so fast they get sick.

Sometimes there's no food at all so the Kens become cannibals. There's a temple in the jungle made from human bones; inside it is a paint-by-number portrait of Barbie, surrounded by darts that didn't hit their target.

I've come for the weekend, and stand beside Barbie at the prow of her shocking-pink speedboat, skimming over the waves home to her island paradise. I'm wearing my favorite Pendleton coat with its deep pockets, red plaid lining, and pickle-barrel buttons.

Barbie smiles as she effortlessly threads her way through the rocks and reef, one hand on the wheel, the other pointing out the undersea grottos where ships were lost and bottlenose dolphins have bottlenose babies. The occasional sea spray glitters her cheeks.

"I have room for you, Lily, even if Judy doesn't." She smiles and passes me the wheel.

Judy and Karla took me to a movie last week. Karla drove her parents' old Buick, smoking and swearing. They thought I'd be shocked but I wasn't.

They didn't want to take me, but I insisted on going even when Mom explained that they were both too old for me and were only being polite. Almost eighteen isn't so old. "So what?" I whined. "I never see Judy anymore."

At the movie theater, Judy didn't see me either.

In the lobby, they stood away from me and whispered to each other; only the tightly rolled ends of their matching pageboys (with the wide white headbands) moved when they talked. They wore identical deck shoes and madras culottes too, blushing when boys looked at them, giggling when certain kids walked by. Once Judy laughed so hard she blew a booger bubble. I've never seen her laugh that hard at anything.

Judy and Karla think they're cool but they're not. When I looked at them, I made fists with my hands and hid them in my pockets.

Two for the Road, with Audrey Hepburn and Albert Finney, was stupid. Karla called it sophisticated and Judy agreed. We were supposed to see *Doctor Doolittle* with Rex Harrison.

I could have ratted on them, but I didn't.

The back of Barbie's bright pink speedboat is piled high with suitcases, hatboxes, and packages with colorful string and foreign stamps. A handsome man with a dark mustache, who looks nothing like Ken, sits next to her, pouring champagne, while Barbie pilots them across my bedroom rug. When they fly over the threshold and land in the hallway, their champagne splashes. They laugh and kiss.

Before they disappear from view, Barbie turns to look back at me. She waves and I wave back.

Later that night I find Barbie's bright pink sports car smashed into a palm tree.

She left her island to the Kens. Several missed her so much they got drunk on mango martinis and took her mangled car for a joyride. After stumbling home they put on her feather boas and sequin gowns, and tried to squeeze their flat boy feet into her teeny-tiny backless high heels.

They took pictures too, but one of them opened the back of the camera, exposing the film.

CHAPTER 13

SOG

Someday I want to ride a camel deep into the Sahara, or take a dirty bath in the Ganges like Jamie did (while dead people covered with lit candles float by), but until then I'm okay to stay home.

"I want to live far away, but I want it to feel like my room," I tell Mom.

"Never gonna happen," she replies, making smudgy paint clouds with her thumbs. "You have to be brave or you'll never leave the house, Lily. It's scary in the real world."

When Dad overhears and calls her "irresponsible" and says that her "duty is to be encouraging, not discouraging," Mom pushes him out of her workroom and kicks the door closed.

She blushes and says, "Things aren't going too well at the office right now. Daddy's a little tense."

I know that. She doesn't have to call him "Daddy" either. I stopped calling him that years ago.

She clears her throat. "Your hands are clean. Would you please take a cigarette out of my shirt and light it for me?"

I'm almost as tall as Mom and look into her eyes as I slowwwly remove the pack from her shirt pocket.

"*Now*, Lily. It's just cellophane and paper; nothing will break."

I stick the Kent in my mouth, flick the butane lighter, and light it.

"Take a small inhale then pass it over, huh?"

While she darkens the gas cloud hanging above the palm trees in the background of her painting, I inhale just a little. Dad would have called this irresponsible too—it smells bad and tastes even worse—but at least I don't cough like the kids at school.

The cigarette makes me feel different. Different like everyone else.

I hand it to Mom.

She smiles. "So, what do you think of my painting so far?"

"Homework, Lily!" Dad calls from downstairs.

It's day four of Mom's nonstop painting of her latest piece, *Dead Vietnamese Woman No. 2,* and he's in charge of dinner, homework, telephone, and bedtime.

Mom rushes past me, throwing open the door with her messy hands. "We're talking! She'll be down in a goddamn minute!"

Lauren and I need a silent language we can use when our parents are fighting. I have a book on sign language and I've been practicing—I even put some in my genuflections—but Lauren said no. She said her brain was already overflowing with school stuff and she needed space for music and fashion.

I told her about Helen Keller talk too, which isn't really a language, just printing on each other's hands. I promised Lauren it wouldn't crowd out important stuff like the Monkees or granny dresses, even though I knew Lauren had memorized almost everything in the stupid Avon catalog and still remembered it after the Avon Lady stopped delivering. Which happened after Mom "read her the riot act" one afternoon.

Mom had been painting and drinking and drinking and painting and "had the blues," she explained to Dad after the head regional saleswoman called to cancel any further business with us.

"You should know that Mrs. White did *not* file intimidation charges against *your wife* even though *your wife* picked up a wine bottle and drove her off the front step with it, swore at her, and refused to pay $23.40 for the goods she'd contracted to buy."

When Dad hung up, he glared at Mom who put her hands on her hips and said, "For God's sake, Paul, it wasn't *that* bad."

Dad bet her a long weekend in San Francisco—"museums, dining, the works"—that she couldn't "give up the easel for three months." Mom said it was just another excuse to gamble and marched off.

I read later that Avon stopped delivery in 1967 but I wondered if other drunk moms didn't chase Avon ladies off their front porches before that and that's why they stopped home deliveries. Mom said the milkman used to deliver glass bottles of milk to our back step, but now you only get pizza deliveries, and Dad said they stand "halfway across the driveway so you won't shoot them for being too close to the house."

Jesus left a pizza at our door once. At least I think it was Him.

By morning it was cold and soggy and an animal had eaten most of it.

Jesus hates being called the "Son of God," so I decide to use the acronym *SOG*.

Acronym means: *An abbreviation formed from the initial letters of other words and pronounced as a word,* Oxford Dictionary.

"Like it? It's an acronym." I prop myself up in bed. Jesus isn't usually here this early. I wait. Isn't He listening? "An acronym means—"

"I know what it means. And no, I don't like SOG. Are you kidding? It sounds like a Japanese movie monster, like Mothra or Godzilla. Call me Jesus, or Hey-Seuss if you want—that's how it's pronounced in Spanish. Just don't call me SOG!"

Maybe I should call Him Mr. Crabby Butt instead.

It's Sunday. Shouldn't He be at church, signing autographs in the parking lot or something?

It seems everyone is grumpy these days—even though the Cold War has warmed up and we don't have to worry about the Russians or Cubans anymore. More people care about the civil rights movement and that's good. They say the war in Vietnam will be over soon. I think we need a royal taster to sample everything—the news, our food, maybe even the air and dirt. Maybe we're being drugged. Timothy Leary said if everyone took LSD, we'd see how crazy life *really* is.

Even the criminals and politicians and dead US soldiers looking out at us from Dad's newspaper each morning seem angry and tired. If life is really that bad, why does Mom want me to get tough and grow up?

As I roll into a fetus, I hear SOG open the window to leave.

Mom knocks on my door. "Lily? It's nine o'clock."

My bed is an island adrift in a warm green sea choked with duckweed. I tried growing duckweed in Mom's rock garden pond but she tore it out.

Why should I get up when the whole world is unhappy? When I start talking, people get nervous; no one wants me around. Mom said that's not true, but what does *she* know? Jesus tucked me in the other morning whispering, "Keep sleeping. You're growing, you need it." Had He turned off my alarm? "Don't go to school. Stay home. No one will miss you."

"Lily!" Mom knocks louder.

SOG is right. No one would miss me. I'm not a jock or a hood, popular or in the school government. I'm not interesting. Okay, maybe I'm interesting.

I smell ocean and hear seagulls call, pop my head through the bedding, and peer across the room. I love my wallpaper with its repeated *tableau* (a French word with four vowels) of Copenhagen Harbor, a section of seawall, mermaids, and fishing boats. This morning, boats bob sleepily in the water while fishermen nap below deck; mermaids stop basking on the rocks and float on their backs in the water, their eyes closed, looking annoyed at Mom's knocking.

I talked her out of painting my room. "Next year," she made me swear.

I roll over again and the bed squeaks. "Are you sick?" Mom asks as she walks in. "What's wrong with you?"

"What's wrong with *you*?" I snap.

She pulls back the bedspread. "Up. Now."

I should be nicer. Since the Savage Boy tried to chew his way into my room, Mom gets nervous when I don't answer the door.

I roll over again and stare at her through my eye slits. Behind her, waves wash lazily over mussels and starfish, and sea anemones affixed to the seawall spit tiny sprays of water from their tiny sandy mouths. Some spit lands inches from Mom's feet but she doesn't notice.

"You can bet Lauren's up this morning!" Mom smiles. "Yesterday was the big hike! Six miles into the wilderness, lunch, then four miles more, dinner, and rolling out their sleeping bags. Hot dogs, s'mores, and ghost stories. Building a campfire and washing dishes in the creek. Doesn't that sound fun?"

"No," I say angrily. Yes, it does, but none of the kids at school like doing stuff with their families and I'm a teenager now too. It's bad enough SOG is always showing up; I'm pretty sure most kids don't have that problem. "No," I repeat.

We drove Lauren to the Outdoor School's bus two days ago. As Mom and I kissed her and turned to go, I heard one of the kids say it wasn't a good idea to wear new boots to camp, but Lauren was already looking for Randy, the boy she had a crush on. Randy was the real reason Lauren wanted to go to Outdoor School, she said so herself.

The kitchen table is empty when I finally get there, just milk, a bowl of fruit, and cold coffeecake.

I pick up the paper, pretending to be Mom and Dad: first scouring the headlines for things to get angry over (Mom) or reciting scores from football, basketball, and baseball games I never watched (Dad). After putting the paper down, I stare out the window. It takes me a few minutes to realize Dad's standing at the edge of the backyard. What's he looking at? What's he thinking?

"Paul?" Mom calls. *"Paul!"*

I knock on the window, waving Dad inside, and follow him to the front door, which stands open.

Mom is talking to a strange woman in the driveway. "It's about Lauren," she tells him, her voice trembling.

"Hold on, Kit. I'm sure it's not that bad." He folds his big hairy arms around her.

"I knew something would happen! We always thought it'd be Lily," Mom says. "Lily always needed all the attention but it only makes sense that something would happen to Lauren."

Doesn't she know I'm here? I'm standing only a few feet away.

The more Mom talks the more excited she gets, and soon she's speaking in . . . really . . . short . . . sentences.

The stranger rocks in place.

"Let her speak, Kit."

Jesus slips His hand in mine, but I shake it off. I heard what Mom said, I know what she meant, but holding His hand doesn't make it better. None of it.

"I'm sure Lauren is fine, Mrs. Asher." The woman is smaller than I am, wears a short Mia Farrow haircut and a lime-green minidress. "I wanted to assure you that—"

"Hold on a minute. You mean you don't *know* if she's fine? She's off in the woods and you don't *know* if she's okay?"

"Is Lauren dead?" Maybe SOG wanted to tell me something earlier.

All three adults suddenly look at me.

"The woods are our friend," I say, meaning to calm Mom. I think of a book she used to read to Lauren and me, and its illustrations of baby animals on rainy days—fawns under giant ferns and raccoon cubs in the trunks of rotted fallen trees.

"Not now, Lily," Dad says.

Sometimes I think my mouth belongs to someone else.

It starts to sprinkle. Is it raining where Lauren is?

The woman steps forward. "If I could come in, I'm sure we—"

"No," Mom says. "I want to hear what happened. Right here. Right now."

"For God's sake, Kit." Dad blushes, then whispers in her ear, "Did you take your happy pill this morning?"

The woman pauses before saying, "Lauren was unable to finish the hike—"

"Unable?"

"Blisters. I think it was her new boots," says the woman quietly.

Mom freezes.

"So our Outdoor School counselors, Tad and Elizabeth, made the decision to leave her in a safe location along the trail. To rest. She had her jacket and sleeping bag, water and a candy bar, and they fully intended to return to her that afternoon, but," she smiled uncomfortably, "they're young themselves and it was their first year as counselors and, of course, their first full day with the kids, so they didn't really know them. And I guess in all the excitement they forgot to count off every thirty minutes as they were instructed to do. And," her smile drops, "one thing led to another . . ."

Mom tenses. She hates that expression. "They *forgot* her? Overnight? Alone in the woods?"

"Lauren will be here in a few minutes; I just wanted to be sure you were home. I'm sure she's okay. Just a little . . . tired, maybe."

Miss Marcus, my sister's favorite teacher, brings Lauren home.

Lauren listed her as an emergency contact (which surprises Mom), and Miss Marcus got the phone call sometime around four a.m., tucked her pajamas into her jeans, and drove to the wilderness area immediately.

She pulls up behind the car belonging to the short woman in the lime-green minidress. The women soon leave, and while Dad carries Lauren inside and I clear off her stuffed animals and open the bed, Mom stands in the garage crying.

Lauren isn't sick but Mom treats her like she is, buying her ice cream, making her macaroni and cheese and grape Kool-Aid (even though it isn't summer). She carefully drapes a heating pad around her bare blistered feet. Every time Lauren needs to get up, she has to call Mom.

Mom doesn't mind. She feels guilty for "not thoroughly reading Lauren's list" that Dad said had "been on the fridge for a month."

I sit on a chair beside Lauren's bed and when she hands me the list, I read out loud: "*Three: wear comfortable previously worn hiking boots. New footwear is prohibited.*"

Yeah, it was right there.

"*Four: new warm clothing is acceptable. Being warm, casual, and comfortable is paramount. A fashionable appearance is unimportant. The goal of Outdoor School is to acquaint student campers/hikers with Northwest flora and fauna and to challenge their outdoor skills.*"

Number four is no problem, but nothing could have kept Lauren warm that night. With her back to a tree, too frightened to move or pee or even look behind her, imagining that every little twig snap or rustling leaf was a wild animal coming to eat her, she didn't sleep, or cry either. Lauren's muscles were so cramped from not moving that she fell to her knees when they first stood her up.

"Shit," said Elizabeth, the new counselor, helping her to stand.

"That's enough from you, young lady," said a worried man in khakis and tennis shoes. Lauren figured he was the boss. "I'll see you in my office." Next to him stood a park ranger.

Once Miss Marcus arrived, she insisted the men carry Lauren out. "You can't expect her to walk! Look at her feet! Poor thing!"

Lauren tells me the story.

When Miss Marcus arrived to drive her home, Lauren was happier to see her than she'd ever been to see anyone in her whole life. "Even Mom and Dad. Even them. Ever."

Ever.

Lauren points at my notebook. "Write down that I want to be a teacher when I grow up, okay? I want to be just like Miss Marcus. Write it down."

I do. Under *Miscellaneous*. I write down everything she said as quickly as I can, listing blame and responsibilities under *Parents, Outdoor School,* and *SOG.*

Jesus isn't getting off this time. That was my sister out there.

That night, I stay in Lauren's room, beside her on the floor in my sleeping bag. I write *I love you* in Helen Keller talk on the palm of her hand, and she does the same on mine.

At midnight I walk through the house checking doors and windows and cupboards, something I haven't done in a while. *Things get out if you're not careful, things get in.*

Mrs. Wiggins and I used to walk through the house together. I concentrate on feeling her wet nose on my bare leg but I can't. I wish she were around to talk to. She watched over all of us—even, for a while, after she died. Now no one does—well, SOG does sometimes, I guess, but He needs watching over too. Sometimes I think the older I get, the younger He gets. Which is weird when somebody is almost two thousand years old.

Back on the floor in Lauren's room, I hear Mom's snores down the hall. She snores when she's had too much to drink.

I hate her so much that night it keeps me awake; I hate both my parents. Maybe Dad feels it. He is up too; I ignore him when he peeks in Lauren's room. Sometimes I think Dad's the saddest one in the family. Maybe Jesus should have crawled through *his* window screen.

If Lauren moved into my room I could keep her safe. She'd never have to go to Outdoor School again, she'd never have to leave my room. And my bed is big enough for both of us.

I watch the clock and each minute ticking off: *Ask her to move in, don't ask her. Ask her, don't ask her,* like pulling petals off a daisy. Sometime after 3:17 I fall asleep.

The next morning, Lauren hobbles into the kitchen on Gramma's crutches, stopping beside Mom at the stove to swing back and forth, her feet free of the floor. "It's groovy, Lily," she tells me. "Want to try it?"

"No thanks."

I feel Mom looking at me, waiting for me to say something sweet and smart and older-sisterish to Lauren, something Lauren and I will treasure when we're all grown up. Sisters are supposed to know each other better than anyone else and stay special to each other their entire lives, like in *Little Women,* but it wasn't like that for Mom and Jamie and it isn't like that for my sister and me either.

I want to say I'm sorry, but I can't. The truth is, I love Jamie and SOG and Mrs. Wiggins as much as I love Lauren, and they're already living in my room.

There isn't space for Lauren.

I'm glad I didn't ask her to move in.

I look down the hall at my room and see that the door is cracked open.

A cold damp mist billows out around it, and inside owls hoot and twigs snap. Trees cha-cha in the wind and cold water rolls over mossy rocks.

A shadow passes over the hall rug.

SOG is back.

I can smell the woods from here and it smells good.

CHAPTER 14

PICASSO'S NOT HOME

"Goodwill?" Mom says, pawing through my box. The brushes in her hair wiggle like insect antennas. "Are you sure you want to donate so many toys? Once they're gone, they're gone, you know."

I know.

"Just because Judy gave everything away doesn't mean you have to."

A minute later I take the bulging cardboard box to the garage where Dad stands at the portable workbench he never uses, digging at something in his hand with a screwdriver.

"Hey, sweetie," he says. His nose flares when he holds his hand under the lamp and pokes the screwdriver into the soft flat place where Jesus has His stigmata. He stiffens and spreads his fingers like the painted hand on the gypsy tent at the county fair.

"I'm giving my old stuff to charity," I tell him.

"Great. You're old enough to appreciate sharing with those less fortunate, I'm proud of you." The back of his neck is red. Whatever's in there must be deep.

"I could get you some tweezers."

"Thanks for the concern, kiddo," he says, walking me toward the open garage door, "but I'm fine. You go play now, and let your old dad build something manly at his workbench."

I'm too old to "go play" and I almost remind him of that when he pulls down the broken garage door. Three-quarters of the way down, it catches. "Like your new bike?" he asks through the garage window. His voice is muffled.

"Yeah."

"Another year or so and you can study for your driver's permit. Imagine that!"

He wants be alone, even if he's hurting himself. I like to be alone too, so I draw giant chalk infinity loops in the driveway and practice going over them on my new ten-speed, getting to "know the bike before you take it on the street," as Dad insisted. Red, my three-speed Schwinn with fat tires, is too small for me now.

Dad's very protective of us.

And he's smart, maybe too smart. They seem to need him at the office all the time these days. Late nights, sometimes even Saturday mornings.

Once, last month, our Sunday drive was canceled when he got a call from the office. Mom said it was a bookie at the track, but Dad said he was needed and had to go. Lauren still gets nervous when they leave her behind. The night in the woods was months ago now and I showed her how long on the paper-plate clock she made me in first grade. Imagining the minute hand as days and the hour hand as months, I turned back time until she said, "I thought you'd understand," and stormed out of my room.

That night I heard Dad and Mom in their bedroom. "We should never have encouraged Lauren to go in the first place," Dad said. "We bought her boots, and told her everything would be fine when we didn't know a goddamn thing about Outdoor School. We let her down. We're her parents and we put her in danger."

Suddenly I heard him cry, tell Mom how he couldn't protect us, how he couldn't be the man she wanted him to be. How he had "one goddamn job" and even that he "can't do right."

Mom didn't contradict him but said, "Shhh," over and over instead, and after a few minutes turned off the light.

I wanted to go in there and tell him that he *is* doing a good job, but then he'd know I was listening. *Eavesdropping:* I like that word, it's Old Norse.

I ride my new bike in smaller and smaller circles watching Dad through the Plexiglas window of the broken automatic garage door he calls a "goddamn waste of money." He glances up at me occasionally but doesn't stop digging.

I should do something. Mom would want me to stop him, wouldn't she? He could get an infection or cut a nerve. He doesn't react when I knock on the garage door window and shout, "Dad! Stop!" Why is he ignoring me? "Dad!"

He waves me off. "Go help your mother," he calls out.

But lunch is over, and Mom shooed everyone out of the kitchen fifty-six minutes ago. Lauren walked to the store with Rusty, and I boxed up my old things. Dad headed to the garage with a bottle of beer; it's still there beside him, he hasn't touched it.

"Dad!" I yell.

He turns off the lamp.

Minutes later, I'm sitting in the family room flipping through TV stations, when I hear Dad lie to Mom.

"Shop accident," he says, explaining the blood-soaked rag in the palm of his hand, but there was no sawing or hammering or nailing. At least not while I watched.

Mom is worried but she's mad too and, after a scene on *Rainy Saturday Movies* where a barefoot princess with a lacy dunce cap and big boobs kisses Victor Mature, I hear her say something about Dad's secretary who "seems to know everything, even why you would cut yourself, for God's sake."

Dad answers, "What the hell does Toni have to do with anything?"

And Mom replies, "Stop hurting yourself, we can work it out," or something like that.

When I take my notebook out of my sweater pocket it's to count how many times Victor's muscles flex when he holds the princess by her arms, how many times she lets him kiss her before she slaps him. I sometimes practice long romantic kisses with my pillow; I want to do it right.

Dad's pacing (I hear his pocket change) as Mom talks about "Portland Meadows," and after a short quiet, he says, "Sure, until we need something for the house."

Mom bursts into tears. Her tears are loud and angry when she races down the hall and throws open the cupboard under the bathroom sink where the medical supplies are stored. Running by me again, she carries gauze, tape, and hydrogen peroxide.

But Dad's already in the car. Heading out to "catch up at work," he yells from the car window, even though it's Saturday on Thanksgiving vacation and he promised he'd be around all weekend.

All.

Weekend.

"At least let me disinfect it!" Mom calls. "Come on, Paul!"

But he's pulling out of the driveway, and all she can do is light a cigarette and shake her head.

I stand behind her, back to back, and grab her wrists, waving her arms up and down like wings. She relaxes her body and lets me do it; we've done it before. Her burning cigarette flies into the air, landing in a rain puddle. Mom's skin is cold, and her wrists are smaller than mine. How tall will I be when I finally stop growing?

"Look!" I call out as we sail above the stone streets and columned buildings of an ancient city in Turkey or Greece. No, it's Rome. Of course! "We're flying over . . . the Roman Forum! What's-his-name is stabbing Caesar! Look, Mom, they just released the lions into the Coliseum!"

I wait for her to tell me what she sees. Usually it's camels and pyramids, white sandy beaches or an exhausted Humphrey Bogart dragging *The African Queen* through mosquito-infested backwaters.

"It's okay, Lily," she says instead. "He'll be back."

Portland Meadows is where Judy said Dad won money for the new binoculars, redwood fence, and dishwasher. It's where Shannon Overbeck's father said my father plays the dogs.

"What kind of dogs?" I asked her. In Lauren's school production of *Peter Pan*, the shortest kid played Nana the sheepdog.

"Greyhounds," Shannon explained. "You know, gambling?"

I guess, but if I didn't she'd beat me up before she'd explain it anyway. Shannon's the tallest girl in school, even taller than I am; she's been held back twice, and she's mad at everybody.

Playing the dogs.

I remember how the neighborhood dogs ran through Crawford Woods once, knocking my family into the bushes. How I felt the dogs' strong fast muscles in my legs and how, for just a minute, I ran with them. It really happened, didn't it? The night Lauren fell into the quarry pit and the sky was full of stars and comets and imagined constellations, racing dogs, and flying carpets?

Dad's been gone five hours.

The beef Stroganoff is good, but we don't eat much.

"I have a surprise," Mom says, drumming her fingers on the evening newspaper. Lauren and I perk up. "I think we've waited long enough for your father." She opens it to the Home and Arts section and spreads it wide. She points at the headline.

"*Artistic Housewife Wins Contest,*" I read aloud. Underneath it is a photograph of an attractive woman in a baggy paint-splattered work shirt and long slim legs, seated at her easel.

"That's you!" Lauren squeals. "What'd you win?"

"Three months of personal instruction, each Wednesday morning, with the Portland Art Museum's new wunderkind, Mark, Marcus something-or-other. Isn't it wonderful?"

"Congratulations," I smile. "Now everyone will know you're an artist."

Mom looks toward the front door.

"*Asher's painting* Si-BI-you Four," I read out loud (the number is in Roman numerals; I love Roman numerals), "*is her first venture into impressionism.*"

Lauren leans over the paper. "*It explores the emotional legacy of being a child in Eastern Europe, during the war.*"

"That's *Sibiu. See-Bee-You Four,*" Mom says softly.

Four? Does that mean there were three other paintings before this one? I've never seen them. Did she throw them away? Were there children in the windows of the houses she painted? Was Mom one of them?

"Proud of me, girls?" she says, and we nod our heads enthusiastically.

"Does Dad know?" Lauren asks.

Mom touches her arm. "Check the phone, will you, sweetheart? It's been acting up lately."

The dial tone is loud and clear.

The Rifleman reruns are on TV and Lucas McCain and his son Mark have come into town for supplies. While they load up the week's staples, the old sheriff tells them about the new gunslinger in town.

I point at the tall bearded bad guy with the crazy eyes. "That's Bruce Dern," I tell my sister. "He's on all the westerns: *Wagon Train, Bonanza.*"

Lauren and I love westerns. *The Rifleman* is especially good on our new color TV. Dad said the star of the show, Chuck Connors, used to be a professional baseball player, like Sandy Koufax and Don Drysdale.

The front door's suddenly thrown open with a bang. Dad's home.

Lauren and I look at each other nervously. I turn down the volume when he opens the fridge, grabs a beer, and pops the cap, letting it fly across the kitchen floor. There is white gauze wrapped around his hand.

Before they were canceled, *McHale's Navy* and *F Troop* were Dad's favorite TV shows. They always made him laugh.

"Kit?"

"Right here," Mom says, walking in from the backroom with the laundry basket. She heads to the stove where she preheats the oven. Dad stands in front of his place setting, staring at the newspaper article she has put there. They mumble something, but Dad's tone is sarcastic when he says, "I *said* congratulations, Kit. Didn't you hear me?"

Mom takes his chilled salad bowl out of the fridge and places it on the table.

"Isn't that something," Dad says, sitting down. "You told a reporter you were born in Sibiu. You even mentioned that your family died in a concentration camp. You won't discuss it with me or Frieda or the girls but you tell the whole damn town?"

"Lily? Close the front door for me?" Mom says.

Outside, steam rises off the hood of Dad's car and rain gurgles through the gutter.

"If you read a little closer, Paul, you'll see that the article isn't really about me. It's about the contest." Mom stands up straighter. "The museum board loved my painting, why shouldn't I be flattered? But their goal is to support local artists. Isn't that fantastic?"

"It's only an amateur contest, Kit. It's not a serious competition."

Mom puts down the laundry basket.

"Hell, tell the newspapers whatever you want," Dad says. "I don't give a damn."

"What's going on, Paul?"

Lauren curls herself around a throw pillow.

"Paul?"

"Nothing's going on. You won a contest. You're a pretty woman so they put your picture in the paper. Happens every day."

I don't have to see Mom's face to know her feelings are hurt. "I see you found someone to bandage your hand."

"There was a first aid kit at work."

Mom sticks Dad's foil-covered dinner plate in the oven and sets the timer.

"The reporter must have interviewed you, what, on Monday? I suppose Connie Marks was in on it."

"*In on it?* You mean the conspiracy to embarrass you?" Mom's hands shake when she stubs out her smoke. "No, Mr. Supportive. I didn't tell anyone because I wanted it to be a surprise. Silly me, I thought it would be more fun that way." She looks my way but doesn't see me. "The painting is in the lobby of the new Bank of America downtown. It'll be there for a month."

There's a better view of the kitchen from the back of the couch. Maybe I'll put this scene in one of the stories I'm writing. Maybe I'll write a play. Mom took Lauren and me to *Charley's Aunt* last week; *Antigone* the week before.

"My painting will be there for a month," Mom repeats. "Maybe we should all pile in the car and go see it."

Lauren claps.

Dad looks at the paper again and asks, "How much longer till dinner's hot?"

When Mom sits down, her shoulders slump forward. She looks tired and small. "Paul?"

"For God's sake, Kit. We don't have money for you to go to art school."

"Who said anything about school? The prize was free classes with—"

"Christmas is next month, and you just bought the new Mediterranean bedroom suite."

"*We* bought the new bedroom suite. We decided together. We had the money, you said. You said you liked it; you said you were sleeping better."

"And what about the house in Crawford Heights? Aren't you still talking to a real estate agent?"

Mom turns pale. "What's going on?"

"Can't you guess, Kit? Do I look like Daddy Warbucks? Do you really think I make enough money for everything we want to do? Think about it, Kit."

"Stop lecturing me and talk to me. You promised me you were done gambling, so what happened? Was it a poor stock investment or something? We'll figure it out, Paul. We can tighten our belts around here."

"A poor stock investment?" Dad laughs. "Jesus, Kit, you're so busy being an award-winning ar-teest that you stopped paying attention. The bank. The checkbook—"

The *checkbook*. I hate that word.

"The girls, Paul," Mom interrupts quietly. "Not in front of the girls."

"Go to bed, kids," Dad says, without looking at us.

He's yelling at Mom—we're not going anywhere.

"Paul?"

"Nothing's going on, damn it." The phone rings. "Jesus Christ, is there something wrong with wanting a little peace and quiet in your own home?"

The phone keep ringing. Lauren jumps off the couch and tears down the hall to our parents' bedroom. All of us listen when she picks up the receiver and says, "Asher residence."

"No autographs!" Dad yells. "Picasso's not home!"

Mom stands up, walks across the kitchen, takes the ticking oven timer off the back of the stove, and hands it to Dad. "When the bell goes off," she says calmly, "your dinner will be hot. Again. The salad dressing is in the fridge door. You obviously know where the beer is." She takes a sweater out of the hall closet. "Ask the girls for help if you can't figure it out." When she opens the front door I hear the rain, falling even harder. "I'll be at Connie's."

"It's November, Kit," Dad says. "You're wearing flip-flops."

"It's just next door."

"Damn it, Kit. You didn't let me explain."

"I gave you more chances than you'd give me. Let's talk when you have a civil tongue in your head." She slips out so quietly no one hears the door open or close.

When Mom returns, Dad's still sitting at the table. Next to him is his cold dinner and the Home and Arts section of the *Oregon Journal*.

He barely touched the beef Stroganoff. His hand must hurt because he made a face when he picked up the fork.

Lauren and I sit in the new love seat thumbing through a stack of *National Geographic*s. I'm reading about Cuban cigars, the migration patterns of hummingbird moths, and staring at the black skeletal wing markings of the North African sphinx moth, when Mom kicks a kitchen chair.

Lauren and I both jump.

"Goddamn it, Paul. Can't you be happy for me? Aren't you proud of me?"

"I am, Kit." His chair squeaks when he stands up. "I'm sorry. Something happened—"

"I figured that. Something big, right? Well, here's something else that happened, Paul. Something else you won't like. When I got to Connie's house, I went to pieces. I cried. I told them everything. I'm sorry if that embarrasses you." The kitchen falls quiet. "How could you talk to me like that? You know how much painting means to me. I don't care about some gaudy bedroom suite."

"I wanted you to have it. I want to give you everything," Dad replies softly.

Mom says the love between a man and a woman is the most important thing in the world. Though I bet right now she'd rather live in an artists' colony, like the childless divorcée in the book she's reading.

Usually after they fight, Dad compliments her on everything for a couple of days. Once, I even heard him tell Mr. Marks how Mom was a "smart, progressive parent" who "reads up on schizophrenia and personality disorders, and signed us up for appropriate treatment."

By *us*, he means me.

They'll be at it for a while, so Lauren and I put ourselves to bed in their new Mediterranean bedroom suite. The lamp is on across the room, and we face each other with our eyes open, but we don't talk. Lauren's face is a galaxy of freckles: some big and close-up, others small and far away. I invent constellations for them: Frieda's Chevrolet, Einstein's Towel Closet, The Dill Pickle.

The night she slipped over the edge at Crawford Quarry—and standing tiptoe on a crumbling shelf, she spoke my name so quietly I didn't hear it at first—I loved her till my heart hurt.

Tonight, when Lauren yawns and rolls away from me, the room fills with the high-pitched purring of giant moth wings, and I say a prayer, thanking God for my sister, even when she's mean to me.

I wake up in my own bed with Mom kissing me goodnight. "How are you feeling?" she asks, happy again.

I touch my tailbone. "Fine." I think of Dad digging at his hand. Everyone has secrets. "What was Sibiu like?"

"It was beautiful. Old and important once, but I don't remember that. I don't remember much—it was such a long time ago."

I reach for her hand, turn it over, and with my finger write *T-R-Y* in her palm.

"All right. Once upon a time . . . wait. You're the one with the imagination," she says. "Why don't you tell me what it was like?"

N-O, I write.

Mom says she only thinks of Romania when she paints, "but I'll . . ." She writes *T-R-Y* in my hand this time. She kicks off her flip-flops and climbs into bed beside me.

"I can tell you that Mother was pretty and our father was tall and handsome like Daddy. Jamie and I never saw them again after they put us on the train for Bulgaria . . . to Sofia actually, the capital. I was the oldest so our parents gave me a little money for food and directions to a Christian boarding school where Jamie and I would live. Everyone was wonderful. Along with our studies, they taught us to sew and cook. We were lucky, Lily, so lucky! Jewish children everywhere were being rounded up and—" She stops. "It didn't matter that we were Jewish; they took care of us. More Romanians than Bulgarians were killed during the war. We were safer there."

"Did you and Jamie share a room?"

"For the first year. After that, they moved Jamie to a dorm with girls her age, but we saw each other all the time. We had dumplings on Sunday, and strudel once a month, and each Christmas we were given knitted gloves and scarves and hats, even new coats if we needed them." She pauses. "Haven't I told you all this before?"

Yes. But I don't want her to stop.

"I was fifteen and Jamie was ten when Frieda's church sponsored us coming to Oregon. We stayed with several nice church families and finished school, but we were too old to be adopted. Jamie earned a scholarship to college, and I worked as a secretary, and modeled for White Stag and Jantzen." She'll never tell me about Sibiu, but that's okay. "Remember how your father and I met when I was modeling?"

Of course. I nod.

"The rest, as they say, is history."

I don't ask how lonely and scared she must have been, or which church families took them in. Or why she doesn't go to the synagogue now that the war's over and she can worship whoever she wants.

It's a good story, but I know what really happened: Wolves kidnapped Jamie and Mom because they were beautiful and smart; they wanted to keep the girls for themselves. While they lived in the forest, Mom painted tiny little portraits of the animals and framed each one with twigs and vines. And Jamie wrote poetry and taught the wolves how to play the guitar so they could accompany themselves when they howled at the moon.

It's Sunday, the last day of Thanksgiving vacation.

Christmas vacation starts in twenty-four days. Next Thursday, Lauren and I open the first window of our Advent calendars. No big deal, it's always a candy cane.

Today is cold and drizzly; yucky weather for hanging the Christmas lights like Dad promised he would. He's been "up since early morning," says Mom, handing me her bathroom wastebasket.

Dad stands at the far end of the yard around the burn barrel, sipping coffee and stirring smoldering leaves and garbage with a pitchfork. An occasional flame stretches above the barrel's rusty lip, brightening his face.

I shake Mom's trash over the fire and look in. Her lipstick-blotted tissues are lightest and burn fastest. A perfect red kiss floats up, suspended in front of me, before turning to cinder, then air. Dad sees it too and clears his throat. "Morning, kiddo," he says. "Warm enough?"

I pull my jacket tighter.

Dad hasn't shaved, or combed his hair. He glances nervously toward the house where Mom stands in the kitchen window, cutting banana slices over Lauren's cereal. He catches my eye then throws a large stained paper bag into the burning barrel.

"Stand back!" he shouts.

Sparks fly, and I smell turkey and know it's the greasy turkey carcass Frieda insisted Mom bring home after Thanksgiving dinner. Gramma hates to waste anything. "This would make a great soup broth," she said. As the carcass burns, the corn stuffing sizzles and smokes. It smells awful.

Dad burns the empty cardboard box marked *Goodwill*. I feel like a traitor to my old toys, but poor kids can love them now. If God really loved us, each child would have something to play with. I toss my crucifix into the burning barrel.

"Lily!" Dad cries, fishing it out with his pitchfork. "What are you . . . ?" He blows on the necklace, and then juggles it back and forth in his gloved hands. After a minute he holds it out and, wrinkling his eyebrows, says, "Here."

I open my hand; he drops it in.

"Whatever you're going through right now, the necklace was a gift from your grandmother. It'll mean something someday. Keep it."

I put the necklace back in my pocket. "It's a crucifix. I didn't even think you liked Jesus."

"What I don't like is you throwing away a present. It was a thoughtful gesture. It cost money. As for Jesus, I never said I didn't like Him. He kept His eye on you at Peace Lake, didn't He?"

Not really. I take Mrs. Wiggins's tooth out of my other pocket.

"The tooth! You still have it. I thought you got rid of it after that . . . incident with the Savage boy."

Mike Savage. His name makes my heart race. "No. Would you make a necklace out of it?"

"Sure. Got an extra chain?"

I nod. "How long will it take?"

"Not long. I'll borrow a bit from the neighbor. I should have it ready by dinner."

"Groovy." I hand him the tooth and he smiles.

"Kind of a lucky rabbit's foot, isn't it?"

"Yeah." I dig the crucifix out of my pocket. "Want it? Maybe it could be *your* lucky rabbit's foot."

"No thanks, sweetie," Dad says, pointing at his wedding ring. "Got one."

I'm not surprised when Jesus climbs through the new window screen that night, snagging His robe, scratching His arms. "Here's the deal," He says. "You've got to cut me some slack. I'm doing the best I can."

SOG drags His fingers through His hair. I read an article in Dr. Giraffe's office about people who have long, thin fingers. *Artistic and sensitive,* the writer called them.

Outside, Mrs. Merton's automatic sprinkler system starts up, which it does for an hour every night, even when it's cold and rainy, because she doesn't know how to turn it off.

"Everyone bad-mouths me," Jesus says, patting His chest. The sound echoes through Him like Mom thumping a watermelon at Piggly Wiggly. "I don't know the answers to everything."

"But aren't you supposed to?"

"It's the tail, isn't it? And the bark?" SOG shakes His head. "Nature's in you up to your eyeballs, Lily. It's a gift."

"No it isn't."

We look at each other for a minute. Then He sighs, and climbs out my window again, squirming and grunting like He's pulling on a wet swimsuit.

Between Thanksgiving vacation and Christmas vacation, I come home from school to find Mom crying three times:

Tuesday, December 2, 3:37 p.m., the same rainy afternoon of the same rainy morning I found her new pillows and bedspread with matching skirt in big plastic bags by the front door. Mom wiped away her tears, but her face was red and puffy.

Wednesday, December 3, 3:42 p.m., when three guys in baseball caps carried the new Mediterranean bedroom suite, the wingback chairs, and the new TV out to the big red furniture truck parked in our driveway. I found Mom crying over the bathroom sink, redoing her eyeliner. Crying. Redoing her eyeliner. Crying. I sat on the toilet and watched.

Monday, December 16, 4:05 p.m., when Mom got off the phone after canceling the check that stopped the delivery order on the new hideaway couch I didn't know we were getting.

"It's foolish to cry; they're just things," Mom said. "I always say that, don't I, Lily? Just things?"

I nodded, but Mom was embarrassed and hoped our neighbors didn't notice.

Judy did. "Got repo'd, huh?" But I didn't answer. I pretended she was talking to someone else, or just moving her lips.

I like ignoring Judy. I like walking away from her too.

I know what "repo" means, and so does Lauren. When Dad told us to think of it as an adventure and there'd be "no TV again until late January," Lauren locked herself in her room. I'm thankful we don't have to watch another *Andy Williams Christmas Show*, especially if Claudine Longet and the Osmonds are going to be on. The Osmonds are creepy, Claudine talks in whispers, and Andy sings "Moon River" on every stupid show.

I'm okay with no gifts or Christmas tree too, but I don't understand why we have to put out Frieda's decorations when she's in Florida this year. On the end table next to the couch is the red felt skirt she made us, with green zigzag rickrack on the hem. And on top of that is a mirror lake, surrounded by a family of pinheaded silver reindeer standing in angel-hair snowdrifts, looking at their reflections. Frieda's crocheted Christmas stockings hang over our fireplace. Everybody thinks they're ugly, but we still use them.

A box came from Florida in the mail last week. "I hope Frieda didn't send another afghan," Mom laughs, and everyone joins in but not too much because "we shouldn't look a gift horse in the mouth, especially when it's been crocheting three hours every night since Halloween."

When we have a tree, it's usually decorated with white, pink, or blue, ornaments, and then covered with lights and ribbons, but one year, my favorite year, we hung homemade gingerbread men from every branch. The treats weighed down the limbs so much that one night Mrs. Wiggins ate most of them. Mom was the first one to step in her barf the next morning.

Lauren and I suggest peanut butter sandwiches for Christmas dinner but Mom digs behind the pots and pans for a jar of loose change she hands to Dad. "Fifty bucks, last time I counted," she says. "Get whatever the girls want," she tells him, and even though she's expecting Chinese food or pizza, Mom's pleased when we return with Swedish meatballs and hot cheese puffs from Rose's Deli; cream soda, popcorn balls, pickles, and Fig Newtons from the store down the street.

She's sitting cross-legged on the kitchen floor, her back against the wall—her sketchpad of neighborhood scenes open in her lap. She tries to get up but falls back. She laughs at herself and my sister glares. "I'm sorry, Lima Bean. I just lost my balance."

But there are tears in Lauren's eyes—angry tears with little fires inside, if you look close enough. Lauren's not allowed to say *drunk*, just like she isn't allowed to call me a weirdo.

After a nap, Mom steps outside for a cigarette.

While she smokes, Dad plays Al Hirt and Ann-Margret—singing "Baby, It's Cold Outside"—and I wonder if Mom told him that she'd given up the contest prize. "There aren't enough hours in the day to be a full-time housewife and an artist," she explained to me.

What about enough hours in the day to be a housewife, an artist, and a drunk?

I'm mad when she steps back inside the house, smelling of smoke, kicks off her shoes, and hurries into Dad's waiting arms. She stands on his feet while they dance, the same way Lauren and I used to before Dad decided we were too old.

Mom doesn't notice that I cleaned the kitchen while she napped, or that I sharpened her favorite pencils and arranged her tubes of paint just like in the color wheel. When Mom doesn't see what's right in front of her, it's called being near-sighted or *myopic*.

I looked it up.

I hate them for arguing.

I hate them for making up.

I hate how no one exists except the two of them.

Out my bedroom window it's a normal Christmas. The Fosters put up more lights this year than usual, and their big plastic Santa with the chipped nose still stands in their front yard waving. Its motor got too hot last Christmas and sparked a small fire at the outlet in their garage that Sherman said smelled "like reindeer farts."

"Girls?" It's time for board games, hot chocolate, and snacks. I bring a clipboard to the table, but no one notices until I ask how to spell *inebriated*. Mr. Alsup, my science teacher, says that to understand something you must observe it carefully, take lots of notes, and record your findings in charts, graphs, and illustrations.

Dad loves *Monopoly*. I hate how boys always win at games, and make a note of it on my parents' chart.

Lauren knocks the clipboard from my hands. "Stop writing everything down! Jeez!"

"Hold on, Lima Bean," Dad says, then puts another house on an already crowded property and lifts his cocoa mug in a toast. "To the richest guy on the boardwalk!" Everyone moans. "All right then," he says, looking at Mom. "To winning another art contest!"

"Yippee!" we cry. Mom holds her cup highest.

"We don't have any money this Christmas so you know what I want for next year?" Lauren says.

"A pala-*mino!*" we all sing. Lauren's shoulders drop like they do when she faces the living room each Christmas morning and doesn't find a horse tethered to the tree. Or tears through her stocking and doesn't find a picture of one with a note that says it's being boarded for her at Horse Heaven Stables (only 1.4 miles away; there's a map on the fridge).

Then Mom announces she's pregnant.

She's pregnant!

That night I put penny candies on my parents' pillows, the way they do in fancy New York City hotels.

Two months later, Mom loses the baby.

Five months after that, she loses another one.

Frieda says Mom's lucky to be young and strong enough to keep trying, but I don't see what's so lucky about miscarriages.

Each time Dad tells Mom, "It'll come to term this time, sweetheart."

I'm never having a child. If I *am* a weirdo and it's in the genes, I could give it to my kids. Bad stuff happens. You can't stop it either—just like the real people couldn't stop the pod people in *Invasion of the Body Snatchers*.

Dad is at a convention the night Mom agrees to watch *Body Snatchers* with me. She dozes off and on during the movie but at the end she sits up, wide awake, and says, "Aren't we lucky we don't live in a world like that?"

"But maybe we do," I say. "Maybe Frieda's a pod person, a body snatcher, and the real Frieda's in her basement, not in Florida. How would we know?"

Mom smiles. "Frieda doesn't have a basement."

"But if pod people have our faces and memories, and nobody believes the real people . . ."

Mom wishes she'd never agreed to watch the movie with me no matter what that magazine article said about "mothers spending quality, individual time with each child, doing something that the child enjoys."

She looks at her watch and announces that it's five minutes to midnight.

"They take your soul—"

"I'm sorry, Lily, but can we talk about souls another time? I'm really, really tired." She flips off the TV and lamp.

"Like *dead* tired?" I ask. Po fell asleep one day and never woke up, maybe Mom will too.

She doesn't answer. I hear her straighten the coffee table, and plump the scatter pillows. Mom has excellent night vision because she eats her carrots.

By March, most of the repo'd furniture is home again.

That spring, Dad makes chili dogs each Wednesday night so Mom can paint until bedtime. While she sleeps in the next morning, he makes us breakfast and gets us ready for school. Mom calls each Wednesday "getting away," and paints Lauren and me little pictures of Chinese pagodas, palm trees, and castles that she slips under our bedroom doors while we're at school.

For a while, Dad listens when Mom tells him that "art has power" and "if more people had painted pictures, written stories, or played music, there'd never have been a Holocaust." She cries each time she says it.

Dad's hand heals, and then one day I see him standing in the garage again, looking at it under the lamp.

I guess the automatic garage door is working now, because it's up.

And anyone can see in.

CHAPTER 15

JARS

Three houses away, Sherman's mom washes her car. A trickle of cold, soapy water kisses my feet on its way to the sewer grate in front of our house. I wore socks and shoes to the mailbox, then took them off.

Mom—who's planting primroses and begonias on the side of the house, and can't see me—won't like it. I've been sick four days and she doesn't know I'm out.

The mail arrives: a bill from Pacific Gas and Electric, Mom's *Harper's Bazaar*, Dad's *Sports Illustrated*. Nothing for Lauren or me though I did receive a *Get well* card from Frieda yesterday. A Jesus *Get well* card. Half the glitter, on the flowers at His feet, was stuck to the envelope, but the message was legible: *I will never leave you nor forsake you. Hebrews 13:5.*

You don't want to give men "big heads," so I didn't tell SOG about it when He sat beside me on the patio this morning.

"Your parents are pretty groovy, sleeping outside with you last night," He said. We both enjoyed watching the sun rising over the roof of my house. Like Kilroy peeking over a fence—all big nose and fat cartoon fingers, the way bossy Louise Lamb taught me to draw him at church camp last summer. Maybe there's only a top to Kilroy and no bottom, like the legless beggar boy on Burnside who uses his knuckles to push his cart around. Bossy Louise is Judy's age. "I'm coming back as assistant counselor next summer," she bragged, "and you'll have to do everything I say." But I won't, because I'm not going back to Lake Little Jehovah. After making a leather bookmark in crafts one afternoon, I found Jesus sitting in the rose arbor and He told me church camp was silly. And, "Louise Lamb?" He laughed. "Come on, Lily. You're smarter than she is." It's hard to be mad at SOG when He says stuff like that.

"Looks like a beautiful day," Jesus said this morning, standing up and popping His knuckles. Mom takes fifty cents off our allowance when we do that, a dollar if we "give her lip" about it.

I looked around. My parents were up, their chaise longues empty, the screen door open to the kitchen, the friendly drumming of the percolator, and the two of them quietly talking. My occasional fevers are a mystery to my parents; they'll try anything.

"Feeling better?" SOG asked. "Did you sleep?"

"Yes," to the first question. Cool night air and moonlight was good medicine; the fever broke, I can feel it. "No," to the second.

I didn't sleep. Mom checked on me every hour with the flashlight, while Dad crept around the backyard (like Vic Morrow in *Combat*) whenever he heard an unfamiliar sound. Which meant he was up a lot. You'd be surprised how much noise there is in a quiet night. Besides sleeping outside for my fever—something Mom swore she'd done when she was a girl in Romania—*Sleeping under a full moon* was the last wish on my Christmas list. Frieda warned against it but they kinda had to do it. Besides, they don't worry about me going crazy since I howl at the moon already.

And jellyfish tides are 68.7 miles away.

As I sit with my feet in the gutter, I concentrate on the soap bubbles sliding over my toes. I concentrate on "be here now," which Jamie said would bring me "inner peace." She said, "Don't worry about what happens next." Of course, Jamie is dead and none of that matters now. She waves goodbye at me from each of the tiny soapy windows.

Mrs. White drives by and honks. School's out and she's off to pick up her youngest, first grader Jack. She's left at 3:20 each day this week.

Suddenly, Judy's front door flies open with a bang, then slams shut again.

"You got her, Rusty?" Mrs. Marks yells, hurrying to the car. Hair in rollers, car keys jingling. "You got her?"

"I got her," Rusty answers. He walks quickly but stiffly, carrying a cardboard box in his arms. It must be heavy. Dad always teases him about hitting the gym.

"Judy!" Mrs. Marks yells. "Get the door for your brother!" They're both home from school? When I finally see my old friend, silently rushing to open the back door of the car, I stand up. Something is wrong.

She puts the box in the backseat and Rusty jumps in. "The street! The street!" Mrs. Marks shouts over the sound of the engine, but Judy's already standing at the end of the driveway, looking both ways, waving her mother out. Connie Marks's biggest fear is running over somebody, or hitting the big maple tree she can't see around.

A car window must be open; Rusty's crying. He never cries, even when Mr. Marks takes a belt to him.

"What is it?" I call to Judy. She doesn't answer. "Judy?" I haven't seen her in months. She looks different. Older.

"Fifi's sick," she calls back. "She won't get up! We're taking her to the vet!"

The car stops beside her and she jumps in the front seat next to her mom.

Four years ago, Judy and I took an oath to always be friends no matter what. "I'm coming too!" I grab my shoes and socks and run toward them.

"Lily!" Mom yells. "No! You've been sick!"

Without asking, I throw open the back door and jump into Mrs. Marks's car. No one reacts. The car is quiet and everyone is numb as Mrs. Marks pulls away. Behind us, Mom stands in the middle of the street, one hand on her hip, the other shielding her eyes.

The car smells odd. Like Fifi's usual poodle farts only worse.

Between Rusty and me is the cardboard box; Fifi lies inside it on a bath towel. She blinks her eyes slowly. One of her ears is folded back and there's blood in its soft pink shell. Her mouth is open, her tongue limp, and more blood is caked around her nostrils and eyes.

"She's bleeding all over," Rusty says.

"She'll be okay," I say softly.

Judy jerks around. "You don't know if she'll be okay, Lily. Maybe she'll die."

"Judy!" Mrs. Marks snaps.

Fifi delivered Caesar's pups without difficulty; what is it now? "Is she . . . pregnant again?" I ask.

"Only if the vet's a quack," Mrs. Marks answers. "We had her fixed months ago."

Ten minutes later, the Markses hurry inside the Multnomah Vet Clinic with Fifi, leaving the car doors standing open. I close them and run in after them.

The waiting room is a sad place. A chubby girl leans on her mother's shoulder, her plump Kilroy fingers gripping the empty birdcage in her lap. Trembling cats and dogs wrapped in bath towels, or whimpering under the chairs of their owners, are everywhere. An old man, with a leash draped over his crossed legs, blows smoke rings over people's heads.

A little girl peeks inside the round hatbox she holds on her lap. "Mabel's my turtle," she tells me.

While Doris Day sings "Que Sera, Sera" on the office radio, the door to a brightly lit room opens slowly on the waiting room. Inside, Fifi's cardboard box sits on top of a steel bed, and the Markses stand around it, talking to a man in a white coat. When Judy throws her hand over her mouth, my heart sinks. I hurry to the door just as the doctor closes it.

"Wait!" I say. "I'm her friend!" But I'm not anymore, and when I tiptoe down the hall, the next door's locked too. "Judy?" I call, but she doesn't answer.

A cat does, though, meowing over and over. I hear voices in rooms around me. A toilet flushes. Across the hall is the *Staff Restroom*; another closed door marked *Kennels*; and an empty air-conditioned science lab with microscopes and cupboards, and shelves that hold jars of . . . I sneak inside for a better look . . .

Dog Embryos.

My heart does a backflip.

Each jar's fetus is bigger than the last, with more detail of dogs' heads, their bodies, legs, tails. One jar is labeled *2 Weeks*, another *3 Weeks*, until the fetus is *5 Weeks* and so big I can't imagine how it got in the jar.

I'm reminded of the photos in Sherman's *Police Gazette*: a murderer's basement refrigerator with "human remains" in jars. *Ball* was written on the jar. Judy says *ball* means *having sex*.

I feel sick. Even more sick when I hear my best friend cry.

An unseen adult comforts her.

What should I do? Judy doesn't like me anymore, and no one asked me to come along.

I freeze in place until another shelf of glass jars wink at me. The shelf is labeled *Dog Hearts* and I stand on my tiptoes, stretching across the clean empty linoleum counter for a better look at the different-sized jars.

Ruben. Two-yr.-old Chihuahua, reads one. *Pokie. 5-yr.-old Collie*, reads another. Thin white shoelaces, like onion strings, run in and out of each heart. There are so many shoelaces in *Frank. 7-yr.-old Lab mix*, it's hard to see anything else.

And then I see *Princess Grace. 8-yr.-old St. Bernard.* Her heart is biggest of all. A single fat shoelace weaves through it. Mrs. Wiggins was a St. Bernard. I'm shaking when I wrap my hand around the jar, feeling its cool pulsing through the glass.

"Heart worms," a young male voice suddenly announces, and, surprised, I scramble back, taking the jar with me. It crashes before I do, spilling stinky formaldehyde and shooting pieces of glass all over the room.

"Shit!" the teenage lab assistant cries. Not much older than me, he looks confused, then offers a hand up. "You okay? You're not supposed to be in here, you know." Mrs. Wiggins's heart lies at my feet, pulsing and reddening in front of me; its white worm, as thick as a pencil, circling through the dark wet tunnels.

I reach down to pick it up, but the pimply faced boy grabs my arm.

"No way," he says. "You cut yourself and I get fired." A nurse appears in the lab doorway, and in the hallway behind her, Mrs. Marks, Judy, and Rusty gesture for me to join them.

"Lily," Mrs. Marks says quietly, "it's time to go."

I stare at the heart.

The nurse adds, "Your family's going home, sweetheart."

"They're not my family," I say, and while the Markses shuffle off, walking like sobbing robots through the waiting room to their car, I stare at the boy who picks up the sacred heart and sets it in a metal pan on the counter. A glowing ring, like one of Saturn's, circles the exact place where it fell on the floor. Some religious people crawl on their knees for hundreds of miles to visit something like this. The least I can do is stand here, right here, for . . . I look at my wristwatch.

"I'll wait for my mom," I tell the nurse when she sticks her head in the room again. I give her our number. After eighteen minutes she returns, telling me she hasn't reached Mom yet. "Why don't you sit in the other room until she gets here?"

I can't move.

Doors open and close. Phones ring, metal cages clatter, and people cry or stomp out of the office. The desk clerk says, "Have a nice week-end," nineteen times. Are there nineteen employees? A chubby woman enters the science lab, stops to stare at me, then smears something on a slide, sticks it under a microscope, and makes a note in a folder before she leaves. The teenage lab assistant leads five whimpering, panting dogs down the hall to the kennel. Voices discuss "surgery on the Johnson terrier," but "nobody expects poor Einstein to make it." Someone named Sandy goes outside for a cigarette, and Joe says, "It's raining like hell," though I can't hear the rain over the fan. People talk to me at first, then finally give up and walk around me.

Maybe I'll make tiny clay sculptures of all the people in the veterinarian's office, and line the walls of a shoe box with them. A stainless-steel operating table (so big it dwarfs everyone in the box) could stand in the middle, and its legs push through the bottom so it wobbles, like a crippled dog, instead of standing up right. On the outside of the box, I'll glue all the wishbones I've been saving.

Except for a few barks and a lot of whining from the kennel, the vet's office is eventually quiet. It's 6:10 p.m. and everyone has gone, except for the fidgety receptionist in her raincoat, who stands in the doorway of the well-lit lab, keeping an eye on me.

"Hello?" Mom finally calls from the other room. "Anyone here?" She blushes when she finds us. "I'm so sorry! I was painting and . . . I thought Lily was with our neighbors all this time . . . You put down their poodle this afternoon?"

She stops to look at me. I know: Fifi is dead.

"Thank you for watching my daughter." Mom puts her hand on my shoulder and heads me toward the door, but the bottoms of my shoes are sticky with sacred stuff and it's hard to lift my feet.

One.

Two.

"Lily?" Mom blushes again. "Can we move a little faster?"

Three times.

The receptionist jiggles her keys. "It's my wedding anniversary. We have reservations. He's waiting for me."

"Of course, of course." Mom tightens her grip on my arm. "Lily's been sick this week."

"Well, *something* is certainly wrong," the woman says, switching off the light. "The front door's locked, just give it a firm pull when you leave."

Lauren's in the backseat of the car, doing her homework.

When Mom stops at the store to get more wine, Lauren asks, "What'd you do this time?" and I show her my fist.

When Johnny Mathis sings "Chances Are" on the radio, Lauren says, "He's got a girly voice," so I slug her as hard as I can.

When I get home I'm sent to my room, but I don't mind. I like my room. I'm in there all the time.

Soon after we've returned home, Frieda calls.

Mom picks up. "Yes, Lily's better . . . Yes, she loves the card you sent . . . What else? Well, you already know that the three of us had a little slumber party outside, right? . . . No, it was a lovely night." Mom lights a cigarette. "A little fresh air never hurt . . . No, no, I don't believe that moonlight . . ." She isn't going to mention the vet's. "No, Paul's still at the office . . . Yes, of course I'll tell him you . . . Listen, I need to go, Frieda." Mom said too much. Now Frieda will call Dad saying she picked a fight.

While our family watches TV that night, I paint a shoe box in pink and white stripes, and glue a small toothpick Eiffel Tower to the top of it.

In the morning I paint white cotton balls black (to look like Fifi) then glue the puffy poodles inside and outside the box and give it to Judy, telling her she can put Fifi's stuff in it if she wants, but she doesn't and hands it back. I "embarrassed her" at the vet's office, she says, but "I guess you can come in. For a while."

"It's okay if we're not friends anymore," I say, wiping each one of my shoes on her welcome mat three times. "I mean, you're older and . . ." Judy walks away. "Maybe you'll want the box later?"

She leaves the door open, and after thirty seconds I follow her in.

We eat sandwiches and drink Coke, and sit together at the coffee table, where we take off our shoes and stick our toes in the thick loopy rug underneath it, just like we used to when Judy still liked me. Not just sometimes, like now, but almost all the time. She sighs when she takes down two old coloring books and the same old crayon box.

"We don't have to color," I say, but Judy answers, "Yes we do. Connie said to be nice to you." I wish I'd never made her a shoe box. "It's fine, Lily. Just don't tell Karla I'm coloring, okay?"

Yes. No. Maybe.

I trace the outline of my circus bear, and then steadily, carefully fill it in with even swipes of burnt sienna. I haven't colored in a long time and I miss the smell of the warm waxy crayons in my sweaty hand.

"Too red," she says, poking my page with her periwinkle crayon.

"Some bears are red."

"Not like that." She pauses. "You're still weird, aren't you?"

"No."

"Aren't you taking pills and seeing a shrink?"

"I *am* taking pills. And I still go to Dr. Giraffe—I mean—Dr. Madsen—sometimes."

"Dr. *Giraffe*? Jesus, Lily, you talk like a baby. I think you should leave."

"Why?"

"Just go home, Lily."

"Go to hell," I say, swallowing my tears. I put my head down and color, adding another layer of burnt sienna to my circus bear.

Suddenly Judy jumps to her feet. "Jesus, Lily, didn't you hear? Somebody poisoned her! The vet said somebody poisoned Fifi."

"Poisoned?"

"He wondered if we'd seen a stranger in the neighborhood, or if we knew someone who might be cruel to animals."

Who would want to hurt Fifi?

The neighborhood boys like the big dogs more—Kaiser, Winston, Caesar, and Uncle Miltie—but they'd never hurt Rusty's dog. And when we were younger and played King and Queen, Fifi was the royal lap dog. She liked to play School too, where she was a nervous but attentive student.

Maybe Judy's dad killed Fifi; he never liked her. Or the Savage Boy— maybe the Savage Boy killed Mrs. Wiggins. And it wasn't me. *Or* cancer.

"My stepdad said that mentally disturbed people sometimes torture and kill small animals."

"So you think the Savage Boy—"

"I'm not talking about *him*," Judy says. "*You're* seeing a shrink, remember? You even said you killed Mrs. Wiggins. Remember?"

"You think I . . . You think I would hurt Fifi?" My heart aches. She thinks I'd kill her dog?

Jesus stands in the kitchen, making a cuckoo sign next to His ear.

"I didn't say you *meant* to." Judy's eyes dart all around nervously. "I don't know, it's just, you jumped in the car when you weren't invited and you made the shoe box for me and I thought . . ."

I hate the stupid pink-and-white–striped shoe box with the Eiffel Tower and cotton-ball poodles. I throw it in the fireplace.

And run out.

My best friend thinks I killed her dog.

Heading back home, I walk five steps ahead of Jesus; I know He's there because I hear His bare feet slapping the sidewalk behind me.

For a while I kept a chart of days Jesus wore His sandals and days He didn't, but He borrowed it to "show someone," and lost it.

Two days later, a box of tall neatly labeled jars appears on our welcome mat.

"Connie's sharing her bounty again," Dad says, the morning paper tucked under his arm. He places the box on the kitchen counter. "For a city girl, she sure loves to can."

"When I grow up, I'm never going to can," Lauren says. "I'm going to be rich and live in the city and have maids. They can can stuff if they want to." She balances a book on her head while eating the three-minute egg and lightly buttered rye toast she asked Mom to make her every morning that week.

"I thought you wanted to be a teacher. Like Miss Marcus," I say.

"Lily," Mom warns. "How about some canned fruit? Anybody?"

Dad holds up a tall golden jar. "Only wish Connie canned meat too. I used to love Frieda's stew meat."

"Meat in a jar?" Lauren makes a sour face.

"Aren't they beautiful?" Mom smiles, placing the jars of pears, tomatoes, and corn in the kitchen window. "Look at the color!"

I watch her, wondering if she'll mention last year's dirt-filled jars from Mrs. Marks, on the shelf above the new ones. Two planted with doll parts. An old Barbie head makes a strange bulb, peeking through the dirt at Mom when she puts on her reading glasses for a closer look. A doll leg sprouts from the top of another. But the jar I'm keeping an eye on is the one planted with Mrs. Wiggins's hair.

Mr. Alsup once said, "The totality of life can be found in a single cell." I guess, if that means all life, then the nucleus of Mrs. Wiggins is in that jar, and if she can be brought back to life, then everything bad that's happened since Peace Lake could change. Aunt Jamie would still be alive, Mom and Dad would stop fighting, and I wouldn't be growing up half-kid, half-dog, all weirdo. It's a long shot, but hey.

Mom catches me looking at her. "I see them," she says. Behind her, the morning sun splashes the shelves. The fleshy pear halves are lit through like one of the jars of murdered "remains" found in the well-lit basement refrigerator shown in Sherman's *Police Gazette*.

"We all see your silly jars," Lauren says. "You're the Queen of Dumb Jars."

"That's enough, girls," Dad mumbles.

"Wait till I tell Simone about your stupid shelf."

"The famous high-fashion model Simone?" Dad laughs. "Isn't she engaged to the Prince of Persia?"

Lauren grumps.

"Lily's shelf is a unique expression of her imagination," Mom says, refilling her coffee cup. "She's an artist."

"It's still stupid," Lauren says, stomping off.

She's in the other room when Mom asks, "Anyone remember their dreams last night?" Her last dream was about a closet of long yellow aprons, and supportive footwear with a blue plastic shoetree nested in each one.

"Dream, Paul?"

"Not this morning, hon." Dad always says that. Mom likes to analyze dreams but Dad says they are just our minds relaxing at the end of the day, and there's no way to interpret them. After a moment he puts down his paper. "Je-sus," he moans, "this goddamn war."

"Don't read about it," Mom says, but he does read about it, swearing under his breath, and soon she's reading out loud over his shoulder. "*PFC Albert Sanchez, 19 years old, Santa Fe, New Mexico . . . PFC Theodore 'Teddy' Jackson, 21 years old. Gainesville, Florida . . .* My God, Paul they're babies!"

"I know," Dad says.

"They're sending them home in pieces! Did I tell you that Mavis's son came back from Vietnam with a human ear? An ear, Paul! He cut it off a dead Vietcong himself. He said GIs take them as souvenirs. Can you believe it? They hang them off their belts, like scalps or something. It's like our soldiers are possessed!" She stomps to the kitchen sink and drinks a tall glass of water. "Babies! They're just babies!"

"Kit?" Dad says, nodding at me.

Ruben. Two-yr.-old Chihuahua.

Pokie. 5-yr.-old Collie.

Frank. 7-yr.-old Lab mix.

Princess Grace. 8-yr.-old St. Bernard.

Mom ignores him. "Murderers," she says. "Butchers."

"They're only boys, Kit. Don't judge them too harshly. Boys living a nightmare."

Slugs and snails and puppy dogs tails, that's what little boys are made of.

"And I'm a mother. A concerned citizen who wants to bring them home."

"Let's not talk about the war, Kit. Lily doesn't need to hear it, and you and I both have better things to do with our time than worry about what our government is or isn't doing. Your work, for one thing, and . . ." Dad looks at me. "And what are you doing today, Hi-Lily, Hi-Lo?"

Hi-Lily, Hi-Lily, Hi-Lo.

The Savage Boy's face pops up in my cereal bowl. I mash him into the soggy lagoon with the back of my spoon, but he doesn't stay down.

Mom lights a cigarette. "Don't be condescending, Paul. We can talk about Vietnam in front of Lily. She's older now, and she's a thoughtful, compassionate person."

"Come on, Kit."

"You started it, Paul! I wasn't going to read the paper today. Besides, why shouldn't every breakfast table across America be discussing Vietnam? How do we stop this madness if we don't even talk about it with our kids? For God's sake, they're the ones who'll fight the wars. Not us!"

"Kit . . . did you take your pill this morning?"

On the shelf over the sink behind her are jars of canned ears. Scalps. Fetuses. Dog hearts laced with worms. There are pieces of bodies everywhere: on shelves in a veterinarian's office, over kitchen sinks, in refrigerator basements, and hanging from soldiers' belts.

Judy said the average American family has 2.3 children. Is our .3 in Mom's belly . . . or one of the new jars?

"Kit, honey . . ."

But Mom's already been to the family room and back, returning with a small stack of *Life* magazines; she doesn't want to listen to him. When she throws the magazines on the kitchen table, a tidal wave hits my cereal bowl.

Dog-eared, coffee-stained, and smelling of cigarettes, some of the pages are loose and slide out.

"Have you looked at Larry Burrows's photographs lately?" Mom asks. "Our government is making our children into murderers, Paul. Our tax dollars are paying for them to be trained to kill people. It's lunacy! It's right to be angry about this war, Paul. I won't apologize."

"Kit!" Dad barks, and Mom marches across the kitchen to the spice cupboard where she takes down her prescription bottle and shakes a pill into her hand. On the shelf above the kitchen sink, the jar with the doll leg sticking out of the top is sprouting green leaves.

I think of Mrs. Wiggins and Jamie. I think about Gramma Frieda's *Get well* card. *I will never leave you nor forsake you. Hebrews 13:5.*

Lauren appears in the doorway. "Are you guys arguing again?" she asks with disgust.

"Just the free exchange of ideas," Mom says, filling a glass with tap water. "While it's still America in this house."

Dad quickly folds his newspaper and grabs his suit jacket off the back of the chair. He's leaving, but he didn't even finish his breakfast.

"It *is* America in this house, isn't it, Paul?"

"Jesus Christ," Dad says, heading out the front door.

Beyond the driveway . . . two strange dogs, on jingling leashes, walk down Aiken Street.

Male dogs . . . (sniff), definitely male dogs (sniff) . . . tall dogs (sniff-sniff); each stream of hot, sour-smelling piddle is aimed halfway up our mailbox post . . . hairy dogs (other smells cling to their coats).

Other dogs bark too.

Alvin, the Pomeranian at the corner, barks his fool head off.

Edith, the dachshund, tries to bark but her voice box has been removed, and she coughs instead.

My throat itches. Saliva floods my mouth. Dogs should, at least, be able to bark, shouldn't they? They give up their freedom to live in human houses, to warn their owners when someone's breaking in, to protect babies and toddlers who pull their tails. It's not fair.

Strange dogs are in the neighborhood. Dogs that don't belong here.

Strange people too.

There are lots of strangers in Vietnam. I bet dogs bark all the time over there.

Fifi didn't bark much. Maybe she was used to people acting strangely: walking around in the dark, going in and out of rooms they weren't supposed to.

It's Sunday and my family watches *Mutual of Omaha's Wild Kingdom* on TV. Lauren leans against Mom who curls up to Dad on the couch.

I sit on the floor away from all of them, hugging my knees.

We each sit this way until animals are run down by predators or start mating, then Dad goes to the kitchen for a beer, Mom giggles, and Lauren covers her eyes but peeks through her fingers.

I just watch, pretending it isn't about me. Pretending I'm not growing a tail or biting my tongue so I don't bark when I hear a siren or a dog howl. Pretending that, if I don't learn to adapt like we learned in science, I won't survive.

I reach for the bucket of cold chicken and give it a shake. The bones knock against the cardboard walls and Mom asks, "Still hungry, sweetheart? There's ambrosia for dessert. Can you wait another half hour?"

I love ambrosia.

Maybe my parents should have left me to die. Some mother animals recognize a weak or diseased pup and leave it alone in the woods to starve to death so it doesn't infect the group or make the family vulnerable to predators. Jim Fowler, Marlon Perkins's assistant, just said so.

I hold my breath until I'm as smooth and cold as the inside of one of Connie's jars.

CHAPTER 16

SLEEPING IN WHAT IS SMALL

Over Dad's punching bag in the garage are two shelves, dusty and stained with the rings of oil and paint cans. They hold his old college textbooks.

I like the small green illustrated book best. *German I*, the binding reads. Inside, the lettering is ornate—dark and pointed like the tiny plastic swords in Mom's cocktails.

I don't recognize anything except for Dad's penmanship in the book margins and how he made the tall loops of his lowercase *h*s, *t*s, and *l*s into ship sails, and traced over and over them. Maybe he was bored. Maybe he wished he was sailing, or had taken a different language.

Like French. Dad says French women are sexy. "Ooo la la," he jokes.

"The illustrations are woodcuts," Mom explains. I love it when she talks art to me. "Pastoral scenes. Spa towns. The Bürgermeister and his Frau." She flips the pages, occasionally leaning in for a closer look. "Too coarse for my taste," she says.

Mom says Hitler went to art school. I imagine him sitting beside her in class. He can't take his eyes off her boobs.

It's spooky the way the picture oozes into the wood grain and small black clots of ink rush in. I stare for a long time at a tiny door on a tiny cottage until it creaks open, inviting me inside. I look away but the illustration goes with me, imprinting a faint version of itself on the garage wall. The doughy face of the German mayor on the next page scowls from Dad's leather punching bag.

Dad studied poetry too. Mom tells me to look on his shelf for a book by some guy with a funny name, Rain-something; Maria's his middle name. When I find *The Book of Hours*, and take it down, it falls open to "I Find You, Lord, in All Things and in All." The first stanza reads:

I find you, Lord, in all Things and in all
my fellow creatures, pulsing with your life;
as a tiny seed you sleep in what is small
and in the vast you vastly yield yourself.

Dad drew a star beside: "as a tiny seed you sleep in what is small."

"Things" is capitalized, which makes it important. Frieda says, "God is in the details." If God is "in all Things . . . in tiny seeds . . . sleeping in what is small," then He's in tears and buttons too, in mouse doors, shoebox crypts, and beeswax cups.

He's in me too, as long as I stay small.

The poem sounds like a prayer, and I memorize it.

Dad doesn't remember it when I recite it to him later. "Rilke, you say? Huh."

I flick the sports page with my index finger, until he suddenly tears it down the crease, and smiles at me with the silly dumpling face of the Bavarian wife in lesson *drei*.

"Tease all you want, Diamond Lil. Nothing can ruin my mood tonight. Your mother and I have wonderful news!"

"Are we going to Paris?"

Lauren rolls her eyes.

"No, no," he laughs. "You'll see. After dinner." He slaps Lauren's leg affectionately. It makes a funny flesh sound and leaves a pink print between her shorts and knee. I watch it fade and wonder how long a fingerprint lasts on dead skin. Gramma Frieda said the Nazis kept records—"lots and lots of gruesome records." Rainer Maria Rilke was German.

When the dinner plates are cleared, Mom brings out a tray of ice cream and cookies. "We have an announcement to make." She winks at Dad. "We're pregnant. We're going to have a baby!"

Again? I thought they were done getting pregnant. I thought it was "hard on Mom."

"Groovy!" Lauren says. Doesn't she remember Mom's miscarriages?

What if Mom loses this baby too? What if it tears her up inside, or makes her sick? "But—"

"But nothing, Lily," Dad says, wrinkling his eyebrows. "Everything's fine. We didn't want to announce it until the doctor saw Kit and gave us his blessing."

I don't like it. What's wrong with my parents, anyway? Haven't they heard of birth control?

When Judy took the same health class I'm taking, she called one night and sang the dirty version of "My Bonnie Lies over the Ocean," laughing at the lines, "*My father lies over my mother, and that's the beginning of me.*" I hung up right away.

"We think three children is perfect," Dad says, kissing Mom's hand tenderly.

Why? Do they want another child because something's wrong with me? If the normal American family has 2.3 kids (and if I'm not normal), then Lauren is one kid, the baby is another, and I'm the .3, right? I stare at the tablecloth, tracing the lacy pattern.

"Lily, aren't you excited about having a little brother or sister?" Mom asks.

"Which one is it?" asks Lauren.

Good. If she's so happy about the baby, she can change its diaper.

"There's no way to know, we'll have to wait and see," Dad says.

"Duuhhh!" I shout.

"Lily! What's wrong with you tonight?" Mom scolds. "I'd hoped you'd be excited about the baby." Is she crying? "You can leave the table, Lily. No TV tonight, either."

I blush and stand up. "Good!" I yell. My chair falls to the floor with a bang. My whole body's mad.

An hour later, the TV chatters and in the kitchen, Jiffy Pop slides back and forth across the burner. I listen as fewer and fewer kernels rattle in the pan, and the aluminum cloud blows up with hot popcorn, reminding me of the atomic cloud they detonated in the Pacific Ocean. I saw a picture of it in *Life*. Mom says that kind of stuff gives me bad dreams, but I have bad dreams anyway.

I love the smell of popcorn.

"It's done!" Lauren cries. "Can I open it?"

Let the brat open it. Who cares?

Across the street, the blue glow of Mrs. Merton's TV silhouettes the lightning speed of her knitting needles. Mr. Garcia drives by. When the

Garcias had their twelfth child, another boy, Frieda said, "Catholics are taking over Washington, DC, and our neighborhood." I like the Garcias.

Mom knocks at my door. "Why don't you join us?" she asks. "I feel bad. I wish you'd . . . I know you're worried about me."

"That's okay," I say.

"But you spend so much time in your room already. Come and have popcorn with us, sweetheart."

I pick up my book—hers actually—it came in the mail today from the Book-of-the-Month Club. "I started *Travels with Charley*. I like it."

"Good. So you want to stay in your room?"

I nod.

"We love you, you know." *We* means Mom and the fetus now.

Why do starving kids get big bellies? There's nothing in there, is there? We made big round beads from baker's clay at school last week. Most of the girls painted the beads and made necklaces for their moms, but I made giant abacus beads.

Suddenly she's sitting beside me on the bed. "You'll always be my firstborn," she says, kissing the top of my head. "You're excited about the baby though, aren't you?"

I nod and keep my mouth shut, posting my smile at its door like a prison guard.

The weather is nice when, three months later, Lauren, Rusty, and I walk home together, talking about the construction work at Rusty's: their family's new swimming pool and bomb shelter. The work won't be done for months, but when it is there will be a neighborhood party to celebrate, complete with a weenie roast and swimming. Everyone's invited.

We'll be back from Lake Tahoe by then.

Dad's car is in the driveway. It's 4:10.

My stomach cramps again. It's done it all day long. I even thought I peed my pants once.

As Lauren and Rusty raid the fridge, I hang behind them, sniffing the air. Something's not right. The room smells of turpentine and hot bitter coffee. Next to Mom's easel is an uncovered paper plate with dried, untouched dollops of oil paint; her brushes sit in a jar of solvent. She never leaves them wet for very long. Where is she?

Out the kitchen window, the garbage can lid is crooked—a broken canvas props it open. The house is quiet; too quiet. No TV or radio. No stereo. Even the phone is off the hook.

Did Mom and Dad go for a walk?

Something's wrong.

"Mom?" I've got to pee. I need to use the bathroom, but what if she's in one and Dad's in the other?

Down the hall, their bedroom door opens and Dad tiptoes toward us. He presses his finger to his lips. All of us stare at him, even Rusty who stops stuffing his mouth. "I need you to go home now, Rust. Something's come up. We need a little family time."

Rusty grabs a soda and stops at the back door. "See you later," he says to no one in particular. He looks sad. He wants to be our brother, Lauren says.

She sucks on a strand of hair while Dad leads us into the living room, motioning us to sit on the davenport usually reserved for company. He squats in front of us, as if we were still little girls, and clears his throat. There are wet circles under the arms of his work shirt. "Girls . . . your mother's been sick this afternoon. She lost the baby."

"But the doctor said not to worry this time. He said things would be fine."

"Is Mom okay?" Lauren asks. Her bottom lip quivers.

I grab my belly and dash down the hall to Mom. I can comfort her. I can say I'm sorry, I can tell her that I'm excited about the baby, no matter what. Lauren and I need a brother or sister. Really. *Three is the perfect number, you said so yourself.*

I stand for a minute in the threshold of their dark bedroom and stare until Mom comes into view. She lies on a towel on the top of the bed. She sees me but says nothing; she says nothing when Lauren walks in too. Dad opens their closet and takes down her suitcase.

"Where are you going?" Lauren asks, hurrying to Mom's side.

"I'm taking her to the hospital, just to be safe," Dad explains. "She'll be fine, girls. Don't worry."

"I'm fine," Mom echoes, only she looks like crap.

Fine, fine, everybody's fine.

Even when they don't mean it. Everything is fine.

Gravity yanks my guts anyway, and a thick liquid, like warm candle wax, moves inside me. I know what it is now: I'm starting my period. I hurry into my parents' bathroom and lock the door.

"Lily!" Mom cries. "Paul, stop her!"

Stop me? Why?

"I'm sorry. I'll be out in a minute," I cry, trying to sound as casual as the other girls who have their periods.

Jesus is in there, standing next to the toilet. He draws a zipper across His mouth, and locking the door, I do the same. "Turn around," I whisper. "I have to pee." But He shakes his head.

"Lily!" Dad says, knocking hard and fast on the bathroom door.

They don't understand. I've started my period and I need to use the bathroom, this bathroom, *now*, because it's close to Mom, and because, because . . . Why is Jesus in the bathroom anyway?

"I can't come out right now."

"Are you sick?"

"I don't know."

"Well, I choose no, Lily. No, you're not sick. So get out here right now." Dad's angry. His voice moves away from the door, saying something soothing to Lauren.

"Lily!" he says again. "Use the other bathroom! Pull up your pants and run. We won't look. Promise."

What's the big deal? I'll be out in a minute.

Jesus points at the toilet, and waves me over.

Something horrible is in there, something I'm afraid to look at but want to see, something that's broken Mom's heart, so I turn away and run my hands through hand-washed nylons draped over the shower rod, instead. While Dad knocks on the door, I also check his suit jacket, thrown on the bathroom floor, for lipstick-stained Kleenex or phone numbers written on matchbook covers. Dad's gone a lot. "He might have another family across town," Judy said once. "Or go to a prostitute. Married men do."

But there's nothing in his pockets.

There's something in the toilet though, and I inch up on It.

Him.

Frog Boy floating in the pink toilet water—the freak from the circus, the mistake Dad and Jamie talked about. Neither boy nor girl, human nor animal, but something in between, something so different it's nearly perfect—floating in a lumpy, soft red feathery mass. My parents don't want me to see the sad ugly beautiful thing that came from inside Mom and died. But I don't mind.

I don't mind at all.

"Isn't it amazing?" Jesus smiles, scooping it out of the pink water that trickles through His fingers like baptismal water. "Life looks like all kinds of things!" He holds out His hand. "Even dead life."

My insides cramp when I look at it, like it came out of my body instead of Mom's.

I smile at Jesus. He's right. Frog Boy makes everything okay. He's the .3 in our 2.3 kids average American family, not me. I'm a whole person, not a half something.

I'm not like Frog Boy at all.

I finally started my period; I'm growing up. Soon I'll be an adult like everyone else.

I smile when I take Frog Boy from Jesus's hand and place him back in the toilet bowl. Until a few hours ago he lived inside Mom, surrounded by stars. I start to tell him about our family when I feel a gush between my legs.

"Can you turn your back?" I ask Jesus.

When He does, I reach into my panties and touch the wet. It's the same watery pink color as the toilet, and it smears my fingers. I tuck some tissue in my underwear. "It matches," I say, smiling, looking at the fetus in the toilet bowl. "It matches. Look!"

"No thanks," Jesus says. He's examining Frieda's Kleenex doll cozy, its white plastic face and big crocheted skirt. "Strange doll."

I finally open the door.

"You okay?" Mom says, patting the bed beside her. "Sit with me before I go." Lauren sits on the other side, her legs stiff and straight, her face red from crying. "Do you know what that was, Lil?"

Of course. I nod, and glance back at the bathroom.

"Never mind that now," Mom says. Her suitcase stands at the end of the bed, her favorite sweater draped over it. "Your father's taking me in. We'll be home before you go to bed."

Outside, Dad opens and closes his car doors, clearing the backseat for her. He stops to talk to Connie Marks.

"Mrs. Marks will stay with you while we're gone," Mom says.

I've been babysitting us for months, but I don't argue. I know it's selfish to think of myself right now. I know that, but I still need to tell Mom what happened. That I started my period and everything is going to be okay. With or without Frog Boy, things are fine.

Fine, fine, everything is fine.

A "tiny seed" sleeping "in what is small."

I recite:

> I find you, Lord, in all Things and in all
> my fellow creatures, pulsing with your life;
> as a tiny seed you sleep in what is small
> and in the vast you vastly yield yourself.

"Dad's poem," Mom smiles. "Rainer Maria Rilke. You memorized it."

"Mom's sick, " Lauren lectures. "This isn't school."

"It's beautiful, Lily. You did a wonderful job of memorizing and reciting. Thank you, sweetheart." When she puts her hand on her belly, a tear slides down her cheek.

"Mom?" I say quietly. "I started my period."

"Gross," Lauren says.

Mom smiles weakly. "We're having quite a day, aren't we?"

I wish I had something to give her. I wish I'd made her a necklace instead of using the beads for my abacus.

"Do you remember what we talked about before?"

"The Kotex? Yeah. They're in a shoe box in my closet."

"Double gross," Lauren says.

"Good girl. I'm proud of you." Suddenly Mom sits up and turns pale. "Damn it," she says, lifting her shirt. She looks between her legs. "I went through *everything*." Blood pools under her butt, soaking her pedal pushers, the towel, and the new bedspread.

Lauren pulls away.

"Don't worry, girls. It's just Old Mom Nature saying, *Not this time, Kit*." She sniffs back a tear. "Will one of you get me another . . ."

Lauren jumps off the bed and grabs a towel from the bathroom. "Thanks, Lima Bean." Mom tucks the towel under herself. "What a mess," she mumbles. "My poor bedspread!"

"Ready?" Dad asks, appearing in the doorway. He looks at Mom and the blood-soaked towel.

"Sure."

"Connie's here, if you need anything, girls." He walks to Mom's side of the bed. "We need to get going, sweetheart. Anything else?"

Mom's voice is clear and strong when she says, "The bathroom, Paul. Flush the toilet, will you?"

"No!" I cry.

"Lily," Mom says firmly, "look at me. Look at me, Lily. I need your help too. Get me my purse. I want to take it with me to the hospital."

"I'll get it!" Lauren calls, jumping off the bed.

Go ahead. Like Kilroy or the beggar boy on Burnside, like Frog Boy, I'm numb from the waist down.

I bet if you look, there's nothing there.

CHAPTER 17
POOR MARTIN HORNBUCKLE

I can't find Mom.

Her car's here, so she's not at the store. She's not painting or cooking or working in the flower beds. She's not with Dad because he's on a business trip. Mr. Marks is recovering from back surgery so he's home, but she's not with Mrs. Marks because Connie took Rusty and Lauren to the zoo.

If I weren't sick, I'd have gone too.

It's nice and quiet outside. The carpenters have left for the day. The bomb shelter will take another month, but the carpenter who wolf-whistled at Mom told her they only needed ten days to finish the pool. "Come over and sunbathe," he laughed. Mom smiled; men always want to see her body. She bought a new swimsuit for our trip to Lake Tahoe, but she's not showing it to Dad until we get there.

"Mom?"

It's the flu this time. I've been in bed two days and promised her I'd stay down until four o'clock when *The Mike Douglas Show* comes on TV, but I can't stand it another minute. Besides, I need to talk to her about Martin Hornbuckle.

"Mom?"

There's no answer so I sneak into the den and grab the *Life* magazine she doesn't want me to see. Stuck between *Sunset*, *Look*, and *Sports Illustrated*, in the fan of magazines on the coffee table, poor twelve-year-old Martin Hornbuckle stares at me from the cover with his eighty-year-old eyes. The same Martin Hornbuckle with the growing-old disease who's coming to Frieda's church on Sunday. "They call him America's Most Unique Inspirational Speaker," she said. "He's addressing several congregations in Oregon. He's a celebrity. We're lucky to get him."

It's spooky, but I want to go. What does it feel like to be a little kid stuck in a body that's dying of old age? And why's he speaking at churches? Church won't help him. Jesus lets people die all the time.

He taps me on the shoulder. "Lighten up," He says. "Martin needs something to believe in."

"Bullshit," I say. It feels good to say it, almost as good as barking.

"I'll let that slide because you're sick."

I flip through the magazine pretending to ignore Him, but He won't let me. In the Record of the Month advertisement, Jesus stands on a surfboard advertising *Jan & Dean's Golden Hits*. On page sixty-five, He pulls up the collar of a London Fog raincoat; He sits in a café smoking a Kool on page ninety-eight.

"Have I got your attention now?" Jesus smiles. "Take the magazine and go back to bed, Lily. We'll talk about poor Martin Hornbuckle when you're better."

I tuck the magazine under my arm and start out of the room. Then I see my opening. "Wait, I want to talk to you about getting us a bomb shelter."

Jesus puts down the *TV Guide*. "I'm not Santa," He says.

"Hardy har har." I roll my eyes. "Sherman's family has one, and the Marks are building one. Dad says the Cold War is over and he's not worried."

"Neither am I."

"That doesn't count; you're dead already. We stopped doing bomb drills at school years ago, but it could still happen, couldn't it?"

I hold my breath. One, two, three . . .

"You worry too much. One day it's Vietnam; today it's Martin Hornbuckle. You've been sick. Go back to bed."

Should I remind Jesus that there's only enough room in Sherman's bomb shelter for his family? What about the rest of us? Of course, if Sherman's blind sister Eva died before the bomb raid, there'd be room for one more. I'm growing taller every day, but I'm double-jointed and I can fold up like a map—no one would know I'm there. Until there's a big deep earth-rumbling sound and it's too late . . . I'm inside with Sherman's family, and outside the bomb has fallen. It's *The Twilight Zone*, *Outer Limits*, and *Alfred Hitchcock Presents* all rolled into one. Time passes. We wait. Open the lid. And *ta-da!* A new family unit.

"Lily," Jesus says. "Lily!"

"Huh?"

He points at the magazine. "It's called progeria, all right? It's a genetic defect, and rare, very rare. Those kids never live past fifteen."

"Fifteen?" Suddenly I'm cold again and drop the magazine. Jesus picks it up and hands it to me. On the cover, poor Martin Hornbuckle presses his eighty-year-old hands over his ears.

"Bed!" Jesus says, pointing me down the hall. "And stay there until your mom gets home."

Back in my room, I set my snooze alarm for twenty minutes; wherever Mom is, she should be home by then.

The Aging Disease, reads the title. Why Martin Hornbuckle? What terrible rotten thing did he do?

Twelve-year-old Martin Hornbuckle: Family Photo. Under the colored photograph of ancient wrinkled Martin, his mom and dad and pretty teenage sister sit on a flowery couch smiling at the camera. Martin looks strange and stupid like a kid-sized cartoon of Jimmy Durante, come to life. Does he have a boy's voice or a man's voice? Does he have hair on his legs and chest, and a grown-up penis? Is he scared all the time or is everything changing so fast he doesn't have time to be afraid?

Mrs. Hornbuckle's smile sits on her face like a broken dish.

Martin's sister isn't dating. "*People feel sorry for me. I want a boy to like me for myself,*" she says.

The Hornbuckles took Martin out of school in November. In March, they remortgaged their house, sold their boat and second car, and went to Sea World, Knott's Berry Farm, and Disneyland on a long family vacation.

"*Might as well walk my check right to the hospital,*" his hardworking father complains. He holds up a framed photo of an unfamiliar boy in a Little League uniform; the caption reads, *Martin, 10 years old.* "*Still, if I could do more for him, I would.*"

Two local banks opened an account in his name. Edie's Nail Salon held a bake sale. The Cub Scouts honored Martin with a Badge of Courage. Willie Mays sent him an autographed baseball.

On page fifty-nine, in each of the four black-and-white portraits in the column on the right, poor Martin Hornbuckle sits on his bed in the same position. He wears the same baseball cap too, but in each picture his body changes: his face sags more, his nose and ears grow bigger, his eyes are sadder. Using the same time-lapse photography they do on TV to show pea vines grow or dung beetles roll poo up a hill, they document poor Martin Hornbuckle's changes: from being a regular ten-year-old kid, to a balding forty-year-old guy, to a jug-eared sixty-year-old, to a wrinkled eighty-year-old man.

He stoops more in each picture, but never changes where he sits on the bed. They've been taking pictures of him since he got sick, like he's a science experiment or something.

I touch my face, half-expecting to find a big nose and basset hound jowls like his. I glance at my reflection in the mirror where I'm sitting on the bed—exactly like Martin Hornbuckle!

I quickly close the magazine.

Who makes up the magazine titles? *Look*? *Time*? I saw Nazis in Po's *True*, and Martin Hornbuckle in *Life*, like bad stuff is always *True*, and little boys dying of old age is just part of *Life*. They say you can't believe everything you read, so how do I know what is and isn't real?

The snooze alarm goes off and I jump. It's been twenty minutes, and still no Mom.

Outside the screen door, I slip my bare feet into her gardening tennies and head for the empty lot next door where she sometimes likes to sketch. No Mom there either. I stand on a rotting log and look over at the houses across the street.

There's no one. Anywhere. The radio is on the Markses' house. Judy's stepdad must be feeling better.

Connie Marks was almost sick with emotion when she came by two days ago. Mom poured them coffee while I sat in the family room writing a book report.

I tuned in when Mrs. Marks said, "For God's sake, who needs a swimming pool in Portland, Oregon?" Her voice trembled. I'd never heard her swear before. I watched Mom put her arm around the woman.

"Judy always gets her way, always . . . I know it's terrible to say, but . . . but . . ."

Connie glanced at me but kept talking. "I'm sorry, Kit," she said, brushing off her lap. "I'm all wound up. I couldn't sleep last night. I must look terrible."

"Who cares, Connie? It's just us girls."

"But you always look good, Kit. How do you do it? You cook and clean like the rest of us." She picked at something on her pants. "My husband says you're the best-looking woman on the block."

"Your husband needs glasses," Mom said, lighting a cigarette.

Connie blew her nose. "He said we'd put the bomb shelter on the north side of the house so it wouldn't tear up the garden. My poor little plants! But *she* wanted a pool and a cabana. She doesn't even know what a cabana is, just that she read about it in one of her teen magazines."

Judy once told me every movie star has a pool with a cabana.

"Now look at the backyard, it's holes, big . . . ugly . . . holes everywhere! And the men working on it trample everything that's growing— they're completely oblivious. Did I mention he's having a barbecue built? With specially treated bricks? My backyard is becoming an amusement park!" Mrs. Marks stood up and walked to the edge of the patio. "Look at it, Kit!"

Mom did.

"My plants, my trees, everything I've been babying for years . . . just torn up and thrown aside!"

Mom patted her back.

"And the money? We don't have the money, for God's sake! Where the hell's he getting the money?"

"And everyone says women are bad with money," Mom added.

Connie was quiet for a minute. "All I do is love my family and take care of them," she finally said in a hurt voice. "All *they* do is . . . take advantage of me. They never ask for my input. I never know what's going on." She turned to Mom and smiled. "Thank God I still have you, Kit. And Rusty."

"The imp," Mom said. Both women laughed. "Screw the coffee. You want a drink, Connie? I could sure use one."

"No thanks. It's tempting, but I should get back. I need to think about dinner."

"Take a day off, Connie. Corral the kids and go to the zoo, take them ice-skating. Get away."

Connie nodded and kissed Mom on the cheek. After she disappeared down the berm, Mom smoked another cigarette and stared at the Markses' house for a long time. When it was done she sat down in a lawn chair and cried.

She cries a lot since her hysterectomy.

By dinnertime that day, Mom was fine, Connie was planning a day at the zoo, and I had a 102.2 fever.

Standing in the lot next door, Mom's tennies smile up at me. Maybe she's taking a walk; it's a nice day for it.

I'm headed back to bed when I hear a familiar voice from Judy's house. *Mom?*

I stick the magazine under my arm again, stumble over, and slip through the patio screen door into her house. Mr. Marks must have called her for help. I hope he's okay even if he's a jerk. Frieda says it's not our job to judge.

I follow Mom's laugh down the hall to the Markses' master bedroom.

The cool turquoise wall-to-wall carpeting of the bedroom stops abruptly at the door where I line up the toes of Mom's grass-stained sneakers and peer inside. The bathroom door stands partly open and lights the floor at the end of the bed where Mom's bra, blue cotton shirt, and the new flip-flops she bought for Tahoe lie in a heap. The rest of the room is dark. I can't see the throw pillows, scatter rugs, and lampshades in greens and blues that Mom and Mrs. Marks shopped for.

Sunlight, through the blinds, stripes Mom's naked porpoise back, and I think of the tropical oceans I've seen in *National Geographic*, and zebra fish feeding in a bed of coral. When Mom leans forward, her butt tips up and I catch a glimpse of mean Mr. Marks flat on his back underneath her. She wiggles the butt of her grass-stained yellow capris, and makes sucking cooing sounds like the babies she never had.

Mr. Marks moans and Mom sits up again, jerking her right arm up and down in short fast movements.

Dave Brubeck's "Take Five" is on the radio. It's my parents' favorite. Mrs. Chester, our piano teacher, ordered me the sheet music.

"Stop . . . stop . . . stop," Mr. Marks says breathlessly, and Mom climbs off his legs and kneels beside him on the bed. "Jesus Christ," he says, dragging a pillow across his forehead. "You're really something, Kit."

Mom gives her pants a tug up so what Dad calls a "plumber's crack" won't show. The room smells sour and sweet at the same time, like dirty clothes. Mom and Mr. Marks are having sex. This is what sex smells like.

"You have amazing breasts."

"Thank you," she says, standing up. Her voice is flat and bored. I've heard it lots of times; she's thinking of something else: a place she needs to be, something she should be doing.

The blue rug seeps through Mom's tennis shoes, chilling my feet and sticking them to the thin metal strip that separates the hall rug from the Markses' master bedroom. The water is cold and begins to rise, in seconds flooding the shoes, passing my ankle, halfway to my knee. My tail snakes down my pajama leg, headed to the sandy bottom of Peace Lake.

And then the strangest thing: a bark.

It's sharp and loud and angry and fills the room.

It startles me. And Mom and Mr. Marks, who turn to look at me.

I drop the magazine, hear it splash, and run home again.

Back home, I place Mom's shoes where I found them.

The house feels funny, like somebody else is living here, someone I haven't met yet. In the kitchen, I pour Mom's last one-calorie Tab over ice and listen.

"Hello?" I call out, and imagine Martin Hornbuckle sitting on my bed. I take a sip and check the doors.

Things get out if you're not careful, things get in.

Except for the screen door, the house is locked. Mom wants me to be safe.

Her kitchen isn't as clean as Mrs. Marks's. The breadboard is smudged with butter, jam, and toast crumbs, a package of hamburger is defrosting in the sink. There's burnt stuff on the foil under the stove's burners, and the teakettle is dull. Mrs. Marks's kettle shines; you can see yourself in it. I imagine Mom's reflection as she walked through their kitchen on the way to Mr. Marks's bedroom. It's like the fun-house mirrors at Pixie Kitchen: distant at first, then coming closer, her head disappears in the kettle's handle and only her belly shows, her sad round soft belly where babies want to grow but can't. It curves like a clef sign.

At Mom's place at the kitchen table are a cup of cold burnt-smelling coffee, a full ashtray of cigarette butts, and her sketchpad. She doesn't want us to look at her new drawings. She calls them "primitive," and says she'll share something with us when she's ready. Dad says Mom has an "exaggerated sense of privacy."

I stand behind her chair and look out the window. Isn't she coming home?

She'll be mad if she catches me drinking her last Tab and looking through her sketchpad.

When I open it, a tear plops on the page. My tear. It darkens the new redwood gate in the first charcoal sketch she made of the Markses' house. The next sketch is almost the same, except an unfamiliar woman stands at the gate smiling. In the third and last one, the redwood fence between the Markses' house and ours is gone, the way it used to be when Mom didn't drink so much and Judy wasn't always angry. Mom drew the toolshed our dads shared because they could only afford one mower, and the rosebushes Mom and Mrs. Marks both took care of. Now that we can afford our own mower and two TVs, we're moving to a bigger house.

After the trip.

After the swim party.

I stick one of Mom's lipstick-stained cigarette butts in my pocket, dump the ashtray over her sketches, and walk away.

Until right now, I didn't want to move. Now, I want to get as far away from the Marks family as I can. I want a new house and new friends. I want new everything.

At the threshold to my room I don't jump over the ocean onto Scatter Rug Island. I walk right in, wading across the shark-filled water to my bed.

Where I sit on it, just like Martin Hornbuckle, and smile for the camera.

Soon Mom is home. When she checks on me, I pretend to be asleep.

She turns on *The Mike Douglas Show* but I don't join her and, when she knows I'm awake, she doesn't ask me to. I like Mike Douglas; he's nice to people—even loudmouth Don Rickles, who isn't nice to anybody.

When my sister gets back from the zoo, Mom makes BLTs and sends Lauren in with a tray and the *Life* magazine with Martin Hornbuckle on the cover.

Mom's been standing on the other side of my door for a couple of minutes. Inside, I stand on my head on the cubit-sized confession rug I cut from Mrs. Wiggins's towel, making jerky dance moves like in *The King and I*, lecturing myself about hating Mr. Marks. When a white dizzy light fills my head, I think of the boy in *Siddhartha* who struggled to be good, and finally getting over his anger and guilt and judgment grew up to be Buddha. There are photos of three big fat smiling Buddhas on the bulletin board in my world history class—two gold statues in India, one carved into a tree in Thailand.

I've taken to confession lately. It doesn't look or sound very religious but I don't care. I'm not Catholic and I'm tired of talking to Dr. Giraffe. It's my room and I can do whatever I want here. I decide what things mean and what matters.

Jesus chuckles. I hate how He reads my mind. He tried talking to me about what happened with Mom and Judy's dad, but it's none of His business. When He said, "You barked again," I listened. I didn't want to believe Him. It'd been a long time since I did something like that, but I touched my throat and my fingers melted through, and when they touched Mrs. Wiggins's wet fur, I knew He was right.

Mom's nervous when she finally walks in. She folds her arms across her chest, which looks weird when you're upside down like I am.

"I didn't know you could stand on your head," she says, trying to sound casual. "You've been sick. That might not be good for you."

I get up, then sit on the bed and look at her right-side up.

I hate Mr. Marks but I'm only mad at Mom. What she did with him even changes the way my room feels, though I'll adapt. We studied "adaptation" in school. Adapting is about change and survival, and I want to survive. I want to live outside my room someday, so I have to.

Dogs learned to adapt when people were cavemen; that's why there are so many of them. I read that there are more animals and insects than people, which means they're better at adapting and smarter than us. They don't care about money or TV or art; they run or fly, and eat, sleep, have babies, and die. That's enough for them—why isn't it enough for us?

"This is your private place and I shouldn't have listened," Mom says, "but I heard you talking to yourself. You have nothing to confess, Lily. You did nothing wrong."

But I barked and it scared her, I can tell. She'll want to take me to the doctor or maybe she'll insist I take more pills, like some of the crazy kids at school. She'll watch me closely for a while, and feel extra bad, extra guilty, for all the stupid stuff she does.

Everybody does stupid stuff, I want to tell her, but I might bark so I keep my mouth closed.

It won't happen again, I want to say, but what if I growl instead?

A tear rolls down my cheek.

"Ah, sweetheart," Mom says, stepping toward me. Her arms open to hug me but then she remembers what happened. "Shall I call Dr. Giraffe? You could talk to him about the barking and," her voice softens, "what you saw." She pauses. "Or maybe you should talk to Jesus—you go to church after all."

Jesus looks up. He's sitting on my desk blotter taking the batteries in and out of my transistor radio. Lately, He's been showing up with grease on His hands and robe, like He's been working under somebody's car. He can't resist taking my radio apart and putting it back together again. Dad says a good mechanic is always in demand. Maybe Jesus should get a job in a garage.

"Of course, He never did much for me," Mom says. "He sure as hell wasn't around for *my* family."

Jesus's face turns white like He's heard a terrible lie, or a terrible truth, and it shocks Him.

She's nice. It's not that Mom isn't nice. "She doesn't mean it," I say to Jesus.

Mom looks His way, but doesn't see Him. "I guess you're busy," she says to me, then walks to the door.

Suddenly I blurt out, "John 1:9 says, *If we confess our sins, He is faithful and just to forgive us our sins and to cleanse us from all unrighteousness.*" I never know what stupid stuff gets stuck in my head, what poems, TV schedules, or Bible quotations.

I feel myself turn red.

Mom stands at the door, her hand on the knob, smiling sadly. "You're a fount of information, aren't you?"

"I'm sorry."

"No, *I'm* ..." She doesn't finish. "Is confession really good for the soul, Lily? Everyone says it is."

201

"I don't know."

"I don't believe we're born in sin," she says. "Most of us are born in innocence. You're the smartest, most innocent person I know, Lily."

It's not true. There's a ball of mean black tar rolling around inside me, she just doesn't know it. Sometimes when I draw something or write a story, or the cracks in the tiles (between the cafeteria tables where I sit for lunch) are a multiple of nine, it shrinks and you can't even find it with a microscope. But it's still there, maybe stuck to an organ I don't need anymore. They say we don't need our gall bladder. Or is it our spleen?

"Is it important to *you?*" Mom asks. "Confession, I mean?"

I shrug. My confession dance is more complicated now that I'm taller. And a teenager. Everything is. Whatever I do, it's important to stay within the cubit-sized square of Mrs. Wiggins's old towel that I keep under my bed.

A *cubit* is a twenty-inch measurement from the Old Testament. The cubit makes every position I squish my 5'6" into uncomfortable and challenging, but things have to hurt if you want them to work. I learned that from *Siddhartha* and the Bible, from werewolves and vampires and voodoo goddesses and twirling dervishes and snake handlers and people who talk in tongues, making themselves crazy with spells, prayers, and entreaties (*an earnest or humble request*, origin late Middle English, Oxford Dictionary). Thomas More, Joan of Arc, and all kinds of people were tortured in horrible ways, some for years. So hurting myself just a little, maybe even hurting myself a little *more* each time I do a dance or pray or bark, isn't such a bad thing.

"Yes it is," Jesus says.

I thought He'd left.

"I'm counting on you not to go battery-cables on me, Lily."

I don't want to go battery-cables, but I don't want to be told what to do either. "I'll do what I want," I say and, gritting my teeth, make three increasingly threatening hisses.

Jesus moves to the windowsill. "Just hang on a little while longer," He says. "It'll all shake out. I promise."

"Doubt it," I say, tucking the sacred square under the bed.

There's a cubby over my closet.

In the back of it, behind old toys and extra blankets, is hunchbacked, prune-faced Agnes, the creepy apple doll Gramma Frieda had when she was a girl. I hear her walk around up there sometimes, hear her dentures click and her knees crunch like Frieda's.

Martin Hornbuckle is old now; do his knees crunch too?

With one foot on the closet doorknob, and the other on an open dresser drawer, I open the cubby door and peek in. When a tiny figure shuffles toward me, I say, in my bravest voice, "I'm not taking you to the new house," and slam the door shut, hoping it blows Agnes, the apple doll, in her dusty flowered scarf and patched black apron, back into her corner again.

Things will be different at the new house. I'm leaving my imagination behind.

There's a knock at my door so I quickly climb down.

Mom sticks her head in my room. "It's eight o'clock," she says, looking at the floor. "Can I get you anything?"

"No thanks," I say, but she leaves before I can tell her that I love her, that I don't care what happened in Mr. Marks's bedroom, that I won't tell anyone, and most of all, *Please don't be mad at me, Mom. Please.*

As I lie on my bed, the light changes and shadows grow long, then shrink up and disappear. The room becomes the inside of a peach, warm and orange-pink as if Mom dipped a watery paint brush into the color and soaked my shelves, dressing table, and closet door with it. As it fades, it becomes the color of Aunt Cass's scalp and the freckled gums of the dog next door; it spotlights the porcelain faces of my Hansel and Gretel dolls too, and the little jade tree that doesn't grow, but doesn't die either.

Martin Hornbuckle's favorite color is green, the article said.

Connie's kitchen counters are green too, green like stuff that gets old and moldy. Mold like the gangrene that's rotting Mr. Marks's back. I draw his face in my mind and give him an extra-big Jimmy Durante nose, even bigger than Martin's. I make Mr. Marks a scared, unhappy little boy trapped in an old man's body, and draw big black Xs on his eyes.

It doesn't matter what happened in the bedroom. Mr. Marks is old and ugly and mean, and soon he'll probably die.

Even-steven.

Lauren and I are surprised when Mom asks Gramma Frieda to pick us up for church the next morning. The house rule is, if you're sick you don't go anywhere. Period.

"Don't worry about getting dolled up," Mom says, pouring herself another cup of coffee. "Just put on some clean clothes. That'll be fine."

"But Lily and me were going with you to the airport to pick up Dad," Lauren says.

Mom turns to face me. There are dark bags under her eyes; her hair's a mess.

"You've been sick, young lady. You're lucky I'm letting you go anywhere." She's talking to me, but looking past me, over my shoulder. "Frieda wants you girls to hear that poor little boy speak at church, and I said fine. Besides, I need some time with your father."

"But Mom, that little kid is gross," Lauren whines.

I grab her arm and pull her down the hall. I want to see poor Martin Hornbuckle. I want to be a good Christian and Buddhist and Hindu too, and forgive Mr. Marks, but seeing him with Mom yesterday reminded me of the time he kissed me.

I made Jesus sit in the closet when I confessed it to Him, whispering it through the door slats. Just like the confession booth Lauren and I played in during the big spaghetti feed at St. Rita's years ago. We took turns playing sinner and priest. "Bad girl," Father Lauren giggled after I confessed to stealing Colonel Sanders's secret recipe. She made me do twenty-five jumping jacks, which I'd barely started when Sister Marguerite chased us back to the dining hall.

Gramma Frieda says Westmont Presbyterian is full of good Christians. She also says they count on her "to keep things rolling" at church.

"I was gone until dinner three times last week!" she says as she drives us to church that morning.

Dad says Frieda's "high opinion of herself" makes him sick. Mom says Frieda's lonely.

She seems to have a lot of friends though. In the church lobby, several frantic ladies approach her. Pastor Mike's wife is eager for Gramma to organize the next potluck. "Have you seen the charity envelopes?" . . . "What's the name of that Indian orphanage in South Dakota?" . . . "One of the deacons is out sick. Could you help with communion today?"

Gramma declines. "I have my granddaughters," she smiles, giving the hem of my dress a tug. "I just love baptisms," she says to no one in particular when we finally sit down. A tiny white-haired woman seated in front of us turns and smiles in agreement. A young man and woman stand at the altar while Pastor Mike draws a wet sign of the cross on their squirming baby's forehead.

Gramma Frieda looks at Lauren. "You'll have a family of your own like that someday," she whispers as the couple returns to their seats. My sister rolls her eyes.

Earlier in the week, Lauren and I decided we're not having kids; we're not marrying men who want kids either. We might not get married at all.

The congregation breaks for coffee and pie, "until we hear what happened to poor Martin Hornbuckle." He's late.

Gramma Frieda asks me to fetch her sweater. Earlier, her sweater snagged her wedding ring when she pulled it off her arm and tossed it to me. "Hang it up, will you, Lily?" she said, strutting into her admiring crowd before I had time to say, *Do it yourself, old lady.*

Not that I would. At our house, Mom makes us hang up our own clothes. I turned Frieda's sweater right-side out and hung it up for her. The sweater's pink shoulder pads are the same color as the underarm pads she pins to her slip, "so I don't stain my church clothes," she explained. Church is the most important thing in Gramma's life.

The pie is good at Westmont Presbyterian, though Lauren and I usually pass after spending Saturday night at Frieda's house. She fills a cookie jar with peanut butter cookies for us, each one with crisscrossed fork marks on top (I line them up and compare patterns).

After dinner she brings out soft vanilla ice cream, "stirring ice cream" she calls it, and Lauren and I fold in fat ribbons of chocolate syrup—or chunks of fresh banana or canned pineapple—with our long-handled spoons. We add maraschino cherries too, from individual jars with our own names on them. We sit on the end of Frieda's bed and eat ice cream and cookies while she watches *The Lawrence Welk Show.* She especially likes it when Mr. Welk dances with someone from the audience, or Norma Zimmer sings patriotic songs.

Seventeen-year-old Marvin Peters, Westmont Presbyterian's most notorious dropout, takes two servings of peach pie, but wrinkles his nose like Elvis when an elder offers him coffee. Marvin makes a late entrance to service each Sunday, popping the clutch and spitting gravel when he enters the church parking lot in his shiny '58 Chevy. He sits on the hood finishing his cigarette before he comes in, slamming the door behind him, embarrassing his mom and dad.

"Always late, always on the aisle," Gramma tsks.

Marvin leans against the wall, stuffing his face, making fun of poor Martin Hornbuckle. "Freaky little fairy probably croaked. That's why he's late," he laughs.

Dad says Marvin ought to be thankful he's got flat feet and a job in his father's garage, so he doesn't have to go to Vietnam. I think Marvin ought to go to Hollywood—he's cute.

I hear Mrs. Marks laugh and look across the room. Mr. and Mrs. Marks each cradle a cup and saucer while Pastor Mike tells them "The World's Biggest Afro" story. He tells it a lot; I recognize his hand gestures. I glare at Mr. Marks, until he looks my way and smiles. When he mumbles something to Connie, she waves.

I look away. I don't remember much about the Afro story except that it wasn't very funny and more unkind than Christian. When Mr. Marks smiles at me, he's being unkind too.

Ten minutes later we're all back in our pews.

Pastor Mike stands at the podium, ready to speak. He nods to Mrs. Chester, the church organist, to stop playing when the church doors fly open with a bang.

It isn't Marvin Peters this time.

"Lily?"

My heart jumps in my throat. *Mom?*

Her voice is high-pitched and shaky. It comes from behind us, from the back of the church, from the aisle where she stands in the same blue cotton shirt and grass-stained capris she wore yesterday; barefoot too, like Daisy Mae, Dad's favorite cartoon "gal" from *Li'l Abner.*

Marvin whistles.

The room is stunned quiet. Everyone turns in my mother's direction, even Mrs. Chester, whose fingers hang over the organ keys like bird talons.

"Lily?" Mom calls again.

"Coming," I mumble.

But when I lean forward to stand up and inch my way down the pew toward her, Frieda grabs my arm and pulls me down. "We're in church, not your backyard," she says without turning around. Her voice is stern. "Sit down. Show some respect."

"But it's Mom!" I say. Doesn't Gramma recognize her voice? Across the aisle, Mr. Marks looks straight ahead too.

"Mom?" Lauren cries.

"I said to ignore her," Frieda says. "You can talk to her later." Her cheeks are red. Mom's embarrassed her.

When I don't sit down, Gramma gives my arm another yank. I jerk away. "Sit *down*," she repeats, talking through her teeth.

"I'm sorry, Lily!" Mom calls again. Her head wobbles nervously as she looks for my face in the congregation. When she sees me holding up my hand, she hurries to our pew. "I couldn't wait until after the service," she says quietly. "I'm sorry but it has to be said now. I don't want another awkward minute between us. I'll confess, I'll do whatever you want me to, Lily."

"Lily?" Frieda says.

"Please forgive me, sweetheart."

"You're drunk," Gramma says loudly. "You smell like alcohol." She looks around, explaining Mom's behavior to everyone.

Lauren stands up beside me and slips her hand through mine. "It's not alcohol, it's turpentine. She's an artist."

"I'm sorry, my darling perfect daughters. I'll be a better person from now on, I promise."

"Oh, for God's sake, Kit," Gramma moans, "must you always make a scene?"

I hate Gramma. Even if it were true and Mom did always make a scene—which she doesn't—so what? It's Mom, isn't it?

Mrs. Chester, the church organist and our piano teacher, hits a chord and everyone looks toward the lectern.

"Mrs. Asher?" Pastor Mike smiles. "Would you like to take a seat and join us? You're always welcome in the Lord's House."

Gramma umphs.

Mom shakes her head and looks back at me. "I love you like crazy," she says, tears rolling down her cheeks. *I love you like crazy* is Mom's supreme compliment. "Crazy's when you got to do it, no matter what," she explained once.

Mom loves me that much; I can't stop smiling. Now everyone will know that—even if I grow scales or a kidney on the outside of my body— she stopped a church service once and told me so in front of the whole stupid congregation.

"We love you like crazy too!" Lauren cries, and the two of us smile and wave like Rose Festival princesses. Our waves are big and wide too, like we're wearing ball gowns and tiaras and sitting in the back of a pink Cadillac convertible with marching bands on either side of us.

"See you at home," I call out.

"See ya," Lauren says, but Mom is already gone.

And we stand side by side. In front of everyone.

During the next hymn, old Daisy Pedigrew touches Gramma's shoulder. "Kit will be fine, Frieda," she says loudly, struggling to be heard above the singing. "It's just losing the babies, Paul's gambling, Lily's problem—"

Gramma's been gossiping. "Shhh!" she spits.

We should have gone home with Mom.

When Pastor Mike finally announces that poor Martin Hornbuckle had to be rushed to the hospital, Frieda stands up and hurries out of the chapel. Lauren and I look at each other in surprise and follow, passing cute half-asleep Marvin Peters who is sitting on the aisle just like Frieda predicted.

In the foyer, she takes a right down the hall toward the women's room, but I throw open the front doors of the church and let them bang against the stops, pretending I'm as brave and beautiful as Mom.

Lauren walks behind me to Frieda's car. We look for our mother's car but don't see it.

"Why did she come to church like that?" Lauren asks as we climb into the backseat of Frieda's old four-door Chrysler.

"I don't know," I lie.

Leaning against the baby-blue vinyl, I press my hands against the thick curved glass of the sun-warmed back window. Overhead, the sky pitches and rolls and Jesus cruises by in a bright red Chris-Craft. His disciples wave their beers at me, while Jesus sings a verse of "99 Bottles of Beer."

My old Sunday school friend, Constantine, who used to be Catholic, says nuns marry Jesus. If you want to be a nun, you wear a white dress, a wedding ring, and a bridal veil, and you lie on your stomach on the ground in front of your family and say a bunch of stuff in Latin and you're married to Jesus forever.

If I married Jesus, I'd never be a writer or an artist or move to France or Greece or Tibet like I want to someday. I'd never open the door to the fancy bathroom of my honeymoon suite and, wearing a low-cut lace negligee, greet my movie-star husband who would hand me a glass of champagne and tell me I'm as pretty as my mother. I'd never do a lot of things.

Dad says it doesn't matter what you look like.

Mom says, "Marriage is work."

Lauren says I was "making goo-goo eyes at Marvin Peters," but she's younger than me so what does she know about goo-goo eyes?

Frieda finally gets in the car. "Anyone for foot-long maple bars?" she asks, starting the engine.

"Me!" Lauren answers. Did she forget how mean Frieda was to Mom? Lauren looks at me and says quietly, "I'm glad we didn't have to listen to poor Martin Hornbuckle. He creeps me out."

I rub my arm where Frieda grabbed it, and for a minute I feel sorry for her. Her friends at Wednesday-night Bible study will ask what was wrong with Kit. And why she left before the closing doxology—nobody leaves before the doxology.

He told me to stay in bed until she got home.

"Maple bars, Lily?" Gramma asks.

I promise to stay in the car while Frieda and Lauren go into the bakery, but I duck into the record shop next door instead.

Ivy's Bakery and Don's Disks share a brick wall. Inside the incense-perfumed record shop, the bricks are painted with brightly colored flowers, peace signs, and words like *Psychedelic*, *Far Out*, and *Viva Che*. Teenagers and longhaired college kids stand over record bins, studying album jackets.

Usually Little Richard look-alike Crazy Ricky is working the cash register. Mom said he's black, gypsy, and Mexican. I like his greasy pompadour, long fingers, and pencil-thin mustache.

No Crazy Ricky today, but Dave Brubeck's "Take Five" is on the turntable.

The turquoise wall-to-wall of Mr. Marks's bedroom soaks my shoes. I kick them off and walk around.

"Shit, Dennis," a chubby clerk says to a guy in wire-rimmed glasses, "what's with the old-fart music? Gramps left ten minutes ago." He jerks the record off the turntable and jams it into its album sleeve. "Don's Disks is rock 'n' roll, man!"

When he puts a Rolling Stones record on, a white boy, with an Afro half the size of the one in Pastor Mike's story, turns and smiles.

The bossy clerk catches my eye. "These yours?" he asks, holding up my shoes.

Back in Frieda's car, I stick the same Rolling Stones album under her nose.

Know-it-all Lauren shakes her head. "You're supposed to be saving your allowance for Lake Tahoe."

I stick out my tongue.

"What is that?" Frieda asks.

"It's the Rolling Stones."

"That's what it's called?"

While Gramma putt-putts through the parking lot, I hum "Let's Spend the Night Together."

Billy Garcia gave me my first French kiss when I was twelve. It was weird, but okay, and we gagged and spit and laughed, and I felt that tickle thing then—the same thing I feel when I push the Rolling Stones record under Frieda's nose, or look at Marvin Peters, or dream that I'm as beautiful as Mom and everyone wants me, even the Savage Boy, even mean ugly rotting-back Mr. Marks.

Let's spend the night together, now I need you more than ever.

"You're going to go blind staring at the sun like that," my sister says from the front seat.

"Groovy," I say, and blow her a kiss with my big Mick Jagger lips.

Mom's ecstatic when, later that week, the Lake Tahoe motel confirmation slip finally arrives in the mail. And the two adult tickets for the Bob Newhart–Vicky Carr show. She calls Dad at work and squeals into the phone.

Copycat Lauren stands beside her, jumping up and down with excitement.

Later in the afternoon, Mom slips an invitation, addressed to our entire family, under my door. *Come to our first annual pool party!* it reads. *Steaks and salad provided. Check out the bomb shelter—in progress!*

She taps shyly on the door. "Lily?"

"I see it," I say from the other side.

"It's the last time we'll see most of the neighbors before the trip. We're moving to the big house as soon as we get back."

"I know." I want to see the bomb shelter. "But Judy and I aren't friends anymore. And I don't want to see Mr.—"

Mom opens my door. "We won't stay long, promise. It'll be weird for me too, but I'll be braver if you're there." She looks different. When she cried after dinner last night, Dad reminded me that she'd been through a lot. "She's changed," he said, "but she'll be fine. We'll all be fine."

Dad looks different too.

Across the hall, their bedroom door stands open. Mom's been cleaning her closet; empty shoe boxes clutter their bed.

"May I have a couple?" I ask.

Inside one shoe box is some tissue paper with zebra stripes, just like the stripes on Mom's naked back.

I glue the tissue paper on its inside walls, place Mom's lipstick-stained cigarette butt inside it, and glue the box shut. I wrap it in rubber bands and Dad's sports page, and stick it in the deep cubbyhole over my bedroom closet. Where Agnes, the apple doll, can't get in it, no matter how hard she tries.

CHAPTER 18

THE SHARK CURTAIN

Lauren and I have been in the Tahoe pool for hours when a busload of square dancers unload in the motel parking lot: men in cowboy hats, women in oversized twirly skirts.

We scrunch down sneaky, and glare at the new patrons who gather around the grunting bus driver unloading their suitcases. The side of their bus reads, *The Cheyenne Squares, Cheyenne, WYOMING*, accented by twinkling silver and red stars. "It's the pool we saw from the road!" a heavyset lady shouts, pointing in our direction.

"How romantic," another woman laughs, nudging her friend with her elbow. "I wonder what their restrictions are on night swimming?"

"Hanky-panky," Lauren whispers.

"Hanky-panky," I echo. It's fun being on vacation.

A third woman grabs a suitcase and walks toward us. She sets it on the prickly fake grass fringing the pool area and pauses to read the sign wired to the fence: *Lifeguard on duty 10 a.m. to 8 p.m.*

She opens the gate, pressing her dance skirt to her sides, and squeezes through. When she walks up to us, Lauren and I sink deeper into the water showing only our eyes and the tops of our heads like crocodiles waiting for canoes of screaming natives to tumble into the water.

Mom warned me to "just be careful. Stay in the shallow end, but try swimming again." She was right. I chased Lauren around the pool doing the breaststroke. The hardest part now is staying in the shallow end.

"My, that looks refreshing," the square dance lady says. The sun at her back throws a wide scalloped shadow across the water. If it weren't for the million stiff net petticoats she wears under it, I could see her underwear.

"I'm Mrs. Ford from Cheyenne, Wyoming." She looks over her shoulder. "We're all from Cheyenne," she says.

"I'm Lauren Asher and this is my sister Lily. She used to be a really

good swimmer. Now she stays in the shallow water." She looks at me bobbing in the deep end. "Sometimes."

Mrs. Ford smiles tentatively.

"I'm getting out," Lauren suddenly announces. She walks up the pool's
concrete steps, tossing her long red hair like she's been doing ever since
a boy at school told her he liked it. Mrs. Ford grabs *my* beach towel off
a chair and throws it to her. Lauren's beach towel lies in a soggy puddle
under a chair.

"Thank you," Lauren says, spreading it across the chaise longue. She
mimics Mom when she crosses her hands on her stomach, then turns her
head to put on her bright pink sunglasses.

"No lifeguard?" Mrs. Ford walks toward the five-foot mark.

I shrug. My voice box was damaged in a fight with a hippo.

"What do you think of the underwater window?" the woman asks,
pointing at the deep end. "It must be wonderful to look out on the street
from underwater." An underwater window? "Everyone on the bus wanted
to stay here. It's the only pool like it in Tahoe!"

I take a breath and stick my face underwater. At the opposite end, a
giant shaft of light splashes the floor of the pool as if it's covered in pirate
treasure.

"Listen," Mrs. Ford smiles, "I'll check on that lifeguard for you, and
then I'm going to go unpack. It's been a long day. See you later?" She is
nice. I like her big yellow skirt with orange polka dots too. She catches my
eye. "Do you like my skirt?"

I nod.

"I wore it at the Elk's Club performance this afternoon. You be careful in there while I get that lifeguard, okay?"

I nod again.

"I have to pee," Lauren says. When she stands up, she wraps my towel
around her.

"That's my towel!" I yell, but it's too late. Mrs. Ford and Lauren are
out the pool gate and heading across the parking lot. Lauren stops to talk
to a chubby girl about ten, while Mrs. Ford continues to the office.

It feels good to swim again.

The pool is as still and blue as the ice rink back home; a bumblebee
skims its surface. I breaststroke around the deep end where I roll onto my

back and float, taking three deep cleansing breaths like the yoga lady on TV.

Suddenly there's a tug on my leg. *Huh?* I sit up in the water and look around.

Nothing's different, no one's in the pool but me. Maybe my leg is tired, and fell asleep and . . . dropped? I haven't been swimming in a long time, and I grew three inches in the last seven months. Relax, I tell myself. Coach Betty said the water would always keep you afloat.

I take a deep breath, roll over, and stick my face underwater.

It's dumb old show-off Jesus, doing a handstand underwater. It startles me at first and the chlorine burns my eyes, but I can clearly see His dry sandals and hairy ankles. His robe hangs straight and dry against His legs too, like paper doll clothes. Which is good, since I really don't want to see His underwear.

Mom thinks I need glasses because I see things that aren't really there, but our entire class was tested at the end of the year, and no one suggested I see the eye doctor, only that I not make up my own hand signals for the eye chart.

"Neato, huh?" Jesus wiggles His eyebrows like Groucho Marx. "Did you notice that I'm not wet?"

"So?"

"Did I scare you?"

"You surprised me."

He smiles mischievously. "You're not supposed to be in the deep end."

I squeeze Mrs. Wiggins's necklace, then stick it back in my swimsuit. What's SOG doing here, anyway? Weird stuff always happens when He's around. I swim away from Him, toward the shallow end, when I feel another yank.

"Stop it!" I cry, louder than I mean to, but when I glance around He isn't anywhere, above water or under. I'm getting out, damn it. I'm definitely getting out. I should have left with Lauren and Mrs. Ford.

I stretch out my arms and lean into them, hoping to break free from my fear and swim away . . . but with only enough time for a quick gulp of air, I'm pulled under again. Suspended between the surface of the pool and the bottom where a big black *6'* is painted on the wall, I jerk and thrash and claw the water but . . .

Don't.

Go.

Anywhere.

Maybe some brain cell has busted, or I just need glasses. And the curtain of water advancing toward me, fluttering like a breeze in Mom's silk curtains or Mrs. Wiggins's lips when she stuck her head out the car window, *is not* a shark curtain at all.

Or an embryonic sac keeping me prisoner.

And the white pointed teeth chomping at its blurry edges, eager to get to me, aren't the Savage Boy's. Maybe I should turn away.

Turn away. Don't be scared. Glug glug.

It's my tail. It has to be. Something growing out of me, pulling me down, keeping me under.

I know this feeling . . . I know this place where things are blurry and I can't breathe . . . I fish the necklace out of my swimsuit and rub her tooth three times . . . *If I should die before I wake* . . .

Back home the prayer train inches out of the roundhouse, Agnes, the apple doll, stuffing its firebox with old sports pages. I miss my room.

Stretch! I tell myself. *Reach* for the dry warm Lake Tahoe air only inches away. I used to be a good swimmer; I used to hold my breath forever. Pull hard, break the grip. If lizards can break off their tails . . . Is my swimsuit caught in the filter? I look around me but see nothing. No shark curtain, no tail . . .

Just me and water. The water and me.

Barely visible through the muddied water is the giant glass window facing the street, and families in Hawaiian shirts, swimsuits, and straw hats . . . moms . . . dads.

Walking. Talking. Laughing. Ignoring me.

Shoe boxes appear on the floor of the pool, adult- and children-sized: some open, some unopened, some I decorated myself. Inside each one are aromas from home: shoe polish, leather, bacon, Mom's cigarettes, and paints. Soggy boxes with air.

I can't reach.

I stretch my arms over my head and wiggle my fingers. I feel the dry warm Lake Tahoe sun on them and, finally tearing a hole in the shark curtain, I hear Lauren cry, "There she is!"

Instantly, the water is an aggregation of movement, a frenzy of kids' legs scissoring the water, of beach-ball jellyfish and air-mattress blimps.

When a horseshoe hits the floor of the pool with a loud echoing clank, I spring to the surface, coughing and spitting.

Lauren stands on the lip of the pool, my towel around her waist. "You better get out of the deep end," she says, "or I'm telling Mom."

I press Mrs. Wiggins's tooth to my chest. The smell of chlorine, suntan lotion, and car exhaust fills my sore lungs. Everything is fine, everything is . . . normal.

"Hey," I cough, "how long was I down there?"

"Like a century." Lauren rolls her eyes at the chubby girl standing beside her. "How do I know? You're the one who always checks the time. Ask the lifeguard."

There's a squeak from the big high chair against the pool fence. It's a lifeguard. He's deeply tanned with white-blond hair, sitting there biting his thumbnail and wiggling a foot.

"Janis," Lauren says, "this is my big sister, Lily Lamebrain. She's not supposed to swim in the deep end."

"Hi," Janis says quietly. She looks nervously at the pool and the yelling, laughing, splashing kids. Mothers in bright summer clothes lounge nearby, reading. Not too far away a boy drinks a grape Nehi and sticks out his tongue. It isn't really purple but his mom says it is.

Lauren sits on the edge, her feet in the water. "Stupid swim party's taking over the whole stupid pool," she pouts.

Everything's okay now, but I'm getting out. I'm definitely getting out, and I swim toward the concrete steps.

Mom talks to the "young couple from Sacramento" we met at breakfast this morning. When she catches my eye, she first mimics taking a picture then holds up five fingers and points to her wristwatch. With a quick goodbye to the strangers she hurries off, calling, "Don't get out, Lily. This is for posterity."

Okay. She'll be back in five minutes. I can do five minutes.

I bob in place looking beyond the pool where a motel maid clatters across the parking lot with a cart of clean ashtrays, bedding, and drinking glasses. She passes the giant terra cotta pots and the two short palm trees, one on either side of the office door.

A boy swims up behind me, yells, "You're it!" and jumps on my shoulders, pushing me under.

I bob back up again. The water doesn't boil and a shark fin doesn't dart through the crowd. Everything's fine. And when Chubby Janis, Lauren's friend, belly flops beside me, I laugh then hold my breath and sink to the bottom on purpose.

I used to love the water. It used to love me.

Across the pool the TV's on, and Edie Adams, in a skintight Barbie gown, takes baby steps toward the camera. When she puffs a cigar and says, "Glub glub," Dad looks up from his soggy newspaper (headline: *Lily Swims Again!*) and wolf-whistles.

Janis is still and floats overhead like a giant cartoon balloon. Her mouth and eyes are open but she doesn't see me, and when I poke her, she bobs like an apple in a barrel.

Janis? Her plump white fingers remind me of the hungry grubs Mom ripped from her roses before we left home. *Wake up! Wake up!* I shake her several times before pressing Mrs. Wiggins's tooth into the palm of her hand.

Suddenly she blinks and jerks away, then falls asleep again.

"Get back!" the lifeguard yells before the water explodes with his dive.

Instantly he surfaces again, rolling Janis on her back and dragging her to the edge of the pool. One of the moms helps pull her up and onto the pavement, gently laying her across the *Do Not Run* sign stenciled on the cement.

Nervous moms and dripping-wet kids watch while Tad (printed on his tank top) gives Janis mouth-to-mouth. Behind them, Jesus bites His lip, and Mrs. Ford hugs this month's issue of *Square Dance International*.

Mom's there too; Lauren's camera hangs from her neck. When she says, "Lily? Stay where you are. I'll help you out in a second," people glance at her impatiently.

On the fourth compression, Janis spews a fountain of water and coughs, and the lifeguard props her up to sitting. A few people applaud.

"Oh my God! Sweetheart!" cries a frightened woman. She kneels beside the girl, wiping her face. "She's epileptic," the woman explains. "She has seizures!"

"She'll be okay," Tad says. "Did anyone call an ambulance?"

"I called, I called!" shouts the pretty young motel clerk threading her way through the crowd. "They're on their way." When she touches the lifeguard's shoulder, I remember that she'd shown Mom her engagement ring when we first checked in.

Janis keeps coughing. "Breathe through your nose," Tad tells her. "That's right, you're doing fine—that's it, through your nose." He holds up his hand and asks, "How many fingers do you see?"

When a toddler answers, "Free," everyone laughs.

Mom helps me out of the pool.

Lauren stands next to Janis. Pee runs down her leg.

Janis pees too: epileptic almost-died pee that soaks the leather sole of Mom's new Italian sandals.

As the family car inches out of the motel parking lot that night, for a fancy dinner at Morgan's Roundtable, Lauren cries, "Mrs. Ford!"

We all look.

"Quite a patriotic outfit," Mom says about the older woman's blue and white dress with red sequin stripes. Seated in a chair next to the pool, she passes a bottle back and forth with a man in a patriotic shirt. When she laughs, her chin disappears into the soft folds of her neck.

Dad honks and Mom whispers, "Paul!" but Lauren and I wave and Mrs. Ford waves back. Without both hands to press down her petticoats, they spring up and she laughs even harder.

Mrs. Ford's legs are short, white, and muscular. I bet she never goes on diets and has never heard of Roman Meal bread. I bet when the Cheyenne Squares vote on where they'll dance next summer, she'll vote yes to coming back to Tahoe, but only if they buy tickets early for the Ponderosa and rent bikes like we were planning to do. *Again.* When Mom's on vacation, it's hard getting her up in the morning, and Dad's already downstairs playing a one-armed bandit when she does.

Mom's neck is as evenly tanned as the rest of her, and the short auburn hairs at the nape all curl the same way. Her nylons *shh* when she crosses her legs and taps the dashboard nervously.

"Morgan's Roundtable is a beautiful place," she says. "I've seen it advertised in lots of magazines. High on a hill overlooking Lake Tahoe—it's a popular spot with movie stars." She giggles. "Aren't you excited, girls? I wonder who we'll see." She clears her throat and turns around. "Kind of quiet back there. Everyone okay?"

I bet Mrs. Ford would have let me wear the dogtooth necklace to the restaurant.

"Is there a square dance tonight?" Lauren asks, as we pull into traffic. "Can we go after dinner?"

"Not this time," Mom says, shaking her head. "I can't imagine coming all the way from Cheyenne, Wyoming, in the heat of summer, in a bus, no less, just to dance at some square dance convention."

"Maybe you should get one of those hootenanny dresses, Kit," Dad teases.

Mom slugs him on the shoulder and smiles. She's beautiful tonight, tall, tan, and busty in her favorite black cocktail dress that's low cut in the front and back. She checks herself in the visor mirror. "Windows, everybody? Just till we get to the restaurant?" Mom worries about her hair.

It's hot, but we roll them up. We want her to be beautiful too.

She takes a long drag on her cigarette, cracks open her window vent, and pushes it through, dropping it on the road.

People stop eating when Mom walks across the large, dark-carpeted room behind the maître d'. A familiar-looking guy with white wavy hair, thick black eyebrows, and a flat nose turns on his barstool to watch her pass. When a woman walks up to him with an autograph book, he smiles.

We're seated at a low round table next to the dance floor, with a little kerosene lamp that lights our silver table settings and linen tablecloth.

"Isn't this elegant?" Dad drapes her black lace shawl over the back of her chair, and lights her cigarette.

I look up at the thick wood beams and say, "I bet it was a barn once."

Dad winks. He likes it when I make normal conversation.

The jazz trio's good; it's fun to watch people dance. I've never seen Mom so happy. She talks about the "beautiful people" and the "gorgeous menus," orders two martinis, dry with a twist, and prime rib, medium-rare.

Lauren orders a small sirloin from the kid's menu and, when it arrives, smothers it in ketchup. She scrapes the sour cream out of her potato and fills it with whipped butter.

Dad orders a T-bone steak with caramelized onions. I stare at the T in the T-bone for a long time, then growl quietly. It's a little growl, but my parents look at me nervously.

I reach for Mrs. Wiggins's tooth, though Mom made me leave it at the motel. The growl is growing inside me, yet for now I can swallow it. And I do—over and over until my dinner arrives, and the waitress ties a bib around my neck. It's my first lobster and I don't know what to do with it.

Mom points at my platter. "They've already cracked it for you so all you need to do is take your nut pick and gently separate the meat from the shell. Cut off a bite with your steak knife, squeeze the lemon wedge over it, and dip it in the drawn butter. Like this," she demonstrates.

When the lemon squirts a sticky stream of juice up Mom's arm, the man at the next table laughs too. He's watching her.

I growl again.

Mom looks at me nervously and wipes her arm on the linen napkin. "I think I better clean up," she giggles. Her nylons *shh* as she walks away.

As she crosses the room, one man's jaw falls to the floor like in the cartoons. He thumps his foot until it becomes a blur, steam shoots out his ears, and the top of his head blows off. Another man's eyes pop out of his head, bouncing off the rug like basketballs, then run up and down Mom's legs, striping them like a barber's pole. "Hubba hubba," a chorus of hungry wolves (in zoot suits) call out.

"How you doing, Lily?" Dad asks. I show him my teeth. "Lily?"

"What sweet young girls," a waitress says, arriving with another tray of drinks. And ice cream. Lauren smiles, but I don't.

I can't. My mouth doesn't work that way.

The sundaes aren't that good. I'm bored and drag my spoon back and forth through the coconut and pineapple making chunky tread marks in the ice cream until Mom tells me, "Stop and sit up straight." I wish we were watching Mrs. Ford and the Cheyenne Squares.

Mom stubs out her cigarette when Dad asks her to dance. "Thank you, sir, I'd love to." As they step on the dance floor, the familiar man with the white wavy hair taps Dad on the shoulder.

"Excuse me," he says. His voice is deep. "May I have your permission to dance with your beautiful wife?"

It's Ben Cartwright.

Mom gasps. "Aren't you . . . ?"

Lorne Greene. Ben Cartwright on TV's *Bonanza*. Father to Adam, Little Joe, and Hoss Cartwright. Owner of the Ponderosa Ranch; widower of three beautiful young wives who died in childbirth. If you're a beautiful young woman, marrying Ben Cartwright will kill you.

Maybe dancing will too.

I stand up and look across the table at the adults. Spit swamps my mouth, a growl sits on the back of my tongue. We should go. "I'm not feeling good," I say.

Mom glances at Dad.

"Why, you must be this young lady's daughter," Ben Cartwright says, first nodding at Mom, then me. "You're almost as pretty as your mother."

Creep. He's just like Mr. Marks. "I'm not pretty," I say plainly. "And my mom's married."

Both men laugh, but Mom scowls. "Don't be rude, Lily," she says.

"That's all right," Ben smiles. "Our show's considered family fare, though children are often scared of me. I think it's the eyebrows."

All three grown-ups laugh this time.

"I'm not scared of you," I say.

Dad grips my arm tightly then clears his throat. "Of course you may dance with my wife. What I mean is, Kit has my permission if she'd like to."

"I'd be honored," Mom says. Dad kisses her cheek and hands her off to the cursed Ben Cartwright who leads our beautiful mother, blushing and giggling, to the center of the dance floor. Where she floats in his arms after two vodka martinis—dry with a twist, of course.

Back at the table, the muscles in my legs flex and tighten, and I imagine bounding out of the chair, pulling Ben Cartwright to the floor, and tearing a hole in his soft white belly. Later, people would read about actor Lorne Greene bleeding to death in a freak restaurant murder.

"*Too bad bo-bad, banana fana fo-fad.*"

"Dad?" Sleepy Lauren says, nodding at me.

"Give her five, ten minutes, Lily, okay?" But it isn't a real question and he doesn't wait for an answer because, like Lauren and me, and most of Morgan's Roundtable that night, he's watching Ben Cartwright press Mom against his chest and whisper in her ear as they float across the dance floor. Couples stop dancing to watch.

Mom laughs her martini laugh across the room. It springs over our little round table to the barstool where Ben would be sitting if he weren't dancing with her. It bounces out the front door, past the teenage boy with our car keys, down the hill to the underwater window and the glittering danger of the shark curtain.

Tonight I wish my beautiful mother looked like Mrs. Ford.

The jazz trio stops playing (to thank the waitress, who hands each musician a drink), but Mom and Ben Cartwright remain on the floor, barely moving, talking and laughing with their arms around each other. Her gold hoop earrings and long tan arms glow. When Ben moves a hand down her bare back, a shark fin breaks through his dinner jacket.

Dad stands up. "Pardon me, girls, I think it's time for our last dance."

The microphone crackles and whistles when the goateed saxophonist announces, "There's been a request." A record needle hits a well-worn groove, and a single drumbeat erupts.

Before Dad gets far, a woman cries out, "Conga!" and giggling, squealing grown-ups pop out of their seats, hurrying onto the dance floor.

A woman signals Mom, who takes the lead with evil Ben's hands on her waist. Mom laughs and shakes imaginary maracas as she leads the snakelike procession around the dance floor. Overhead, a spinning ball of colorful lights splashes the conga line, and I remember the striped blinds in Mr. Marks's bedroom.

Ben is striped too; only it's one wide stripe down his back like Pepé Le Pew.

Cowboys on *Bonanza* say *skunk* instead of *coward*. Ben Cartwright is a skunk. When he can't get a wife of his own, he steals other men's wives. Is there a ring in his pocket? Has he asked Mom to marry him yet?

My teeth itch, the hair on my neck stands up, and I crouch in my chair, ready to pounce when Ben Cartwright dances by. I feel the glance of the baldheaded man next to us. Dad sees him too.

"Sit down, Lily," Dad says sternly. "Don't you dare ruin this night for your mother."

"Sit down, weirdo," Lauren adds.

I want to, I really do, but I can't. I know that what's going on between Dad and Mom and Ben Cartwright is about sex and none of my business, but I have to protect Mom. Mrs. Wiggins is inside me, and she took care of *all* of us once.

Things get out if you're not careful, things get in.

The bark is building up inside me. I bite my tongue to hold it back, but it doesn't help. It hurts and a tear rolls down my face. *Please*, I pray, but the prayer train's been racing around my bedroom since Ben Cartwright first showed up, and it just flew off the track and out the window, landing in Mom's rosebushes.

My lips twitch and my nose flares.

The conga line is coming. As it nears, Mom sees me crouching in my club chair, frowns, and shakes her head.

I see me in her eyes—a pretty, tall, teenage girl in a turquoise dress (she didn't want to wear), baring her teeth and squinting her eyes as she hugs her knees.

Mom tries to steer the dancers away from our table, but Ben is flirting with the redheaded woman behind him, and the laughing, dancing procession plows on, pushing Mom ahead of it. Someone in the conga line has a tambourine.

The room is loud, even louder when I bark. Two short angry barks, startling Dad and Lauren and even me. A leave-my-family-alone bark, a somebody's-breaking-in bark.

Dad can't reach me before the third bark but Lauren hits me with her ice cream spoon. There is no fourth bark, only panting and coughing, only my red-faced Mom (with Ben Cartwright beside her) who says, "For God's sake, Lily." She takes a deep breath. "Apologize to Mr. Greene."

"That's all right," he says, wrinkling his hairy eyebrows. "She's just feeling the music. Like Spike Jones."

The conga line continues, weaving in and out of tables. People laugh. A woman with an autograph book taps Ben's shoulder.

"To whom should I make it out?" he asks.

"Apologize to Mr. Greene!" Mom snaps.

"I'm sorry," I mumble, but she can't hear me over the music and drunk giggling. I ruined Mom's dance with Ben Cartwright; I ruined our trip to Lake Tahoe. The conga line passes by. Waving martini glasses and high heels over their heads, the dancers don't notice us at all.

"Lily?"

Everything is different now. I barked in public. "I'm sorry," I mumble again. Then, "Sorry, Mr. Greene."

"Now, sit down properly, please," Dad says.

"Do as your father says," Lorne Greene adds.

My parents instantly glare at him.

"We'll discipline our daughter, Mr. Greene, not you," Dad says. "This is family business, *our* family business." He slips his arm around Mom's waist and pulls her close. "Ready, sweetheart? Shall we head back?"

Mom nods. She's embarrassed; the tear in her eye is embarrassed too. Over her shoulder, Jesus stands behind the bar, garters on His shirt-sleeves, wiping glasses with a clean towel like the bartender in *Bonanza's* Silver Dollar Saloon.

No one stares at my beautiful mother when Dad covers her trembling shoulders with her black lace shawl. No one looks at me strangely, either.

By the time we pay the bill, Lorne Greene has signed another autograph. And someone else is sitting at our table.

I pretend to be sleeping when we drive back to the motel.

"He did not," Mom whispers.

"You may not remember it, you may not have felt it," Dad says, "but I saw it. That man, that television star, touched your ass, Kit. I saw it. Lily saw it. The whole damn restaurant saw it."

Mom opens her purse, shakes a pill into her hand, and swallows it.

"I don't know how you can do that without water," Dad whispers. He taps the steering wheel nervously, then throws me a glance in the rearview mirror. He thinks I'm sleeping but a dog's eyes are always open a little. "What should we do about—"

"I'll call Dr. *Fraud* in the morning," Mom says. "Of course, he'll probably say what he always says. That she'll probably grow out of it. That she's not dangerous. And not to anticipate. Lily can't predict what she'll do next any more than we can." She pauses. "I thought we were past Peace Lake and Mrs. Wiggins." She lights a cigarette and rolls the car window all the way down. She doesn't care what her hair looks like now. "What if seeing a psychologist isn't enough, Paul? What if she gets worse? Tonight was . . . embarrassing."

Dad remains quiet.

"Weren't you embarrassed?" Mom asks.

A car joins us at the intersection. The driver honks and looks over. "Hey, baby," he says to Mom. "You busy tonight?"

She drops her cigarette to the street and rolls up the window again.

"I'm sorry, Paul," she says.

And crosses her legs with a gentle *shh*.

"They've moved."

"Excuse me?"

"The Markses." Mom points the flashlight toward Judy's house. "They didn't answer the phone so I walked over. They left our mail in the milk box."

"What?"

"They're gone, Paul. The house is empty, the garage too."

"Maybe they're away for the weekend or bug bombing the house."

"You're not listening. There's not a stick of furniture, not a note on the door. Even the backyard construction projects—nothing is finished. No one is living there. They're gone."

Dad stands on the patio sipping a beer. He looks over the rosebushes Mom and Connie Marks once shared, past his new toolshed (with the new lawnmower) to the Markses' abandoned house.

Lauren stands next to them. "Rusty too?" she asks. Mom touches her shoulder.

"Your manuscripts came back, Paul. Unopened. I put them on the kitchen table."

Dad shrugs.

They act like they don't care, but they do.

He sends out the same two manuscripts every six months. Mom posts them with the most interesting stamps she can find. She says he writes like Gay Talese, whoever that is.

Gulliver, Rusty's old yellow cat, crawls out of Mom's hydrangea, meowing hungrily. Lauren smiles and kneels beside him. "Rusty is gone," she tells him, walking inside for a dish of milk.

It's the last week of our last summer on Aiken Street. I hear sprinklers, car radios, and squeaky screen doors. I smell kerosene and burning charcoal. I'm glad I'm going to a different school where no one will know me as Judy's crazy neighbor, the "retard" who killed the family dog, got the Savage Boy in trouble, and barked at Ben Cartwright. When we get to the new house, I don't know what I'll be, but I won't be that person anymore.

Suddenly more tired then I've ever been, I sit down at the picnic table. In the dusking light I hear Mom sob.

"I'm sorry, Paul. We loved this house. This isn't the way I wanted to end our time here."

"Nothing happens in a vacuum, Kit. Especially marriages."

They're quiet until Mom says, "I know you had . . . relations with your secretary, Paul. It's okay. After all I've put you through—"

"I had *cards*, Kit. I had craps, poker, Portland Meadows, even the horses a couple of times, but I never had Toni, or any one else for that matter. Why would I want another woman when I can't take care of the one I've got?"

In the movies, people usually hug when someone says something like that, but in real life people stand silently side by side.

Next door in the overgrown lot, a young buck stands in the dappled darkness of the trees. It catches me looking at it and makes a break for it, leaving its safe camouflage to bolt past Mom's roses to the rock garden pool—where it pauses to take a deep noisy gulp—then trots down our driveway, past the family car, finally disappearing into the neighborhood. In the ten short days we were gone, it grew accustomed to passing through.

And Judy moved away, as if my family and I never lived here, and she was never my best friend.

Dad's eyes burn a hole in the Markses' house. "It's over then?"

"There never was an *it*, Paul." Mom's shoulders droop and her voice falls down her throat. "Just that time . . . I told you about . . . when Lily—" Her breath catches. She holds out a hand to Dad. "I'll miss Connie and the kids."

"We were moving anyway," Dad says. "It doesn't matter."

Mom spreads her fingers wider. When Dad slips his hand in hers, she cups it but leaves it loose, like the broken catch in the redwood gate.

"Let's never lock it," Mom said to Connie the day the fence was built.

Dad throws his empty beer bottle at the Markses' house. "He always was a bastard."

CHAPTER 19
PRETENDING

Dr. Giraffe told Mom to never confront me directly. "Be matter-of-fact," the psychologist said, "pretend you're making a suggestion to a friend," which explains why Mom didn't look at me when she cleaned her paintbrushes in the kitchen sink.

Mom pretended not to confront me twice this week already. Once while folding clothes, another time unloading groceries.

This time Mom has more to say. She says I've been spending too much time in my room, and when I'm at the dinner table, I'm usually daydreaming and not paying attention. She says I'm too serious and don't laugh enough. She wants me to get more fresh air, join the chess club, or play tennis after school. Maybe even get back into swimming.

"Didn't you love it in Tahoe?" she asks.

"No," I answer.

Everyone's pretending today. I'm pretending I didn't like Tahoe when I did, pretending it didn't feel good to bark at Ben Cartwright or help rescue Janis.

Mom pretends she took her happy pill when I saw her throw it away.

Dad's pretending he can help Lauren with "new math," and Lauren's pretending the lightning and thunder don't bother her. A bad storm has been parked over Portland since breakfast and our parents have unplugged almost everything electric.

The house is growing dark inside. The radio says the storm will be gone by dinner, but what it if isn't? What if the storm never goes away?

The house is half-packed; it's been that way for a month. The original deal on the new house fell through at the last minute, but the new one stuck. The moving trucks will be here in ten days.

"You need to get out of your room, Lily," Mom says. "It's not healthy to spend so much time inside. Look at Lauren, she gets out." Lauren stays over with girlfriends almost every weekend. She went to a slumber party last night.

"I get out," I whine, but when I try to remember where and when, all I can think of are scenes from books or TV. "I'll get out at the new house."

"You're old enough for dances, shopping, hanging out with your friends." Friends?

I don't do those things. Mom doesn't either. Mom likes her studio like I like my room, and she hasn't had a friend since Mrs. Marks moved away. Which I blame on evil Mr. Marks. I write *S-E-X* in my left hand under the table.

"Lily's fine," Dad says. My folks take turns arguing about me. "Look at her. She's healthy, and isn't she pretty? She's like you, Kit, pretty and artistic. What's wrong with that? She'll be dazzling the boys in no time and then you'll wish she *was* spending too much time in her room."

"Lily's a nerd," Lauren says.

"Lauren!"

Mom gets "directed" when she paints, productive, "hyper," and Dad says he wishes she'd start drinking earlier in the day. Mom's father was the same. "Everybody's a slouch next to her old man," Dad told me once. "There weren't enough hours in the day. He was hard drinking but productive. He could do anything, fix anything, build anything. He even played the violin. At least that's the story."

He doesn't know many other stories about Mom's father. None of us do.

Mom says, "All stories are secrets first," so for the longest time we didn't know that Mom and Jamie were once little girls on a train. They had nothing when they were first sent away, but when they left the orphanage years later—with steerage tickets to America in the pockets of their donated coats—Jamie had a notebook and pencils, and Mom a cigar box of new paints. They had a future. They had secrets, stories, and dreams. Mom says that they pretended a lot; that pretending helped them survive. Pretending to be happy when they weren't, not happy when they were. Pretending they didn't remember their parents waving goodbye to them at the train station. They were brave. How did they leave "home" twice? How did they leave even once?

I'm growing up. I need to know.

I follow Mom upstairs. We have to talk but I don't know where to start. Instead, as Mom stares at her easel, with its portrait of a dead Vietnamese woman, and lights a cigarette, I pull the pocket-sized notebook out of my notebook-sized pocket and add another hash mark under today's date.

"Must you, really?" she asks.

Back in my room, I open my closet door and stand there, smelling the smoky remains of the desiccated jungle.

It used to smell rich and wet, like dirt and licorice and dewy summer mornings, but one night I woke up to the heat and crackle of a dying fire in my closet and, pulling aside the sliding doors, saw burning villages on the floor there, American helicopters hovering in my hanging clothes and frightened villagers hiding in my shoes. Actually, I didn't see the villagers but I knew they were there. When I closed my eyes I recognize their faces from Mom's paintings. They were Vietnamese.

"Be matter-of-fact," the doctor told Mom, so I was too, gave the burning villagers their privacy and closed the closet doors. There was nothing I could do anyway. Death is a personal thing: no one ever understood what happened to Mrs. Wiggins, even when I tried to explain it.

Within hours the jungle's lushness was dried up and only a sour bitter smell remained. It's still there when I open my closet.

Mom says it's my collection of old gym shoes, but I disagree.

On the shelf above my clothes is the box with the mask from Aunt Jamie. Beside it is a stack of letters from her—the African stamps are beautiful, bigger and brighter than American stamps.

Until Jamie died, Africa was the most beautiful place on earth.

When the package first arrived, Mom wanted me to wait until Dad got home to open it, but I tore into it. The carved wooden mask jumped out at me and I laughed.

"You laugh at the weirdest stuff," Lauren said, opening Jamie's note and reading it out loud: "*Lily, it's made of tree bark. Wear the mask when you don't want people to see you.* Well, duh!"

But I smiled so big you could hang wooden masks off each ear.

"Great," Mom mumbled.

At breakfast the next morning she told me to take it off. "No, Lily, absolutely not. We just got rid of that damned Big Bad Wolf outfit . . ."

Just? Sure, I remembered the costume, how it stuck to my body and melted into my legs, arms, and teeth, but that was a long time ago and I'm older now. "It was a *werewolf* costume," I said in a muffled voice from inside the mask. I smelled the paints that colored it and the dusty, spicy air of the African village where Jamie found it, tried it on, and knew the mask was for me, even if it meant wrestling it away from the local witch doctor.

"It's Lily's!" Jamie cried, and upon hearing my name the witch doctor smiled and motioned his guards to put down their spears.

"Lil-ee," he nodded, and the others did too. Everyone knew my name. It was carved centuries ago—in ancient trees that scratched the clouds—by ancient ancestors who rode giraffes and lived underground. My name was heard in songs sung by beautiful black girls dancing in formation, and in the dreamy howls of wild dogs sleeping in the bushes.

Lil-ee. Lily's. The mask was meant to be mine.

The following week I tried sneaking it to the Portland Public Library, but Mom caught me. She convinced me to leave it at home and did a quick sketch of the mask instead, and the two of us researched African iconography (*the use or study of images or symbols in visual arts,* Oxford Dictionary) at a long table in the library's biggest room where a handsome man stopped to ask, "Sisters, or mother and daughter?" Mom blushed and said something about visiting the library more often, but we never did and we never found the mask's design either.

Near the library was the natural history museum where a docent looked at Mom's sketch. She said she'd seen a mask just like it in an import store across town, but we knew better.

Mom filled a new sketchbook with pictures of the mask. She wanted to do "something new, something abstract using the mask. Maybe a collage?"

"Hurray!" Dad said, tearing up the newspaper and throwing it in the air like fat confetti. Mom called it "trying too hard," which he does when the two of them are fighting or he's been away on business.

"Are you being sarcastic?" Mom asked, but Dad only joked about "naked native titties in *National Geographic*," then stomped around the kitchen "like a Bantu," thumping the broom handle on the floor, calling for a hula with Mom who'd be the "most popular girl at the fertility dance."

Dad confused everything: Africans don't do hulas, and there are millions of Bantus in Africa and most of them don't do fertility dances either, but Mom put down her sketchbook, kicked off her shoes, and, wiggling her boobs at Dad, took tiny barefooted hula steps toward him, both of them laughing till their faces were red and Lauren ran to her room to call a friend.

I thought of the girl whose parents chaperoned the Harvest Dance at school that fall. While I sat, fully clothed, on the toilet reading before class one day, she stood in the restroom crying, two friends patting her on the back. "They actually danced!" the girl said. "It was so embarrassing!"

I took out my notebook and wrote, *Never ask Mom and Dad to chaperone. Especially on Luau Night.*

When they wiggled their way to the middle of the kitchen, my parents fell in each other's arms, and turned to look at me.

"Lighten up, Lily!" Mom laughed. "Honestly, I don't know how we raised such modest girls, do you, Pablo?"

"*All day, all night, Marianne,*" Pablo sang, giving Mom a twirl.

Have I mentioned the basement before?

I like its damp sawdust smell and the single bulb lighting the floor-to-ceiling shelves on three of the four walls. Sometimes I sit on one apple box and write at another, getting up every so often to swing the lightbulb back and forth like it does in old movies. I don't go down there much, but when I do and I'm not writing, I like to arrange and rearrange the shelves of canned food. Alphabetically, or by fruit or vegetable. Mom doesn't notice when they're out of order, but I do. I check on them once a week and when Jamie's Special Jams get pulled forward, I hide them behind the others again. If no one opens them, they'll last forever.

Yesterday I only went halfway down, and sat on the steps in the dark listening to Mom and Dad dance overhead. Halfway down is as far as SOG ever goes, and when I saw His sandals and the hem of His robe over my shoulder, I wasn't surprised.

I wasn't surprised when He was gone either.

There's something about basements.

Maybe if I spent less time in my room and more time in the basement, Jesus would give me some privacy. I decided to do my homework down there on Tuesdays and Thursdays, but imagined Mom freaking out about it. Then Dr. Giraffe would want to talk to me about that too.

Forget it.

Later that night, after everyone went to bed, Jamie's little red house with the yellow shutters on the old coast highway burned down.

We read about it later, how the growth around it was too wet to take a spark, so the outbuildings were safe and the neighbors were able to "tamp out any errant flames."

"*Errant flames*, huh?" Dad read. "Who writes like that? Must have been one of her poetry students."

Yesterday upon the stair,
I met a man who wasn't there.
He wasn't there again today,
I wish, I wish he'd go away.

When I came home last night at three,
The man was waiting there for me,
But when I looked around the hall
I couldn't see him there at all!
Go away, go away, don't you come back anymore!
Go away, go away, and please don't slam the door.

Last night I saw upon the stair,
A little man who wasn't there.
He wasn't there again today
Oh, how I wish he'd go away.

"Did you write it?" I asked. This was two years ago.

Jamie is dead now but I still remember the poem. I remember everything.

"No. Somebody named Hughes Mearns," she said. "I always wondered what he was like." She tucked the red velvet bookmark back in her journal. "I memorized it for drama class when I was about your age."

We sat up together in her bed with the Lincoln Log headboard, pressing hip to hip under her Guatemalan quilt, sharing the same long pillow that stretched the width of her bed. She'd sewed two regular-sized pillows end to end, and made a pillowcase out of moth-eaten wool sweaters. She called it her winter pillow. It was cold that winter in her little yellow house with the red shutters, especially since she wouldn't date the guy who delivered wood so he only left half a cord.

She'd paid for a full one. Dad threatened to call the cops but Jamie said no.

"Shall we?" Jamie cleared her throat. "*Yesterday upon the stair . . .*"

"*Yesterday upon the stair,*" I repeated.

"*Yesterday upon the stair, I met a man who wasn't there,*" Jamie recited. She paused and reached for the glass of warm sake beside her bed. I felt her thoughts wander. "I still don't know how he got in. I never gave him the key."

What's she talking about? I looked at her but she was pretending I wasn't there. Like the man in the poem.

"There was a staff meeting after school, and I grabbed some groceries on the way home. I was late," she said. "He was sitting on the bedroom stairs."

When I came home last night at three, the man was waiting there for me.

"The dogs went crazy when they saw me drive up, but I wasn't paying attention. I was stupid for going inside. I could have been killed." She looked across the room at the matching *His* and *Hers* bathrobes hanging on the coatrack.

Did Kevin know?

"I don't know why I went through with it. I mean, he was cute and there'd always been a . . . a . . . vibe between us, I guess. But I was never going to do anything about it."

So she knew him? Mom says all stories are secrets first.

"There was sawdust in his hair," she continued, "and he smelled like freshly cut wood . . . and beer. That night he smelled like beer too."

She had told me things before, things she knew I wouldn't repeat, things she wasn't sure I understood or even heard her say. Mom does the same thing. Dr. Giraffe says they're taking advantage of me, and suggested I tell them to stop, but I don't care. Their secrets are like chapters in someone else's book, with characters I'll never know and questions that will never be answered. Mostly I just run out of space in my head. I keep so many secrets I can't hold them all, and once in a while one slips out an ear or the corner of my eye so I don't have to worry about remembering.

"He never did it again but now the peace is gone, you know? The house isn't mine anymore, not since then. There's something else living here, something else."

"*He wasn't there again today,*" I said, remembering the poem.

She looked at me, alarmed. "He didn't hurt me," she added. She was explaining herself again.

I stayed quiet, then repeated: "*Yesterday upon the stair, I met a man who wasn't there.*"

Jamie smiled. "*He wasn't there again today, I wish, I wish he'd go away.*"

Go away, go away, don't you come back anymore! Go away, go away, and please don't slam the door.

She was talking about sex, wasn't she? Not love. Not marrying Kevin.

I took her hand, turned it over, and wrote *S-E-X* in Helen Keller, then added a question mark.

She wiped it off on the bedcovers and looked away.

Wait, I didn't mean anything by it. I was just being stupid.

Stupid and weird.

I decided to write *S-O-R-R-Y* in Helen Keller, and reached for her hand, but she jerked it farther away.

I quickly recited, "*Yesterday upon the stair . . .*"

"*I met a man who wasn't there,*" Jamie said, her head still turned away. She sniffed. Was she crying?

I took a deep breath. "*He wasn't there again today . . .*" I turned away too, so only the backs of our heads were looking at each other, and waited, silently reviewing the poem in my head.

The room was quiet.

"*Go away, go away, don't you come back anymore!*" I said in a witch's voice, putting a spell on the dark places in Jamie's house, the places where something else lived. Then I turned back.

But she was gone, and in her place: nothing. Not a creased sheet or a dent in the winter pillow.

I listened for her footsteps but only heard my heartbeat knocking on the front door, and a tiny squeak when I pushed the door open.

"Hello?" I heard myself call out. "Anybody here?"

CHAPTER 20

THE SLAP

We move into what the *Oregonian* classifieds call "a charming sixty-year-old Cape Cod in Crawford Heights" on August 25. Lauren and I are enrolled in school by September 1; and by the end of the month, Mom has introduced me to most of the women on our block as "my beautiful older daughter." When one of them smiles and says, "Why yes, she looks just like you, Kit," Mom pulls me close.

I hate that. No one knows what I look like, not really; not where it counts, not on the inside.

Mom says moving to the new house is a chance to "start fresh." She even asks us to write a "New House Resolution."

While our parents both want "more family time," I'm not sure what I want, only that for a while it had to do with the lump of gray-white clay I kept in a bread wrapper on my bed stand.

Mom says I read too much, but if I didn't I wouldn't know about golems: how their spirits live in clay and mud, and if you perform the right spell, they'll come to life and do your bidding, like Frankenstein's monster.

Mom bought me the clay but she didn't like the idea of me building a golem. "There are things you play at," she said, "and things you don't," which Dad called "being superstitious." I didn't worry about it until I came home from school one day and found the entire ball of clay gone. The wrapper too.

A small white clay horse stood in its place.

When I ask Mom about it, she smiles and says, "What horse?"

Mom's a good artist, and it's nice of her to make me something, but the clay was mine. I was still designing the golem's face, and writing the spells I would give it. I wasn't *playing* at anything.

The next day, when everyone is out of the house, I call a synagogue—a lot of people in Crawford Heights are Jewish—and I talk to the assistant rabbi. I tell him I'd read about a golem who, even now, is said to live in the attic of a really old house in Prague. He murdered a bunch of Nazis up there during World War II.

Mom always says, "Never be afraid to ask," so I ask him why the golem didn't kill *all* the Nazis. "It could have saved the Jews," I say.

"Let me get this straight," he laughs over the phone. "You're not Jewish? How old are you?"

"Does it matter?"

"Okay, so maybe you're a teenager. And you're not Jewish?"

"I live in a Catholic neighborhood but I'm Presbyterian. Kind of."

"Do your parents know you're calling?"

It's not a golem, but I like the clay horse. When it falls over, I stand it up again.

Dad suggests my New House Resolution should be to "write down or illustrate every wild thing that crosses your mind for a year." Mom says he is being cruel, and makes a joke about reams of paperwork.

Lauren's resolution is "to earn enough money to buy an entire set of Bonne Bell cosmetics. She tells me people call me pretty because they feel sorry for me. She says I need lots of makeup and that's why she gave me a sack of little half-used Avon lipstick samples she and her friends use at school.

After looking at them under Jamie's microscope, I determine the lipsticks are covered with germs and dead skin cells, so I rename each tiny tube (*Monkey Blood, Cat Splat, Crushed Crusader*), rubber cement them to the outside of a red-and-white–striped shoe box, make big papier-mâché lips for the top, and give it to Lauren as her future cosmetics case.

She just stares at it. "You are so weird."

Mom loves it. She calls it pop art.

I don't think there's much pop art in our neighborhood. Even though the new house is only a mile or two from the old one, and a couple of blocks from the entrance to Crawford Butte, it's in one of the nicest neighborhoods in Portland. At least that's what Mom says. Ten years ago, our house was featured on the cover of *House Beautiful*. The magazine liked the English ivy crawling up the chimney, the perfect little smoke tree in the front yard, and the apple tree on the side of the garage.

Mom keeps the outdated issue of *House Beautiful* on the coffee table in the living room for all to see. Some of the neighbors still remember the photo shoot, but Mom walks them through the house anyway, magazine in hand, pointing out where we'll make improvements.

In our living room there is "faux marble" wallpaper; in the TV room, real brass nautical fixtures; in the basement is a games closet, and a recreation room with a built-in bar and refrigerator. When I noticed a dog leash on a nail at the top of the basement steps (like Santa's cane in *Miracle on 34th Street*), I wondered out loud if Mrs. Wiggins led us to this house, but Dad said the "previous owner had dogs, that's all." He suggested I write a newsletter featuring movie trivia, though.

When Dad first saw the pilot maps of South Sea Islands, tacked to the basement wall behind the built-in bar, he told Mom he'd put his desk and file cabinet downstairs. "It's a man's space," he said after filling the bar fridge with beer, beef jerky, and a jar of pickled eggs.

I like the floor plans of the house Dad found, illustrating its closets and crawl spaces, even a room off the kitchen that was never built.

What was it for? Why wasn't it built?

In the morning, I use Dad's tape measure to trace the invisible 10' x 12' room onto the grass with chalk. Mom watches from the kitchen window where she cleans everything before the maid arrives. Though later, after meeting Mrs. Rudman who was recommended by a neighbor, Mom decides against hiring her.

Mrs. Rudman is twenty years older than Mom and looks like Frieda. "I can't have her cleaning up after us, like we're her children or something," Mom explains.

"But you wanted more time to paint," Dad replies. His eyes glaze over.

"It's all right, Paul. A little elbow grease never hurt anybody."

Since finally moving to Florida, Frieda doesn't call much. Last time she called she said she'd "never seen so many attractive retired men in one place." She doesn't like the weather though; "too muggy," she said.

She doesn't mention the heat in the postcards she sends.

One arrived today. I found it on the kitchen counter after riding my bike home from chess club. Mom says if I stop thanking Frieda for sending "those syrupy cards with Bible illustrations, she'll send something else," but I don't mind. I cut out the little pictures of Jesus and put them in collages, some including Willa Perkins and me. Willa is the prettiest girl in high school. I was walking behind her when a sheet of little school pictures slipped out of her notebook. They were good too; looked just like her. "Excuse me?" I said, but she ignored me so I kept them for myself. Did I mention Willa Perkins is the world's biggest snob?

It's 5:30 p.m. but no one's downstairs, nothing's on the stove, and the evening paper sits unopened at Dad's chair. Upstairs there are angry voices. I pause at the top of the stairs to listen.

"Psst." Lauren motions me to her door and whispers, "He's doing it again."

"Gambling?"

Suddenly our parents' door flies opens. "Lily?" Mom calls.

"Yes?"

"Thank God you're home. Where were you? Why didn't you call? I went to pick you up but Mr. Ruff said you'd left on your bike." Mom's confused again. Her voice is strained, her face red.

"I told you that you didn't have to. At breakfast," I remind her.

Lauren appears next to me. "I heard her, Mom. You said okay."

Mom finally replies, "I guess it must be true then," and heads down the stairs.

"Kit?" Dad calls down after her.

"Don't push it," she says over her shoulder. "It's the end of the day, Lily's home, and I'm going to pour myself a drink. Maybe two."

"Kit!" Dad starts down the stairs after her.

"If you want to join me, fine," Mom says, reaching the bottom of the staircase.

They turn to face each other. Dad says, "This isn't the way to handle our problems, honey. Booze, pills."

Stop arguing!

Lauren doesn't pay attention. Whenever our parents fight, she goes in her room, locks the door, and calls Simone. They laugh and talk for hours.

"How dare you broadcast your sanctimonious pop psychology to the entire house!" Mom says. "Under the circumstances, it's a little hypocritical, don't you think? A little obvious? We were repo'd for months, or don't you remember? I will not let you lose this house!"

She glances up the stairs at me. "After school snack, Lily?"

"That's okay, I'm . . ." Do I follow?

On their way to the kitchen, my parents pass through the fancy un-used dining room, where an Easter brunch, with individual hand-painted flowerpots of paper whites and a centerpiece of flawless white lilies ("Hot house," Mom called them, "no Oregon rust on those babies"), was once set for *House Beautiful*.

I listen at the kitchen door when Dad says, "I'm not your average insurance executive. I'm not hitting the strip clubs after work with busi-ness associates. I drop by the track sometimes, but I've stopped most of it. I've changed, Kit, you know that. I come home to you and the girls every night."

Ice cubes drop in a glass. "Here," Mom says. I picture her handing Dad a drink.

"Now it's the cold shoulder? Kitty, please. We've been through a lot the last few years. We can get through this too."

"Excuse me, Paul," Mom's voice is high and she's talking fast, "but what have *you* been through? Did *your* sister die? Did *you* have three miscarriages?"

"Come on, sweetheart. You're all wound up. I'd rather have you read me the riot act than—"

"Would you? That's wonderful, but I haven't heard you actually say it yet. Say it, Paul. Admit you still have a gambling problem. Admit that you're not Mr. Perfect."

"I'm *not* Mr. Perfect. I said I was sorry. Don't lecture me like I'm a child."

The freezer door opens again. I hear its motor.

"Did you know I painted a portrait of Lily? I took a picture of her working on a shoe box. She braided her hair with strips of rags and drew designs on her hands and feet. She's an original, Paul, like Jamie always said."

More ice in a glass.

"And the portrait? Gee, thanks for asking."

"Jesus, Kit, come up for air! Give me a chance to respond . . . I don't remember you showing it to me. Did you show it to me?"

"It's good," she sniffs. "In fact, I liked it so much I entered it in another contest—no, no, don't touch me, Paul. Why must you always touch me when I'm trying to talk to you?"

"What the hell do you want from me?"

There's a scary pause before Mom answers. "I don't want you to grovel."

"Then tell me what you want. I don't understand what's going on."

I understand. Their words are teeth and they're tearing each other apart.

"You don't understand? That's funny, I always thought you were the smarter one. I guess I'm wrong; I guess you don't understand. Maybe you've sat at that big desk for so long your brain's gone soft." Her voice is as cold and wide as the Pacific Ocean. "I didn't go to the track, Paul. *You* went to the track. You went to the track because you're," she pauses, "weak."

There's another scary pause before Dad says, "Damn it, Kit."

And then he does it.

He slaps her.

I try to make the sound into something else, but I can't. Mom immediately gasps. I imagine her putting her hand to her face.

I gasp too, and cover my mouth. Then run upstairs, past Lauren's room to mine, where even after turning on every light, it's still as dark as Crawford Quarry on a new moon.

I hate it here.

An hour later, I tiptoe past our parents' bedroom, downstairs, through the kitchen where a cartoon bubble with the word *slAAPPP!* (in angry black letters) bounces between the ceiling and the floor. Peering outside, I see the bay window of Dad's study and his favorite chair, where he sits with his head in his hands.

I sneak into the garage and grab my bike and flashlight. It's almost dusk, and as I ride through our new rich neighborhood, looking at all the big cars and bigger houses, I wonder who else was slapped tonight.

What's happening to my family?

I used to think that everything that went wrong was my fault, but maybe my parents fight so much because they shouldn't stay together. Jamie once said women shouldn't get married, but she ran off with Kevin, and look what it got her.

Something small and dead lies ahead under a streetlight. A possum, her guts dark and open, and little possum babies—curled up like tiny autumn leaves—spill out of her pouch. Possums are nocturnal. Was she taking them to safety? I gently pick them up, and place them in the bushes.

A cat meows. He'll eat the dead babies the minute I ride off.

Was the meteor show at Crawford Quarry the last time my family was happy? Every August, when the sky is full of meteors, I ask to go again. But Lauren doesn't want to, and Mom says, "Ask your father."

There's a hole in our family that's getting bigger every day.

The sky's a bowl. If you turn it upside down, it's a hole too.

I race along the sawdust trail that narrows and widens, narrows and widens, breathing with me like the giant walk-through lung at the science museum.

Up ahead is the basalt quarry, the bombed-out crater, the hole all the way to China. Up ahead is the quiet openness of the pit and the early-evening sky.

Up ahead are Mr. and Mrs. Waterston, out for their daily constitutional. I ring my bell in warning. I smell White Shoulders when I pass; Frieda wears it too.

"Lord's sake, Lily," Mr. Waterston scolds.

Would *he* slap his wife?

Trees fly past. Darkness leans over me, but suddenly I'm there and rest my bike against a tree. I'm alone with the stars and the quarry until . . . a horse nickers.

A horse? At the quarry? "Careful, Beauty, care-ful," the rider purrs. "Not too close." The horse whinnies, throwing back its head, as the girl pulls it away from the lip again.

When they stop under the North Star, I see them both: the tall white horse and the girl with the blond hair and sunglasses. Bareback, just reins.

A white horse!

Then they're heading toward me. I freeze in place until, only feet away, the rider pulls up on the reins and says, "Whoa." She sits back and listens. "Is someone there?" She's pretty, prettier than snobby Willa Perkins any day.

Sunglasses. Is she blind?

"I'm here," I say, stepping in front of them. The horse snorts loudly. "I didn't mean to scare you. I'm sorry. I didn't see you at first."

The girl lowers the reins and pats the horse's thick white neck. "Did you hear that, boy?" She laughs. "*She* didn't see *us*."

Is she making fun of me? "You shouldn't walk your horse so close to the edge," I say in my know-it-all voice. "It's dangerous."

The girl drops her smile and sits up even straighter. "You're right. I'm blind, and Beauty's old. We should be more careful."

Beauty snuffles my sweatshirt with his big soft nose. When he gets a snoot-full, he snorts loudly and I jump. The girl pulls back on the reins and Beauty steps back.

"He likes the pit," she says. "He likes to walk along the edge. Horses have their own personalities, you know. Like people."

"I was rude. And bossy. Sorry."

"No, no, you're absolutely right. It *is* dangerous. Usually I feel the air rising up from the pit and steer us away, but not tonight. Everything's so still and warm. I heard the bats, and the quarry office radio. I should have heard you too, but I didn't until Beauty led me this way. He must like you."

I reach out without thinking, to touch him.

"Go ahead," the girl says. "Beauty won't mind."

How does she know I reached out?

My hand is dark against the short white hair of the horse's chest, feeling the warm firm muscles underneath.

"Can you keep a secret?" the girl asks.

"Yes," I quickly answer.

The girl leans forward. "I'm not supposed to be here. But Beauty and I don't like being told what to do. I live with my grandparents; they own the butte and the quarry. During the day I ride with someone, but at night, while they entertain their friends, Beauty and I sneak out. I can saddle him myself, but we like going bareback. The security guard doesn't care if we're here. This is a groovy place, especially at night."

I pat Beauty again.

"No one knows what to say to a blind person. Thanks for talking to me, uh . . ."

"Lily."

"I'm Allison." Beauty nickers. "You must think it's special too, to be out here at night. Alone."

I don't say anything.

"I live around a lot of trees. Sometimes I feel them breathing and I get claustrophobic, so I come here where the air moves. I can feel the sky here too."

I smile.

"I feel you smiling, Lily." She pauses. "I wish I could see the stars."

"They're beautiful," I say. Then, "Sorry."

"Why? Because I'm blind and can't see them? Maybe I can see things you can't." She pauses again. "Do you like to read?"

"I love it. I like to write too."

Allison laughs. It bursts like milkweed and floats into the sky.

"I write poetry," she says. "I've even written about the pit."

"Really? I'd love to read it."

"You could give me your phone number."

But I'm not supposed to be here. What would I tell my mom when she called?

She waits. "Or," she says quietly, "maybe I'll meet you here again. I'll put it in my saddlebag. We try to come here every Wednesday night."

"Okay," I say. Like we made a plan. Like we could be friends someday.

"I love words." She smiles. "Each one is full of mystery. You can make them whatever you want them to be."

"You *are* a poet," I say.

"You know, there's an expression I heard in Mexico," Allison says, patting the thick white neck of her horse. "*Emptiness pulls.* The pit pulls Beauty and me. Maybe it pulls you too."

The air is spicy. Crickets sing in the bushes.

I think of the clay horse Mom made.

Across the pit, Mom and Dad and Lauren count the meteors overhead. "Comets!" Mom calls. "Doughnuts!" yells Lauren. Her cheeks twinkle with powdered sugar that floats off her face, joining the star show overhead.

"Why are you here, Lily?" Allison asks.

"My parents argued," I blurt out. "Tonight my dad slapped her." *Really smart, Lily.* It's nobody's business. Now Allison will think Dad's a bad guy, and that I'm from one of those families that beat up on each other all the time. "It's complicated," I add.

After a long moment, Allison whispers in the horse's ear, "What do you think, boy?" She blows gently and the horse nods. "Beauty agrees," Allison says, sitting up again. "Would you like to climb up behind me and ride around with us?"

"Okay," I say excitedly. "But how do I—"

"Give me your hand, then kind of jump, and I'll pull you up. I'm stronger than you think." She is too. Once I'm settled behind her, she asks, "Ready?"

"Okay," I say breathlessly. "But not too close to the edge." It's funny how I can see but I'm scared, and Allison can't but she isn't.

We walk around the quarry, a safe distance from the lip of the pit.

The White Horse.

The Blind Girl.

And me.

Lauren is sitting on my bed when I tiptoe in. "Where were you?" she asks quietly. She's been crying.

I sit down beside her. My heart beats like crazy after sneaking up the stairs. "What happened?" I ask, pretending I don't know.

"He hit her." Lauren chokes back the tears. "She didn't say he did, but I saw the marks on her face. She was in our bathroom washing her face. She told me not to worry. She said they loved each other and everything would be okay in the morning."

Without asking, Lauren climbs under my covers. "I thought you ran away," she says softly.

I glance at the white clay horse on the nightstand, and hold a strand of hair under my nose, sniffing the night air.

"If you run away, you'll take me with you, won't you, Lily?"

"Sure. We'll run away together."

Lauren scoots down in the covers and yawns. "I like your shoe box."

She means the new one with the papier-mâché house, painted yellow with red shutters. And two blind llamas—Ray, and the friend he never had—one at each end.

"Really?" She never likes my shoe boxes. I kick off my tennis shoes. "It's for Aunt Jamie's ashes. Do you think she'd like it?"

"Yeah. It's neato. Maybe you'll be an artist like Mom someday."

"Maybe."

"Lily? Did Dad slap her when we lived on Aiken Street?" My sister has the same deep crease in her forehead as Dad.

"I don't think so," I say, turning off the lights, slipping out of my jeans. "No. I'm pretty sure he didn't."

"That's good," my sister mumbles.

I watch my radio clock and wait 3.7 minutes before I whisper, "I have a secret. I met a beautiful white horse at the quarry pit," but Lauren's already asleep.

I wonder if we'll like each other when we're grown up.

That night I dream Mom walks across the pit on a tightrope. Lauren and I sit on the edge, our feet hanging over, applauding her.

"Emptiness pulls," Allison said.

CHAPTER 21
THE REPORT CARD

I wish we'd moved to Paris instead of Crawford Heights. Kids my age wear berets, drink coffee, and smoke cigarettes in Paris. They read poetry out loud to each other and argue about God. Art books show photographs of couples kissing in Paris, usually with the Seine in the background. People make out like crazy over there.

I walk home from the school bus every weekday—and pass the same boring colonial homes with used brick, fancy bay windows, and big green yards—but they never look familiar.

I think I'd recognize a windmill though, especially if it was sitting at the edge of a windy slough with ponies grazing at its feet and snow geese flying overhead.

I'd recognize a neighborhood of whitewashed houses on a Greek island too, and wave at the short gummy-mouthed old woman in black, who stands at her stone fence petting a goat named Socrates. "Good day at school?" she calls. A telescope is strapped to my back. I'm hiking to the top of a rocky white hill to watch the stars.

It's fun to daydream as I walk home. Dr. Giraffe says daydreaming is okay; it's the other fantasies that get me in trouble.

Mrs. Bennett honks as she passes. It startles me and I drop my report card.

Mom doesn't like Mrs. Bennett. After she called one of Mom's recent canvases "nice," Mom grumped about it for days. "*Nice*? What the hell does that mean?"

When I bend over to pick up my report card, another car drives by and some stupid jerk yells out his window, "Nice ass!" Sometimes I wish I weren't "becoming a woman," and could be something in-between or no sex at all.

Sometimes I don't think Mom likes being a woman either. My report card should make her happy though.

246

When we moved to Crawford Heights, she told me she didn't care what grades I got as long as I was "happy and healthy." The family always celebrates Lauren's good grades, so when I asked if we could go to Van's Drive-In when I improved my grades, Mom said, "Sure, whatever you want."

I want to be rewarded, like Lauren is. I want to be a regular freshman at Crawford High School and not some weirdo who used her drowned dog as a flotation device. I want my family to hug me and congratulate me on the 3.8 report card I'm holding in my hand. I want them to gush at the As I got on makeup work, the special comments from my art teacher, and my English teacher's suggestion that I work on the school newspaper next year.

"Mom!" I call out, standing in the foyer. "I want to show you something!"

Harry and Bess, the matching cockatiels she got for her birthday, screech at me from their cage in the kitchen nook. "Upstairs," Mom finally answers.

She's painting. She'll be in a good mood.

Dad gets home around six. I'll show him my report card, and the four of us will pile into the car, singing songs and playing car games like we used to. We'll pass the Grotto with its Stations of the Cross, the furniture factory, and then, *ta-da!* Van's Drive-In!

I hit the stairs running.

Extra-tall chocolate shake, thin-cut curly fries, burgers, and corn dogs.

At the landing I call out, "Guess what?"

Lauren slams her bedroom door. She's on the phone, of course.

Mom sits at her easel staring at a blank, framed canvas. Her back is to the door, and the room is thick with the blue smoke of cigarettes. A half-empty bottle of vodka sits on the windowsill. Without thinking, I hold my nose high and sniff for danger.

"Do you smell it?" she asks me.

"Do I smell what?" My hands are sweaty and the corner of the report card bends where I hold it. My heart beats so hard it lifts my sweater.

"The blood," she says, impatiently. "The blood of the Vietnamese. Even the cigarettes don't cover it."

Not tonight, Mom, please.

Pinned to her empty canvas is a photograph of a crying woman bent over a dead baby. Except for a bright red cloth in the background of the picture, everything is dusty, even the woman and child. Usually Mom wouldn't paint something like that; there's not enough color "to make the subject pop." But she's not painting anyway, she's drinking, and when she turns to look at me, I see that she's been crying too. Her eyes are swollen, and what remains of her makeup blotches her face with black smudgy hyphens.

I got an A minus, technically an A hyphen, in world studies. I hold out my report card and stare at her. She doesn't see it.

"Don't you smell it, Lily?"

I don't smell anything. I'd rather cut off my nose than smell blood thousands of miles away. Maybe I'm just taller these days, but Mom's smaller than she used to be. Crying shrinks her, draining off her 86 percent water inside, and once she starts she cries for everyone: Vietnam and Romania, Jamie, her lost Jewish family, kids dying of hunger and disease.

"Mom? *Mom!*" When she finally looks at my hand, a question crosses her face. "You promised," I say quietly.

"You raised your grades? Congratulations, Lily!" She buttons her work shirt. "Van's, right?" She smiles, briefly sober and pretty, then frowns. "Sure, we can do that, but . . . but can you imagine how much rice a Vietnamese family could buy with the money for a burger and shake?"

I drop my hand.

SOG should be taking care of the Vietnamese people, not me.

The room is suddenly noisy with the sound of Mrs. Bennett's gardeners. The lawn-care specialists come every Thursday afternoon, filling the block with the racket of lawn mowers, rakes, and electric hedge trimmers. Mom says we moved to an affluent neighborhood because that's what you do when you start making money. Lauren's friend Simone lives up the street in the house with the big white columns and a wraparound porch. They used to have a black maid, but since the March on Washington they have a Mexican one. Except for being closer to Crawford Butte and the Grotto, I don't like it here.

"Let's talk about it downstairs, shall we?" Mom says.

No we won't. Mom won't snatch up my report card, dancing me around the room. She's not going to say, *I always knew you could do it*, then try, in vain, to talk me into dinner at Oscar's instead of Van's.

248

Downstairs, in the kitchen, Lauren doesn't notice my report card either. "Dinner at Van's!" I say, holding it up.

"Can't. I'm eating at Simone's; tell Mom, okay? We're on the same math team and we need to study. This chapter's really kicking my butt."

Maybe it's wrong to want a hamburger, but a deal's a deal. At least it is when Lauren makes one. I set my report card on the counter. "But the whole family's going to Van's."

"Not me," she says, skipping out of the room.

I alternate sitting on the third, sixth, and ninth steps while I wait for Mom to come down. I cross and uncross my legs, roll and reroll my jean cuffs, and pick at the scab on my elbow until it hurts. When I hear the vodka bottle fall off the windowsill, I slowly walk upstairs again. My left foot is angry, my right foot scared.

Angry.

Scared.

Angry.

Scared.

"Mom?"

She's covered the easel with a sheet; the bottle's in the trash. She locks the door and leans into me as we walk downstairs.

The more I think about the night Dad slapped her, the more certain I am that it didn't happen. It was a rip or something, like the awful sound cloth makes when Mom tears it and it hangs like a broken wing in her hands.

She smells of Doublemint gum.

"Do you miss Aiken Street? Do you miss the old house?" I ask. Gulliver disappeared after we moved here. We were all homesick at the beginning. Then school started, and Mom had more time to paint; and I spent every Tuesday and Thursday after school in the art room making stuff.

"Not really. Do you?"

No. Yes. "No," I answer. "Have you ever been to Paris? I mean, when you were little and lived in Europe?"

Mom turns to me and smiles. "No. Have you?"

"How about Greece?"

"Wouldn't it be wonderful, Lily? We could both set up our easels on some rocky beach, and snorkel in undersea caves." The worry lines in Mom's face clear, the bags under her eyes fade. "We're alike, you and me," she says. "I know you don't think so, but we are. We understand each other."

But I don't want to understand her. I don't want to agree with her when she says the world is full of uncaring people and it's just a matter of time until we blow ourselves up. I don't want to be reminded of the quiet skinny kid at school who always gets beat up on his walk home. I don't know his real name; everyone just calls him Cry Baby.

Dr. Giraffe said that a clinical study just came out about genes and alcoholism and "addiction is both inherited *and* modeled."

When Mom suggests we wait at the kitchen table "for your father to come home," I do the crossword in the *TV Guide* and don't say a word.

Dad holds up my report card. "There's our little scholar," he beams, and jingles his car keys. "Ready, Freddy?"

Mom says Dad should have been an actor because he can change his emotions on a dime. Or a trial lawyer. Or a fairy-tale knight, because he thinks people ought to act better than they do. Years ago, at a parade downtown, Dad suddenly grabbed a stranger by the collar and marched him up to a policeman. The surprised man had a little mirror taped to the tip of his shoe; he used it to look up women's dresses.

Mom touches my arm. "We're so proud of you, sweetheart."

My stomach growls. I try to unknot my fists but I can't.

"Van's Drive-In, here we come!"

Mom steps back.

"You're not going?" I ask.

"It'll be more special without Lauren and me. You and your dad never have enough time together."

Dad's outside honking the horn.

She hands me my coat.

"But . . ."

"You earned it, Lily, now go enjoy yourself. And I'm . . . sorry about earlier." Dad honks again. "I'm a little drunk. You know that, don't you?"

Yes. A blind girl riding a white horse would know she was drunk. I look toward the door. I thought I was done with it. I thought I didn't care anymore if she was drunk or sober, but I guess I do. I guess I do.

"I'll be fine."

Who cares?

"I'll be fine," she repeats.

But Dad isn't. He drives too fast. Forty-five miles per hour down a thirty-five-miles-per-hour street. When I mention it, he scowls at me.

I cross my arms against my chest and push my fists into my boobs. I don't want boobs. I don't want boys looking at them, or honking at me when I drop something. I don't want to have an artistic temperament like Mom.

It's a longer trip to Van's since we moved to the other side of town. 136th has been widened, digging into people's yards with only a thin strip of gravel and litter separating them from the road. It must be strange to walk out your front door and watch people race through your yard. Someone threw a sack of empty beer bottles in front of one house. A mangy-looking dog tied to a rope makes a big dirt circle in front of another.

"It's pathetic," Dad says. "It used to be such a nice neighborhood." Then he bangs on the steering wheel and mumbles to himself. We're going fifty miles per hour now. At the next light he sits back and takes a deep breath. "Hungry?" he asks.

I nod.

"Me too." He looks tired.

I don't know what to say. "Hard day at the office?"

"Yep," Dad smiles. "But this is your night, Miss 3.8. Tell me about school this term. What do you like best?" He tries to sound upbeat but there's a twitch in the outside corner of his eye. Mom calls it the Kit Twitch.

I like lots of stuff. Especially when no one makes fun of me. "Math, of course," I tell him. "Science. Literature. I like learning about the Industrial Revolution. I like writing stories and art. Art and writing are my favorite subjects."

"You know, Lily," Dad says, "I read that some geologists believe the earth is three and a half billion years old. How 'bout them apples?"

"Cool."

Dad loves geology. Rocks, minerals, shale, volcanic refuse from the lava beds upriver, fossils with embedded seashells, all that stuff. He collected samples when he was a kid; there are boxes of it in the garage.

"Three and a half billion years old," he repeats, shaking his head with wonder.

My fists relax. I'm glad Mom and Lauren aren't here.

A school bus pulls into the lane ahead of us.

"Do you think we're alike?" I ask.

"Who?"

"Mom and me. Do you think we're alike?"

"No," he says right away. "Not at all."

Good. I look at Dad and sit up straight. I'm fifteen and nearly as tall as Mom. With the flat of my hand I measure the distance between the top of my head and the ceiling of his car.

"You're getting tall," he says.

"Yeah . . . from the top of my head to the tip of my tail." Did I say *tail?*

"Jesus," Dad says, laying on the horn. The school bus is right in front of us; it's creeping along. When the fat boy in the backseat hears Dad's horn, he flips us off then pulls down his pants, mooning us. Raindrops on the steamy window make his white butt looks like melting candle wax.

"The perfect end to a perfect day!" Dad says, honking the horn again. "Some juvenile delinquent flashes his bare ass at us."

Now all the kids in the backseat make faces. "It's okay," I say nervously. "I'm not in any rush."

It's raining hard, and Dad turns up his windshield wipers. "Goddamn it, Kit," he mutters as he pulls around the bus.

Up ahead, on the right, is the bright red neon spaceship of Van's Drive-In.

"There it is," I point.

It happens in a flash.

A blue metal blur slides into us, and Dad slams on the brakes. The sound hurts my fillings. Dad throws his arm in front of me, like the gate at a railroad crossing. It thumps my chest, but the sudden stop pushes me through it, and I slam into the dashboard.

I hit the windshield and am thrown back again, knocking my breath into the backseat.

Where's my seat belt?

I smell the brakes. And oil.

Dad?

The car has stopped, but I'm still moving. My head bobs like the bobblehead figure on Frieda's old dashboard. My head has a mind of its own . . . that's funny, isn't it.

Dad?

The blue metal blur comes to a stop in the gravel beside the road too, spitting rocks at our car, making little dents in its freshly waxed hood.

I think I should be hurting but I don't feel it yet.

"Dad?" When I open my eyes the light burns, so I close them again.

He moans and swears. Then says my name. When he kicks open his door, cool air fills the car. It's still raining.

The car seat moves; he's gotten out. Gravel crunches. The car rocks when he briefly leans against it for balance. More gravel crunches as he walks to my side.

I hear strange voices in the background, footsteps running toward us and, in the distance, a siren.

"Lily!" Dad struggles with the door handle, yanking it open, swearing. Then he clears his throat. Men always clear their throats before they say something important. "Daddy's here, Lily. Don't move . . . but if you can hear me, honey, wiggle a finger for me. Just a finger. Wiggle a finger for Daddy."

I taste salty blood in my mouth. Doll-sized breaths make me sleepy. My body is heavy. Something hurts, somewhere far away inside me, maybe Greece, maybe Paris.

The pain gets closer the more I concentrate on my father's voice.

"Lily? Can you hear me?"

I'm a little burger, short and stout . . .

Spaceships and french fries float through the interior of Dad's car.

Here is my handle, here is my spout . . .

A chocolate malt. A dipping tray, please.

The earth is three and a half billion years old. How 'bout them apples?

Someone is moving me. It hurts like hell. "It hurts like hell. Can I say that? Can I say it hurts like hell?"

"Sure. Go ahead," Mom says. "It probably does."

I open my eyes. A crack. Just a *crack crack bo-back, banana-fana fo-fack . . .*

I'm in a hospital.

Or on the set of *Dr. Kildare.*

Or in poor Dorothy Gale's bedroom at the end of *The Wizard of Oz*. *And you, and you and you were there*, I say in my mind, pointing at each member of my family.

Only my hand is a paw and my index finger a thick black nail like Mrs. Wiggins's. Did the doctors find my tail? Did it break off during the accident? Was it shoved inside me with the impact of the crash?

"Welcome back, sweetheart," Mom says. She sits in a chair next to my bed.

Lauren looks up from a copy of *Vogue*. "Hey, klutz," she says.

Dad explains that the accident was yesterday. He has cuts and bruises, especially on his arm, and for a month he'll have to wear a stiff white neck-thing that makes him look like one of those long-necked African women in *National Geographic*, but he'll be okay.

"You broke your arm and suffered a concussion. It rattled you up pretty good, Lily Lou."

"You've got an egg on your forehead," Lauren says, still flipping pages.

An egg? On my forehead? What's an egg doing there?

"We weren't wearing our seat belts, Lily," Dad says. "Neither one of us buckled up. We were talking and forgot, I guess. I should have checked, I should have—"

"It would never have happened if I'd gone with you," Mom interrupts. "Or if we went to Van's the next day, or waited until I . . . felt better."

"I drove too fast and totaled the car." Dad sniffs. "The whole thing is my—"

"Stop it!" Lauren cries, jumping to her feet. "Everybody did something wrong. Jeez! Lily's awake, so can we please go home now?"

Someone places Mrs. Wiggins's tooth in my hand, and curls my fingers around it. The room turns foggy and milky white.

I stand in the bushes as Beauty walks toward me. He lifts his head and sniffs the air.

"It's just a little morphine, sweetheart," Mom whispers. "Just sleep. All you have to do is sleep."

A gum bubble pops nearby. It startles me awake and I imagine flying off the bed, running into one wall then another like a pinball.

"Lauren, please," Mom says.

Snap. Crackle. Pop. The cereal elves tie me down like Gulliver in

Lilliput, doing cat's cradles with my tubes, and somersaults off my drip.

Drip.

Drip.

"Aren't you better yet?" It's Lauren, standing next to me.

"She's coming home tomorrow, remember?" Mom says. "The doctors want to be sure. We want the doctors to be sure."

How long have I been here? "How long have I been here?"

"Three days. They were worried about the concussion. Get all the sleep you can, Lily. You're back in school on Monday."

"You ruined my slumber party," Lauren glares, "and Mom won't let me see Simone until next week! I have to come here every afternoon after school, even when you're sleeping."

"Sorry," I say, only it doesn't sound like "sorry," and Lauren rolls her eyes.

"Quit bothering your sister," Mom says.

My beautiful barefoot mother sits in front of her easel on a rocky beach in the Greek islands. Canvases are everywhere, catching in the wind, flying into the sea. Two large, white, paint-splattered wings fold neatly against her back. Her hands are a blur as she covers one canvas after another with bright colors. Her face is tan, her cheeks speckled with freckles like Lauren's. Her teeth are white; she can't stop grinning.

"Doesn't your father seem happy?" Mom asks me. She points her paintbrush at Zorba the Greek, dancing at the ocean's edge. "Lily, where's your easel?"

"Ah-CHOO," Lauren sneezes.

Amen.

Ah, Man.

Lauren left her spiral notebook here, accidentally-on-purpose. It's full of doodles, spelling tests (one B minus, two Cs), and a half-finished essay on our trip to Lake Tahoe. Lauren loves talking on the phone, so she drew a receiver in the upper left-hand corner of the page, and a thin telephone cord that curls all over the things she wrote about: the restaurants, the gift shops, the trip we finally took to the phony-baloney Ponderosa Ranch.

She didn't write about the pool; or how Mom danced with Ben Cartwright and everyone in the restaurant watched while she fell in love with him and wanted to run away with him, run away from *us*, even if it was only for a few minutes.

Lauren didn't mention Mrs. Ford either, so I added:

Mrs. Ford and her boyfriend sit together on the square dance bus.

On the drive to Lake Tahoe, he gives her the seat by the window, and they share the meat loaf sandwiches (lots of ketchup, no lettuce) Mrs. Ford made for them. Afterward, he falls asleep with his head on her shoulder. She smiles and looks out the window at the cacti and jackrabbits and the beautiful deep red canyons, and imagines wagon trains seeing the same things on their way to Oregon. Mrs. Ford's boyfriend doesn't sleep long and when he wakes up, she digs a sack of sugar cookies out of her knitting bag and gives him three (no, four) before sharing the rest with the bus.

Mrs. Ford doesn't care what her hair looks like. She doesn't worry about her weight. She doesn't like one-calorie Tab or Roman Meal bread. Inside her fridge at home is whole milk not skim, packages of thickly cut pepper bacon, and sticky jars of homemade blackberry jam she puts on pieces of potato bread with the crusts cut off.

She rescued two long-haired dachshunds and a three-legged cat from the Humane Society. She knits hats for orphans all year long and she plays bridge at least once a week. She likes the Three Stooges (even though most grown-ups don't). Mrs. Ford knows the first and last names of every clerk at her favorite grocery store, sends brand-new twenty dollar bills to each one of her grandkids on their birthday, and gets her hair done every third Wednesday morning at Betty's Beauty College. The last thing she looks at, when she crawls into bed at night, is a framed photo, on her bed stand, of the late Mr. Ford. She's danced with the Cheyenne Squares for fifteen years, and only missed two performances: when Mr. Ford died, and when she had her appendix out. Her new boyfriend and dance partner is Mr. Ed Boetcher (pronounced "Butcher"), the man on the bus.

Maybe they'll get married someday and take long summer bus rides to square dance conventions all over America.

Maybe they'll even fly to Paris and dance in front of the Eiffel

Tower, where dark handsome men in turbans and beards, and graceful women in kimonos (with chopsticks in their hair), will clap for them and take pictures.

I glance at the wall clock at the end of the bed. It's 10:32. My door is closed and the blinds are drawn. It's late, way past visiting hours.

Mom said I'm going home tomorrow.

Next to me on the bed is an empty shoe box. Inside it are two handwritten notes. The first one, in Mom's writing, reads, *This coupon is good for one UN-BIRTHDAY lunch with Mom, any restaurant you choose. AND,* which she also capitalized, *fifty dollars worth of art supplies. Coupon good until December 31, 2050.*

She'll be dead by then.

PS, Mom also wrote. *I know you'll make something amazing with the shoe box!* Then, *PPS. I promise to get help for my drinking.*

I give Mrs. Wiggins's tooth a squeeze. Don't count on it, it squeezes back.

The second note, on pink stationery with a gold embossed *JC* at the top of the page, reads, *You're my miracle.*

Stay out of my shoe boxes, SOG! "I'm not your miracle!" I scream. "I don't belong to you! I don't belong to anyone!"

Jerk.

His note flies out of my hand and under the bed when the nurse bursts in.

"Lily?" she says, rushing to my side. "You were screaming. Are you all right?"

My head hurts. She gives me an aspirin, turns off the bed light, and props the door open when she leaves. In the hallway, she greets another nurse and they both laugh.

"Close it!" I yell, and throw the shoe box on the floor.

CHAPTER 22

GOD BLESS THE MIDWAY

Mom says I should write an article for the local paper about all the crappy TV I've watched since the accident: game shows, talk shows, soap operas, cartoons. *Dark Shadows* is okay, but I get tired of Jesus showing up on it. He thinks it's funny to creep up behind Barnaby Collins and bite his neck when the aging vampire's not looking. But I'm not laughing. It isn't funny when He shows up scrubbing toilets or selling cars during commercials, either.

Most of all, I hate that weird European clown with the white leggings on *The Ed Sullivan Show*.

"Why, you sound like a teenager, Lily. You hate everything these days." Mom looks up from her darning. Dad's long toes wear holes in his socks all the time.

"But he's not even trying to be funny," I say, pointing at the TV.

"Not all clowns are funny."

"Then what's the point?"

I like Emmett Kelly better, even though he just mopes around. Mom told me he paints too, only it's always the faces of sad clowns. Kind of spooky, I think. Rod Serling should write a story about him for *The Twilight Zone*.

Mom kneels beside the TV and flips the channel. On the next station, David Niven pops his monocle at platinum-haired, big-boobed Jayne Mansfield. Mom says I've inherited Frieda's body type, which means I'll be tall and skinny, get arthritis, and never have big boobs like Jayne or Diana Dors. Or her.

"Remember Manners the Butler?" Mom asks. "You loved him when you were little. Didn't he have a monocle?"

My heart jumps into my throat. "You mean the TV commercial? The little butler who stood by the dining room table and handed you a paper napkin when yours slipped off your lap?" I stare at the cover of *Vogue:* a super-tall, half-clothed, lion-maned model barely fits on the cover. "No. No monocle."

"You remember!" Mom says. "I'm surprised. You were hardly more than a baby."

Of course I remember Manners the Butler. He moved in under my bed when I started my period; he even moved with us to the new house. He's always quiet and never complains. When he can't sleep I read him Tom Thumb, or something from *Gulliver's Travels*; he likes hearing about other tiny people.

"The man who played Manners was a good actor," Mom says, "but the ads were popular and he was typecast as an English butler and couldn't find any other work." It must be hard when you're fifteen inches tall. Still, I made a list of all the TV and movie butlers I could think of and slipped it under my bed for him: William Powell, Leo J. Carroll, and Alan Napier, the actor who played Alfred the butler on *Batman*.

Move to Hollywood! I wrote. Maybe Jesus could go with him.

Mom puts down her darning and begins sketching my hands. She likes variety; she likes to keep busy. Frieda says, "Idle hands are the devil's workshop."

"Manners is weird," I say.

I hope he hears me; I want him to go away.

Mom grabs a poker chip off the coffee table and, using it as a monocle, mumbles, "I say, I say," in a bad English accent.

I found a pair of my panties under the bed, covered in dust bunnies. Manners is usually very neat; I think he didn't want me to find them.

The butler list was under there too; a tiny teacup stain in the corner told me he'd read it.

Lauren said it was spider poop.

I dream that Mom's the fat lady at the circus.

She sits on a throne in the Midway, surrounded by trash, with tufts of angry grass pushing through the straw. Emmett Kelley and the weird clown with white leggings sit on bales of hay on either side of her. I'm there too, crouching behind her Eva Gabor wig and thick dimpled arms.

Manners, the miniature butler, stands on her knee, lifting her skirt for anyone who'll pay. Her legs lead to something too dark to see, but the men still want to look, and passing by slowly they stop to check their pockets for change.

Actor David Niven pays. So does Santa Claus.

I run to the man with the waxed mustache who keeps the ponies for the kiddy rides. I help him brush them, and braid their tails. He pats their flanks and smells their ears. "Sweet," he says.

When the pony man's wife goes to bed, I sit between his legs facing the campfire, and we talk. I tell him stories about Captain Nemo, Tarzan (Lord Greystoke), Robinson Crusoe, and Sherlock Holmes. The pony man tells me about the love affair between the Bearded Lady and Cleo the Pygmy Contortionist, how one of the Flying Dutchmen has three nipples ("Guess which one!") and all the clowns are drunks.

With his arm around my waist, the pony man holds me against his pinstriped vest. I don't mind. He presses his nose in my hair and whispers, "Sweet." His breath quivers. His mustache twitches.

He prays in a language I don't understand, but then says in English, "God bless the Midway." Sparks from the fire snap and fly, landing in the soft duff around us. "Watch over my ponies," he adds, then moves his warm hand between my legs. "And the fat lady's beautiful daughter."

I know the dream is about sex, but Mom calls sex "hormones." She calls everything hormones.

Now that I'm fifteen, she's even more afraid that I'll embarrass her. She blushes when I ask for more information, even though Dad and Lauren are out of the house and I'm only writing it down on my clipboard.

"It doesn't matter," I say. "Nobody will want to have sex with me anyway."

"Yes they will. You're going to knock them dead," Mom says, which doesn't make me feel better. Since Jamie died, nothing about death makes me feel better.

I don't sit on the end of my bed anymore either, petting an imaginary Mrs. Wiggins, howling at the moon. Instead I sleep with my head under the pillow, and bite my tongue until it bleeds. Sometimes my tail throws back the covers, slips over the edge, and thuds to the floor—fleshy, thick, and heavy—taking me with it.

The school nurse told us that teenagers need at least eight hours of sleep every night, but my body doesn't listen to anyone.

The car accident makes me sleepy at the craziest times. Like falling asleep during dinner. Other times I can't sleep at all.

Tonight I lie in bed, rubbing my bare foot on my leg stubble for thirty-six, er, thirty-seven minutes. I rub my leg clockwise, then counter-clockwise, then clockwise, then counterclockwise . . .

"You'll never catch any z's if you don't get up and shave."

"Manners?" I've read to him, but we've never actually talked. I lean over the bed, pull up the dust ruffle, and whisper again, "Manners?"

No answer. He must be out. I hope he's looking for another flat. That's what they call apartments in England.

I fill the bathroom sink with warm tap water and soap my legs. Thin islands of scum spread over the water, reminding me of the islands on the flight maps Dad found in the basement. Dad loves those maps. Last Sunday, he pulled up his favorite overstuffed chair, drank beer, and stared at the maps for most of the afternoon.

"Up kind of late, aren't you?" Jesus asks, suddenly appearing in the doorway.

Startled, I drop the razor and bang my hospital bracelet (*Head Injury, Possible Seizures*) on the enamel basin. I look for Jesus's reflection in the bathroom mirror, forgetting He's half-vampire and doesn't have one.

"Late?" I ask. Which isn't really a question, and I pick up the razor and draw it the length of my leg. When I look again, He's tossing a baseball hand to hand. "Besides, you're dead. Dead people know nothing about time."

"Dead?" Jesus says, pretending to be shocked. "Nobody told me I was dead."

"Hardee-har-har," I say, and promptly cut myself. I'd like to ask why He's dressed like a baseball player, but I don't want to encourage Him.

His cleats snag the pink bath mat when He sits down beside me on the edge of the tub. I blot at my leg with toilet paper, and He takes off His catcher's mitt.

His stigmata is bleeding again. "Damn thing," Jesus mutters.

"Want some?" I hand Him the hydrogen peroxide. Not because I've forgiven Him or even want to talk to Him; not because my head isn't right since the car accident (like Lauren says), or because He's SOG, either. I just want to be a good person.

"Son of God, huh?" Jesus says, reading my mind. "Until the crucifixion I was just Jesus of Nazareth, the blowhard know-it-all. The Pied Piper of the Lost and Disenfranchised."

Jeez, did He have too much communion wine?

"I should have stayed dead. Being on earth for thirty-three years was good enough; being mortal was great. I misled everyone with that Heaven business." Jesus sits up straight and shakes His head. "Woulda, coulda, shoulda, huh?" When I turn and look at Him, His dull halo glows. He's like the brother I never had: an older brother who leaves his dirty clothes by the bathtub.

Dad makes a loud rutting snore and two smaller ones. The headboard slams the wall when he rolls over.

Okay, I'm asking. "What's with the mitt?"

"It's a prop," He says. "Seeing that you were up and everything, I thought it was a good time for the 'Who's on First?' speech. But, uh, I don't think you want to hear it."

There's a quiet knock at the bathroom door. "Lily? Who are you talking to in there?" Mom asks.

"Kit?" Dad calls from the master bedroom. "Everything all right?" Since the concussion, he's worried about me all over again.

Jesus quickly writes, *I'M NOT HERE*, on the steamy surface of the mirror.

"No one," I answer them. "Just me." Mom walks away and I turn back to Jesus.

"You're familiar with Abbott and Costello's 'Who's on First' sketch, right?" He waits for a second. "Well, just substitute *me* for *who*."

Huh?

"Abbott and Costello?"

"I don't like them. Got any Marx Brothers?"

"Never mind," Jesus says. "I was trying to be clever. You know, find an entertaining way to remind you that, no matter how crazy things get, I'll always be here for you?"

What time is it?

His shoulders sag. "I'm keeping you up. Go get your eight hours of sleep."

"Actually," I say, rinsing off the razor, "it'll be more like four hours."

"Right, right." He nods and stands up. "You went to bed at 9:30 . . . you read for two hours, and rubbed your legs for . . . It's 2:35 right now . . ." He slips in and out of the ether, and I remember that He isn't good at math either. "You're shaving your legs. Growing up. I know you started your, you know, awhile back."

"Period?" I stare at the bathroom trash basket that includes today's *New York Times* crossword puzzle, which Mom does in pen. Must be a big deal, because Dad always brings it up at cocktail parties.

Getting my period is the only thing I have in common with the other high school girls, and it's kind of big if you think about it. I mean, girls bleed five days every month for forty years, whether we like it or not. Boys don't have anything like that.

Jesus follows me to my room.

"You said you'd always be there for me?" I ask. "You'll always be around?"

"Yep."

"Until when? When am I going to die?"

Jesus gets drifty-looking. "Everybody always asks me that question . . . How would I know? Lots can go wrong, just don't sweat it." He turns off the lamp beside my bed. "You'll wonder what's the point of living when you're only going to die, but you'll figure it out. I'll help you."

"But if you're with *me*, then who's with everyone else?"

Jesus: "Think of it like this: every department store has a Santa, right?"

Me: "Yeah, only I'm too old to believe in Santa."

Jesus: "Well, anyway, it's like that."

There was something in Santa's lap last time I sat on it. When I told Mom about it, she cleared her throat and said, patiently, "That's called an erection." Then she walked right up to Santa and slapped his face.

I'm standing on the narrow outside ledge of a skyscraper, pressing myself against its massive façade. Next to me, written on a steamy window, are Jesus's words: *I'M NOT HERE.*

A seagull lands beside me, and begins to preen. "God bless the Midway," it squawks, spitting truckloads of feathers that float to the garbage-strewn sawdust boulevard below.

* * *

The Midway.

At one end are the carnival rides. At the other, the circus Big Top stretches into the sky. Inside, the clown with white leggings towers over the crowded bleachers, a huge leg in each ring. Below him, twin white horses—with purple plumes on their bridles—trot around the inside of each ring with ballerinas on their backs. The crowd gasps, sloshing sodas and spilling popcorn, when the girls disappear behind the clown's enormous legs. They whistle and applaud when the girls reappear.

The horses' tails brush the giant's ankles, making him smile. They feel like butterfly kisses, the kind you make with your eyelashes. His shoulders support the tent's highest riggings; his head bursts through the top. He describes cloud formations (a bunny, a train engine, George Washington), and bellows changes in the weather that echo throughout the fair.

I sit on a throne under a banner that reads, *Circus Fat Lady.*

Mom crouches behind me shaking a can of loose coins, then looks away when the Three Stooges lift my skirt for anyone who'll pay.

My legs lead somewhere too dark to see, but men check their pockets for change anyway.

Emmett Kelly sits down in front of me. David Niven looks over his shoulder. Another man joins him, and soon every man on the Midway stands behind them. Cleo, the Pygmy Contortionist, and the Flying Dutchmen are there, Abbott and Costello, and all of Elizabeth Taylor's husbands.

Stop looking at me! I try screaming, but the words don't come out. Only the words of the pony man, who pushes through the crowd holding out a bit and halter and, kneeling between my legs, mumbles, "God bless the Midway," as he runs his thick calloused hands along my thighs.

I sit up with a start. I'm trembling all over.

"Good," Mom says, inching into my bedroom. "You're awake." My bed's center stage in a pool of morning sunshine; I squint to see her through the glare. "I've been calling you for ten minutes. Thought maybe the bed ate you up."

I blush. I'm wet between my legs, but it's not my period. The pony man's hand rests on the place between them. His fingers twitch.

"Must have been quite a dream; your bed's a mess." She gives my room a quick glance before sitting beside me. "I had crazy dreams when I was growing up too. Hormones, I suppose."

She kisses the top of my head and leaves, stopping at my door first to say, "Breakfast?"

I nod.

The Mamas and the Papas sing "California Dreamin'" on Lauren's radio. Dad's electric shaver groans as it fights his thick black beard. Under my bed, Manners shines his shoes, polishes his pocket watch, and practices rolling his bowler hat up and down his arm like Red Skelton does on TV. He wants to look nice for our date tonight. Climbing hand-over-fist up the blankets, burrowing through them to my new warm smells, shaved legs, and . . .

The sun slips behind a cloud, erasing everything but the smell of burnt sugar, popcorn, straw, and hot grease. Everything but the abandoned trapeze ropes that hang from the ceiling, like spiderwebs on TV's *Dark Shadows*. And—in the Midway dirt beside my bed—my mother's footprints that glow when I slip my feet inside them.

CHAPTER 23

EMPTINESS PULLS

It's late Saturday morning and our parents are gone when Lauren comes barreling into my room.

"Lily!" she shouts. I look at her over the top of my book. "Some kid riding by on his bike just said a horse fell in the Crawford pit! I think it's your horse, Lily! The white horse."

Beauty!

The book slips to the floor when I jump off the bed. "When? Right now?"

"I guess. I don't know."

I touch my desk, dresser, and bed with the pointer finger of each hand, then, scrambling into my tennis shoes, glance at Lauren. She hasn't moved an inch. Just when she's the jerkiest sister in the world, she turns all concerned and sweet. I kiss her cheek as I run out of my room.

"Mom's entertaining the new neighbors tonight," she calls after me. "You better not be late. I'm not doing your chores no matter what Mom says."

Across the street the Bensons' twin shelties, Elmer and Floyd, rush to their living room window and whine.

I feel brave and foolish as I ride through the block on my ten-speed, Mrs. Wiggins's tooth bouncing against my chest.

"Emptiness pulls," Allison told me. Did it finally pull Beauty over the edge? Is it drawing me there right now?

Lauren dreams about falling into the pit, only in her dreams she never touches bottom. I heard you die if you hit bottom, but I've dreamed of dying lots of times, and when I do I break into knobby little pieces that skitter around sideways like crabs.

And it doesn't hurt, it doesn't anything.

I'm almost to the quarry's *No Trespassing* sign before I remember how I got there: Tearing through the neighborhood, just avoiding the lady

Mom calls "Big Hair" as she pulled out of her driveway. Shaking and excited, I fell off my bike twice. And flying down the trail through the woods, I nearly ran down Sister Mary Joyce on her daily walk.

Finally, only yards from the entrance, I hear Beauty and I know it's true.

He's fallen.

He's suffering.

His cries echo the same high-pitched scream as a rabbit being killed, or a turtle ripped from its shell—sounds I've heard on TV nature shows.

He's dying.

I can't see him yet, but Beauty's tears already soak my hair and handlebars, and the ground under my bike like the overwatered terrarium at school where the Cracker Jack man lives. If "tears are protein," like Mom says, the thick vine across the path at the entrance to the quarry must be really healthy. With more tears it could cover everything in Crawford Woods, and it wouldn't matter what happened to Beauty or Lily Ashes-to-Ashes; they'd find us years later, like an ancient ruin you read about in *National Geographic*.

"Emptiness pulls," Allison told me.

E-M-P-T-I-N-E-S-S, I spell over and over, breathless and afraid, as I walk my bike into the barren opening. I put it down and look around.

Ahead of me is the pit. Quiet sad-faced people stand around its rocky rim like game pieces. Some I recognize, most I don't. Some cry, while others hug themselves, but no one looks away.

Quarry men walk around the edge in hard hats and denim jumpsuits, smoking cigarettes and speaking into walkie-talkies.

Where's Allison? Did she hurt herself in the fall?

Mrs. Garcia, from the old neighborhood, catches my eye and waves. I haven't seen her in months. I wave back, then stick my hands in my pockets and stare self-consciously at the little zits of earth between us. I wish I was back home and didn't know that Emptiness won and pulled Beauty in after it.

Suddenly I hear his terrible cry again, gurgling up from the bottom of the pit.

Allison hears it too. I see her across the hole—she's covered in dust, her dirty face striped with tears. "Beauty!" she cries.

The hair stands up on my arms and legs.

Tapping the ground with her riding crop Allison inches toward the edge, and I start running toward her.

Suddenly Mrs. Garcia is next to her, touching Allison's forearm, gently guiding her a safe distance from the rim. She slips her arm around Allison's waist and whispers to her, like Allison whispered to Beauty the night I met them, and the frightened girl relaxes. Neither of them notice the dusty saddlebag at their feet, its flaps open, the spilled pages around it. Poems Allison wrote, poems she promised to bring to Crawford Quarry, poetry she wanted to share with me.

How many Wednesday nights did she ride to the pit and call my name?

We could have been friends. For two hours every Wednesday night we could have been friends.

I look at the ground at my feet. The earth is gray and cracked like an open sore on the surface of the moon, and so ugly even the trees stand back farther than they need to. Does Emptiness stop pulling when you're already down there, or are there deeper, emptier places?

Maybe it's not so bad at the bottom. Maybe Beauty wanted to fall. Allison said he was old.

Finally I stand at the edge with everyone else and watch as, across the pit, Allison stretches out an arm and holds her hand steady, waiting to feel the air, the heat, Beauty's movement below.

He's talking to her with his breath. She's reading it with her hand.

When Allison screams, "Oh no!" my heart sinks. She doesn't need eyes to see Beauty.

I inhale the gritty metal of his blood when I finally look over. I can't make him out at first, just the jagged jutting basalt walls blotched with his shiny blood. The muscular white horse and scraped-to-the-bone gray-white floor of the quarry camouflage each other. But then he's there, like Frieda's photoflash, a pulsing spot at the bottom of the sun-washed crater; his long face, almond-shaped eyes, and black steaming nostrils jump at me from the dust.

His legs and side, covered in a thin frothy lather, are cut and bloody. Bits of cloudy, gravelly grit rain on him from the rim, and with each wheezing, strangled breath, his chest heaves and his flesh quivers.

He's broken and drowning inside.

"Don't move, boy," Allison says. "Help is coming!"

But hearing her, Beauty tries to get up, and he throws himself against the rocky interior with a heavy thump. Grunting, he presses a bloodied shoulder into the rock, tucks his trembling legs under him, and pulls himself to a leaning-stand against the quarry wall. An English saddle hangs from a single strap under his belly.

Daylight. Saddle. Beauty walked too close to the edge, lost his footing, threw Allison, and pitched over. He never fell when they rode bareback at night. Was he blinded by seeing too much?

"Look!" someone says. "He's trying to stand!"

"Beauty?" Allison smiles.

But the horse can't get his footing and his back leg slides out from under him again. He collapses with a deep meaty thud, first on his haunches, then on his side. A rib, like a broken steak knife, has torn through his chest.

People gasp. A woman turns away in tears; a couple walks off. Allison presses herself into Mrs. Garcia, who leads the sobbing girl toward the quarry office. A golf cart suddenly appears in the thinning crowd. An old man drives, while a younger man in a hard hat, tie, and short-sleeved white shirt walks beside the cart talking to him. He carries a megaphone.

"It's Old Man Crawford," someone says. "The blind girl's his granddaughter."

"*Folks,*" the quarry boss says into the bullhorn. Beauty jerks with the sudden sound. His eyes bulge, the whites brighten. "*Please, folks. This is private property. Unless you have permission to be here, you need to leave.*" Quarry men walk through the crowd, pointing at the trailhead.

A worker picks up the saddlebag and poetry.

In the giant hole, propped against the wall, Beauty looks small and forgotten, like a dirty white sock in the back of my closet. He snorts, making miniature sandstorms with his breath. Dark tearstains sit under each black dusty eye.

"I'm here," I say to him, lying down on my stomach. "I won't leave you." I hang my arms and head over the crumbling lip, reaching for him like I reached for Lauren two years ago. "Shhhh . . . shhh."

Minutes pass. I make myself invisible, and for ten minutes or so I succeed. No one sees me except Beauty.

Emptiness pulls. Beauty knows he's dying. And I know why he couldn't stay away and Allison kept coming back. I know why I'm here too. "Good boy," I say. "Everything's going to be fine."

Fine, fine, everything is fine.

Someone has to lie to Beauty.

The steam whistle sounds for lunch.

"Hey, Savage!" a man calls to a young quarry guy. "Ask Bob, in the truck there, if he brought his hunting rifle."

Savage?

"Savage!" the voice repeats. "Ask Bob to get his rifle. Orders, from the old man."

Savage pauses before walking back to a dump truck where he raps on the hood.

The figure in the driver's seat shakes Himself awake and steps outside. A lopsided halo wobbles over his head. The men talk briefly, and SOG glances toward the pit. He lights a cigarette, grabs His hard hat from the truck cab, and heads to the parking lot.

What's He doing here?

The Savage Boy moves around the pit toward me.

"Hey, kid!" says the megaphone. *"Get out of there!"*

Is he talking to me?

"I won't let them hurt you," I tell Beauty. "I'll be right here." Tears roll off my face into the pit. "I'm going to sing to you, okay? *Beauty beauty bo-beauty, banana-fana fo-footie . . .*" It's not a real song but it's all I can think of.

"Lily," Mike Savage says softly. He stands several feet away. Gravel kicks free under his boot. It catches in the rocky ribbed walls of the quarry pit, like a marble skipping along the roulette wheel where my beautiful mother and Sean Connery (as James Bond) play, his eyes glued to her big breasts. They smoke Turkish cigarettes and toast each other with martinis. "Shaken, not stirred," Mom says when she orders another round.

"You have to go," Mike Savage says. He holds out his hand.

I ignore it. "I know who you are too. You looked in my window." I'm not afraid. I came for Beauty.

"I remember. I'm sorry," the blond boy says. "I've straightened out. I'm going to school and working this job."

"I know who He is too," I say, looking at the figure carrying a rifle at His side.

A dog barks in the woods.

"You know Fred?"

"Hey, girly!" Jesus calls out. He's red-faced and overweight. "Get the hell out of there!"

"Get up, Lily. Go home," Mike says nervously. "Something bad's going to happen. You don't want to be here."

I'm on my belly on the edge of the pit just like I was when Lauren fell over. "No! Go away! I'm not afraid!"

Across the way, Allison stands in the doorway of the quarry office. She must have heard my voice. "Lily? Help me, Lily!" she calls. "Beauty fell! They're going to shoot him!"

I never should have come.

Jesus followed me here, and now He's going to do something terrible.

"Lily!" Allison screams. She holds her body stiff and waits for my answer. "Lily?" she calls weakly. I feel my heart break into little knobby pieces.

Allison listens to the silence between us, then collapses against Mrs. Garcia.

I lied to Beauty, and now I've lied to Allison. I'm a liar and a phony. I scoot away from the edge, press my ear to the ground, and listen to the Savage Boy walk away.

"She's confused," I hear him say. "Just give her a minute, Fred. She'll leave."

But I don't, and when Jesus sets the rifle on the ground beside me, He slips a meaty arm around my waist and yanks me to my feet. "Skinny little thing," He says. He smells of cigarettes and BO. "Didn't hurt you, did I?"

The phone rings in the quarry office.

The golf cart heads toward the parking lot. Allison sits alone on the back, staring blankly toward the pit.

My heart beats so fast I'm dizzy. "Please don't kill him. He didn't do anything."

"The horse is dying. It's unfair to let him suffer more," Jesus says.

"Now get out of here before you fall and I have to shoot you too . . . Just kidding."

I stare at Him. "Why do you follow me? Why do you always hurt people?"

"I haven't hurt anyone. And I sure as hell ain't following you!" He glances at my medical bracelet. "You sick or something?" For a second he looks like any of the other quarry guys. "Listen, kid, I've got a job to do and you're in the way." He picks up the rifle. "Hey, boss!" He yells across the pit. "She doesn't want to leave. Better call the police."

"Jerk!" I yell. "I hate you!"

I jump up and run to my bike. Dump trucks and steam shovels wave goodbye.

I don't look back as I ride away. But I do.

I don't hear Him cock the gun. But I do.

I don't hear the fatal shot, or Beauty's last high-pitched cry for Allison.

I should have stayed with Beauty.

I should have climbed down in the pit and refused to go. That's what Reverend King would have done.

A long lean dog appears on the trail ahead of me. It's feral and hungry, I can see its ribs from here, and I yell for it to get out of the way. It joins me instead, running beside my bike, growling, panting, yipping as I sail through potholes, fallen branches, and the mangled guts of something wild and partially eaten. The dog tells me I'm free and I don't have to go home; I don't have to return to the pit or see Allison either.

"Mrs. Wiggins is inside you," the dog reminds me. "Join us." And for a minute I imagine myself as Dog Girl, running from one dark treelined panel to another, like a hero in a comic strip.

But Lauren is waiting, and I told her I wouldn't run away without her.

I speed off and finally, unable to see through my tears, I hit something. And fly off my bike.

"You okay?" Jesus asks, offering me a hand.

"Go away, asshole." I've never used that word before.

"I'm afraid I can't do that. It's not in my job description."

"You don't like your job description, so why do you care?"

"Can I walk you home?"

"I'm not walking, I'm riding."

"Don't be mad at me. Sometimes there's nothing you can do."

"Too bad for Beauty, I guess."

"Wait," Jesus says, holding my handlebars.

"You killed him!" I scream. "He was beautiful and Allison loved him and you killed him!"

Jesus looks around nervously. "Can we talk about this later?"

"No! I don't want to talk about it. I don't want to see you. I want to stop seeing you!"

"Can't I come by tonight? We can talk about it then."

"No!" Jeez, we're not going steady. "I'm busy tonight." I think of Gidget and Moondoggie when they've had a fight. "I'm busy every night."

"You sound like a teenager."

That's what Mom said.

"*You're* the teenager!" I say. "You're the selfish, lying, phony brat!"

His face grows red. "Correction: you sound like an *angry* teenager."

Two boys ride by on bicycles, competing to sing "Kumbaya" as loudly as they can. I recognize them from the quarry pit. Singing and laughing, they've already forgotten the horse.

Beauty stands off the trail, nibbling a clump of grass. He sees the boys and runs off, the English saddle flapping under his torn belly.

Jesus is quiet.

I don't want to be mean, I just want Him to go away. It's fine for some people to see Jesus. Saints can see Him, and the Pope I suppose. Poor little starving kids in Europe a hundred years ago saw Jesus at the bottom of a well, and they weren't crazy. But girls like me, "weirdos" who live in Crawford Heights, aren't supposed to. "Please go away."

The birds stop chirping when I say it; the clouds stop darting through the trees.

"If I go, you'll be alone."

"No I won't. I'll have my shoe boxes. And my family. And my books. And Mrs. Wiggins."

"Mrs. Wiggins?"

"Go."

"But . . ."

"I know what I said."

"I'm sorry," He responds sadly. "Sometimes doing the right thing feels wrong, Lily. Please don't send me away, I need you. If you don't see me, I'm not sure I'm here."

Dad wrote something like that on a valentine to Mom once.

Jesus lets go of my bike. When a tear slides off His face it turns into a diamond, just like in fairy tales.

"There are lots of other girls to bug," I say.

"But I like bugging you."

I'm tired and my voice is soft when I say, *Thou shalt not kill*, remember? You could have saved him, but you didn't. You only do miracles for other horses, and other girls."

"That wasn't me back there."

"You kill everything I love."

"It wasn't me, Lily. You were hallucinating. That wasn't me."

I'm hallucinating? Maybe Dog Girl was a hallucination, but the man with the rifle?

An overweight woman rides by on her bicycle. I know what it looks like: I'm alone in the woods, talking to the trees.

"Everybody thinks I'm crazy." A cartoon anvil falls from the sky, flattening my head into a disc. A cartoon bird lands on it and, using his beak as a record needle, plays sad Gypsy music.

Jesus swallows. "I know. I'm sorry."

I don't know why I ask, but I do: "Can you make them stop?"

"You mean the people?"

"Yeah."

"No," He says.

"I didn't think so."

CHAPTER 24

CLAM DIP

Mom meets me at the door. "You're a mess. Where have you been?" She's impatient and looks me over. "Are you hurt?"

I shake my head.

"Lauren said you went for a bike ride . . . You're okay, right?" She knows something's wrong.

I look at Mom's flip-flops and her freshly painted toenails. If she catches my eye she'll see Beauty, and I can't talk to her about it. "I left my watch at home. Sorry."

Mom walks to the kitchen and I follow. She picks up a shiny pickle fork and starts polishing it. "All right, Lily. We'll talk about it tomorrow." She's mad at me but trying to stay calm. "Did you put your bike away?"

"I think so." It's hard to remember. I'm empty inside.

"You *think* so?"

"Do you want me to go look?" I close my eyes and see myself in the garage, leaning it against the lawn furniture. I usually put it there. Everything's the same. Except me. "I put it away."

"Good. Now run upstairs. I need you to clean the bathroom before you change your clothes." Behind her, the counters are full of her best glasses and dishes, antique china (which she bought on a "long weekend" with Dad) etched with rosebuds and sprigs of mint. Fancy canapés are arranged under plastic wrap. Unopened bottles of vodka, gin, and whiskey stand next to a big silver ice bucket.

"Lily?" Lauren calls from upstairs. She listens, then slams her bedroom door.

Mom glances toward the sound and scowls. "Your sister is not a happy camper. You stuck her with your chores again. You better get up there and apologize." Mom looks at me nervously. "Something happened, didn't it?"

She gives me a quick hug. "Damn it, Lily. What can I do about it when the Hendersons will be here in, in . . ."

I look at the wall clock. "An hour and a half. Give or take."

Mom smiles crooked. "Give or take, huh? Nothing more specific? Guess we can call that progress." She polishes the fork even harder. "Your father's at the drive-in grabbing you two dinner. He'll be back anytime."

"Van's?"

"Tik-Tok, or Yaw's. No Van's, remember?"

"But I'm fine now and—"

"End of subject." Her hands shake when she unties her apron and sticks it in a drawer. "I'm not happy with you rolling in here at the last minute, either."

"I know."

"Go, just go. Clean the bathrooms." She wipes out a dry water glass. "You know how I like things organized before we have company. I don't want to have to worry about you being gone, being late, wondering where you are." She looks at me again and her eyes soften. She knows I'm keeping something from her. "Maybe I should cancel—I mean, the Hendersons aren't here yet. We could always have them over another time." She puts down her towel and touches my face. "What's wrong, Lily? Should I cancel? Would you like me to cancel?"

"Have your party. I'm okay."

It's what she wants to hear and she exhales deeply. "All right then," she says, and looks around the room. "What do you think? Everything look ready to you?"

It's not a real question. "Yep," I answer.

She looks at me with her why-are-you-still-here eyes. "Bathrooms?" she asks. When she doesn't take her happy pill these days, Mom gets all tug-of-war inside, happy one minute, wound-up the next. Dad warned her against taking it if she was going to drink with the neighbors tonight. "Pills and booze don't mix," he told all of us. "It's one or the other, Kit."

On my way upstairs, I pass the family room where a TV game show is on, no volume. Someone has won a trip to Busch Gardens, Florida, where gaudy water shows include tiers of smiling bikinied showgirls balanced on the shoulders of other water-skiing showgirls. They turn their heads and wave at me, one-handed.

Maybe I could tell *them* about Beauty.

The living room smells like warm beeswax candles. Ella Fitzgerald's on the stereo. The stairway banister is already polished; usually that's my job.

At the top of the stairs is Lauren's bedroom. She sticks out her foot to trip me and then slams her door again.

"Stop slamming the door!" Mom yells. "Lauren!"

My sister opens her door but she doesn't answer.

Mom stomps up the stairs. Her eyes are black and stormy. "Do I need to take it off its hinges? No door to your bedroom—would you like that?"

Lauren glances at me quickly then shakes her head. "No," she answers timidly.

"So stop!" Mom rears back with the door, and slams it shut . . . "Slamming!" She slams the door again. "Your . . . door!"

Lauren crawls on her bed and hugs her pillow.

"Okay?" Mom asks breathlessly. She's sweaty and panting.

"Okay," Lauren says quietly.

Mom looks at the back of Lauren's door and her lucky jump rope hanging on a hook. Mom starts untangling it, but my sister's been practicing macramé knots and it's knotted pretty good. The more Mom works on it, the more the wooden handles with the metal hardware bang against the door.

Mom puts her hands on her hips. "Okay, okay, just hang it up in the garage and stop banging the door, all right?" She's quieter now, calmer. "Can you do that for me, please?"

"But I want it in my room."

"The answer is no, Lauren. No, you may not keep it in your room. No, you may not slam the door. Why doesn't anyone listen to me?"

"But it's my lucky—"

"You make your own luck, Lauren. Haven't you heard?"

Bully. "No," I suddenly say. "It's Lauren's lucky jump rope. She's leaving it there."

And then I see it. It's not about pills, painting sad pictures, or arguing with Dad. Mom gets stuck like I do. Only different, of course.

Did she always get stuck or did I infect her with my weirdness? Maybe real weirdness is a germ or a disease, maybe it's airborne, and if you're already dying, like Beauty was, it's fatal. I imagine each breath of mine taking microscopic parachutes down the quarry wall. Maybe Beauty was dead before Jesus pulled the trigger. I know I killed Mrs. Wiggins, but maybe I killed Po too. Maybe if they put me under a gi-normous microscope I'm teeming with weirdo bacteria.

Mom steps back. "I'm sorry, girls. I guess I'm a little nervous about the party." She looks at Lauren. "Oh, Bean," she says. Then bolts downstairs.

I follow her as she heads to the kitchen, turning smaller and smaller with every step she takes. I want to tell her that I'm sorry too, but I'm already counting by twelves as loudly as I can, and Mom will be the size of a mouse by the time she reaches the kitchen. She likes the mouse hole I painted (over a wood knot on the paneled wall of the kitchen), but I'd rather she yelled at us all day long than live in the wall.

In cartoons, every house has a mouse hole. There were no mouse holes in our perfect house, so I made one. The hole is a foyer, really, to rooms where mice sleep in matchbox beds, or nap in cushioned thimble chairs with tiny newspapers in their tiny laps. In other rooms, mice outfit themselves in climbing gear, hat-pin swords, and sewing-thread lariats for a midnight raid on the kitchen counter. Swashbuckling their way to the lip of the breadboard, they'll fling themselves onto the counter, careful to dodge Mom's ashtray and lipstick-stained wineglasses while looking for cheese scraps from her cocktail party.

We pass the family room where a police show is now on TV.

Mom collapses on the floor behind the kitchen table and pulls her knees to her chest. "Jesus, Kit," she scolds herself.

I sit down beside her in my loose-fitting mandatory TV cop pants with three inches of thick white leg showing above the mandatory black socks. I'm overweight and bored, and three hours into the stakeout.

"Sometimes I don't know what gets into me," she says.

I take her hand.

"As long as the party's a hit, right?"

She wants an answer but I'm only a cop, gnawing on the end of my blue-black mustache, sucking on the shoe polish I use to touch up the gray.

Dad brings Lauren and me cheeseburgers from Yaw's. We eat them in my room that night, and when we're done I wipe off the checkered wax paper and put it with my scrapbooks.

We don't say much until Lauren asks, "Did you see the horse, Lily? What happened?"

"He's fine," I tell her. Someone has to lie to Lauren. "Everything's fine."

I'm still on page twelve of *The Doors of Perception* when, four hours later, Mom knocks on my door. The pages are too heavy to turn, line after line of black ink tiers down the page, like striations in the walls of the quarry pit. Each white space is Beauty's crumpled body.

Mom tucks her head inside. I smell Chanel N°5.

"May I borrow—ohhhh, damn it, what's that record with the song about the restaurant and the garbage dump? Alice something?"

She's tipsy. Not drunk, just tipsy.

Jesus walks down the hall behind her, a drink in one hand, a potato chip—with a huge shovel of clam dip—in the other. When He slips into the bathroom, glancing at me over Mom's shoulder, there's no recognition.

"Lily?" Mom repeats.

I open the door wider. "You want to borrow *Alice's Restaurant*?"

She's wearing her new black dress with the low-cut back, and the rhinestone earrings Dad calls "candelabras." She's already taken off her high heels and rubs one stockinged leg against the other.

"Well, don't look at me that way," she says, her voice a little slurred. "I just thought it would be fun."

"You look pretty," I say when I hand her the record.

She wrinkles her nose self-consciously and looks at Arlo Guthrie on the album cover and smiles. Arlo smiles back from his Thanksgiving dinner table, wearing nothing but a clean white napkin and a bowler hat.

"Thanks, sweetie," she says, kissing my cheek. Then she drops her smile. "I know something happened this afternoon, Lily. When you were out. Should we call the doctor about it in the morning?"

"I'm okay. Are you having fun? Are the Hendersons nice?"

That perks her up. "Oh yes, they're very nice. We're having lots of fun." She looks at Arlo again and giggles. "Thanks, kiddo," she calls over her shoulder.

The stairs are freshly waxed. I hope she's careful.

SOG flushes the toilet, but He doesn't come out. Cabinet drawers open and close, tubes and bottles of stuff, toothpaste and makeup, knock against each other as they slide around. What a snoop! What's He doing at Mom's party, anyway?

Wait! I should rush after her and explain to everybody that *Alice's Restaurant* is an antiwar album. That Arlo Guthrie is Woody Guthrie's son, and while it's a funny record, it's not funny ha-ha. Definitely not funny ha-ha.

But I stay in my room instead, and when I hear Arlo's guitar intro roll out, I lay on the floor listening through the grate.

A moment later, when the bathroom door opens, I imagine tackling SOG, then making a beeline for the living room where I'd tear the record off Mom's new stereo—but I don't. It would just embarrass my parents, and no one would say, *Thanks for telling us about* Alice's Restaurant, *Lily. You are certainly an articulate young lady.*

It's too late to rip the record off the turntable.

Too late to tackle SOG who'd mumble, *Gross,* when He wiped the clam dip off His face.

Too late to save Beauty.

Check out the album cover, Mom will giggle. *Look at that hair!*

When *Alice's Restaurant* finishes, and there's a smattering of applause with requests for more drinks, I feel like a traitor.

Later that night, I find the record slipped under my bedroom door. I don't turn on the light when I stick it in the back of the closet.

Behind my clothes hangers and a mountain of empty shoe boxes is a hole as deep and wide as Crawford Quarry. It holds the things I say, and the things I don't. Its walls are ribbed like the inside of my mouth; I feel them with my tongue.

I listen for the record to hit bottom, but it keeps falling.

CHAPTER 25

FROG BOY

I was quieter in OE (oral expression) than the rest of my classes. In math and spelling, I was quietly confident and I quietly smiled, but in OE (Dad calls it "speech") my tongue curled up like a potato bug in the back of my throat. I calmed myself by doing times tables on the bright red abacus in my brain, visualizing first odd then even multiplication tables.

Earlier in the week our teacher, Mrs. McGivens, gave us an assignment to "write an essay about someone you find interesting."

Mrs. McGivens is a newlywed. If she were writing an essay, it would be on her husband who brings her back and forth to school each day, kissing her hello and goodbye in the car. The popular girls use binoculars to watch them from the science lab. Dad calls her husband "a kept man." Mom called Dad "jealous" and said everyone deserves to fall in love.

I wonder if I'll ever fall in love.

I briefly considered writing about Jesus, but last time I mentioned Him at school someone called me a "Jesus freak," which I'm not. He's a jerk a lot of the time—rude and bossy, demanding I pay attention to Him even when I'm busy. "You're trying to ignore me," He says, but I couldn't if I wanted to. No matter what direction I turn, He's bull's-eye, smack dab in the center of things, like a bad actor who won't get off stage.

Then I remembered the shoe box. Frog Boy!

Of course!

I thought of the *Look* magazine photograph inside it, the picture of Frog Boy—the circus freak, the "mistake," the fleshy little lump of life sitting, slumping actually, in Floyd Halverson's big calloused hands. I'd dug the magazine out of the trash after my folks and Jamie argued about sharing it with me.

My teacher said to write about someone interesting. Frog Boy was the perfect candidate.

Even essays have beginnings, middles, and ends. Whatever happened to Frog Boy? A cat could have eaten him. Or he might have fallen in the trash and no one would have noticed, only he probably didn't, and because he didn't, and girls feel sorry for ugly little things, one would have fallen in love with Frog Boy.

Mom jokes about bald rich fat old men getting the prettiest girls, so I sewed Frog Boy tiny clothes (like Cinderella did for her mice friends)—including a top hat and a wedding tuxedo with an extra-wide felt bib, and waders in case he went fishing on his honeymoon—and put everything in a shoe box I painted bright green with potato-stamped webbed feet all over it. Mom said the box wasn't my "best work," so she left it alone and never looked inside, and I never had to explain who it was for. It's been in my closet ever since.

I think Frog Boy and I could have been friends. Physically, he must have gotten stared at a lot; girls my age get stared at too—we have that in common. Only where my legs and arms reach each nook and corner of my bedroom—stretching like sticky octopus tentacles, preventing me from leaving it sometimes—Frog Boy's tiny arms and legs, his big belly and surprised incomplete little face, kept him from nothing. He was small and Floyd took him everywhere, and everywhere the world called him a freak and thought how ugly and pitiful he was. While no one spits at me like they spat at him, Frog Boy saw the world through the same eyes I do.

Inside we're even more the same: our hearts were born broken, our brains on fire.

Each week my OE class draws straws. Long straws "orate," that's what Mrs. McGivens calls it. I drew a long one this time, which means it was my turn to stand in front of the class while every inch of me crawled with clammy nerves, and my voice cracked, and I pretended I'd memorized my assignment so I could recite it in front of twenty- . . .

Five.

Kids.

(Gulp.)

I walked to the podium in front of the blackboard and, while some kids were graded on "Eye Contact with Audience," "Confidence," and "Projection and Tone," Mrs. McGivens simply said, "Just read it, Lily. Don't worry about the class."

I felt their eyes and restless bodies when I did.

Oral Expression
5th Period
Mrs. McGivens
April 12, 1968

Essay: FROG BOY

"Frog Boy" (cowritten by June Boy) tells the story of Frog Boy's life after pulling himself out of the primordial ooze of the popular La Brea Tar Pits, and dashing (as much dashing as he could do covered in tar) through traffic to a sideshow tent across Wilshire Boulevard. There, he was first observed rolling under the tent skirt like a sneaky tumbleweed. "Observed" because no one except his future wife June or his manager Floyd Halverson EVER had a relationship with Frog Boy. He wasn't around much so you didn't make a coffee date with him or run into him at the store. One year in one town was enough, and he hid out between engagements.

It looked like Frog Boy would be a bachelor until a stage bit in Reno when he was wheeled out on a platform (a gift from the Fortuna Flea Circus) and Floyd held a microphone to his tiny mouth. When the room fell silent he sang "Somewhere over the Rainbow" without accompaniment. His voice was small but in tune and crystal clear. No cameras were allowed so only newspapers told the story of how a parade of bare-chested showgirls introduced him as "The Biggest Little Man in Reno" and with a hand on her sequined hip, each kissed the whiskery knobby little head of chinless Frog Boy. He made a purring sound when they did, which the paper insisted was proof he was either a deformed cat or a windup toy. When showgirl June (a former magician's assistant) said his whiskers felt like armadillo hair, Frog Boy fell in love with her immediately.

"It was her honesty," he wrote later. The broken pieces of his heart instantly melded and his heart grew to a threatening size in his teeny-tiny chest (a pushpin could have killed him). It stayed that big all the years they were married.

They dated quietly first, of course, until a midnight wedding ceremony under a sandy tiki lamp on Padre Island. "You're dead to us," wrote June's embarrassed parents of their only daughter's only choice, though they sent a nice punch bowl the following week.

There were rumors that FB hung out with movie stars, was the toast of Hollywood parties, had a star outside Grauman's Chinese Theatre, and was carried around in drunk women's cleavages—for someone the size of a guinea pig with water retention, that would have been dangerous. No one really knows how old Frog Boy was when he died, but he was a performer to the end. His shows were rare but celebrated: six months of highly publicized performances in the Curtis Wilkin Freak Show, private parties in Boca Raton and Acapulco where he performed in the living rooms of drunken millionaires, and three Las Vegas shows (opening for Jack Jones, Dr. Irwin Corey, and Tiny Tim), before disappearing into the desert of the American Southwest with June.

"I feel safer in the open," Frog Boy wrote of all that sky and not-much-else. Nobody knew where that was until a lone Australian tourist turned down a dirt road in the middle of nowhere. With a dust storm on his tail he almost didn't see the rusty mailbox painted "F. and J. Boy" or, in the distance, the geodesic dome they called home. June made the stranger dinner but FB wouldn't come out of the workshop where he was building more bookcases.

When Frog Boy "croaked" nobody knew his real name or even if he had one. For some reason the Retired Circus Freak Association (RCFA) wanted nothing to do with him.

June remarried several times but always unhappily.

"Rib-bit," someone said from the back of the room

A few kids giggled and I felt myself turn red.

"That's enough, class," our teacher said, standing up.

Tanya Richards, who's also in drama and debate, waved her raised hand. Without being called on, she blurted, "Mrs. M., Mrs. M., is that a *real* essay? Because it kind of sounded like a book report, and then—"

"Yes, Tanya, all right." Mrs. McGivens promised Mom she'd treat me like any other student and not "sugar coat it," which sounded ominous (*threatening; inauspicious*, Oxford Dictionary). She paused to gather her thoughts. She does that when she really likes something (or doesn't). "You have a wonderful imagination, Lily, but I asked for an *essay*. Your piece starts off as a book report then changes into a short story. Only it reads like reportage. You're all over the map with tense, and—"

Huh? She didn't like my essay?

"It's not a short story," I interrupt. I wasn't nervous now and stood taller behind the podium. "It's nonfiction. Essays are nonfiction. Frog Boy is nonfiction."

"Lily."

The whole class would have laughed if our teacher hadn't just lectured us about picking on the handicapped and retarded kids in school. The kids rolled their eyes and looked at each other with nervous smiles, confirming that I was seriously odd, which is kind of like being retarded. While she wrote the definition of *nonfiction* on the blackboard, the rib-bit boy said, "Rib-bit," louder than ever.

This time Mrs. McGivens ignored it.

Back home, Dad was out of town and Mom didn't have time for my essay. She was finishing a painting of a dead bloody soldier and couldn't get one of his dead eyes right. Lauren and I had learned there was no budging her until the last detail was done, plus thirty minutes of her walking around the easel talking to herself and smoking.

She was in her studio for hours this time, so Lauren and I did our homework, made ourselves dinner, and took baths. Before going to bed (on time), I placed "Frog Boy" on her nightstand.

Her door was closed in the morning but there was a plate of french toast and scrambled eggs staying warm in the oven, and Lauren and I loaded up.

"If I don't fall in love," my sister said to me, "and I'm poor and don't have money for my own house, we could live together." She traced Mrs. Butterfield with her sticky finger. "Maybe you won't fall in love either, Lily. I could take care of you."

Lauren wants to be a nurse after winning a scholarship as Miss Oregon (but losing Miss America) and working in a veterinarian hospital every summer she's in high school.

"No thanks," I answered. Frog Boy needs taking care of, not me.

Lauren and I heard the stairs squeak when Mom snuck upstairs to her studio, and when we opened the front door to leave for school she called down, "Have a good day, girls!"

I checked her nightstand before going. "Frog Boy" was still there, only with an ashtray and wineglass stain on top.

Mom says love is sometimes stronger when the "object of affection is gone." Or dead. She always misses Dad when he's gone; she paints like crazy, never makes their bed, and they have long phone conversations in the middle of the night. I hear her cry sometimes when they talk.

She says Jamie's fiancé Kevin is more in love with Jamie now than he ever was. I hope she was really dead when they buried her. I read that back in the 1870s, people sick with cholera were buried alive all the time.

Jesus was buried then rose from the dead. He died so we would have Eternal Life, but He really meant Eternal Death because we have to be dead to get it.

If Kevin loves Jamie more now that she's dead, would I love Jesus more if He were alive?

Did June love Frog Boy more when he was just a framed photograph over a teeny-tiny casket?

I lifted Mom's ashtray off my essay.

Oh well. Jamie will like it. Even dead she'll like it better than Mom ever would, and I grab a big manila envelope from Dad's desk, and even though it won't get there, even though there's nowhere to get, I address it:

Aunt Jamie
Ethiopia
Africa
Southern Hemisphere
Earth
The Solar System
The Milky Way Galaxy
The Universe
God
Heaven (if it isn't a lie)

CHAPTER 26

NAILS

At the end of St. Rita, not far from our beautiful magazine-featured house at the foot of Crawford Butte, is the woodsy candlelit grotto.

Nuns run the souvenir shop but there are never enough personnel to chase the horny teenagers away. They start making out the minute they park, then nearly run over the contemplative Catholics moseying along the narrow paths serving the fifteen Stations of the Cross.

Between Stations Nine and Ten a deer path veers off into the bushes, one of the more popular necking locations in the grotto.

> *Station One: Jesus is condemned to death.*
> *Station Two: Jesus carries His cross.*
> *Station Three: Jesus falls the first time.*
> *Station Four: Jesus meets His mother.*

I read that Mary stood in the crowd with three other Marys, weeping as Jesus walked by dragging the cross. He paused to say something to them, but later, in the New Testament, neither Matthew, Luke, nor John could agree on what it was.

If I were Mary, Jesus's mom, I'd have left my girlfriends at home, and as Jesus stopped to say goodbye, the crowd would step back. It'd be just the two of us then, and I'd look at Him and finally say a few things that needed clearing up. Like, *I'm here and I've always been here. I love you so so much.* And, *That stuff about being a virgin? It's crap. I'm as human as you are.*

Maybe I'd say the rest with my eyes so no one else could eavesdrop.

> *Station Five: Simon (or Simon of Cyrene) helps Jesus carry the cross.*
> *Station Six: Veronica wipes the face of Jesus with her veil.*

I don't know Simon from Station Five (or the Bible or the trail placard noting the stations and park benches), and the only Veronica I know is comic book Archie's girlfriend (old comics Mom gave me when I'd read every book in the house) who's probably Jewish (because she's pretty like Mom).

Station Six says, *Veronica wipes the face of Jesus with her veil,* but when she felt Him trembling and saw the fear in His eyes, she'd have followed Him to the Mount too. No one should be that frightened and alone and I'm right behind her. We're all there: Mom, Jamie, Veronica, and me.

Maybe a Roman soldier would tell us to move and the four of us would say, *Hell no, we won't go,* too loudly, too sure of ourselves, and people would stare and complain so the Romans would arrest us and throw us in a cave that no one would walk by, check on, or write about later because women were second-class citizens, especially back then.

Somewhere, among the grotto's Stations of the Cross, there should be another cave and through its tiny *Flintstones* window, people passing could see the four of us crowded together ignoring the cries of our hungry babies and husbands because the voices inside us are louder. Jesus's body was gone in three days, but our bodies are still there, huddled together like those ashen figures at Pompeii. Mom, Jamie, Veronica, and I didn't go anywhere, except to die right there and be delivered to the ground and the ground was sacrosanct (*too important or valuable to be interfered with,* Oxford Dictionary) and we were its offerings.

Station Seven: Jesus falls the second time.
Station Eight: Jesus meets the women of Jerusalem.
Station Nine: Jesus falls the third time.

Jesus fell three times on the way to Cavalry. At least that's how the story goes. Three times for the Father, the Son, and the Holy Ghost? There's something about adults falling and skinning their knees that's sad and pathetic and Jesus falling three times as He carried the cross makes me especially sad. The meanest people threw spitballs, peed on Him, and called Him names; soldiers poked Him with sticks. "Stand up, you piece of shit!" someone yelled, and everybody wondered how the Son of God could be clumsy. God wasn't clumsy, was He?

Jesus fell for the last time, knowing He wouldn't do it again and nothing would stop Him from reaching the crucifixion mount. And even though millions of people would someday go, *Wow, He loved us that much!* and Jesus could have cried His eyes out and it wouldn't have mattered, He didn't. Men are private and proud and stuff their feelings down inside themselves (which is why they die younger than women), and Jesus loved being mortal—at least that's what He told me—so He choked back His tears too.

The Maharishi Mahesh Yogi taught the Beatles deep meditative breaths, so I vibe Jesus to do the same.

Except for the cruelest of the cruel, the crowd wept when He finally stood up under the weight of the cross again. Helpful hands flew out, but their bodies stayed with the others, like canned sardines or pencil boxes, and not a single fingertip touched Him.

Maybe they were afraid that what He had was contagious, that whatever was wrong with Him was already living inside them and if they touched the naked weirdo it would burst out of them, like spores exploding under pressure, pollinating everything. Jesus could have fallen five, seven, eleven times (all prime numbers), even more, but He didn't.

Still, each time the purpling bruises spread across His legs and arms and as the sky rumbled and the storm mounted, He realized He was already dead. And rotting. It started when God condemned Him.

God gave Jesus life then took it back, gave Him the chance to go fishing and eat chocolate cake and kiss pretty girls and bust up the marketplace, then took it away from Him. I'd have yelled at God from the cross too. Even louder.

Station Ten: Jesus's clothes are taken away.
Station Eleven: Crucifixion—Jesus is nailed to the cross.
Station Twelve: Jesus dies on the cross.
Station Thirteen: Jesus is taken down from the cross.
Station Fourteen: Jesus is laid in the tomb.
Station Fifteen: Resurrection—the resurrection of Jesus.

The Romans didn't need to take His clothes (Station Ten), leaving Him embarrassed, skinny, and cold in that big origami diaper. Wasn't it enough that they were killing Him?

If I were Jesus, and knew what was coming, I'd have sent my disciples all over Jerusalem buying, stealing, and hiding the nails.

Still, Jesus said it had to be nails because it had to hurt; it had to hurt so much that people got sick to their stomachs just thinking about the pain. It had to hurt so much that nobody killed anybody like that ever again. It's like naming your baby Adolf Hitler—no one ever did that again either.

The really bad stuff shouldn't be repeated, though during Word War II President Truman bombed two cities in Japan, one after the other, wiping out everyone and everything. Dad said it had to be done to end the war. He said more bombings were planned if the Japanese didn't surrender, though that was a secret at the time.

On the school bus, boys talk about the war in Vietnam and pipe bombs full of nails; they mimic exploding sounds, laugh and fall back against their seats, pretending to puke blood and die. They talk about their fathers and brothers "in-country," how the jungle is a massive clusterfuck but furlough is the best with its *boo-coo* drugs and *poontang*. They say they can't wait to be drafted and fight the *gooks*.

I close my eyes and see bloody nails everywhere; they're shot out of cannons into rice huts. They fly through bus windows—we walk over them on the way to class.

Jesus stands next to my locker ready to help with the lock. It's not that I forget the combination, it's that once I turn the dial and feel the tumbler click, so many combinations are possible. "You're going to be late," He nags.

He's mad at me; I see it on His face. "You worry too much," He says. On the way to first period, He takes my books.

The books aren't heavy, the nails are.

Yeah, we're going to be late. The halls are empty except for chubby sneezy Brian who's in the "slow" class upstairs. He runs past us going *beep-beep* like the roadrunner.

"So we can't talk about the *Why hath though forsaken me* moment?" I ask Jesus.

He shakes His head no.

Everybody has their secrets.

I have mine too.

Making out with Luca, the Swedish exchange student, is one. He didn't know many kids but he'd said he liked me. He was only going to be in town three more months, and he stood up for me in class, so when he asked me out I took him to the grotto. I'd rather have made him a shoe box than kiss him, but we had no choice. Parents forget that there are things teenagers have to do—whether they want to or not—even weirdos like me. Maybe especially weirdos like me.

Mom and Dad used to make each other laugh using bad Swedish accents. *Da-OO, da-OO,* was usually in there someplace, like a stuttering owl trying to learn English.

Luca and I leaned our bikes against the souvenir shop and, hand in hand, headed toward the Stations of the Cross.

"Aren't we going to stop someplace?" he asked after a while.

But I didn't answer and stared at statues of Jesus instead. In the first four stations, the sculptor gave Jesus a thumb and three fingers not four, and His hair is red, not black or even chestnut. His cheeks are either fat, like he has nuts in them, or starvation thin, and his skin is powdered-wig white.

"Lily?"

I turned to face Luca and kissed his cheek.

As he hurried us along the trail, looking for the deer path between Stations Nine and Ten, I felt cameras on us, like we were actors in a film and nothing was real, nothing familiar. Until Luca and I sat Indian-style in the bushes and he pulled me toward him, and with one hand on the back of my head and his tongue scraping my teeth, I felt the Stations of the Cross press in around us, crowding us like the angry apple trees in *The Wizard of Oz.* I don't know this for certain, but I think the Stations of the Cross embarrass Jesus—all that attention over something He'd sooner forget.

He paced nearby, impatient for me to finish so we could head home again.

And after nineteen minutes (a prime number of course) the movie men put down their cameras, the Stations of the Cross returned to duty, and I stopped kissing tall blond big-nosed Luca from Sweden. I liked kissing him, but not that much.

I was myself again: Lily Asher of Crawford Heights, Portland.

Racing Jesus home.

His sandals slapping the pavement behind my bike.

CHAPTER 27
RED STRINGS

It's raining when I step off the school bus and walk to the entrance of Crawford Woods. I consider going in, then change my mind as elderly Mrs. Singer hurries by with her umbrella.

"For goodness sake, Lily!" she says, slipping her arm through mine. "Let's get home and out of the rain!" Mom's trained the neighbors to look out for me, and Mrs. Singer is the most conscientious. She drags her basset hound, Edgar, behind us.

"The woman has an unerring way of walking me just before a cloudburst," Edgar says, with quiet contempt. Edgar's never talked to me before. I can't place the accent.

Edith Singer's yellow plastic galoshes belonged to her dead husband. They're too big for her, and make a squish-fart sound when she walks in them.

Lauren's home; her wet umbrella's in the laundry sink along with the empty birdcage. Harry and Bess Cockatiel died over the weekend, victims of a contaminated cuttlebone.

I grab a towel from the dryer and hurry inside.

In the kitchen, a bubbling pot of spaghetti sauce shoots little red strings all over the white stovetop. I turn off the burner, move the pot to the back, and cover it.

The house is quiet. No jazz on the hi-fi, no Mom on the phone, no last-minute chores before Dad gets home. I remember the last time the house felt this empty: Mom's miscarriage (the one before the hysterectomy), and Frog Boy floating in an ocean of stars.

"Mom? Lauren?"

Next to the stove is the wall phone and, below it on the counter, an ashtray with a dead lipstick-stained cigarette, most of it ash. The phone book is open, and on the page titled *Pharmacy* lies an empty Valium bottle.

292

"Mom?"

"Come here," Lauren says. Her voice is dull and sluggish, like she can hardly be bothered to speak. I follow it into the family room, where she stands over our mother.

Mom lies on the carpet, her back to the TV, her arms and legs extended, her body relaxed. She blinks but doesn't change expression. On TV Mike Douglas laughs with actors Vincent Price and Dick Shawn, then holds up the new Turtles record.

I look at Mom again.

Then Lauren.

And back to the TV. I like the Turtles.

"She won't talk to me," Lauren says. "I was telling her about something at school, then the phone rang. I thought it was Simone so I grabbed it, only it was Dad saying he was going to be late." Dad's not supposed to be late anymore. "Then she put down the oven mitt, and walked in here and laid down." She points at Mom. "Just like that."

I know I should be frightened but something's always wrong with Mom.

"At first I thought she was looking for something under the couch," Lauren continues, "but then she didn't move. I turned on the TV because I thought that maybe, maybe she'd like it and sit up." Lauren taps her bottom lip; it's what she does these days instead of sucking her thumb. "What do we do, Lily?"

Standing over Mom like this, it's a long way down. Like the view from the top of the rope in PE. Or Mike Savage's roof before he launched himself into a mountain of old mattresses and furniture cushions. Like the quarry pit, and the white horse.

"Lily?"

"She's blinking," I answer. "That's good."

"Yeah, that's good."

"Mom?" I say, touching her shoulder. Her hair is a mess.

"Look at her lipstick," Lauren whispers.

"It's smeared."

"I'm going to fix it. Mom would want me to fix it," Lauren says, hurrying out of the room.

"Don't!" I cry after her.

"But Mom wouldn't like it if we . . ."

293

Boo-hoo! I want to scream. *Boo-fucking-hoo!* But instead I say, "It's okay, Lauren. Mom will fix it when she gets up. She doesn't need makeup to rest."

But she does. She needs makeup and brushed hair and big beautiful terrible boobs and big beautiful terrible paintings. She needs people to think she's gorgeous even when she's selfish and drunk, and making spaghetti and calling in prescriptions and even talking to her youngest daughter is too much work. Maybe *way* too much work, so she lies down on the floor . . . right there . . . scaring her kids, stopping the clocks. Even Mike Douglas gets out of his chair and knocks on the TV screen asking if she's okay.

"What if it's more than just pills?" my sister whispers. "What if she's really sick? Like neurologically." Lauren can spell the word too. She's the second-best junior high speller in the district.

"Maybe we should put her to bed," I say. "We're not supposed to call 911. Remember what she said when we moved in? She doesn't want us to draw attention to ourselves."

"But what if we shouldn't move her? Talk to her, Lily! Try talking to her!"

"Mom," I say, kneeling down beside her, "do you want me to call an ambulance?"

"Nooo," she slurs. "I'll beeee ohh-kay in a minnn-it." Is she drunk? I don't smell the booze.

"She said no." I stand up. "But you could get her a drink of water if you want to. Put a straw in it."

My heart is pinched and frostbit from holding Mom too close. She doesn't get to be beautiful and tired of doing married-mom-stuff at the same time.

Not this time anyway.

When I call the racetrack, we get a recording.

We don't call the police or ambulance. We don't throw out her pills because we don't know which ones she needs. We don't interfere with the scene of the crime, move the body, or touch the evidence, like they say on detective shows. We don't answer the phone when it rings or collect the evening paper.

We don't get up until after it turns dark, and the only light inside comes from the television.

We kneel beside Mom instead and take turns holding her hand. In the next forty minutes, she sits up twice, mumbles about spaghetti sauce and making dinner, tells us she loves us, then lies down again.

Rain blasts the windows. It fills the quarry pit, rinsing Beauty's blood off its rocky walls. It knows Mom is sick and Lauren and I are alone with her.

"She's going to be okay, right?" Lauren whispers.

Maybe Mom's had a stroke. Maybe somebody poisoned her like someone poisoned Fifi.

"Sure," I say as I gather up the liquor bottles. "Besides, Dad will be here soon. He'll know what to do."

Glug, glug, glug, down the kitchen sink.

"She'll be mad," Lauren says.

"So will Dad," I tell her. "Booze is expensive, but it doesn't matter. Maybe it was a bad batch and it made her sick. We have to protect her."

If Mom lies there much longer, she'll sink through the carpeting, through the house frame, into the soggy ground where the water table leads to Crawford Woods and the quarry. Where the rain collects at the bottom, puddling where SOG shot Beauty, and angels stand around a giant doughnut hole in the sky looking down at all the stupid stuff people do on earth. There's a picture like that in one of Mom's art books.

I feel SOG's hands on my shoulders but I shrug them off.

I told Him to leave me alone.

Dad insists on an ambulance, and after the paramedics leave, he sticks TV dinners in the oven and puts Mom to bed.

"Exhaustion," he explains, which means we'll never know for sure. Sometimes Mom reminds me of the rose in the bell jar in *The Little Prince.* "You girls can tuck yourselves in tonight, can't you?" Dad kisses us both. "She'll be fine, don't worry. We'll all be fine after a good night's sleep."

Fine, schmine.

Lauren falls apart. She cries for three minutes and five seconds without blowing her nose, even after Dad gives her his hanky.

"And you, Lily?" he finally asks. "You haven't said much."

I shrug.

"Kit said something happened to you yesterday. Can you tell me about it?"

"No, nothing happened. I'm good." And press Mrs. Wiggins's tooth to my chest.

Lauren and I play three games of *Yahtzee* before the rain stops.

A scratch at my window makes me jump, but it's only a branch. Maybe I shouldn't have been so mean to SOG. Maybe I should have been meaner.

"I'm tired," Lauren says, lying back on my pillow.

I sleep until 11:40 when I sneak into her room, untangle her lucky jump rope, and tiptoe downstairs with it. "Me too," I mumble.

Me too: *M* is the thirteenth letter of the alphabet, *E* the fifth, *T* the twentieth, and each *O* a fifteen. Thirteen plus five, plus twenty, plus thirty, equals sixty-eight.

We live at 1968 Crawford Heights Boulevard. Mom married Dad when she was nineteen. There are numbers that represent times and places, dates that tell you when things will happen like Jamie's astrology charts. Numbers have colors, even music.

It's sixty-eight steps from my bedroom, down the stairs to the laundry room, where moonlight splashes the wet clothes sitting on the dryer and an unpacked grocery sack stands on the washing machine. Inside it are a bottle of bleach, a can of Insta-Starch, and two nooses of clothesline.

I grab the clothesline and a flashlight, then throw the lucky jump rope in the basket of my ten-speed.

I know what I have to do.

It's the last time I'll ride my bike to the quarry pit.

Promise.

CHAPTER 20

SPIDER EYES

It's 11:32 p.m. when I rocket through the dark neighborhood to Crawford Butte. The drying streets are empty.

Behind me is Mom.

Up ahead is the basalt quarry, the bombed-out crater, the hole all the way to China. Up ahead is the quiet, cool openness of the pit and the star-filled sky overhead.

Behind me is Mom.

Up ahead is Beauty's ghost.

I race along the sawdust trail that narrows and widens, narrows and widens, breathing with me like the giant walk-through lung at the science museum.

The woods are cold and black, but I don't care. Emptiness is easier to see in the dark.

I stick the dogtooth necklace in my pocket. I know what I have to do. Since I can't take back the lie I told Beauty, I'll do the next best thing: I'll give him my most prized possession.

Starting today, I'll be a better person. I'll take care of Lauren and love my parents less.

I'll stop talking to Jesus. If He says something, I'll ignore Him. I'm a little shaky on what to do if He never leaves me alone, but as Frieda says, "We'll cross that bridge when we get to it."

The shimmering song of the bike's wet tires fills my ears; the bouncing flashlight lights the bushes and trees off the trail. When it turns its blinding beam on me, I stop to readjust it, and shine it into the dark woods.

You're almost there, blink spider eyes in the bushes.

Every branch points to the pit up ahead.

Is that Wolfman Jack on the radio?

At the chained barrier that reads, *Stay Out! Trespassers will be prosecuted!* I lift my bike over, lean it against a tree, and walk into the clearing where the dark sleepy shapes of Crawford Quarry dinosaurs sit in the shadows: long-necked earth shovels, snaggle-toothed rock crushers, big slow dump trucks. "Start your engines!" Mom jokes when the men begin their noisy day. Sometimes she swears she can hear them "open a lunch box."

Hurry! Beauty is waiting. A soul stays in the place where it died for sixty-two hours, or sixty-two days, depending on which book you read.

If Wolfman Jack is on the radio it must be past midnight. The witching hour. Besides, the office door is open and a man sits inside listening to the radio and smoking a cigarette. If he sees me, he'll kick me out and I'll never have a chance to set things right with Beauty.

I keep an eye on the office as I tiptoe to the center of the clearing and look into the giant black bowl.

"The Wolfman's next dedication goes out to Sis in Baltimore. That's right, you knooow who you are." Wolfman Jack howls and I get shivers. "On your six-month anniversary," he growls, "Tony says . . . 'I Got You Babe' by Sonny and Cher."

I hold out my hands over the pit (like Allison did) to calm the dying horse.

"I'm coming," I say out loud.

They say our love won't pay the rent, before it's earned, our money's all been spent . . .

Something flies past me and I flinch. It's a bat, and a second later a bat cotillion, diving and dodging and dancing midair. The pit echoes their high-pitched chirps.

"Stop it," I say, waving them off. "Stop!" even louder. They'll scare Beauty. "Leave him alone!"

The guard turns off the radio and listens. I dart behind a dump truck and watch while he flips off the office light. He stands in the doorway looking for movement in the dark. Satisfied there is none, he turns on the light and radio again.

The closest thing to the rim of the pit is a deformed gnarly old tree. In the dark it reminds me of an enchanted tree from fairy tales, but tonight it has to get me to Beauty, and as I talk to it softly, I tie Lauren's jump rope around its trunk, knot one clothesline to the end of it, then another to the first, pull out the kinks, and slowly lower myself over the edge.

I got flowers in the spring, I got you to wear my ring . . .

Step.

By.

Step.

Down.

The.

Wall.

Angry.

Scared.

Angry.

Scared.

I got you babe . . .

Billy Vega calls me "babe." He's the biggest flirt at school. It doesn't even bother him that I'm a weirdo.

. . . got you to walk with me . . . you to talk with me . . . kiss goodnight . . . hold me tight . . .

The tune fades as I climb further into the quarry pit. My hands and back hurt, but for a moment I'm braver than I've ever been, braver than Dog Girl or Wonder Woman. I'm a girl version of Trevor Howard in *Von Ryan's Express*, following some stupid order from Frank Sinatra that will probably get me killed.

My skinny-girl muscles gleam with sweat as I lower myself down the side of an old Italian villa that's crawling with Nazis.

Inside, Jesus instructs his aide, "Kill every white horse you see. And when you're done with that, kill all the Jews."

"But sir . . ."

Jesus grabs the halo off His head and sticks it in His young assistant's face. "See this, soldier?" He spits. "I'm your superior, damn it!"

Only suddenly it's a swastika. Maybe it always was a swastika.

It was silly to think a lucky jump rope and two lengths of clothesline would be enough to get me to the floor of the pit.

I fall and, before I can catch my breath, land with a thud.

On my side. On my arm. And without thinking, I roll, for good measure, roll like a potato bug or a hedgehog, roll like they taught us in fire drills.

The pain is immediate, but it doesn't matter. Beauty suffered more. Jesus suffered too, but He wanted mortality so let Him have it. Mom says men never suffer as much as women do, anyway.

My whole body hurts. Taking shallow little breaths, I inventory each part: feet, legs, hips, chest, back, hands, neck; everything's fine except my left arm. Mom's going to kill me. I broke that arm in the car crash; the cast just came off three months ago.

How many times can a person break the same arm before it decides to grow in a different direction?

The ground is hard. My sweater and windbreaker won't be warm enough tonight; it's cold at the bottom of the pit. When I roll onto my knees, the monstrous outline of a steam shovel stares at me.

The pit is filled with big machines, their powerful jaws lifted in mid-bite.

I hold my arm against me and try not to cry.

I came here for a reason, right? Concentrate, I tell myself. We have business. Do what you have to do, then somehow get out of here and go home.

Where is the . . . I left my flashlight on the rim. Good thinking, Lily.

Lily Lily bo-billy, banana-fana fo . . .

I smell the gunfire and taste the cold sour metal of Beauty's blood in my mouth. He's close.

Emptiness pulls, and I know where I'm going.

Beauty's ghost lies on his side, his legs extended, his body relaxed, his head turned away from me, just like Mom this afternoon. He's not surprised to see me but even with the necklace in my pocket I don't know what to say to him at first, and the minutes pass slowly.

Minutes, or what pass as minutes after I broke my wristwatch in the fall. I hold it up to the starlight. Its face is cracked.

When I visualized us resting in front of the fire in my favorite Little Golden Book, the words came out: I confessed to barking in the bushes when I first met Beauty. I sang, *"Beauty's only skin-deep, yeah, yeah, yeah,"* and I pointed out the constellations, both the real ones and the ones in Lauren's freckles.

We talked quietly for hours, and I made up stories, but Beauty's favorite story was my favorite too:

Dad is in the lead with the flashlight, a paper roll of star charts crin-

kling under his arm. Mom follows, the picnic basket with sandwiches, doughnuts, a thermos of hot chocolate, and tin cups knocking against her leg.

Lauren and I giggle excitedly as we carry the blankets each of us will lie on when we stare at the sky counting meteorites out loud.

"I love my life!" Mom calls out between the thirty-fourth and thirty-fifth.

We all join in: "Me too! Me too!"

"I love doughnuts!" Lauren yells.

"Hot chocolate!" Dad says.

"Comets!"

"Meteors!"

"Painting!" "Newspapers!" "Babies!" "Summer!" "Monopoly!" "Princess phones!" "Shoe boxes!" "Gramma Frieda!"

We list everything we can think of.

We love the big stuff and the little stuff.

We love the cold ground that burns through our blankets and gives us goose bumps all over.

We love each other.

Beauty's ghost is still. He's tired, like me.

At home, my family's asleep and don't even know I'm gone. The house is quieter than usual with Mom sick.

My arm stops hurting but I'm sure it's broken again. If Beauty and I fall asleep, I hope Jesus doesn't cover us with a blanket of moonbeams or some corny poetical thing like that. I don't want Him touching me. I'd rather be cold.

I'm uncomfortable but I like it here in a strange way. At home I don't know what I feel.

If Jesus were here, I'd say: *I'm sorry bad stuff happened to You when You were human, but that's not the Jews' fault, or the kids in Hiroshima or Africa with flies in their eyes. It's not Mrs. Wiggins's fault, or Jamie's, or Judy's, or Beauty's.*

I'd say, *I don't believe in you anymore. I'll be my own savior, my own Jesus, but I won't die in pain making everyone feel guilty. I won't die at all, none of us will, if I'm the new Jesus.*

At least not until we have a chance to start over—not in Heaven but here on earth. I think everyone wants to. I'm pretty sure Mom does.

I'll start over too and be braver next time.

As brave as the blind girl.

As brave as Beauty.

His ghost quivers under the stars, like a heat mirage.

I lean forward, patting the hard dry ground around us for a rock. When I find one, I dig underneath it, deep enough for Mrs. Wiggins's tooth which I slide off the chain and bury there. "It's yours now," I tell Beauty.

An owl hoots nearby.

Merlin's owl was Archimedes, the most beautiful bird in *Camelot*, Mom's favorite movie.

What if Mom wakes up in the middle of the night and I'm not there to recite a poem or show her a scrapbook?

Overhead is the Big Dipper, shaped like her cocoa pan with the chipped red handle. Mom didn't replace it when we moved to the new house. She said it only gets better with age and makes the chocolate sweeter.

I forget about my arm when I stand up to go. Then it hurts so bad I cry out, and slump against the quarry wall again. Overhead are either stars or spider eyes; it's hard to tell when you're dizzy and cold.

"Baby," I lecture myself.

I think of Lauren spending the night in the woods, alone and scared.

"Hello?" a voice rings out.

Footsteps.

"Anybody there?"

Is that the Savage Boy's voice? Is *he* the night watchman?

A flashlight beam crisscrosses the dark sky. The pit is bottomless. I know he won't be able to see the dead horse, but I lie on top of Beauty anyway, covering him with my body.

CHAPTER 29

HEY SEUSS

Someone drapes a blanket over my shoulders. Its sudden warmth surprises me, and I open my eyes.

"Good morning, Lily," says the quarry boss, standing in front of me. I recognize his plump red face, hard hat, tie, and short-sleeved white shirt. A bullhorn hangs off his belt.

"Hi," I mumble. How does he know my name?

Where am I?

A large dark-skinned man stands next to the quarry boss. Behind them is a steam shovel; a guy in a hard hat sits in the cab, his head out the window, watching.

The quarry boss turns, looks up, and raises the horn to his mouth. *"She's conscious and talking."* On the rim, half a dozen men in work clothes applaud.

"Mom?"

The man smiles and lights a cigarette. "I'm sure she's wondering where you are too. We called an ambulance for you. How you doing?"

I smell coffee. The morning sun is low, but there's enough light to see the steaming coffee mugs of the two men in front of me. While the men on the rim put their gloves and hard hats on, another walks off speaking into a walkie-talkie.

"You want some coffee or something? Water?"

"No thanks." My arm hurts. It's swollen to bursting in my pink windbreaker. When I try to lift it, it hurts like hell and I remember the fall.

"Don't try moving it, kid, I'm afraid it's broken. Doesn't look like you broke anything else though. You're a lucky girl." *Lucky.* Where's Lauren's jump rope? Boss looks nervous and spits. "Jesus found you first. He's got the first aid kid around here. Said you're going to be okay."

Jesus? My heart jumps, though slower than usual. My body is cold and empty like one of those abandoned refrigerators they find dead kids in, and I pull the blanket tighter around myself.

"It's Hey-SEUSS, boss," corrects the big Mexican guy standing beside him. I stare. Jesus can be anything He wants, right? "You're going to be fine," he says to me. Smiling.

I know I should keep an eye on Him, but I'm tired and warmer and I can't help closing my eyes. Just for a sec.

"Don't fall asleep, Lily," Boss says. "Stay awake, all right?"

Just for a sec.

My eyes are shut when I hear him say, "What do you think: a concussion? Great, fucking great. *She* falls in but her folks will sue the pants off Crawford, and I'll lose my goddamn job." He spits again.

"Maybe you should wait for the EMTs to move her, boss. I mean, in case something else is wrong with her."

"You're probably right, Jesus, but you checked her out and she's been down here too long already. Screw the regulations . . . Lily? Can you hear me? We're not waiting for the ambulance; we're getting you out of there right now, okay? Lily?"

Oh yeah, Mike Savage probably told him my name.

"Polanski, throw Jesus another blanket!" Boss calls through the bullhorn. *"Daniels, bring her bike to the office."* He takes a deep breath. "I suppose we should be grateful it didn't rain after midnight," he says to someone nearby. "At least her clothes are dry."

"She'll be okay."

"Better be." Boss clears his throat. "We need to get her out of here. We're behind schedule. What do they call the pit, Martinez? *An attractive nuisance?*"

"That's right, boss. But it's also a work site and well-marked."

"We'll see, I guess, huh? . . . Goofy kid," Boss says quietly. "I knew I should have slept in this morning." The ground crunches under his feet, and he lifts the bullhorn again. *"All right, gentlemen, let's get this show on the road. Hoffman, start your engine in three! Gently. For God's sake, be careful!"*

"Lily?" It's Jesus. "Don't know if you can hear me but we're going to start up Big Betty. I'll crawl into her with you and we'll ride her to the rim together, okay?"

Huh? Who's Betty?

"Once you're on top we'll take you to the office and the medics will look you over. You with me?"

The prayer train picks up speed as it takes my bedroom corner, only Aunt Jamie is at the wheel. I don't hear a prayer, or recognize my own voice when I recite:

> *Yesterday upon the stair*
> *I met a man who wasn't there.*
> *He wasn't there again today*
> *I wish, I wish he'd go away.*

"Keep talking, Lily. That's right."

My words are little blocks sitting beside each other in an ice cube tray. I feel my lips move though the rest of my face is frozen.

My lids are heavy but I finally open my eyes.

"It's going to be loud when they start her up," Jesus says, walking away, "but don't be afraid. I'll be with you, just like I said."

I will never leave you nor forsake you, Hebrews 13:5.

"No!" I cry. I don't want to go anywhere with Jesus. I try standing up but my knees crumble.

"Hold on, kid," Boss yells down. "You'll be out of there in no time."

Halfway across the pit, Jesus stands in front of the steam shovel and smiles at me, holding out His arms like He does in the Bible pictures. "*Mi amiga!* Ready for a ride? It'll be fun!"

The pit spins when I shake my head back and forth. On every rotation, I look for something familiar but nothing is.

A siren screams into the area and stops.

Boss raises the bullhorn and counts, "*Three . . . two . . . ONE!*" And the steam shovel engine roars to a deafening start. A cloud of black smoke bursts from its exhaust pipe and the long rusty arm of Big Betty rattles and moans as it pulls free of a mountain of earth.

"Cover your nose!" someone yells, but it's too late. A curtain of thick dust rolls toward me, filling the pit, and through it, towering over Jesus, is a giant silver shark mouth with painted serrated teeth as red as Mom's lipstick.

Go away, go away, don't you come back anymore!
Go away, go away, and please don't slam the door.

Tears roll down my cheeks. The engine roars, and the little chimney spits more thick blinding smoke. I pull up the blanket and stand, my body shaking with pain. The only way out is the steep dirt ramp behind the advancing monster. Was it always there?

Should I say a prayer? I can't think of one.

I scoot farther back, but I'm already leaning against the wall.

There's nowhere else to go.

They say I took a roundhouse swing at Jesus Martinez, but I don't remember doing it. Or being lifted in the mouth of the steam shovel, either.

The medic looks familiar, though. When he treats me in the quarry office he says my arm has a clean break. "Been broken before?"

I nod.

He looks at my medical bracelet and makes a note. "How old are you, Lily?"

"Fifteen." Dad says people should be careful about giving out personal information.

The quarry boss smiles. He sits at a cluttered desk, filling out a form. "A *young* fifteen," he says, arching an eyebrow at the medic. Then, "Teenager, huh? I have one of those at home." Mike Savage steps into the office. "Hey, Savage! How old are you?"

"It's right there on my pink slip, boss. Twenty next month." He lights a cigarette and looks at me. "You okay, Lily?"

I nod. Carefully.

Boss hands him the paper. "Take this to your PO."

Mike shrugs. "I guess it doesn't matter that I thought I heard something and came out to look but—"

"Sorry, kid. But if you can't do your job, you're a liability. Being sued is not an option around here."

"It's not his fault," I say.

The Savage Boy didn't do anything. SOG shot Beauty. That's why I was at the bottom of the pit.

I see Mike's face at my bedroom window. He can't help it if a shark's inside him.

"It's not his fault," I say again, but the Savage Boy is gone.

Dad sighs when he opens the front door and sees me standing on the porch between the medic and Old Man Crawford.

"I just checked your room," he says quietly. "I thought you'd . . . I thought something had happened to you." Dad looks at the strangers and clears his throat. "Thank you, gentlemen. I'm sorry for the bother. We'll take it from here." His face is red; I've embarrassed him again. "You scared your mother half to death," he says. Which (I will remind them later) isn't possible if no one was up yet.

"I'm sorry," I mumble. But if Dad looks into my eyes, he'll see Beauty and the night our whole family went meteor watching, and he'll know it was important that I go to the quarry last night. Look, Dad, look in my eyes.

"The soul lives for sixty-two hours after . . ." I start to explain. "Maybe it's sixty-two days, I'm not sure. One book said . . ." My voice gets smaller with each word.

Mom steps forward. She wears a robe and Dad's pajama bottoms and wrinkles her forehead when she says, "Lil-ee? Who are these people? . . . What's going on?" She looks at the strangers then at my arm. "Your arm! Again?" Her cheeks are flushed but she's not wearing makeup. She never goes to the door without her makeup.

Lauren's there too, and reaches over to touch the splint.

"Lily's all right, Mrs. Asher, just a bit shook up," Crawford says. "Had herself a little slumber party at the bottom of the quarry pit last night." He puts his hand on my shoulder, then passes Dad his business card. "Hope you haven't called the police yet."

"Actually, we just realized . . ." Dad reads the card. "Gaylord Crawford! For goodness sake!" Dad shakes his hand, he's impressed. "You've been very kind. Lily is our oldest and, well, something of a handful."

Gaylord Crawford smiles. "I have children too. We do the best we can to keep them safe, but they have minds of their own." He hands Dad another card. "My lawyer."

"I'm sure there'll be no need."

"That's all right—you may change your mind later."

"We tried reaching you by phone," the medic says, "but then we real-ized you only live a few blocks away."

"We took it off the hook so my wife could sleep. She's been . . . a little under the weather."

The medic clears his throat. "Lily broke her arm. It isn't a bad break. We put a temporary splint on it in the ambulance." He motions toward the driveway. "Gave her a Valium, also for the pain. We were cognizant of her health issues."

"Excuse me?"

He nods at the medical bracelet I got at the hospital after the car accident: *Head Injury, Possible Seizures.* "After Lily gets some sleep and something to eat, you'll want to see the family doctor. He'll put a proper cast on her arm and check out her bumps and bruises. She may have a slight concussion, I'm not sure."

Now I know why the medic looks so familiar. I see it in Dad's eyes too. Mom would be mortified if she knew that the very same emergency guy was here last night. Twice in twenty-four hours, and Mom didn't want to make a scene in the new neighborhood.

Lauren looks scared. "Are you okay, Lily?" she asks. "Does it hurt?"

"Yes. Yes." One for each question. "You were outside alone overnight, and now I was too." It shouldn't matter but it does—at least for a while.

Mr. Crawford hands Dad the clothesline and Lauren's jump rope. "We brought back Lily's bike. Her flashlight is in the basket."

"You have my jump rope," Lauren says, taking it from the strange man. She looks at me and smiles. "Did it bring you luck?"

"Yeah."

The newspaper boy steps around the men standing at our door and hands Dad the morning paper.

Mom turns to Dad, and wraps her arms around him. "What hap-pened, Paul?" she whispers. The back of her hair is flat; her scalp peeks through.

"We'll be going," Mr. Crawford says. "You folks take care."

Dad shakes both men's hands again and watches them walk away before gesturing for me to step inside. "Lily," he says sternly, then closes the door behind me.

He wears the same wrinkled dress shirt he had on last night, the same pants, and yesterday's Gold Toe socks. He must have slept in his clothes. He hasn't shaved either and stares somewhere over my shoulder, deciding what to say to me next.

"Groovy," Lauren says. "You're the only person I know who broke the same arm twice. Too bad it wasn't your right arm, then you wouldn't have to do homework." I smile at her. "Can I use the phone?" she asks Dad.

I don't care if she tells Simone. Everyone at school will know soon enough, anyway. Simone and Lauren are best friends; they're the only ones who signed my cast last time. Someday I'll have a best friend again.

"It's too early."

The house is quiet: no percolator, no morning radio, running water, crinkly newspaper.

"Okay, I'll wait. What time is it, Lily?"

I take the wristwatch out of my pocket: *12:23* reads the cracked face. "It's broken," I say. "It broke when I fell."

Dad glances at the wall clock. "Six thirty," he says. "You can talk to Simone at school later. Just no family gossip." He hugs Mom tighter.

"I know."

"I mean it."

"All right. Jeez. Don't have a cow!"

"Lauren!" Mom snaps.

"Don't be mad at me! I didn't do anything, Lily did! I was home all night, remember?" She slugs my good arm, then runs upstairs and slams her bedroom door, but this time no one minds.

"Look at you," Dad says to me, impatiently. "You're cut and bruised and covered in dirt. What the hell were you doing at the rock quarry all night?"

"Paul," Mom says calmly, "she's home now."

"You broke your goddamn arm again!" Dad's eyes grow black. "How could you do this to us after last night? Weren't we giving you enough attention? Your mother was sick! That registered with you somewhere, didn't it?"

I lower my eyes. Mrs. Wiggins nudges my leg.

"I'm fine now, really," Mom says.

"No you're not. You have a fever. You should be in bed."

Mom touches his back, but he doesn't feel it.

"I don't want to know what you did," Dad goes on, "or why you thought you had to sneak out! I don't want to hear anything about your fantasies . . . your fairy tales. I'm tired of all of it!"

"Paul!"

"You either want to be part of this family or you don't."

Are they kicking me out? Should I leave?

When Mom touches him again, he takes a deep breath and turns to face her. "I know, I know," he says, patting her hand. "It's just so damn frustrating."

It's always been the two of them. Maybe they never wanted to have kids. Maybe Lauren and I were accidents. They'd probably be happier without us. Maybe they'd live on a tropical beach somewhere. Mom would paint all day and Dad would learn to play the ukulele.

"We love you, Lily," he says. "We were worried about you. That's not so hard to understand, is it?"

"I love you too."

"Good. Now take a shower and go to your room." Dad rubs the back of his neck.

"Keep the splint out of the water," Mom adds.

Later, Dad writes me an excuse, and Lauren takes it to school where she'll tell everyone that her weirdo sister spent the night at the bottom of the quarry pit.

I stay in my room and read.

By ten a.m., Mom's temperature is normal again and Dad goes to work. After lunch, she takes me to the doctor who puts another cast on my arm. He's surprised to see me again so soon, and when he says so, Mom blushes.

I have a slight concussion, but it's "nothing a few days of rest won't cure."

I'm still in trouble when we get back, so I'm sent to my room. Mom brings me dinner, magazines, and aspirin. Finally she reads me a chapter from *Robinson Crusoe*, but I still can't sleep.

Because my arm hurts.

Because it rains, and it's a beautiful sound, and I don't want to stop listening.

Because it's a full moon and I love full moons.

I sit at the end of my bed, petting Mrs. Wiggins. We both bite our tongues when a fire engine races through the neighborhood. By my radio alarm clock, it's 2:00 a.m.

Exactly.

Beep . . . beep . . . beep.

The sun is rising. I rub my eyes, get out of bed, and walk to the window.

"Back her up . . . back it up . . . a little more . . . little more," Howard, the garbage man, calls to the driver of the truck. "There you go. You got her."

Dogs bark. Cans rattle and bang. Howard looks around self-consciously. He's making a lot of noise, and it's early.

A dark blue Cadillac inches down Crawford Heights Boulevard, then stops in front of him. The driver points at his sandals. Both of them laugh.

"Whatcha looking at?" Dad asks, walking into my room. His cup of coffee smells good. He looks over my shoulder and laughs. "Holy Howard loves his sandals, doesn't he?" He takes a noisy sip. "Hair's getting long; sure wish I could let myself go. Maybe if I quit my job and put you kids up for adoption." He blows on my ear. "Just kidding, Lil."

I swallow a tear. "I want to be part of this family," I announce, strong and clear.

Dad kisses the top of my head. "I'm glad," he says.

The garbage guy looks at my window and waves. Dad waves back; I give Howard the Vulcan greeting with my good hand, then take a deep breath and ask, "How's Mom?"

"Still cutting the old z's. She isn't going to be happy about that, though." He reaches over my shoulder and traces the masking tape letters in the window. "*I'M . . . NOT . . . HERE,*" Dad reads. "Bass-ackward."

"I'm . . . not . . . here," I echo.

"Who did you write it for?" Dad asks, taking another sip of coffee. "Or is that *whom?*"

"No one." It's my first lie of the day.

"*I'm not here* sort of announces that you are, doesn't it?" He looks concerned. "You must have written it for someone."

Lauren stands in my bedroom doorway. Her red hair is in curlers;

it's picture day at school. "She wrote it for the exchange student," Lauren says.

I did not. "I did not."

When my sister rolls her eyes at me, cherries, bananas, and apples spin like a slot machine. "Mom says Lily's been smiling at that Luca kid who's staying with Mrs. Lockhart."

"Scram, Lima Bean."

"He's Scandinavian," she adds.

Dad's face relaxes. "Scandinavian, huh?"

I shrug.

"That makes sense. You like Victor Borge. And Hans Christian Andersen, of course; he had a big imagination too."

"Only those guys are Danes and Luca's Swedish," I say.

He smiles, happy I'm acting like other girls my age.

Dad's okay. Maybe I'll tell him about Jesus someday. How I used to believe Him when He said He loved me, but I don't anymore.

"How's the arm?"

"All right." I look out the window as the garbage truck inches down the hill. Holy Howard grabs a handle and hooks a ride.

"Scrape off the sticky tape stuff before your mother sees it," Dad says from my doorway. "If you don't, she'll—what do you kids call it?—freak out. Yeah, that's it." When was I ever one of the kids? I guess Dad figures now that I'm fifteen, even a *young* fifteen, there's an even smaller chance he'll understand me.

The garbage truck has stopped. The gears squeak and growl as it backs uphill and stops in front of our house again. Did they forget something? Yeah. One trash lid is crooked, but the other isn't. They forgot a can. Only this time Holy Howard doesn't pick it up, the driver—the outline behind the steering wheel—does.

Jesus.

Not Hey-Seuss, but the real one. SOG. In His long tattered robe, beard, and stringy hair. He looks at my window and waves.

I freeze in place, staring at Him. If I don't blink or move, maybe He won't see me.

Stop looking, I tell myself. He isn't there anyway.

But He is. Bending over to pet Edgar.

It's going to take time, but "nothing worthwhile comes easily," Gramma Frieda said in her last letter from Miami. Of course, she was talking about the three months left until eighty-year-old Lou Merkin's divorce became final and they would be free to move in with each other. "*Sans* marriage!" Mom scoffed. "Must be putting LSD in the water down there."

"Lily? One more thing?" Dad sticks his head in my room again. "Your mother and I talked, and things are going to be different from now on."

"Yeah," Lauren says, suddenly digging through my sock drawer. "They're locking you up."

Outside, the garbage truck honks. I smile nervously.

"School, Lauren? . . . No one's locking you up, Lily. You're staying right here. We're going to take better care of you, that's all. Maybe get you another prescription, something that won't interfere with your schoolwork but will help you sleep through the night. Help *all* of us sleep through the night."

I'm better, I want to say. *I won't bark or act strange anymore. I'm kissing boys now. I don't need more pills. I'm even writing a story about Beauty and Allison—one story, not a hundred. And next time SOG shows up—*I glance outside. Jesus is hitching a ride on the garbage truck, holding His free hand over His eyes to shield them from the sun, looking for me at the window—*I'll pretend I don't see Him and He'll go away.*

"But Dad, I won't—"

"No buts, Lily."

"Okay. I guess."

"Jah?" Dad says in a corny Scandinavian accent.

"Jah."

CHAPTER 30

ON MARS

I'm drawing when my family leaves the house to go shopping. Dad is home early today. He hates the stores and Lauren hates to tag along, but they do it anyway. Mom insisted. "Teenagers need their privacy," she said. Meaning me.

She left a note on the kitchen table, under a new flashlight with a tag that has my name on it. It's a family rule that we all have workable *torches*. That's what they call flashlights in England, you know.

The Besiegers gave away three hundred autographed *torches* at a concert in Blackpool last year because the fire marshal didn't want people waving lighters and matches around. I heard one autographed torch later sold for two hundred dollars.

Back by 5, the note reads. *No sweets. Dinner at 7.*

The drapes are closed, each door is locked. The house is dark, quiet, and cool. I walk through the kitchen, opening and closing each drawer and cupboard like I used to.

Still do.

Sometimes do.

Things get out, I remind myself, *things get in*, but maybe I don't believe it anymore. Some things are born in you—determined to keep you company, while other stuff can't get in no matter how much it tries. For a long time my body needed to do the opening-and-closing thing every night. It was like eating or peeing, even waking me up if I forgot.

Buddha said, "Everything changes."

On the front porch, the mailbox is stuffed to overflowing. In addition to the bills, and the latest issues of *Sunset* and *TV Guide*, there is a postcard to Mom from Connie Marks in Puerto Vallarta. She doesn't mention Rusty or Judy or her mean old husband, just getting sunburned, drinking margaritas, and some guy named Bill. She sounds happy, and signs off, *Nice to hear from you.*

Mom knows where the Markses live?

My grades are in the mail too, but I don't open the envelope. I'm not worried; I get good marks. Since the car accident, my teachers mail home a progress report each month. They occasionally complain about things like my "stubborn lack of participation in group projects," but admire my "unique take on almost every subject." My English teacher once called me, "naïve and willful, but romantic and artistic too." Mom smiled when she read that part, but Dad didn't like it.

I place the mail beside me on the uncomfortable wrought-iron love seat he gave her for Valentine's last year and stick my fingers between its lacy patterns. Closing my eyes, I trace the leafy curves with my mind. I'm almost asleep when I feel someone standing in front of me.

A quarry man in coveralls. "Excuse me," he says, holding out the dog-tooth. His halo winks under the bright yellow hard hat. "We found this at the bottom of the pit, and figured it was probably yours."

"We?" I stand up and look at him. The raised porch makes me taller than my almost five-foot-nine.

His work clothes don't fool me. "First you're a garbage man, then you're a quarry guy? This isn't Halloween. I know who you are."

SOG shakes His hand with the tooth in it. Holding out His arms in that familiar, "Blessed are the children for they shall inherit the Kingdom of God" pose, His teeth twinkle like a Pepsodent ad, and at His feet are plump awestruck curly haired white kids, more like cherubs than the Israelites we learned about in scripture class.

He shakes the tooth again.

"I don't want it," I say calmly. "I left it there on purpose."

He's nervous and fidgety. He shakes a leg until His halo slips down His pant leg, then picks it up and sticks it in His pocket. "Damn thing," He mumbles.

"Didn't you see my message?" I step off the porch and point to my second-story window with the sticky tape residue of *I'M NOT HERE.*

Not that I expected Him to read it. Not that He ever pays attention to His flock. That's what he calls us, you know: flock, sheep. No one seems to mind that sheep are dumb, but I do.

He still holds out the tooth.

"I said I don't want it."

"I know, but it's yours." He tosses it to me, and walks off. I follow Him a few yards.

"I gave it to Beauty!" I stop to yell. "Put it back where you found it!" I throw the tooth at Him but it lands in the boxwood where it glows like Kryptonite.

Yeah, I throw like a girl, so what?

No one would ever lock Jesus up, stick Him in pajamas or wire jumper cables to His head. If He sees the Son of God, He's only looking in the mirror. I'm already a weirdo. Dr. Giraffe hasn't threatened to put me in a big white house with nurses and crazy people yet, but I've seen enough TV to know how it goes.

"Go away," I yell, "and never come back!" The words burn my lips and dig little quarry pits in my heart. "I'm not your friend. I won't be crazy! And you can't make me!"

Neighborhood dogs bark. The mailman, walking down the opposite side of the street, stops to look at me. My whole body shakes, though I don't cry.

SOG walks toward me again.

The phone rings. I let it. It's only Mrs. Singer checking up on me. The family car is gone, and I was shouting; I'm a troubled kid. "A little confused, a little disturbed," Dr. Giraffe told my parents. "Some people are. It's a disturbing world, why shouldn't they be? Treatable, definitely treatable."

Mrs. Wiggins's tail slats the front door behind me.

Does SOG hear it too? He stops a couple of feet away and stares over my shoulder. He looks angry close up. Has He always looked mad but I never noticed?

Mrs. Wiggins gave me her tooth. She gave me her last breath. Even dead, she saved my life, bringing me back to shore alive, while Dad rowed around in circles. Okay, the boat only had one oar but Jesus could have helped. He could have created another one; what kind of miracle would *that* take?

When I look, she's not there. When I don't, she is.

I'm alone with her. I'm alone without her.

Mrs. Wiggins can be my god, *she* can be my Jesus. "She's all I need," I say to SOG. "You can go."

"False prophets," SOG replies, smiling sarcastically.

"*False prophets?*" He rarely talks Bible-ese. "Are you quoting yourself? Didn't You tell me You don't remember saying half that stuff in the New Testament?"

"I'm sorry if I've disappointed you, Lily."

Disappointed? I never considered that. Wasn't He just being Himself? He always hated His job description.

"Go away, SOG." He still flinches at the nickname. "I can't worship someone who doesn't worship me."

I don't know why I said that, I don't even know what it means, but I wish I'd said it to Grandma Frieda too, to Mr. Marks, to Judy, to the mean kids at school and every jerk who ever treated me like I was some kind of dummy.

Jesus whistles the theme to *The Andy Griffith Show* as He stumbles down our street and His boots and coveralls melt away, the same old yellowing robe, bare feet, and halo appearing underneath. Dad's new red Pontiac drives past Him, the silhouettes of my parents and sister framed in the midafternoon light, the backseat full of grocery sacks.

They've been shopping for tomorrow, my sixteenth birthday.

On my last birthday, Jesus popped out of the cake the way strippers do in old movies, but He left a huge hole in the top that collapsed it. No one noticed and Mom cut irregular slices. I know it shouldn't matter, but between that and Jesus sticking the birthday candles up His nose, I excused myself and went to my room.

If I'd only ignored Him when He first crawled through the tear in my window screen; not listened when He told me everything was fine, that "the kids who call you *weirdo* don't have jungles in their closets or bulters under their beds, that's all." If Jesus had gone away for a month or two, maybe fishing with Mr. and Mrs. Potato Head like He does in Chapter 3, instead of coming and going from my room anytime He wanted to, I might be an almost-normal almost-sixteen-year-old.

Jesus is off to another neighborhood, another house, another girl's bedroom.

At her window, He'll dazzle her with His sharp white teeth, then wiggle through an insect-sized rip in her window screen. He'll entertain her with hand shadows and tell her stories she's never heard before.

It's the first time she'll be alone in her room with a boy.

When Jesus acts sad, she'll feel sorry for Him, like I did, and try to help. He'll convince her that she's special, and she'll believe it until something terrible happens.

Something He could stop but doesn't, because Jesus keeps His miracles close to His chest.

And none of them are for you.

My room is enough (for now).

Its sky is wide, blue, and warm. Its horizon cluttered with windmills, pagodas, circus tents, and palm trees.

Books are enough. Poems. Stories.

Paint. Pencils. Paper.

Numbers are enough.

Patterns.

Luca says I have the mind of a scientist. "On Mars!" he snorts.

The Swedes have a strange sense of humor.

When I asked if he'd left the rose on my windowsill, Luca said no. Dad hadn't either. I dried its petals and glued them in my scrapbook.

When a rose appeared on my windowsill each odd-numbered day after, I left them there to dry and blow away.

On the coldest day of my sixteenth year, a heart appeared on my frosty bedroom window, with *pi = 3.142* written in the middle.

The next day I cut out a life-sized paper lab coat—with the name tag *Dr. Lily Asher, Scientist, Stockholm General Hospital*—and taped it to the closet mirror. Each day I stand before it and recite:

Dr. Lily Asher.
Former weirdo. Present weirdo.
Brilliant, tall, and exceedingly well read.

With thanks and love to:

My mom, dad, and sister. I was so lucky to have such a loving family! Thank you all.

Kid Cadillac. My daughter, my heart.

Readers of early drafts of *The Shark Curtain*, who believed in its good bones and urged me to continue—you know who you are.

Ursula K. Le Guin, who taught me the only rule to writing is "numbering your pages; the rest is up to you." Thanks for taking me under your literary wing a millennium ago, for flattering me by arguing with me about a poem I wrote (the bullet in my purse, the merit of the word "Polaroid"), for strolling with me along the beach. You liked my work and treated me as an equal. Mind. Blown.

Tom Spanbauer, who schooled me at Haystack then invited me to join his Dangerous Writing table in Portland. Thanks for your support and encouragement, for your exceptional gifts as a writer and a teacher, for your courage, modesty, and generosity.

LitChix pals Val Brooks and Patsy Hand. My talented "sisters" in work, in soul, in play, who keep me honest and challenge me to invest each page with hard work, imagination, and clarity. I love you madly.

My agent Carrie Howland, who loved *Shark* from the beginning and worked hard to find it the right home. How can I thank you enough?

Jessica (J.L.) Powers, a beautiful writer and editor extraordinaire. Brilliant, caring, accessible—you knock me out. Fingers crossed I'm lucky enough to work with you again someday.

Johnny Temple and Johanna Ingalls at Akashic Books. How did I luck out to have rock 'n' roll publishers who print smart, edgy, original work? I'm flattered to be on your roster.

Lily Asher, my fictional heroine. Thank you for trusting me. I hope I haven't embarrassed you or sold you short.